AL

"This book evokes the feelings of young school kids in an absolutely unique situation at a time of great worldwide change. The happy and not-so-happy times are faithfully remembered and the setting of the great plains of central Tanganyika (Tanzania) in an era before television, cell phones, reliable electricity supply or decent transport, makes for a book that one cannot put down."

— Graeme Berry (an alumnus of that place and times), United Kingdom

"Brilliant! Having lived in Africa for 40 years, during and after colonial rule, I avidly search bookshops, now that I have returned to Britain, for books about life on that continent. There are many available, written by short term visitors to Kenya, South Africa, the Congo and elsewhere but they seldom convey what life was like for people living in these places during the past 60 years. "The Slope of Kongwa Hill", like "Africa House" by Christina Lamb, falls in to a very different category. The author experienced life as a schoolboy in East Africa, with many good times but also a lot of hardships. He describes a way of life that will never be repeated but is a part of history for every African Nation. Compared to the life of the average schoolboy in Manchester or Toronto in the 1950s, Kongwa probably will sound exciting, but with parents seen perhaps twice a year, no television, wild animals and life-threatening bugs in large numbers and, later, terrorism, life was not a bed of roses. Sadly, the number of people still alive to remember life in East and Central Africa during the early post–Second World War years are becoming fewer and fewer with each passing year but they, and anyone else with an interest in Africa, will find this an enthralling book."

— John Harrison, United Kingdom

"The author captures a fascinating time in East African history. Travel with him into the richness and adventure of a boarding school in the wilds of late colonial Tanganyika – a great read."

— Elvin Letchford, Salt Spring Island, Canada

"An unusual British boarding school in the middle of nowhere, Africa, was brought to life for me by the author's memories and astute observations. What a remote and wild place to grow up!"

— Leona Bridges, Alberta, Canada

"It is the landscape that remains with me still... the heat, the sand, the isolation. And how a boy's experiences begin to reveal the hidden secrets of that vast and empty space."

— Heather Birnie, Alberta, Canada

THE SLOPE OF KONGWA HILL

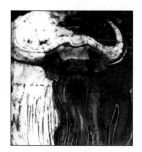

A Boy's Tale of Africa

ANTHONY R. EDWARDS

PUBLISHING HOUSE

Agio
PUBLISHING HOUSE

151 Howe Street, Victoria BC, Canada V8V 4K5

© 2011, Anthony R. Edwards.
All rights reserved.
Web: slopeofkongwahill.com
E-mail: theslopeofkongwahill@gmail./com

Cover illustration – batik by Imelda Edwards.

For rights information and bulk orders, please contact
info@agiopublishing.com *or go to* www.agiopublishing.com

The Slope of Kongwa Hill (2nd Edition)
ISBN 978-1-897435-65-6 (trade paperback)
Cataloguing information available from
Library and Archives Canada.

Agio Publishing House is a socially responsible company,
measuring success on a triple-bottom-line basis.

10 9 8 7 6 5 4 3b

"Memory always distorts, and memories of childhood, tinged inevitably with nostalgia, distort most of all. You remember women lovelier, men nobler, houses loftier, horizons wider than they really were."
—Elspeth Huxley

ACKNOWLEDGEMENTS

THANK YOU SO MUCH TO ALL THOSE good souls who have been so helpful in their material contribution, photographs, commentary, support or encouragement, and have helped improve the revised edition to this book. In alphabetical order:

Kenneth Aranky, Nadia Aranky, Aurelio Balletto, Chris Beck, Adrian Begg, Graeme (aka Stewart) Berry, Philippa Bianco, Leona Bridges, Tony Bruce, Elaine Anderson, Nigel Butterfield, Morag Cormack, Ian Cook, John Cook, Paul Dodwell, Lawrie Fegan, Fiona Firth, Glynn Ford, Monique Gibeau, John Harrison, Massowia Haywood, Valerie Hext, Neville Hoy, Sigurd Ivey, Thadeo Kavishe, Clive Knight, Barbara Laing, Monika Laing, Tricia Lane, Martin Langley, Steve Le Feuvre, Maria Letailleur, Elvin Letchford, Beryl Lloyd, Morgaine Longpré, Donald McLachlan, Graeme Maclean, J.Y. Madinda, Alan Moore, Silvia Papini, Corinne Poetker, Hazel Redgrave, Judi Moore, Marie-Louise Sandberg, Irene Stacey, Margaret Thomson, Heather Tickner, Michael Warren, Denton Webster, Ted Weir, Douglas Westley.

DEDICATION

To my friends and former colleagues
of Kongwa School.

And to my ever-loving wife, Imelda,
who has been a bit of a writer's widow for these last few years.

KONGWA

Kongwa is a dry place
Very, very dry
Where the sun is always shining
And no clouds are in the sky.

There are no flowers to look at
But only prickly thorns
And when the day is ended
Your clothes are rather torn.

But Kongwa is a nice place
And 'tis a happy school
And although the children have to work
There is some time to fool.

—K. Bakewell, 3A Juniors (1955)

CONTENTS

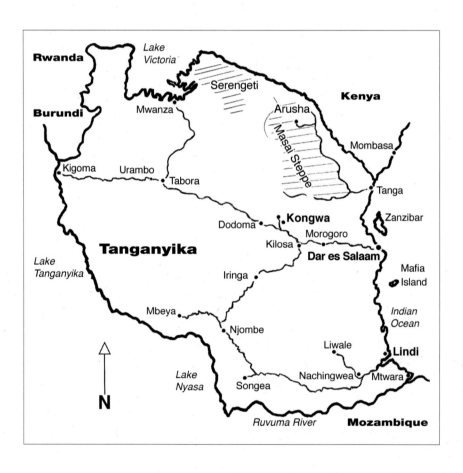

Rwanda

Burundi

Lake
Victoria

Serengeti

Kenya

Arusha

Mwanza

Masai Steppe

Mombasa

Kigoma

Urambo

Tabora

Tanga

Zanzibar

Dodoma

Kongwa

Morogoro

Lake
Tanganyika

Tanganyika

Kilosa

Dar es Salaam

Mafia
Island

Iringa

Indian
Ocean

Mbeya

Njombe

Liwale

Lindi

N

Lake
Nyasa

Songea

Nachingwea

Mtwara

Ruvuma River

Mozambique

PROLOGUE

KONGWA, Tanganyika Territory, 1950

T HE BULLDOZER'S ENGINE WHINED AS ITS EXHAUST coughed a stream of black smoke skyward. Then the complaining, war-surplus Caterpillar D7 veered off-course with a seized left track and, with a muffled thump, collided with a massive baobab tree. John Sorrel, wrestling with the beast in blinding dust, cursed his luck as he anticipated another delay in the day's work.

The burly Sorrel, heavily muscled, and deeply tanned from exposure to Kongwa's burning sun, was muddied with sweat, wearing only his shorts and 'tackies' on his feet. As with many of the men, the discomfort of a shirt that would fill with dust, yet be wringing wet, led him to do away with it when working on a 'Cat.'

They'd been using D7s for knocking-down smaller baobabs, so hitting one wasn't the problem. But this had proved inefficient for clearing thousands of acres in the unending bush of central Tanganyika. That's why the new technique had been adopted. Two Cats ran parallel, a hundred feet apart, tethered by the world's toughest anchor chain. The D7s bulldozed their way through the bush, dragging the chain between them creating mass clearings, at the same time using the rippers on the machines' rears to churn the soil.

The chain was snagged. Sorrel hadn't been quick enough to cut the motor. Now, with the transmission lever still engaged in 'forward' and the left track seized, the rear of the giant machine, still tethered to the second D7, dragged off-course.

"Oh no! Bwana, no!" Sorrel's gogo assistant cried out as he realized, too late, that the tree they'd hit held a huge bee's nest in its upper branches. In moments, twenty thousand killer bees swarmed. Seconds later, large numbers descended upon Sorrel and his assistant.

Sorrel reached desperately for the throttle so he could stop the dozer, but before he could, the swarm swirled about his face, completely distracting him as he swatted frantically at the angry bees. At the same time, the D7's right track kept on rotating, creating a dense, red dust-cloud as it skidded on the rock hard earth.

"Jump, man, jump!" Sorrel yelled.

The two leaped but were overwhelmed by bees before they hit the ground. They ran, howling, trying to get away from the swarm, waving their arms furiously, shaking their heads, trying to cover their faces, rolling in the sand, anything, to escape death by a thousand stings.

From his position fifty yards away, mechanical engineer Harry Miller and his assistant had been working on a field repair of another D7. At this moment they were hunched against an intense, swirling, deep-red dust devil some one hundred feet high. The sandpaper-like vortex engulfed them, tore at their flesh and threatened to pull them off their feet. Then it was gone and the men straightened, coughing and rubbing dust from their eyes as they became aware of the yells from the men under attack from the bees. They watched, for a moment frozen in horror, powerless to do anything. Then Miller ran to his Rover parked in the shade of a nearby acacia tree. He reached over the Lee Enfield carbine, set ready in the event of an altercation with lion or rhino, grabbed a walkie talkie, and called urgently: "Hello, Base, this is Miller, are you there? Come in – come in!"

"Go ahead, Mr. Miller," came the startled response from a recently-married young English lady newly arrived from Britain, and guarding the radio at Kongwa's base camp. She, with her hitherto soft, pale English complexion, was busy rubbing another dollop of Cold Cream into her arms in her attempt to control her dry skin.

"I have an emergency," Miller rattled off. "Sorrel and his assistant are being attacked by killer bees. Their damned Cat's stuck in drive, out of control. I need medical help for the men and any help I can get to shut down the

Cat. I'm not jumping on that bloody thing until help gets here and I'm buggered if I know what else to do. Just get people out here – now!"

"That's just terrible, Mr. Miller, I'm so sorry," the suddenly alarmed
radio lady responded, hastily setting aside her jar of Pond's. "Where are you?
Where should I send everyone?"

"Number five unit, north-west quadrant and hurry for Chrissakes or these
men'll be dead."

"Yes, Mr. Miller. I'll get help right away. I'll let you know when they're
en-route."

THAT HAD BEEN A MOST UNWELCOME COMPLICATION in Harry Miller's bad
day, yesterday. It had taken forty minutes for the emergency crew to arrive at
the scene. Miller, along with the other Cat driver had done what they could
to comfort Sorrel's assistant but it was too late for Sorrel. There was not a lot
they could do. You couldn't equip, never mind train, hundreds of engineers
and field operatives on how to guard against every danger. With big game,
insects and reptiles you took your chances. It was a hazard that came with
working in the bush.

The bees that had not stung the men had disappeared; those that had were
dead, lying on the sandy terrain in dark, furry clumps but mainly on the faces,
necks and backs of the prone men.

John Sorrel was pronounced dead at the scene, death later formally determined as a result of anaphylactic shock. He'd received over nine hundred
vicious stings all over his largely exposed body. His African assistant, more
dead than alive, had received three hundred or so and was rushed back to
Kongwa's new hospital. It appeared, a day later, as though he would survive.

That darn D7 was still bucking, trying to get somewhere when the emergency crew had arrived. They'd noted the bees' nest, abandoned for the
moment, swinging precariously and about to be completely dislodged. Two
of the men, in a feat of some daring, had half jumped, half climbed aboard the
bucking bulldozer in order to get at the controls and shut it down.

Now, this morning, Miller had been called – well, *summoned* might be
a better word – for his second round of bad news. He was to appear at the

office of the man in charge of Kongwa's ground operations, Major-General Desmond Harrison, formerly British army, desert campaign.

When Miller arrived, he found Harrison in the dubious protection of his white-ant-eaten, tin-roofed, office building, seated in his captain's chair, relighting his burled, walnut briar and exhaling roiling clouds of smoke into the turbulence of the ceiling fan. On his desk, a multitude of papers rustled vigorously in their attempt to escape the breeze, but were retained firmly in place by a veritable landslide of mica rocks, enthusiastically retrieved from the slopes of nearby Church Hill.

"Ah, there you are, Miller," he gestured with his pipe for the new arrival to be seated, while withdrawing a grubby handkerchief from a pocket to wipe his neck of sweat. "Bad affair that incident with Sorrel," he said. "Damnably bad actually. Fine man, Sorrel. Shouldn't have been driving the bloody Cat. Not his job, you know. Fine engineer, not a driver."

"Well I—" began Miller, swatting at the cloud of flies that had descended on his sweaty face and shirt while he attempted to respond.

"—I know, no need to say anything, he was helping out, shortage of drivers and all that. Must get more Africans driving the Cats, don't you know? I'm accelerating the training program immediately. Soon have sufficient numbers that way, wouldn't you say?"

"Well, sir, I'm not sure that—"

"Anyway, 'nuff of that. How's your wife? All right, is she?"

"Hazel's doing very well, sir. Helping out with teaching the children now that a proper school opened in the classroom you set up, sir. Good move that—Goddamn these flies!"

"Big improvement from the tent, what? That's what you get, when you've got resources. Bringing in Welch, last year, made the difference. Glad you approve. He'll probably expand the school if we get any more children – even take in boarders. You have a daughter, don't you?" Harrison squinted through swirling smoke.

"Yes, sir, two actually. The older one, that's Hazel, she's nine—"

"—Wife's Hazel, first daughter Hazel? Bit confusing, I should have thought. Oh well, what the heck, easier to remember, I expect."

"Well, actually—"

"—Anyway, 'nuff of that. None of my business. Not what we're here to talk about. Now here's the thing, Miller. I'm transferring you to Mkwaya."

"Mkwaya? Never heard of it, sir. Where is it?"

"On the coast, don't you know? Southern Province, down near Lindi, Mikindani, Mtwara, that area. Staging post, what? The brass at the OFC wants to get Nachingwea going so I need good mechanics down there. Roads impassable. Vehicles can't handle the conditions. Need good engineers and you're the best. Thought you might like it. Later on, when the railway from Mikindani to Nach is complete, we'll move you up there... Plenty of action there too."

"Actually, sir, I was rather looking forward to some long leave next summer. I'd like to take the family home for the Festival of Britain. I've not been able to get away since arriving here in '48.

"We'll talk about that nearer the time, Miller. Should be able to work something out."

"Then, there's the question of schooling for my children, sir," Miller went on. "With Hazel being nine and all...? And she's not the only one I know of, there's the older of the Begg brothers.... I don't expect there's any sort of a school in Mkwaya. Soon she'll be old enough for secondary school and, as you know, there isn't a boarding school for Europeans in Tanganyika. Unless Dr. Welch gets something going in time, it looks like I'll have to send her out of the country; Nairobi, maybe. Right now we've only got the one classroom for all ages."

"We're planning on a second class, Miller, and more besides. We'll soon split up the ages a bit; build dorms for boarders; Get the little whipper snappers set up properly. Can't manage with all age groups together. No, you'll see, we'll soon have a proper school up and running – probably by the time your eldest's ready for high school. When we do, you can send your children up here. Put them on a plane from Nach to Dar; overnight train ride to Kongwa and – *voilà!*"

PART ONE

THE FOREIGNER

CHAPTER ONE

TRAIN TO KONGWA

January, 1952

THE SHRILL WHISTLE FROM THE PANTING STEAM ENGINE alerted us to our imminent departure, then a disembodied voice intoned over crackling speakers that we were about to leave and for all to "stand clear of the train."

"Goodbye," I sniffed.

The guard waved his green flag, his whistle shrieked, then with a barely perceptible jog against couplings, the train nudged forward. The carriages were crowded with two hundred or so European children; four, five or six little bodies leaning out each open, wood-framed window. Tearful mothers reached up lovingly, some jogging alongside, oblivious to jets of steam from the train's exhausts that embraced them as they clung to their children before fingers were torn apart by the train's inexorable progress. The pall of engine smoke left hanging in the still air had been stirred by the movement of the carriages beneath, enveloping those on the platform in clouds of muddy darkness as it created roiling eddies of light and shade and left some rubbing eyes from coal smuts. With Mum and Dad two hundred miles away, I'd hung back from the window, leaving the strangers to it. I'd managed a polite goodbye to Mr. and Mrs. Kherer, the colleagues of my dad who'd been looking after me. Then I'd blinked back my tears, hoping no one would notice. *Boys don't cry. Boys don't cry.*

Feeling lost, hot and uncomfortable, I'd sunk back into the maroon leather bench seat, already sticky with someone's sweat, and watched in dismay the departure activity around me.

I became attuned to the slow *click-click* of the wheels over the rail joints as it built faster into a *clickity-clack* when we passed through marshalling yards and picked up steam. I felt forlorn and took no notice of the boys around me as I sat in the silence of my heartbroken world. The others, who had quietened down once we'd left the station, slowly came out of their dismal silence and started finding something to talk about. I just sat there watching them, amazed they could so quickly forget leaving their parents, knowing they would not see or talk to them again for nearly six months.

Presently our modest pace slowed to a sedate *click-click*, as the train rolled through a sun-baked shanty town with its flaring shelters of corrugated iron, battered metal signs, flattened cardboard boxes, and palm-thatched roofs. Tall and stately coconut palms reached snobbishly for the sun way above the desolation below where dried-out, scrubby thorn bushes survived, rooted in baking white sand.

I was wide-eyed at what I was seeing and how different this was from my cloistered experience in England. Less than a week ago I had been in London town, with its bustling shops and noisy traffic, its historical buildings and dirty factories… and its rain. Now this. *Where am I?* I asked myself. *What am I doing here? I came to Africa to be with my parents, not go off on a train into the middle of nowhere with people I don't know, or care about.*

I stared out the window lost for words. Throughout the passing village smoke from the cooking fires hung like a pall, diffusing sunlight into dark grey shadows. Large and buxom African women draped in gaily coloured kangas, heads covered in kilembas tiny watoto swaddled on their backs, squatted by open fires stirring their pots of posho, the staple for the evening meal. Chickens, disturbed in their grazing by a cyclist, scattered, letting out irritated clucks before returning to that patch where food had seemed plentiful. Shenzi dogs, bedraggled, flea-bitten and bearing wounds from recent fights with their canine neighbours, slunk between dwellings, searching endlessly for something, anything to eat. I didn't feel for the dogs. I cared only that I was alone in myself and no one cared for me.

The train slowed to a crawl and I watched in amazement as older African boys ran alongside. They were dressed in binding seams, all that was left of a vest, and khaki shorts filled with holes and ripped with tears that revealed smooth black bottoms. *Crikey, they're almost naked; is that allowed?* I wondered as the sight of them intruded on my sad thoughts.

The children held out their hands as they caught my eye.

"Baksheesh, baksheesh," they called, through radiant smiles and glistening white teeth, hoping I'd be the generous bwana mdogo who would toss them a ten cent coin or two, those ones with the hole in the middle. But not me. Not today.

The repetitive chuffs of the locomotive grew louder and faster as the maroon-painted Garrett locomotive of East African Railways and Harbours (E.A.R. & H.) was given its head and our speed picked up. I stared with indifference at the change as our route became lined with vegetation. Thick, impenetrable-looking forest bordered the line a verdant green, with huge, soggy leaves, damp with humidity, tied together with lianas as thick as a python and as long as the train itself.

I should have been interested but I wasn't.

I missed Mother and Father terribly. Funny how you can miss something you've rarely had. Because the climate in Nigeria, where they'd lived, was so unhealthy, my parents left me in England, at age three and a half, to attend Cable House, a boarding nursery school. As if that wasn't bad enough, I often remained with the principal and her family (she owned the school) during the holidays when my parents couldn't get home from Nigeria, which was more often than not. I don't mean to be unkind. She was a dear lady who was always very good to me. But, it's not the same as your real parents, is it?

I remembered well that first day at Cable House even though I'd been so young. We must have travelled by train and bus because I was being carried by Allan, a friend of my parents whom I heard talk of in later years, as we walked down the country lane to the school which occupied a former stately home. I do not recall if they told me where I was going or whether I understood it from their conversation but I was bawling my eyes out. I knew I was going to be left behind.

At age seven, I was moved – attending Allan House, a boarding prep school with strict discipline and the first of many experiences of being caned for the slightest behaviour infraction, imagined or real.

Parental visits from Nigeria were few in my first nine years of life and could be counted with three fingers where my father was concerned. Now, I was in Africa at least, but not much better off.

I cannot know how I would have developed had we remained in England and experienced a normal home life. I do know, as a somewhat delicate child because of severe asthma and a skin rash – something that did not elicit sympathy from most other children – that I became somewhat reclusive and a loner. I would make friends but usually only a few. Otherwise, even though surrounded by others, I preferred my own company whenever I could get it. Which at boarding school wasn't often.

The other boys in the compartment got noisier, snapping me back to the present. I ignored their talk, instead taking notice of my surroundings. I scanned the polished oak walls and fittings. Brass fixtures flared a sharp brilliance as shards of afternoon sunlight streamed in and shadows traced themselves according to the train's direction. High on one wall was a map of the rail route from Dar es Salaam to the end of the line at Kigoma, on Lake Tanganyika, some seven hundred and eighty miles away. I peered closely and noted disappointedly the spur that led off the main line at Msagali. There were two stations on the spur, the first Kongwa, the second Hogoro. The map confirmed we were on the correct route. I felt even more down, and sighed; we would reach Kongwa eventually. I turned to the opposite wall and gazed at a landscape print of a passenger train crossing the savannah, with graceful giraffes necking under flat-topped acacias.

When one of the boys said, "Come on, chaps, let's see what it looks like with the bunks up," I took notice.

As I stood, I asked the one who wanted to put the bunks up, "Why do we need bunks?"

"To sleep, of course. We'll be all night on the train," another boy answered for him.

"Oh, yes," I said. "I'd forgotten. So when will we arrive?"

"It takes about twenty-two hours to get there," said a third. "It's a long way, you know, and it depends on what happens along the way. These trains don't run faster than twenty-five to thirty miles an hour. My dad says the problem is the rail lines are narrow gauge."

"What does that mean?"

"Well, the lines are too close together, of course. They're a little over three feet apart; most rail lines are about five feet. I don't know why they build it that way 'cept it's cheaper or something. Anyway, my dad says trains that run on narrow gauge mustn't travel fast or they'll tip over on the curves."

"Really?" I asked, elated with the idea of our carriage rolling onto its side and wondering, hopefully, if that would mean Kongwa was cancelled and I could return to Lindi.

The first boy was leading the way in raising the bunks. We lifted the back rests of the bench seats to make a third and fourth. Then the others climbed on those two to lift a fifth and sixth above them. With them in position the first boy lay down on one of the lowest and called, "I bags this one."

"I bags the other bottom one," called the second and promptly laid out on it to establish his claim.

"I bags a top bunk," I called out before I was left with no choice and hastily scrambled up high to claim my territory.

"Let's lower them again," the fourth suggested after surveying the assembly with five of us in place. "It's way too early for bedtime and we haven't got anywhere to sit, man."

I was encouraged to join the conversation. Several of us were new to the school and didn't know what to expect.

"My name's Edwards," I said, after a little coaxing. "I arrived from England six days ago. My home's in Lindi now. That's where I've been for the last five days 'til I flew to Dar es Salaam to catch this train."

Kenneth Aranky, who was slim and tallish, with dark, almost black hair, olive skin and a long but angular face, told us who he was. Tony Shed explained it was his second term and his nickname was Sheddy. He was about my height, lightly built yet muscular and quick to smile. He was self confident and acted like everything was under control. His dad was an engineer and worked on projects in Dar es Salaam harbour. Sigurd Ivey followed Sheddy in turn, then Mike Jenner and the evidently brainy one of the group, Stewart Berry. It turned out I was the only one recently from England.

"You flew to Africa, eh?" asked Ivey. "Boy, I sailed on a ship with my mum. My dad was already here. I don't remember a whole lot about it 'cos I was only eight, but I liked it a lot. I want to be a sailor when I grow up."

Ivey had moved from Britain two years earlier. He had ancestors that may have hailed from Norway but he wasn't sure. He was taller than any of us and had a smiling, V-shaped face that displayed an easy-going nature.

He was wearing school uniform like we all were, khaki shirt and shorts with khaki socks and brown shoes.

"Did you have a celebration on the plane when you crossed the line, Edwards?" Ivey asked. "Like we did on the ship?"

"What line?" I asked.

"You know, when you cross the equator, they have this celebration with the old man of the sea, Neptune and his helpers, and you get dunked in water and covered in coloured paints made with ice cream and stuff. Boy, it was fun."

"No, they didn't do that on the plane; although there was a sort of celebration of two New Year's Eves."

"Two New Year's Eves?" chipped in Jenner. "How can you have two New Year's Eves?"

"Well, the captain told us when the clocks were chiming midnight in Dar es Salaam and then, again, three hours later when it was midnight in Britain. Some of the grown-ups asked for more drinks when he did that."

"So where do you live?" asked Sheddy who seemed not to recall I'd already mentioned Lindi.

"Lindi," I repeated. "That's south of Dar es Salaam. I've only been there five days and we haven't got a house to live in so we stayed in a hotel. I left yesterday by plane. It was my third flight this week."

"Wow, what's it like?" Jenner wanted to know. "I've never flown in a plane."

"I haven't been to Lindi," Aranky interrupted. "I remember once being taken to Malindi but I think that's in Kenya. Do they have ice-cream shops in Lindi?"

"No."

"They only have one in Dar," Berry interjected with a knowing air, "and that only opened about four weeks ago. I shouldn't think they'd have one in Lindi."

"Well, I know about the one in Dar," retorted Aranky. "It belongs to my parents."

"Golly, really?" we enthused as we stared at him in admiration. "Can you eat as much as you like any time you want?"

"No. My dad says the ice cream is for sale and if I want some, I must use my pocket money like anyone else."

That didn't sound quite so much fun; *what a mean dad*, I thought.

"I don't think we've even got a toy shop in Lindi," I changed the subject.

We resumed our stares out the window to contemplate our deprived life... and I my new world.

At dinner time, the restaurant car's portly and superior-looking maître d' – dressed in his bleached white kanzu and a green, velvet waistcoat with brass buttons, crimson lining and gold braid, his head topped with a scarlet fez – walked the length of the train's long corridors tapping his xylophone in a lethargic diner's concerto. There was a general every-boy-for-himself movement into the train's corridor, causing teachers to flatten themselves against the windows before they recovered their composure and asserted their authority.

"Everybody just stop where you are! Back to your compartments, please! We'll let you know when it's your turn."

It was going to take many sittings for all to get a meal. When our turn came, we hurried through several carriages to reach the restaurant car; scurried by the galley kitchen with its indescribable heat and the clatter of feverish activity through the open doors, and then into the dining area.

I found a seat next to a window. The table for four was covered with a brilliant white tablecloth adorned with matching serviettes sporting the E.A.R. monogram. Two small lamps with tiny shades and tassels were mounted on the wall and another stood in the middle, flanked by small vases displaying posies of carnations. Four place settings of heavy, monogrammed cutlery completed the table top. There was warmth about this car with rays of a vivid sunset streaming in on the polished oak reflecting a deep, golden glow that I liked. Tony Shed slid in beside me but there were two boys already at the table, so that split up our group.

"Hello," said one as we sat. "I'm Grandcourt, and this is Keller."

Keller acknowledged me with a nod; we recognised each other. Keller, with his bleached white hair and I thought Scandinavian appearance, turned out to be German. He'd flown from Lindi with me on the same plane but we'd not spoken.

"His name's Edwards. I'm Shed."

The waiter was not long coming. I noticed grown-ups ordering from menus while we were brought our food directly, no choice, just eat what you're given. It was roast beef and Yorkshire pudding with new potatoes, veggies and gravy served on heavy, monogrammed china; it was good so we had no complaints. The four of us got into conversation but soon the two of them were talking to each other, with Sheddy and me doing the same.

The clickity-clack of the wheels, the rocking of the train and the pitch blackness outside that followed the golden sunset, made the restaurant car warm and comforting. It was a strange feeling really. I had left home, no doubt there, but I wasn't at school yet. I was in a kind of no-man's-land, a nether-world where, I liked to think, school jurisdiction – and discipline – were not quite yet in force.

If only I could enjoy school as much as I'm enjoying this train ride, I thought.

Sheddy brought me back from my daydream.

"So, with you being a new boy and all, do you know what house you're in?"

"Yes, my dad received a letter from the school. Uh, Livingstone," I said tentatively. "Does that sound right?"

"Yes it does, jolly good. I'm in Livingstone too. I wonder which house you'll be in."

"But I just said Livingstone."

"Yes, I know, I didn't mean that sort of house. We live in individual houses in Kongwa. There aren't any big school buildings like in England. The houses we live in used to belong to families that have gone and so now they're used by the school."

"That sounds nice," I said. "With kitchens and sitting rooms?"

"Not any more; they did have. They still have the rooms, of course, but now they're all bedrooms. The bedroom has four beds in it; the sitting room has four beds in it, and what was the kitchen has one or maybe two beds in it, depending. It's the prefects' room. You know about prefects, I suppose?"

"Yes, I bloody-well do," I felt irritated at the thought. "I was at boarding school in England and they had prefects. Mean ones, too."

"Did they make you fag for them?" Sheddy asked.

"Of course… and sometimes, even when a prefect had nothing for you to do, they'd make you stand there and wait until they thought-up something."

"I hate that so much."

"These houses," I asked, "are they like we had in England, you know, were they all joined up in long rows?"

"No, they're individual. They were for married people, pretty small. Most are about fifty yards apart with a choo in between."

"What's a choo?"

"A toilet, you know, a big drop. It's also called a dub."

"What big drop?"

"There's no flush, no water, just a hole in the ground."

"You mean they don't have real toilets, not even in the house?"

"No, well, a few of them do, but most don't, it just depends."

"Oh."

"And we walk a helluva lot."

"What?"

"We walk miles and miles and miles every day."

"Why?"

"Because, like I said, the houses are far apart. So are the classrooms. They used to be offices; so's the Head's office and the mess and the sports fields. The girls are miles away from the boys, obviously, and the Seniors are miles away from everybody, so we have tons of walking to do. And that makes fagging even worse, 'cos if a prefect wants you to fetch things that are far away, you have to walk all that way, man."

"So how big is the school?" I asked.

"I dunno; maybe a mile long. My dad says the school area is two hundred and seventy acres big so whatever that is in miles, you know, square miles. It's not all being used yet, there're still a lot of empty buildings, but the school is growing so fast it'll soon use them all. The grown-ups that used to live in the houses probably didn't mind all the distances 'cos they had cars. I'm telling you, it's big. Soon as I'm in Seniors I'm bringing my bike."

"You can bring a bike?"

"Yup, once you're in Seniors. And it's bloody hot in Kongwa; you'll be asking your parents if you can bring your bike too."

"But I haven't got a bike," I said, embarrassed. "My mum won't let me have one."

Sheddy stared at me, clearly amazed.

Not being a bike owner, I lapsed into silence again as I thought about how unfair she was.

✦ ✦ ✦

BY 8 P.M., THE CONDUCTOR, IN HIS uniform of grey jacket embroidered with a crimson East African Railways logo, and grey trousers, was moving through the train asking about bedding requirements. Not long after, shoeless train porters, in khaki shirt and shorts, were lugging large maroon canvas bags containing rolled up bedding, squeezing down the pinching corridors and into each compartment, there to make up the bunks. Our four companions had disappeared again.

Sheddy and I stood in the corridor gazing out the open window into the pitch-black, catching sight of fireflies or sparks from the engine, I wasn't sure which. The chuffing of the engine noise, the hooting as we approached unguarded crossings, the smell of coal smoke, all wafted in on the train's slipstream. Then Sheddy was called by someone and wandered off. It struck me that I'd never seen darkness like this before. Perhaps if I'd been old enough during the war with its black-out? But I was only little then. Now in England everything was lit up at night. But in this moonless African night it was definitely black.

By the time I returned to my compartment Berry and Jenner were on their bunks, noses into books.

"Have you seen Sheddy?" I asked.

"He's a couple of compartments along," said Berry. "I think he went to listen to Grandcourt play his mouth organ."

I wandered the corridor until I heard the music. The bunks were not made up. Grandcourt was sitting in a far corner against the window, right foot drawn up, his heel resting on the bunk he was sitting on, both hands cupping the mouth organ to his lips in a loving clinch as melancholy sound filled my ears. He was playing country and western music and this was the first time in my life I'd ever heard it. I found the music bitter-sweet. It lifted me when Joe played *Hey, Good Lookin'* or dropped me down again with *My Heart Cries for You.* It made me yearn for Lindi where I could be with Mum and Dad. Sadness gripped me even though there was no one to sing the words, so I wasn't sure whether to like it or hate it.

"Everyone back to their compartments!" called a prefect dressed formally in school dress uniform of white shirt, long grey trousers and a striped school tie that matched the zebroid, green, black and gold stripes of his blazer. His uniform was finished with posh, brown, polished shoes. "Come on now, everybody back. The 'boys' can't complete making up the beds with you lot blocking the corridors. Besides which it'll soon be lights-out so we want you in your bunks... now!"

One chap, three compartments away thought the rules didn't apply to him. "C'mon, Ian," he said, "I'm older than this lot; I'm going down the end to see the others."

"You'll do as you're bloody-well told," responded the prefect. "Or explain yourself to Fergie. Now get in there and settle down."

"Who's Fergie?" I asked of no one in particular.

"Mr. Ferguson," said Sheddy. "He's Livingstone Junior boys Housemaster as well as an English teacher – and more likely to find a reason to cane you than any of the others," he added as an after-thought.

"Oh no, not again," I shuddered, as I thought about Allan House.

Minutes later, having shed our clothes, we'd squeezed flat into our bunks, with barely enough height to rest our heads on upturned palms, as we read. Then I had a thought to do with the prefect who'd barked the order down the corridor.

"Who was the one who ordered us to bed, Sheddy?" I called down to him.

"You mean Ian Longden?" Sheddy asked, sticking his head out the side of his middle bunk as he looked up. "The one dressed in blazer and all?"

"Yes, that one."

"Ian's Livingstone house prefect and one of the highest prefects in the school. A chap called Robin Hoy is Curie's house prefect but he's also Head Boy. We haven't got an official second to Robin. Ian would probably be considered for Head Boy if Robin left. He won't get a chance now."

"Why?"

"This is his last term. Many of the top Seniors will leave in June when school breaks up. Ian'll be leaving then, I heard. It's a pity in a way; the chaps like him."

Lights were switched off. The clacking of wheels and motion of the train brought on drowsiness, then sleep... for the others. Why I had to be the exception I didn't know. I'd finished reading and was content with the ride. My mind was in turmoil as my thoughts ran with the excitement of the day, yet also was haunted with sadness at being far from home. If the train journey didn't come to an end, then maybe everything would be all right.

My thoughts drifted to my new-found friends. Sheddy seemed to like me which was nice. He was a good-looking boy and I could see how he would be popular. I was amazed at how easily he beat another boy at arm wrestling even though the other chap was bigger and heavier. And when he talked about some of the things he built with his dad at home I knew he must be pretty clever.

Berry was different. We hadn't talked much yet but I liked him too. He was of light build and I thought it wouldn't take much to knock him down. His arms and legs were thin. He had thin, blond hair and an angel face. He seemed brainy though. I recognised him as similar to a boy I'd known at Allan House; always reading, seemed to be good at learning, popular with the teachers. I guessed I'd be asking him for help with maths prep from time to time.

Aranky was good at sports. Sheddy said Aranky usually got to be captain of any football team he was playing on. I don't suppose he'll be pleased with me not joining in on account of my asthma.

Ivey I thought of as organised; everything for him had to be just so. He was tall and I thought probably strong; he appeared happy with a constant smile. I judged he was a practical sort, probably less daring than someone like Sheddy? I hoped we'd become friends.

It was cosy in my bunk on the train. Occasionally it chugged along at quite a lick. At other times I'd wake because there wasn't any movement. We'd stopped again at one of the numerous halts that governed this train's progress. I heard hushed conversations outside our window and the squeak of a trolley. Peering out I saw a high pole and a lamp smothered with insects. It spread a pool of yellow light over a couple of bodies prone in a sleepy haunch. The cicadas were shrilling. Far away, a cockerel crowed. A full moon had risen to my surprise after the earlier blackness. Now its luminescence lit the scene. I heard, from way up front, the impatient hissing and clanking of a steam engine anxious to be on its way. After a while I grew weary, settled back and closed my eyes.

CHAPTER TWO

ARRIVAL

I'D BEEN DREAMING ABOUT MY FLIGHT FROM London. We'd taken off from London Airport North in the morning of New Year's Eve and flown first class. We'd landed to refuel in Rome, Cairo, Khartoum, Entebbe and Nairobi. The journey was luxurious and infinitely exciting. People look back now and call the '50s the golden age of air travel. They're right.

Even though I'd heard Africa was hot I was amazed to discover just how so in Cairo at 2 a.m. and how stifling the air could be when mixed with mosquito spray that Egyptian ground staff used when they came aboard. They walked up and down the aisle and sprayed something called 'Flit' in the air all over us. The sprayer had a hand pump like for a bicycle with a tin can at the end out of which the spray came through a nozzle. "It's to keep the mozzies at bay," I was told.

It had been a thrill when I'd spent time in the cockpit with the captain while the first officer socialised in the cabin. And oh, the excitement after that thirty-hour flight when we'd circled Dar es Salaam and I'd first set eyes on millions of coconut palms. It had been super meeting up with Dad. Here I was, in Africa, with both parents and the promise of a family future for the first time in my nearly ten years of life… together at last.

That joy had lasted an hour or two before my heart sank.

Mother and Father had met with a business colleague of his who lived in

Dar, Franz Kherer and his wife, Jean. I'd been exploring the hotel when Dad called me over to join them in the lounge where they were having drinks. After ordering me a lemonade, he'd said, "There's something we want to ask you, chum. Seeing as you'll be leaving for school in Kongwa by train, from here on January 7th, we wondered whether you might prefer to remain with the Kherers for the duration of the week rather than journey to Lindi with Mum and me. You'll be in Lindi for only a short time, it seems hardly worth it?"

My heart sank. I'd been in Africa only a few hours when Mother and Father were going to leave me already!

"When will you be leaving?" I'd asked, looking sadly down at my hands.

"Tomorrow morning, chum, very early. Plane takes off at six."

"How long will I be away in Kongwa?" I'd followed up, tears welling as the full appreciation that I'd soon be far away in boarding school once more, finally sunk in.

"Well, Kongwa School has just two terms a year," he'd said, "so you'll be gone five-and-a-half months."

"Five-and-a-half months!" I'd reacted wide-eyed in horror. "And I'll have seen you for one night!"

"The time is short, I'm afraid, but that's the way it worked out."

I'd taken no time at all in reaching my decision. I'd wiped the tears from my cheeks as I told Dad, "I want to travel with you and Mum to Lindi, even if it is for just four days, and I don't care how early I have to get up."

THE TRAIN SHUDDERED AS THE CARRIAGES JERKED against their couplings. Perhaps I'd slept and was dreaming as I woke because I hadn't realised we'd stopped. Wondering what station this was, I moved to peer through the window. I caught sight of the moonlit sign on the fence at the end of the platform as we rumbled by; 'MOROGORO,' it read.

I think someone told me Morogoro's about half way, I muttered to myself. I glanced at my watch with its luminous dial. For a moment I thought I'd forgotten to wind it, then I realised it was reading four in the morning. It was early still.

A little after six, I was awakened by the noise of others. With golden sunlight spilling through the shutters and the chatter of voices in the corridor, there wasn't to be any sleeping in. Stewart was first to the hand basin, standing there naked as he washed his face and hands and then under his arms. I'd noticed the night before when we got undressed that the others weren't wearing a vest or underpants; I was the only one who was. Well, you had to in England; it was so cold most of the time.

"It's too hot here," I was told. "You don't need them."

"Well, if you others aren't wearing any, neither will I," I proclaimed and shed mine there and then.

As we struggled about getting dressed with no room to do it in, we heard girls in the corridor on their way to breakfast. Ivey thought that the right moment to drop the louver blind on the compartment door that hid the interior from passers-by in the corridor and through which piercing rays of sunlight had been filtering. The thud caused the girls to glance in, where they saw the naked Stewart, spotlighted in the newly-released sunlight, glancing quickly and nervously around at the sound. The girls broke into convulsions of laughter at seeing a naked boy. Hands to mouths they giggled their way down the corridor. Ivey was impressed with himself and laughed out loud; we joined in as Stewart frowned in annoyance while hauling the blind back into place.

"I s'pose you think you're really funny!" he said.

Jenner lowered the blind on the other window revealing a wonderful view. Stretching as far as the eye could see, bathed in the glow of this brilliant sunrise was countryside of burned gold. Scrub grass dotted with golden acacias intermingled with msasas and a few mopani trees, all rooted in Martian red soil, seemed to stretch forever. Breaking the horizon were the necks of a squad of giraffes, but much closer in zebra and wildebeest in their thousands mingled and grazed in an orgy of perpetual motion.

Most of the animals displayed a studied indifference to the train's passing, but not so the Thomson's gazelle that had been drinking at a water hole. Heads erect and alert, ears twitching and noses taking the air, these gazelle were not so blasé and began moving off to give us distance. I was disappointed when we lost sight of the herds and were left with only the long shadow of the train bouncing over the uneven earth and the now empty savannah beyond. Except, that is, for a pack of jackals trotting purposefully in the direction of the animals we'd left behind.

Sheddy was last up and slowest to get ready, so when Stewart asked me,

"Want to go for breakfast?" I nodded and we swayed our way down the narrow corridors to the restaurant car.

"You're too late for this sitting," asserted Miss Strong, the Senior Mistress. She had assumed command on behalf of the girls who had, through their wisdom and foresight, taken over the restaurant car completely. "You'll have to wait. I suggest you go back to your compartment and wait for the gong."

We beat a hasty retreat from all this female flesh, two of whom I recognised as they eyed us and whispered to each other, hands cupped to ears. The one was Annelize Van Buuren whom I'd teamed up with, along with her brother Egbert, in Lindi. She thoughtfully decided not to acknowledge me now that we were on the school train. Her friend was the other girl, perhaps a year or two older, whom Annelize had sat with on the plane to Dar. It would not be good to be seen in female company. I thought I heard the whisper from Annelize though, "See, Hazel, he was on the plane with us, the one I was telling you about."

We returned to look for the others and found a compartment where bunks had been returned to daytime positions. There was space to share company with Alder, Maclean and Neil Thomson, a Junior's prefect, who was regaling those two with his adventures hunting with his dad.

"Yes, come and join us if you want," he invited. "I was telling this lot about some of the hunting trips I've been on with my dad up in the area close to the Ngorongoro Crater and the Serengeti Plains and—"

"—Where are they?" I interrupted.

"Up in the north of the country," Neil answered. "You know, west of Arusha. You know where that is, I suppose?"

"No, I'm new to Africa."

"Oh, well, that's where they are. Anyway, that was how we bagged the elephant," he said, turning back to the others. "I'm telling you those tusks were huge. I couldn't lift either of them no matter how hard I tried."

Neil was a good-looking boy, quite tall, with a continuing smile and a quiff in his honey blond hair that made him seem a friendly sort.

"What did you do with them?" inquired Alder.

"My dad sold them to some Indians, man. They do all those carvings out of ivory like you see in the shops. I think they probably sent the tusks to India where they do the work; I dunno really, something like that. I'm not much interested in the ivory; it was just the excitement of the hunt."

"Did you see the zebra and wildebeest we passed some way back?" I enthused, not wanting to be left out with my observance of wild animals.

"Yeah, man. They're nothing, man. You can see those animals and more besides almost anywhere, man. They're two a penny; you don't even bother with those, man. Now if you want to talk lion, that's something else."

I listened entranced as Neil told us a story of a lion kill with his dad. I was kind of fascinated with the detail but also disappointed at the same time. I couldn't see the point of killing animals and, surprising for me, I spoke up and said so.

"What's with you, man, you some kind of sissy? That's what a man does, man, he hunts. It's the challenge of man against animal with all their cunning and ability to survive in the bush. It's tough, eh, I'm telling you, man, it's not easy. You need to grow up, man."

Chastened, I kept quiet after that and listened a little longer until we heard the xylophone. I leaped up, grabbed Berry and headed for the restaurant car.

There were two spaces left, at different tables. Robin Hoy seemed to be organising this shift, "You, what's your name?"

"Berry."

"You sit here, man...You?"

"Edwards."

"Take that seat there and join in with them, see?"

I found myself at a table that included Ivey's familiar face.

"Hello, I'm Edwards."

"Lugt."

"Meyer."

The two older boys looked down at me in a pitying way.

"Where've you been?" whispered Ivey.

I told him of my visit with Berry to Neil Thomson's compartment, and the stories he was telling about hunting with his dad.

"He's a good sort, Neil, you know," said Ivey. "I've heard about him and they say he's jolly decent. Not like some prefects."

"What's for breakfast?"

By the time we'd finished and were returning to our compartment, the train drew into Kilosa. Sheddy was close behind.

"We can get off the train for a bit," he said. "It'll be in Kilosa for a while. Let's go for a walk and see what we can see, eh?"

"Are we allowed to do that, you know, get off the train?"

"Oh yes, it's allowed in Kilosa."

"All right, you lead. We'll follow."

Sheddy opened the door at one end of the carriage and descended the steps. Ivey and I followed, me feeling nervous because we would be in trouble if the train started up again and we couldn't get back on.

"Don't worry about that, man, it'll be here for a long time; it was last time. They have to wait for another train coming from the other direction to pass us and you can see it's not here yet."

I felt better as I noticed other boys and teachers had got off too. Soon there was a crowd milling about in the red dust.

Sheddy led us through a door to the station's waiting room where there were a number of parents with children ready to join us on our school-bound trek. One little girl, too young to be coming to Kongwa, was crying, it seemed because she was about to lose her brother to this inland migration. Sitting at a bench was a boy I judged about my age, with thick Coca-Cola glass spectacles, looking grim and tearful as his mother attempted to comfort him with words like, "It won't be so long and soon you'll be home again."

As if five-and-a-half months isn't long, I thought. *His parents are lying to him too.*

There was a counter behind which an indifferent looking Indian was standing, the proprietor of the biltong he had for sale. Sheddy spotted it, crusted-looking strips of antelope meat that had been hung from trees to dry, burned by the sun while being marinated by flies. I thought it looked revolting but he got excited and said he must have some.

"Ten cents, plis?" from the Indian.

Sheddy hunted for change but couldn't come up with any.

"I'll lend you ten cents," I said.

"Oh, would you, that's jolly decent," said Sheddy. "Thanks a lot, man… I'll pay you back, do you want some?"

"No, thanks."

I didn't say anything but to me biltong looked like something you might sweep up off the floor and place quickly into the dustbin.

We wandered through glass doors into the blinding sunshine. I screwed up my eyes, gradually letting the light back in. There was a row of cars parked on the sandy street. Most seemed to be Peugeots but there were several Land Rovers and one or two others like the Austin Hereford, looking amazingly clean given its surroundings, and a shiny new Vauxhall Cresta.

I became vaguely aware that, somewhere far away, a whistle blew. Sheddy was gnawing on his biltong and had got Ivey to try a piece.

"Look at this rattle trap," I said.

I'd spotted a Land Rover that must have come off safari not long since. It was caked in dried mud and was open to the world without a windscreen and no rag top and no cushions to sit on. It had flat iron seats and a slightly curved iron back to lean against, both welded to the chassis.

"Boy, they'll need cushions or something for those seats. Imagine bounding around in the bush with no springs on that lot," said Ivey.

"They're tough, man, those Rovers are built tough," Sheddy said again, as he tore at the solidified biltong like a lion with a new kill. "They're designed to stand up to the East African roads and there's not a car in the world that's tougher."

"What about a Jeep?" I asked, having seen a Hollywood war movie, in which the military dashed around the front lines in Jeeps, with no doors and no roofs and no windscreens.

"Oh, they're not a patch on a Rover," asserted Sheddy. "They're pansies in comparison. There's nothing can touch a Land Rover."

"Where've you been?! What're you doing? Do you want to miss the train?"

Mr. Chambers rattled off the questions in agitation with Hoy by his side. The two had burst through the station's exit searching for us and had come panting up at a sprint.

"The train was about to leave and someone said you weren't on board, so we had to stop its departure. Now come on, the three of you, hurry now, run and don't stop 'til you're back on the train!" he called breathlessly as he clipped me a clout on the back of my head (against which I had ducked, but alas not quickly enough). We ran for the train in full flight.

"And don't get off again 'til we arrive in Kongwa!" he called after us.

We jumped on the steps along with Chambers and Hoy further along. Even as we climbed on board the train inched forward.

By the time we'd returned to our compartment amid the buzz of boys wondering what trouble we'd be in, the bedding had been removed and the upper four bunks tucked away. Our friends were not there so we sat facing each other at the window, watched the unending landscape of savannah, and talked of things that matter to nine-year-olds.

"That was funny, Ivey, when you lowered the blind on the door and made Berry jump with those girls looking in. They laughed all down the corridor."

Ivey smiled. "I couldn't resist it," he said glancing at Sheddy. "Berry strikes me as a bit shy or something. He's a decent chap but needs to open up a bit."

"I like him," I said. "Seems to be brainy."

"Me too," said Sheddy, "but I tell you what. I wish someone would lower the louvers in one of the girls' compartments so we could see in on them when they're naked," he laughed.

I smiled but wasn't sure I agreed. I hadn't discovered girls and the idea of them in the buff held a little curiosity perhaps but no great appeal. Ivey changed the subject.

"I've got a Hornby Dublo electric train."

"You have?" I exclaimed wide-eyed. "Boy, you're lucky. Do you have it set up somewhere or do you have to put it together each time?"

"Oh it's all set up," said Ivey with a grimace as though that should be obvious. "I have a table-top set-up on a ping pong table. It has landscaping and marshalling yards and freight trains and passenger trains and all sorts of things, with signals and level crossings and bridges."

I was almost breathless with excitement. "I haven't seen anything like that outside of Hamley's," I said. "That sounds spiffing!" Then I fell into silence for a moment. "I haven't got an electric train," I confessed ruefully. "I did have a clockwork one in England but it got left behind."

"Clockwork is old hat. If your parents ask you what you want for Christmas, you jolly well tell them you want an electric gari-ya-moshi," he announced with a head toss. "They're smashing."

"Gari-ya-moshi?"

"Yes, that's a steam train like this one. I s'pose you can't speak any Swahili being new from England?"

"No, I know 'Jambo,' and that's about it. Do they teach it at school?"

"They don't give Swahili lessons anymore. If you like I'll teach you a bit now," Sheddy offered. "I speak it well. I was raised by my ayah, that's an African nurse who takes care of you. Saved Mum a lot of work."

And there followed my first Swahili lesson with Sheddy and Ivey outdoing each other to teach me as many expressions and as much vocabulary as they knew and could think of in the enthusiasm of the moment. "Lete chakula tafadhali (bring the food, please)." "Mimi nasema kibanda kiko wapi?" (I said, where is the hut?)

We stopped at tiny villages that looked as though they hardly warranted a stop. There might be a few tidy-looking kibandas. There were always the shanties. There was nothing else here. No reason to live here, it seemed, except this was the way it had always been. But what depressed, now in the brilliance of the African sun, were scenes of horror. I looked out at ghastly examples of injured or malformed humanity; people who appeared as though they'd be better off dead.

"Why have we stopped again?" I asked, feeling uncomfortable at the sights. "We always stop at these places but no one gets on or off, near as I can tell."

"Well, it's a long train," replied Sheddy. "You can't see either end. Maybe they're refilling the water tender for the engine. If you were at the back, at the guard's van, you'd probably see a few letters or parcels being unloaded for a nearby mission, something like that."

"I can't believe the horrific things that have happened to these poor people. Oh my gosh, look at that man there with the huge leg and foot."

"It's called elephantitis," said Sheddy. "I've heard it's terribly painful. I don't know how he gets around."

"Elephantiasis," corrected Berry. "There's only one 't'."

"You sure?" asked Sheddy.

"Yes, believe me."

"Elephan... what?" I asked.

"Never mind."

"How about that poor bloke over there, seems to have lost both eyes and a foot? What could have happened to him?"

"And what about that chap?" asked Sheddy, pointing. "Look, over there."

I followed Sheddy's finger. There was a boy, about thirteen, with his skin covered from head to foot in the most awful rash, with open sores, bleeding and suppurating wounds being plagued by flies. I turned away. I couldn't look as I thought about my own skin rash which wasn't a patch on what that African was enduring. I wished the train would leave. I felt sorry for them yet I didn't want to see their misery.

It was a relief when we ambled forward. But even as we did, there was a late arrival of younger watoto carrying sugar cane and fruit. These runny-nosed boys ran beside the train as it picked up speed calling out, "Muwa, Muwa," in their attempt to sell lengths of cane to hastily bargaining school children leaning almost too far out the windows to reach the fruit below them. And there were others bearing oranges that could be bought for a bargain, green skinned and tasting delicious. "Machungwa, Machungwa," the dusty watoto called as they ran, clutching hand-woven baskets to their heads as they tried to look up and keep up.

Lunchtime came, with more juggling of people and tables for the restaurant car. This time I was seated opposite Venables. I'd noticed him up and down the corridor; he was the one with the weeping sister I'd seen in Kilosa. But he seemed shy, even more than me, and we'd not got talking. Now here he was, peering at me across the lunch table through his thick spectacles.

"Are you a new boy too?" I asked.

"Yes."

"I'm a new boy and I'm new to Tanganyika. I haven't been here a week yet, out from England."

"Oh."

The conversation went one-sided for a while before I decided I was not so much the quiet sort in comparison. It might take a while to get him going. But, it was lunchtime, so why not try? I told Venables of my experiences in English schools and how little I saw of my parents. He seemed impressed and loosened up after a while.

"I only know Africa," he said. "I've been at a day school in Arusha, but my parents have been transferred to Kilosa and now this'll be my first term in a boarding school. I'll be a Junior."

"Me too."

After lunch I followed Sheddy to explore the train. In a carriage mostly devoted to Wilberforce house, we came across a compartment with a number of boys sitting talking. Sheddy knew the prefect/house captain who was with them.

"Ah, Shed," called Glynn Ford, 'Your dad still with the Harbours lot?"

"Yes, Glynn. But what are you doing here; I thought you moved to Urambo?"

"We have. But I may be staying-on in Kongwa after I leave school In June, to work on their experimental farm project and needed to go to Dar. I was able to cut out a lot of travelling by returning to school with you lot."

A boy jumped in, "Glynn was telling us a bit about how the school started, why don't you join us, Sheddy?"

"Okay. All right with you, Edwards? This is Edwards, by the way. New boy this term."

"Yeah, well, so what was I saying – I arrived just before the second school year started, in October 1949. I was a day boy, we all were. Boarders started in 1951."

"Were there girls, Glynn?" Sheddy asked.

"Oh yes, plenty of girls," he smiled. "Matter of fact one of them still at the school is my girlfriend, Rena Neish. Then there were others like Beryl Lloyd and Ann Kenny. They were like twins those two, always together."

"Did you get into much trouble in those days, Glynn?" asked another boy trying to change the subject from girls.

"Oh, yes. More than you lot, I hope. I've got quite a funny story actually. We got into swiping our parents' alcohol. I mean, after all, they all drunk all the time, so why shouldn't we have some. Least ways that's the way we saw it. Anyway, by now Mr. Moore had arrived and he caught us one weekend in the Kongwa Club drinking Port. When we arrived at school the following Monday we were told to report to the Head. He gave us a lecture on drinking alcohol, mostly why we shouldn't, of course. But his parting words were funny: 'And always remember,' he concluded as we left the room, 'You don't knock back Port like a double Whisky – You sip it.'"

We broke into laughter.

"Anyway, to get back to the beginning. The school officially opened on the fourth of October 1948. There were forty-seven kids, together with most of their parents, gathered in the Kongwa Club for the opening of the new school. Normally, schools smell of ink wells and chalk and empty milk bottles. This one, of course, smelled of stale beer and ash trays."

We found that hilarious and broke into laughter. "Did they get beer to drink at break instead of milk?" asked Sheddy.

Glynn tossed his head in a smile, "I don't think so. I imagine the smell was about as close as they got. Anyway they were milling around and then the Head called them to attention and said he would begin the first roll call."

"Who was the first, Glynn?" Robert Seabrook asked enthusiastically.

"You should know, you were there," Glynn responded. "Well, let me put it this way, you should know who *would* have been the first."

We frowned, "who *would have been?*"

"The first name to be called was a chap by name of Begg. Nice chap, younger than me; one or two of you may remember him, although he left Kongwa a couple of years ago. His first name was Adrian. He and his brother had recently flown out from England in a converted Lancaster bomber left over from the war years." Glynn chuckled, "I remember Begg telling me the bomb doors were still in place and he'd worried all the way to Africa what would happen if the doors suddenly burst open. They'd been instructed not to walk on them, you see – just in case – but to walk around them when they went to the toilet."

We exchanged faces with each other. "Whoa."

"Now, this chap Begg was aged eight, I think, or may have been seven come to think of it, and wasn't much used to schools at this point and was a bit fearful. Mr. Whitehead solemnly began to read from the list of names.

"Begg, Adrian," he intoned, looking expectantly at the group, obviously expecting a, 'Here, Sir.'

"It was Begg's big moment. His chance to be recorded as the very first pupil of the new Kongwa School, but it was all too much for him. He fled. Out of the Club, through the courtyard where a couple of 'boys' were stacking the empty beer bottles from the previous night, and into the embracing freedom of the bush. Dr. Welch, the Overseas Food Corporation's chief education officer, was present on this opening day. Mary Welch, his wife, was not. She was tearing through the bush in hot pursuit in an effort to recapture the seven-year-old who had evidently decided that he had come out to East Africa to avoid all this sort of thing. Not having been in a school before, he concluded that he was now too old to start and headed for home by the shortest route."

We laughed as we imagined the scene.

"Did they catch him?" asked Tommy James.

"Oh yes, eventually, but only after being coaxed out of hiding by his parents."

"Did he get the cane?" asked another.

"No, I don't think so. Not that time anyway. It was his first day, it was only a day school then and he went home to his parents that evening."

At that moment Mr. Chambers stuck his head through the door. "Ford, have you got a minute?"

With Glynn disappearing down the corridor, Sheddy and I wandered off.

It was close to two-thirty when we steamed into Gulwe. This was the closest point of population to Kongwa, I was told, and the place where the train would be split into the carriages that were going to Kongwa and the carriages of the mainline mail that was en route to Kigoma.

"Come... take a look," Sheddy called me to the window on the corridor side. There in the distance was a mountain range. "They're the Kiborianis," Sheddy assured me with a shove of his chin. "We'll be going in that direction soon. Kongwa's on the other side of the mountains."

"Why are we waiting?" I asked. "We seem to be just sitting here... again!"

It wasn't long before, with an extended whistle followed by some friendly toots, our train ambled forward. Not much later we heard the stilted and deliberate click-click, clack-clack as we crossed the points at Msagali, diverting off the mainline of rail and heading towards those distant mountains. We arrived at about three-thirty amid much engine whistling. After winding through the hemming Kiboriani foothills, the hillsides covered with scraggy and denuded forest, the landscape abruptly opened to an expansive vista. No savannah, no trees but the occasional baobab, nothing but aloaceous scrub stretched north into the haze of mountains at the distant horizon.

With a final whistle our train came to a squeaky halt.

"Everyone remain on the train until you're told to disembark," a disembodied voice called down the corridor. Then the locomotive was de-coupled, switched tracks and departed, racing back to Gulwe, there to re-link with the mainline mail.

Sheddy and I leaned out the windows on the southern side of our abandoned coaches. Looking forward, we could see a small, shoe-box building some hundred yards distant. It was standing close to the rail line in the rich, red sand, amid a huge, whirling dust devil and blowing tumbleweeds.

"Look at that dust devil," I remarked. "Gollee, that's something, eh?"

"That's nothing," said Sheddy. "We get those all the time. Just wait 'till we get a dust storm, then you'll know all about it."

"A dust storm?"

"Uh huh. You see it like a dark cloud on the horizon and it's as wide as you can see. Then it gets closer and closer until you see the sky is filling with red. And everything goes still, eh. Quiet. No birds, they've all ducked for cover. It's kinda eerie actually. Then it hits. Oh boy, then you know, eh, I'm telling you. It's hard to breathe even. The air is thick with sandy dust you have to hold your hanky to your mouth and keep your eyes closed if you can. It can last for hours when you can't hardly see anything around you."

"Wow! Really?"

"Yup. You know what a thick fog is like in England; you came from London, didn't you?"

"Yes, I did. We had thick, dirty, 'smogs' they called them. You couldn't see your hand if you held it out in front of you."

"Well, imagine the same sorta thing, but red dust and it stings when it hits you."

I looked at Sheddy in amazement as he shook his head. "I'm telling you, man."

I returned my interest to the station building. I guessed it was the official terminus. It was built with hollowed concrete bricks the same colour as the sand blowing around us. The tiled roof was coloured similarly. Under the apex of the roof, facing the direction from which we had arrived, a large engraved concrete sign set into the bricks proclaimed the legend: 'Kongwa.'

CHAPTER THREE

THE SCHOOL
AT THE END OF THE LINE

FOURTEEN MILES SOUTH OF THE TRAIN SIDING, the low, blue Kiboriani Range stood shimmering in the late afternoon heat. "Those mountains were climbed by Stanley during his search for Livingstone," said Sheddy. "You know about Stanley and Livingstone, I suppose?"

"David Livingstone, I presume?" I responded holding out my arm for a mock hand shake.

Lying half way between us and those mountains was a low hill.

"That's Kongwa Hill," said Sheddy, "and the school buildings are along its base."

"But I can't see anything."

"I know, everything's pretty small, but between here and the hill is where the school is and that's about all there is to Kongwa. See over to the right, that big hill, that's Leopard Hill. And can you see the little one in front of it, it's quite small from here, looks almost hidden but anyway, that's Church Hill."

"Hello, chaps," Anthony Paton from the third compartment joined us at the window. "What are you looking at?"

"Sheddy's telling me about Kongwa. I learned in geography in England that this part of Africa was savannah but it doesn't look like what I expected savannah to look like from the pictures in the books."

"Well," responded Paton, "there are mostly msasa and acacia trees and savannah bush between Kongwa and those mountains, but...."

"The hills are covered in trees," I said.

"Pretty scrubby ones, yes, that's because, well, you can't see from here," Paton continued, "but from around the base of Church Hill there's a donga, it's quite—"

I frowned.

"A donga, you know, a ravine," Paton said. "You know, rain water from the hills runs down and forms a river; dried up most of the time. So anyway, I suppose because of the donga, it's sort of forested around the base of the hills, if you can call those trees, sort of like what we just came through on the train. But from here on north it's just bush and baobabs, nothing else. Mostly that's because the baobab trees and the scrub were cleared for groundnuts."

Berry caught up with us, and joined in as we gazed out the window.

"What groundnuts?" I asked.

Berry jumped in. "After the war, the British Government had an idea for farming this area and other parts of Tanganyika for growing groundnuts. You know what groundnuts are, I suppose?"

"Yes, I do. My dad told me. We called them peanuts in England."

"I know," said Berry.

"They're also called monkey nuts," added Paton.

"Anyway," Berry continued, "the Groundnut Scheme was to be massive so they could grow millions of tons of nuts, three million acres in fact and maybe even more after that.

"Come off it, I queried doubtfully, as I thought about how if you put all of England's farms together in one big patch it would probably be less than three million acres.

"No, I meant three million. Anyway, after four years the government gave up on it on account of no rain."

"If there's hardly any rain where do they get water from?" I asked. "Is there a lake?"

"No, there isn't," said Berry. "There's an underground spring or something in Sagara, about forty miles away, so water gets piped from there. My dad says the development here should really have happened in Sagara but no one seems to know why Kongwa was built instead."

"There's a lake in Mpwapwa," added Paton.

"Anyway," continued Sheddy, "everyone left Kongwa and all the buildings and equipment and stuff were left here. You should see the graveyard. There's a dump where all the abandoned bulldozers and graders and ploughs and all sorts were left. It's out of bounds, of course, but there's tons of stuff to raid if you want."

"And they wrecked the land and drove the animals away," Paton added with a frown. "My dad and I hate that they frightened the animals away."

"Come on," said Sheddy. "There was nothing here to wreck. They tried to cultivate the land for everyone's benefit. I know you like animals an' all, but there's plenty around still. They didn't go killing them all off."

"Enough of them," retorted Paton with a sniff.

Berry continued, "So anyway, with all those old buildings it was decided to make a school out of them. I mean, they'd already started a school and there were plans to build more buildings but then they didn't need to on account of, like Sheddy said, everyone left Kongwa and all the buildings that were already here were abandoned."

"How do you know all this stuff?" I asked.

"My dad has a book about it, that's how. He told me to stop reading Louis L'Amour and read something intelligent. Do you chaps like L'Amour? I think he's the greatest Westerns writer ever. Anyway, the book about Kongwa was kind of boring but my dad wanted me to know about it. You're going to school there, he said, so you ought to know something about where you'll be living and studying, blah, blah, blah."

We paused to ponder Berry's words and the pressure from our dads to learn about such things.

"There're plenty of animals still," Sheddy continued, "although, Paton's right, not as many as there used to be. But that's because they drifted away, not because they were all killed. Anyway, nuts aren't grown here anymore; maybe that's why the animals are returning."

"They are?" queried Paton. "That's not what my dad says."

"Alan Wood," said Berry.

"What about him?" I asked. "Who's Alan Wood?"

"The bloke who wrote *The Groundnut Affair*, the book I was telling you about."

"Before the land was wrecked," Paton persisted, "there were tons of wild animals here. Lion, leopard, elephant, buffalo, rhinos, as well as zebra, gnus and antelope of all sorts."

"What's a gnu?" I asked.

"It's another name for wildebeest," said Paton.

"Don't forget the crocodiles in the rivers," added Sheddy.

"Yes, along the way," Paton agreed, "but not here, there aren't any rivers near Kongwa. Anyhow, now there's only a few animals in the area. If they weren't killed then they moved away because of the activity. My dad's a game warden, you know, he knows about this stuff. I go into the bush with him all the time when I'm at home. If there's any animals left when I grow up I'm going to be a game warden too, or maybe a vet."

"You're laying it on a bit," said Sheddy. "I've seen herds of impala and gazelle and antelope, even Eland and waterbuck. Oh, and giraffes when we've gone on school outings. You see hyenas nearly every night from our houses; you watch tonight, Edwards, you'll see."

"And there're baboons," Berry added.

"And more dudus than you want to know about," said Sheddy.

"Dudus?"

"You know, insects – mosquitoes that give you malaria; there's all the flies in the world here, well, most of them; horse flies that bite like a horse and stink bugs."

"And," said Berry rising to the occasion and joining in the let's-scare-Edwards-undercurrent,' "don't forget the tsetse fly that gives you sleeping sickness, the hornets, and the killer bees – the Africans call them wembembe. They'll kill you, man."

"That's right. Tons of workers died from killer bee attacks during the Groundnut Scheme," Sheddy confirmed with a serious nod to Berry. "Well, maybe not tons, but you know… you've got to be careful when you see their nests in the baobabs. Don't go close, don't even walk under them. The bees might attack even without a cause."

My jaw dropped. "Blimey, you chaps are giving bloody good reasons not to come here," I said. "How does anyone survive?"

"Most don't," said Sheddy. "There's only a small percentage'll make it out alive!"

I frowned.

"I'm joking."

WITH THE DYING ECHOES OF THE STEAM ENGINE disappearing behind the hills, boys, girls and teachers returned to the silence, punctuated only by the clack and whir of a solitary locust. We'd been told to disembark and now milled around on the sun-baked sand, hunching our backs to the rust-coloured dust devils, and contemplating the newly abandoned train carriages standing so out of place, in the middle of nowhere. Far down the end, the girls were gathered around the tiny station building. As we talked I stared incredulously at this new scenery. What a difference from England. The chaps at Allan House would never believe it.

"There's no one to fetch us," I said. "Have we arrived early?"

Aranky, who'd caught up with us, jumped in. "They'll have waited 'til they heard the engine's whistle. That lets the staff know we've arrived. There's no telephone here but they'll have heard the whistle and then they'll come."

He turned out to be right, for several open-back, decrepit, Bedford lorries rolled up about a half hour later, driven by masters who must have arrived days earlier. The war-surplus lorries were in bad shape, tail boards were flapping loose and their disintegrating wooden siding looked barely strong enough to retain anything.

At the other side of the station building I saw what looked like buses arriving but I wasn't sure in the swirling dust. The girls were being herded that way.

"Attention, everybody," called Ian Longden. "Select the closest lorry and climb aboard. If one is full, find another or, if they're all full, wait your turn. They'll be coming back for another load."

"Come along, Venables," I called as Sheddy disappeared in another direction. "Let's get on this one."

We scrambled up, followed by dozens of others, found a spot to stand, and awaited the next move. At the last moment Sheddy came running up and squeezed onto the packed lorry as it pulled away on a sandy, corrugated track.

The gari's complaining engine groaned under our weight, packed like sardines standing up, but headed resolutely for the school. The sun beat down, blinding us in its late afternoon angle to the horizon. The track's loose, red sand was kicked up in a roiling, unending cloud that swirled about in our slipstream. The jarring of the corrugations rattled the bones as we swayed from side to side trying not to fall off, chorusing extended whaooooos and aaaaaahs as we clung on to each other.

There were small, one-level buildings as we turned south onto tarmac and drove up the gently rising slope towards the western end of Kongwa Hill. It was a half mile of the only paved road in Kongwa. We passed a shack or two then a cluster on our right; "That's the hospital," said Aranky. Next to it was a small, green oasis surrounded by hedging.

"What's that?" I asked.

"Kongwa Club," responded Sheddy, who'd squeezed his way close to us. "Only for grown-ups, of course, except we'll be going there for swimming lessons next year when they've built the pool. It'll be the only one in Kongwa. Last term we went to a pool in Sagara, the place Berry told you about, but that was the only time. The Club's got two tennis courts, if you wanna learn to play."

Kongwa Hill had become prominent. There, at its base, were the posher houses of Millionaire's Row that Sheddy had pointed out to me from the train as well as the row of flats that some juniors would be housed in. We turned left, onto sand and came to a stop among a wide-spread collection of single-level, L-shaped buildings. As we piled off the lorries, we were directed to a particular building some thirty yards away.

"That one over there with the slab in front is the mess," a prefect pointed. "Dinner is waiting for you. It's a bit early but that's the way it is for today. So, go find yourself a table or go where you're directed by the prefects up there."

We strolled toward the mess gazing at the large slab with a drain in the middle that was located outside the kitchen but hesitated as we rounded the end of the building, not sure where to go. I looked around and asked, "What happened to the girls? First they were all over the train, now I can't see any."

"The dames eat at the other end there," said Sheddy, "and its doors are on the other side, so they were probably taken in their buses 'round the back. You won't see much of them except in class; there's not supposed to be mixing outside the classrooms 'cept maybe on sports days."

"That was something," I said. "We were loaded into those rattletraps while the girls got what looked a bit like buses. They weren't much good either but seemed in better nick than our lorries."

"Yes, well, the dames always get favoured treatment," said Sheddy. "They're girls, after all."

"What are those buildings down there for?" asked Goggles. (Venables had already been tagged with this nickname on account of his thick spectacles.) We were looking at several, single-level, dark wood structures with flaring, corrugated-iron roofs that were blinding if you caught them at the right angle to the sun. It seemed like there might be something like six rooms in each. The buildings had open air corridors built around their front.

"They were offices, now they're classrooms for Seniors mostly. That one over there, see, to the right of that smaller baobab, that's administration. The Headmaster has his office in that building… and his kiboko."

"What's a kiboko?" I asked naively.

"It's like a cane, only it's a whip. Not one like Lash Larue uses, you know, the cowboy in the comics?"

"Lash Larue's smashing, man; he's got a bull whip."

"Well, not that sort of whip," continued Sheddy. "A kiboko is about yeh long," he said stretching his arms wide. "My dad says it's carved from one piece of hippo hide. At the tip it's not much bigger than a screw driver, 'cept it's rounded, and then its shape widens until its big enough to grip like a handle the other end. If you get beaten with that it's a thousand times worse than anything else."

I felt chilled; so they whip boys here! "How do you know?" I asked. "Have you been whipped with it?"

"No, they don't use it on Juniors. I asked my dad about it in the hols because two Seniors got a public caning with it last term because they'd run away from school. They were caught by the conductor on the train 'cos they'd not bought tickets. Anyhow, if you watched those two when they got six of the best, well, you'd know why you wouldn't want to feel it."

As we loitered around the mess, prefects dressed for dinner in long grey trousers, tie and blazer beckoned us indoors to find a table. Glynn Ford directed Goggles, Sheddy and me. Sheddy was allocated the last seat to be filled at a table for seven at the far end, while Venables and I were the only two to be sat at an unoccupied one. The table was covered with a muslin netting to keep crowds of flies off. Underneath we liked what we saw: plenty of spam and salads, bread, butter and that sort of thing. Every table was similarly dressed. As we sat down and removed the net I noticed the walls. On each side of the mess, for its entire length, were mounted growling and snorting heads of lion, leopard, water buffalo, rhino, eland, kudu and others. Paton was right, they had been shooting animals. Later I learned the creatures had been shot by former employees of the scheme as well as Senior school boys and teachers on their hunts for meat for the school. The heads were mounted on wooden shields, made by boys in the woodwork class.

No sooner had we sat down when we were approached by a teacher. "Everyone has to take anti-malaria, quinine pills. Here's your first Palludrin, see you swallow it right away, please. In future you'll find one to take with your lunch every day."

Goggles and I, still the only two at the table, tucked in. Having got over my amazement at the animal heads, I focused on how this room was full of small tables, rather than extended trestle tables like I knew from my previous schools. It looked like a restaurant in here. Venables guessed that this was because the mess had belonged to the Groundnut Scheme, which he knew lots about from his dad who was employed by the Overseas Food Corporation (O.F.C.).

"The mess was probably a cafeteria, open most of the day for family meals or small groups; that's why the individual tables."

"Oh, I get it."

Now, because every table had to have a prefect, a place was set for a seventh person at one end.

"It's good scoff," I said.

"Plenty of it too," Venables replied. "Not the piffling amount my dad said we might get because of the famine in Tanganyika. He said it was especially bad in Kongwa on account of no rain. I once heard him talking with mum saying they'd been having trouble getting enough meat for the school."

"What does your dad do?" I asked.

"I don't really know, something to do with supplies, I think; doesn't tell me much. How about yours?"

"He got a new job, working for a Dutch company. It's called – let's see if I can say it in Dutch – Twentsche Overzee Handel Maatschapij. Well, something like that anyway. They call it T.O.M. for short. Anyway, he'll be importing and exporting stuff, I think; that's about it."

We kept scoffing until the second convoy drew up and off-loaded a new surge of arrivals. A number of them, including a Junior's prefect, were directed to our table. As the boys arrived they reacted in horror. But for a few scraps, Venables and I had enjoyed a good repast and eaten nearly everything.

"What do you think you're doing, you bloody idiots?" the prefect yelled. "You've eaten all the food. Don't you know this table was laid for seven, not two? How could you eat it all and leave us hardly any?"

"I'm sorry," I said. "I didn't know, no one told us, we didn't know, did we, Venables?"

"No, we didn't know, no one told us. Can't they just bring more?"

"You greedy bastards," growled another who looked aggressive and I instinctively knew would bring me much trouble. "They need beating up, man," he said and turned to the prefect.

"Shut up, Viljoen," said the prefect as he turned back to us. "Now what are we supposed to eat? Where do you expect us to get food from now you've had our shares? You know you've eaten almost all the food for seven? Godverdomme, man, you piss me off, eh."

We were stricken at this attack and instantly ashamed, as our conversation about plenty of food and the famine among the Africans suddenly took on new meaning. My averted eyes came to rest on the lion head on the wall behind the prefect's head, its mouth open in a roar, its massive fangs I could just imagine dripping blood, adding to the menace that I now felt. Goggles and I shrunk into our seats.

"Why couldn't someone just bring more, like they do at home?" I repeated Venables' question.

"Because they've already put out food for seven, they're not going to bring anymore until tomorrow," the prefect snarled. "They haven't got any more food, dom." His voice became louder as he shouted at us in his Afrikaner accent.

Just as I thought he or Viljoen might lay into us with a punch, a teacher came scurrying over to find out what the noise was about, now that everybody in the mess was looking over their shoulders in our direction.

"These two greedy bastards have eaten all the food, sir. There's none left for us, sir. So now I suppose we'll have to go hungry tonight, sir."

I had the frightening thought that my first caning in Kongwa was imminent.

"You will not swear or use the word bastard," the teacher asserted to the prefect with a frown, an angry tint to his voice. "I don't want to hear language like that now or at any time! Is that clearly understood?"

"Yes, sir. Sorry, sir."

"Now calm down and be quiet."

Turning to Venables and me, he asked with a kindly squint, "You're new boys, aren't you?"

"Yes, sir," we admitted in duet but in relief at his tone.

"Hmm, don't suppose you know the routine yet." He turned to the prefect. "An honest mistake, I'm sure, but do not concern yourself; we can get more food sent out. You five should take your seats and I'll arrange with the kitchen to have your table replenished. Now, let's not hear any more noise, please. This was an unfortunate mistake, not intentional, so just cool down, will you?"

"Yes, sir," the boys grumbled.

As soon as the teacher disappeared in the direction of the kitchen, we were glared at by the five as they took their seats. The prefect shook his head. Still angry but in a subdued voice, he seethed, "You're lucky. Shutty saved your bacon. I hope you're not in my house because if you are it'll be the worse for you. Anyway, now you've finished eating you can leave, get out of my sight!"

We hadn't finished and still had a few scraps but were not about to argue. Venables and I left, glad to be out of there.

After dinner, Juniors were called to form crocodile lines by the Housemasters for Livingstone, Wilberforce, Nightingale and Curie. There were twenty-seven in each line. Although we were Juniors we would share the same phase as the Senior boys but would be in different houses consisting of more or less our own age group. Mr. Ferguson led the way to our houses following a lengthy walk. Even though I'd been warned of this I was surprised. "Are we going to be walking this far all the time?" I asked Venables.

"I don't know, man, I'm new like you, but Sheddy told us everything was far from everything else."

As we arrived at phase 3, I and several others nearly jumped out of our skins at the raucous shrieks that accompanied our arrival.

"Oh golly, what's that?"

"Only tree hyraxes, they won't hurt you," said Sheddy. "They just make a helluva din when they're startled."

"Yish."

Then I got refocused as I discovered the houses. Rows of small houses were now our dorms, if that was the right word. There were nine of us allocated to a house and that included the prefect. Our prefect was Clive Knight.

"You didn't see me on your train because I wasn't on it," he replied to my question. "I live in a place called Urambo, further west from here, past Tabora if you know where that is."

"But how did you get here?" I asked.

"By train from the opposite direction; from Urambo to Dodoma, then by bus to here. I, and others from up-country, arrived earlier this morning."

Clive was only about six months older than me but he was senior to the rest of us and he held a prefect's authority. I took a liking to him. He seemed different from the prefects I'd been used to.

The other boys in our house included: Sheddy, Goggles, Berry, Gunston, Aranky, Maclean, Jenner and Priestley. The first thing I noticed was that there was a toilet in the house.

"We're lucky this time," said Sheddy, "may not be in future terms."

Once we knew our beds and unpacked our cases, we rushed out to play. I noticed we were close to a hill. Sheddy said, "It's Church Hill, the one I showed you from the train. It's the one with the donga at the base, just at the end of this row; I'll take you there soon as we get a chance."

Having eaten we had time to spare. I didn't join in any games but when I noticed Venables wasn't around I went looking for him. He was lying on his bed looking forlorn. He'd been crying and when I spoke he started again. He was trying not to but he couldn't help it. I sat on his bed next to him; I was feeling low too. A feeling of melancholy washed over me, not helped by these Spartan rooms and the memory of my happiness in Lindi just two days ago. I put on a brave face.

"I say, cheer up, Venables, old chap. I know how you feel, really I do, I feel pretty rough myself, but it won't do for the others to see you blubbing."

I expected he would be teased; I'd had enough of that at Allan House and had no reason to believe it would be any different here.

"I say, why don't we go outside and walk around like the others, see what gives and all that."

"I don't want to go outside! I don't want to be here! I hate this place!" he shouted with unexpected venom. "I hate it, I hate it, I hate it! And I want to go home!" And with that Venables burst into another fit of sobs and buried his head in his pillow.

I didn't know what to say. We were all right for the moment, with the others outside. Then I heard quick footsteps and a rather tanned Matron came bustling down the corridor. She wore a white housecoat and on her head full of short, brown curls, a small cap I suppose you'd call it, not unlike nurses wore. She was slim, probably middle aged, although all adults look old when you're nine or ten, with a bit of a stern face; a bit like Mrs. Stick in one of those Enid Blyton books. I stood to meet her.

"Please, Matron, my name's Edwards. I'm afraid Venables here is very sad and is crying."

Matron assessed the scene and when she spoke you couldn't miss her German accent. "You may leaf us, Edverds, vile I haff a talk vis Venables."

"Yes, Matron," and with that I wandered through the door and onto the stoep.

Not much later, with the last shards of sunlight having blinked out behind Leopard Hill, it was dark. The noise from the insects' chorus and the hyrax's shrieks were drowning as Matron called us out for a nightcap. We brought our fat, general issue china mugs with us and she poured us either hot milk or Ovaltine. I selected Ovaltine as I couldn't stand drinking milk, much less hot.

While we were standing around drinking in the spill of light from a nearby house, there was rough play going on between a couple of boys. One of them backed into me as I was taking a sip from my mug, bumping it into my teeth.

"Ow!" I howled, clutching my hand to my mouth to catch the chipped china that I'd felt break away on contact. "Be careful, you clot, this is hot and now you've made me break my mug."

"Sorry, Edwards," Viljoen laughed. "Maybe that'll teach you not to eat everybody else's dinner."

Matron came hurrying over to check on me.

"Dit you spit out ze china fully?" she asked.

"Yes, Matron."

She examined the mug then said, "Let me see your mouse. You vill show me your teese, ya?"

I gave a cheesy smile.

"Zat's not china you spat, Edverds. Zat vos a piece of your front teese. Doz it 'urt?"

"No, Matron."

"Goot. Vell, finish up your Ovaltin. Come on, efrybody, drink up, bet time."

Back inside, I sat on my bed in pyjamas, examining the itching around my ankles. My skin not only had the rash to cope with but was aggravated by burrs from the long grasses. The scabs had brushed off and my raw skin had stuck to my socks. I sat on my bed, gingerly peeling the socks down, trying – without success – not to open up the sores. But as the sock was peeled away it took newly-forming scabs with it and opened several wounds.

"All right, everyone," called Clive. "That's enough noise. You all need to calm down. I want you to brush your teeth and get into bed."

It wasn't long before Matron arrived for inspection. After a quick scan of our room and its state of tidiness, her eyes came to rest on me.

"Vat is wrong mit your ankles, Edverds?"

"Please, Matron, I don't really know. But I did have this skin problem in England, actually it was worse than it is now, it seems to have healed a bit, but anyway, my ankles still have these sores and they're really itching because of the prickly things in the grass."

"Hmm, Vat do you put on zem, zie ointment of zome sort?"

"No. Fuller's Earth, Matron. We stopped using ointments, didn't seem to help much."

Matron moved in to take a closer look. "Sprinkle your powder on zen. I vant you to come see me before baas time each day so I can zee zoes ankles. Iss zat understood?"

"Yes, Matron."

"I see you have ze problem on ze back of your 'ands too?"

"Yes, Matron."

"Anyvear else?"

"Behind my knees, Matron. But my knees and hands aren't as bad as they were. They seem to be getting a bit better."

"I don't vant those sores going septic, zo mind you come see me each evening. Now listen, boys, I vant you to settle, please. Iss efryvun all right?"

There was a chorus of "Yes, Matron."

"Goot. Lights out now. Gootnight."

" 'Night, Matron."

I'd watched Venables whenever I'd looked up from sock peeling. I'd not seen him crying anymore although he was still withdrawn. Matron must have got him to feel a little better. He'd been watching me with my socks and gave me a weak smile in the grey darkness as he pulled his sheet over himself and said, " 'Night."

Days later and it was laundry day. Clive told us to place our washing in the dhobi bags we'd brought with us to school. "Matron will come around and check them before they're picked up," he told us.

When Matron arrived we tipped everything out again for her to check against our list: "Vun shirt, vun short, vun half-pajama." (Which says a lot about our clean clothing as it was a weekly wash!)

CHAPTER FOUR

DREAMS AND DONGAS

I COULDN'T SLEEP. AFTER THE EXCITEMENT OF the day, reality had caught up. I sympathised with Venables and now my emotions were running high too. I felt miserable as it all sunk in. I was stuck here for months. If it was anything like Allan House, who knew what misery lay ahead, especially with those blokes at the dinner table, and that one, Viljoen, who was in Livingstone too although not in my house, thank goodness. Thanks to him I have a broken tooth already… on my first day! Worse yet was what Sheddy had told us about the kiboko. It wasn't hard to imagine that one teacher or another would find a reason to use it on me sooner or later. Tears of sadness ran down my cheeks and I dried them off with my sheet. After a couple of sniffs I nearly gave the game away.

"Is someone blubbing?" Sheddy's sleepy voice came out of the darkness.

No one answered, least of all me. I stifled my sniffling and finished wiping my tears so no one would know.

I tried changing my thoughts to happier occasions but could only come up with Miss Evans, in England. When the parents didn't come home on leave from Nigeria, which was most of the time, and because neither my grandparents nor any other family member were in the position to look after me, my parents had to find somewhere else for me to stay during school holidays. Allan House could not take me in like Cable House had done, so

I travelled to Miss Evans' boarding home, alone on the train, with a label round my neck, under orders from the guard to remain where I was until I was escorted off the train in Bournemouth. Amazing that I should think of that place as a happy time! But there had been some fun, especially when we went out in the pony and trap.

I remembered helping harness the pony and backing him into the trap. The trap could seat the six of us and have room for Miss Evans too. As we stepped on the bottom step, the trap would tip on its axle with those huge wheels rimmed with metal felloes. Miss Nash, who was Miss Evans's assistant, always went on ahead in her Austin 7, taking the picnic basket with her.

I loved those pony rides. Perhaps it was the unhurried clip-clop along sequestered country lanes in the New Forest with its umbrella chestnut boughs that would let shimmering specs of sunlight dapple through, or coming across an open glade with its green, undulating and sun-drenched countryside sentineled with fine old English oaks and elms, watercress-lined streams and bringing to mind thoughts of Robin Hood and the Sheriff of Nottingham (although that took place in Nottingham Forest, of course); or further along peeking through breaks in high bracken, hawthorn and wild rose, or thickets lined with blackberry, brilliant yellow gorse, elderflower or the many purple shades of heather. Of watching cows chewing the cud, and the grass in the fields alive with buttercups, clover and daisies with furry bumblebees flitting from one to the other; of looking for a way to cross streams with sparkling dragonflies and thick with bulrushes and later drawing up to an old stone church that had stood there a thousand years – all induced an unhurried charm toward life.

We'd walk the farmers' fields keeping closely to the bridle path and along the fence lines, clambering over stiles and nervously making sure the cows were not hiding a bull among their number who would chase us away from his ladies. We gathered buttercups and held them under each other's chin to make sure we were as nice as we thought we were, while others made daisy chains for fun or perhaps to give to a girl a boy was sweet on. Later, back at the summer home, we loved looking after the pony, grooming him, feeding him carrots and lettuce or an occasional sugar lump, and hitching him for rides into the village where we might be treated to delicious Wall's ice cream, if we were really good. But these thoughts didn't help much. I was too hot and threw off my blanket as the memories of England lingered and my mind wandered to home, which for me was wherever my parents happened to be.

I barely knew my dad. He hadn't even seen me until I was two-and-a-half. We'd been together while he was on long leave on three occasions during my nearly ten years of life. I'd seen a bit more of Mum but not a lot, not compared with my friends who seemed to have parents all the time. My mind wandered again, this time to our plane landing in Dar es Salaam. *Golly, it was only a week ago.*

After we'd landed, we'd got through customs and immigration in seconds and into the reception hall. Happiness! There'd been Dad, a beaming smile; hugs all around; together at last. Dad was dressed in the de facto uniform of colonial Africa, white short-sleeved shirt with two breast pockets which carried a diary or notebook and an array of coloured pens; white shorts, white long stockings or socks up to the top of the calves and brown slip-on walking shoes. Casual wear was khaki and short brown socks, if any, and sandals.

Trunks were collected and loaded into the boot of the Peugeot, and off we'd driven to the city centre, where we'd stayed at the Metropole Hotel. Dad recalled how, while he was in England, I'd gone on about wanting a 'bus 'n coach 'n jeep.' To greet me, he'd tried to find a toy that would impress and had come across in Dinky Toys a double-decker London bus, a motor coach and a Land Rover. I'd found those three awaiting my arrival in our hotel room. They were accompanied with an apology, "Sorry, chum, I wasn't able to find a Jeep. I hope a Land Rover will be close enough."

"They're smashing, Daddy, thank you very much, they're just super!" Then, not long after that, they'd sounded me out on remaining in Dar with the Kherers for those few days before leaving for school. Well, I'd had my say about that.

✦ ✦ ✦

THE DOUGLAS DAKOTA OF EAST AFRICAN AIRWAYS had lumbered lazily down the runway and lifted off in the cool dawn air at 0600. That flight to Lindi was the first hop on a milk run that took the plane around the bush stations of the southern province, before returning to Dar es Salaam that night. It made the trip three times a week. The languid climb gave opportunities for views of the larger city as it clipped the coconut palms, catching sight of the beautiful homes and crystal beaches of Oyster Bay, while streaks of sunlight penetrated the early morning cloud cover.

"Look," said Dad. "That's the Kherers' home over there, near the corner of those two roads."

Alas, I hadn't picked it out in time before we flew on.

Gradually, the plane had gained altitude and edged over the aquamarine coral waters, to follow the coast on its southerly flight, to its first touchdown, Lindi. That early-morning flight had been a smooth ride. Dad pointed out Mafia Island looking like an atoll in the azure blue sea off to the east, and I studied every inch of the coast as we followed its endless miles of unpopulated, sandy beaches. There were bays recessed into the land protected by rocky outcrops; further on mangrove swamps would pervade with their thick, bushy leaves and grotesque roots shooting out of sodden sand to the point of high tide water. Wild coral reefs abounded.

The Dakota banked inland to line up over massive sisal plantations that stretched seemingly forever, before landing in Lindi – an hour and a half since we'd left Dar es Salaam. Mr. Salvini, a tall, young, wiry-built and bespectacled Hollander, sent out from the Netherlands to assist my dad, greeted us. He would provide our lift into town in a small, red, Austin pick-up with just enough room in the front to seat my parents in addition to himself. We hung around waiting until a couple of African servants – who they called 'boys,' which I thought funny because I was a boy and they looked like grown-ups to me – filled the pick-up with boxes and cartons from the plane. Those were followed by our suitcases, all dumped in the open back. To my surprise, Mr. Salvini told me, in his thick, Dutch accent, "You should hop in the back, Tony; there's not enough room in the front."

I gladly did so, thinking *this is going to be fun*, and the 'boys' followed. I nuzzled a wedge between a couple of the larger cartons or cases where I expected I could sit and enjoy the ride. I'd never ridden in the open back of a pick-up, so didn't know what to expect.

The twenty miles drive to town through sisal estates was corrugated and dust-laden. It was rutted, pot-holed and intersected with, for now, dry river beds. Progress was slow to preserve springs and shock absorbers. Eventually, battered and bruised, we found tarmac on the edge of town, then wound the last few hundred yards along a beach front drive, and came to a squeaky halt outside the Beach Hotel.

The Van Buuren couple, who were Dutch, were the hoteliers of 'The Beach,' and, expecting our arrival, they came out to greet us. They were trailed by a curious daughter, Annelize, a year or two older than me, her brother Egbert some five years younger than her, a hanger-on or odd job man, Tony, and a mutt named Binty.

"Leave everything in the pick-up for the 'boys' to attend to," counselled Mr. Van Buuren.

So, I'd disengaged from lettuce, carrots, squashed tomatoes and other produce that had been my cushion for the journey, hopped the sides and followed the entourage through the solid, not to say sombre-looking, double doorway with its understated sign immediately above, *Beach Hotel – Right of Admission Reserved*.

I have to say that the building from the outside looked decrepit, even foreboding, but, in the colonial style, once inside, the hotel was wide open. Doors, walls and windows were few and far between, replaced by arches and open corridors that encouraged the flow of sea breezes. It was all so different from the tiny homes and shops of England, mired under rain clouds, cold, with tiny rooms and doors from which hung draft curtains. The wide-open patio, overlooked by a long bar with its listless fans, was in such contrast, so different, so inviting. It presided over the sun-drenched beach and the ocean shore that washed gently beyond. The palm fronds rustled in the breeze, creating a cooling effect from the broiling heat and humidity.

I couldn't remember much about the hotel's services but know I enjoyed being there, and wished it would last forever. I'd noticed my father and others refer to the hotel as 'The Dysentery Arms.' I've since learned it was a term of endearment, as it was a mnemonic attached to many bush hotels. I was thoroughly happy. I was with my parents, it was hot, there was sun, sand and sea, and there were two other children to play with. I was there almost five days and enjoyed every minute.

Mum and Dad and I sat around talking for a while after dinner that first night. Dad asked, "So, chum, what did they teach you at Allan House about East Africa, or Tanganyika, once they knew you'd be moving here?"

"Well, Dad, they told me how it's the largest country in East Africa and we looked at it on an atlas. They said Tanganyika is larger than France and Germany put together. They told me it's a protectorate, not a colony, whatever that means. It was explained that East Africa is the name given to Kenya and Uganda as well as Tanganyika, the three countries together, you know?

"Uh huh, what else did they tell you?"

"Really, Les," chipped in Mum. "You're putting him through his paces a bit, aren't you? He's only nine."

"He goes to school to learn. I would expect a prep school like he went to should inform him of this sort of thing; it cost enough, goodness knows."

"Well, Dad," I continued, "they told me about those countries because they're all three linked by things like airlines and railways, like East African Airways, right, the plane we flew here on?"

"Right," said my dad. "What else?"

"They said Africa's countries are going to become independent some day. See, I asked them about Nigeria and the Gold Coast where you used to live, and they said they might be the first to be independent."

"What do you know about the Africans?" asked Dad.

"They said there are a lot of tribes in Tanganyika, I forget how many, maybe fifteen or twenty, I think."

"And?"

"The tribe where my school is, is called Gogo but they're a smaller tribe than some of the others… Oh yes, and they also told me most of the country doesn't have people because it's too arid and kind of deserty… no water."

"Uh, huh, anything else?"

"Well, there's lots and lots of wild animals which I have to be very careful of, like lions and elephants, especially here in Tanganyika where there's a large area called… hmm, let me see, what was it called… Ser… I don't know, Ser something."

"Serengeti," said Dad, "the Serengeti Plains. It seems they got you off to a good start. We may talk on this a bit more tomorrow."

"It's getting late," said Mum. "Time for your bed. Come on, give your dad a hug and I'll take you to your room."

Although I'd gone to bed late it was difficult to sleep. The bedroom was large but featureless – just four walls and a ceiling fan that revolved squeakily and didn't seem to help. A white cone mosquito net shrouded my bed. There were louvered French doors that opened to the balcony. After Mother had left, I got out of bed to step out onto it. There I'd stood gazing at the stars and the sea. The sky was so clear, so sparkly. The moon was nearly full. Down below, just the other side of a low concrete wall that divided the grounds from the beach, wavelets bathed in moonlight washed in endless repetition.

My ears filled with the amazing sounds of the night, dominated by the chirruping of cicadas, punctuated with the croaks of bullfrogs and backed up by countless insects singing in harmony. I'd returned to my senses when I heard the interweaving contrails of a mosquito zeroing in. It went into a dive, like a German Stuka and landed in an explosion of silence on my neck. Instinctively I slapped at it as I retreated to my bed and the protection of the net, there to think on the excitement of the day until the slowly revolving fan mesmerised me to sleep.

ANNELIZE AND EGBERT SEEMED GLAD FOR MY company. They were the only two European children in Lindi beyond infancy. That first morning they'd taken me in tow to show me around. As we passed any African pedestrian they would mutter something about elephants.

"Why do you keep talking about elephants to those people?" I'd asked.

"Elephants? We're not talking about Jumbo's!" Egbert had replied with a chuckle. "We're saying hello or good morning in Swahili. 'Jambo' means hello, why don't you try it?"

I'd smiled, feeling a little foolish, but after a while plucked up the courage.

"Jambo," I said to a passing native.

"Jambo, bwana mdogo," came the reply. "Habari yarko?"

All I was looking for in response was 'Jambo.' But no, the chap responded asking questions in Swahili that I couldn't understand. I'd kept to English after that. We'd explored the beach and picked for shells. I'd rolled up the legs of my long, grey, warm, winter trousers, slipped off my shoes, peeled away my socks from the sores on my ankles and broiling feet, and paddled.

"Mind out," Egbert had yelled at one point. "Don't tread on that!"

I'd frozen and looked down at a huge jellyfish.

"That's a Portuguese Man o' War," Egbert told me as I'd stared at it, caught in the shallows and washing ashore.

I stepped quickly aside when he'd yelled, "Those things sting bad," and remained on the dry sand where I could keep a close watch on where I was treading. The beach was alive with crabs and we'd had fun chasing them.

We'd still not caught any when we heard the urgent call of the parents. "Annelize, Egbert, Tony, where are you? Lunch time."

It had been a good lunch. A seafood concoction of Mrs. Van Buuren's, served in a large clam shell, was delicious. Lobster, prawns, clams and barracuda were caught close-inshore by local fishermen who could be found daily touting their fresh catch for sale. I'd never eaten anything like that in England; this sort of food simply wasn't available, well, unless you had an awful lot of money. Food had come off the ration from the war years only two years earlier but that didn't mean that exotic food of this sort could be readily come by, or afforded.

During lunch we'd been warned not to walk the beaches in bare feet: "The 'jiggers', you know."

"What's a jigger?" I'd asked.

"A jigger is a tiny worm-like sand flea," said my dad. "The female burrows into your foot and can cause an infection. It can be serious because you can end up with lost toes or tetanus."

We'd worn slops after that, bought that afternoon when we'd gone to The Lindi Store to buy me suitable clothes. We'd emerged with me sporting a khaki, short-sleeved shirt and shorts.

I'd stayed at 'The Beach' for what was left of the week, but my parents said they'd be living there many months. Letters home were to be addressed care of the Beach Hotel, until they'd registered a post office box.

There wasn't any vacant office space either. Father and Salvini had taken over a bedroom in the hotel, and made it into an office. T.O.M. was building a block of flats that would house us and other employees on the top floor, with office space on the ground floor. We'd visited the block under construction. It was there I'd met Carlo, an olive-skinned and handsome Italian bachelor with a sparkle in his eyes and a character full of charm. Carlo was the local builder and would tell me, in time, many stories of the great engineering legacy of the Italian people.

In discovering Lindi with Annelize and Egbert, I'd talked with some of the Indian proprietors of the larger stores, they being surprised to note a new European child in town. In this simple act of exploring I'd found freedom, a huge change from the cloistered and oppressive boarding environment I'd been used to all my life. It had been exciting being out with my new friends; no grown-ups holding hands or telling us what to do or where to go. I was nearly ten and it was the first time in my life I'd done that; but it was short lived.

There'd been brief confusion a couple of nights earlier, whether I would have all day of Sunday, the 6th in Lindi, a chance to delay departure by precious hours – or virtually no time at all.

"As you now know, chum," said Dad, "East African Airways' three-times-a-week flight alternates its timetable. On the one run, the plane lands in Lindi on its first call of the day. On the alternate trip, Lindi is its last stop of the day at about five in the afternoon. Depending on what it's doing, you'll have to leave pretty early on Sunday or quite late in the day. I'll be popping around to the EAA office in the morning to find out."

Oh, what happiness. It turned out I'd have the better part of Sunday to spend with parents and my new friends, rather than taking off at eight in the morning. That 5 p.m. flight would fly direct to Dar. If I'd gone on the milk run, I'd have had an all-day, hedge-hopping, and air-sick flight to Mtwara, Nachingwea, Songea, Iringa, Mbeya and finally Dar es Salaam. Dad told me I could expect taking the roundabout route might happen from time to time, on future trips.

SUNDAY LUNCHTIME HAD BEEN AND GONE. ANNELIZE, who was also going to Kongwa, had left with her parents for the aerodrome along with Egbert, not quite six or old enough to attend, tagging along. He would start school in September. Behind them, we'd pulled out in the pick-up. We hadn't been long at the aerodrome before we'd spotted a plane descending from the south.

"That's not the usual E.A.A. flight," Dad said with a frown as it touched down. "It should be a Dakota, not a Lodestar."

"And it doesn't have any E.A.A. markings," I said.

"The plane has been borrowed while the DC-3 is in for service," said a man who overheard our conversation and seemed to be in the know.

Hugs and kisses, but bravely no tears, were dispensed.

"Bye, darling, write soon," said Mum.

"Cheerio, chum. See you in June," said Dad giving me a brief hug.

Then I'd climbed a couple of steps into the fourteen-passenger Lockheed Lodestar. It had arrived with a few people on board, one a girl wearing Kongwa school uniform. I judged her to be a year or two older than me. Annelize knew her for she immediately went and took the seat by the older girl's side where they were instantly into non-stop chatter punctuated with frequent squeals of laughter.

Soon we were airborne. Sitting alone, I gazed out the window at the infinity of Africa below. I was amazed at the clouds above us. As far as the eye could see, tiny puffy well-spaced clouds filled the sky, breaking up the deep blue heavens and casting tiny, dark shadows on the ground. It was to become a source of amazement for me over the years to gaze upwards from a walk and see these thousands of cotton swabs that seemed never to cast shade when you were on the ground, for the sun seemed unrelenting.

The Lodestar ferried us safely to Dar es Salaam, where Mr. and Mrs. Kehrer met me and took me to their lovely home lost among the acres of palms of Oyster Bay. I thought about it, with its rancher style, terra cotta tiled roof, white, smooth, stucco finish, large, open windows protected by wrought iron burglar bars, spacious, nicely furnished and beautiful in the evening, with the indirect lighting of the table lamps that Jean Kherer favoured. My bedroom annex was connected with the main house by a breezeway that caught the fresh ocean wind and lowered the humidity. The insects had been loud, and the curtains rustled constantly in the breeze. I'd climbed under my net and was tucked in.

WE WERE WOKEN BY MATRON. "VAKEY, VAKEY. Time to get up, everyvun. Come on zen, up you get, no sleeping in. Zere's not much time 'til breakvast."

There was a scramble for use of the bathroom, with two if not three trying to wash themselves and brush teeth at the same time. We were not long getting ready. I stepped into the already hot sunshine and was rustled up by Clive to join the line for inspection. Matron checked our hands and behind our ears for tell-tale dirt and looked for a presentable appearance. As she did so we glanced up at the noisy chirruping coming from squadrons of gaily-coloured birds flying overhead.

"They must be parakeets," I said to Goggles. "They're so beautiful."

"Kasukus," he replied. "The Africans call them kasukus."

The line moved out, following the beaten path to the mess. As we walked, in between glancing up at the extraordinary numbers of kasukus flying noisily above, I thought about the dinner table following our arrival yesterday.

"Gosh," I turned to talk over my shoulder to Sheddy, as I kept my eyes open for Viljoen further back in the line, "I hope we don't have the same prefect at the table as when we arrived. He really yelled at Goggles and me."

"We weren't divided by houses then," Sheddy replied. "We were allocated the nearest tables available. Now it'll be organised by house. Those blokes weren't even in Livingstone, were they?"

"The prefect wasn't, I haven't seen him again, or the others, except for Viljoen. He's in Livingstone and was one of them."

"Don't worry about him," said Sheddy. "Our prefect will almost certainly be Clive."

"What's for breakfast, do you think?" I asked.

"Oh they have all the usual, you'll see. Sometimes they give us Marmite; do you like Marmite?"

"Love it."

"Well you can have mine. They have this concoction of margarine and Marmite mix; can't stand the stuff. And watch out for the corn flakes if they have them... sometimes they have weevils in them."

"Really? Yuk. Why?"

"It's on account of they come by boat all the way from England, then sit around the docks in Dar, with all that heat, then they come here by rail. So, who knows. But if you do eat them they won't hurt you."

Our Juniors' classrooms, Forms 1 to 4, were close to Church Hill and the Donga. They were housed in three oblong buildings. Fergie brought us to attention sharp at eight-thirty, rapping his desk with a blackboard pointer.

"All of you just settle down now. I want quiet, please. You boy," looking directly at me, "what's your name?"

"Please, sir, my name's Edwards, sir."

"Edwards, yes, a new boy," he said. "Who else here is a new boy or girl?" A bristling of arms went up. He wrote down the names then said, "Right then, here's what we're going to do. Firstly you'll go to the storeroom at the end of this building. There you'll be handed text books, exercise books, pens and nibs, pencils and rubbers, geometry squares, together with any other items they may have for you. I want you to go and fetch everything, and return immediately. I expect you back within a few minutes."

When we returned and settled down Fergie told us, "Among other things, I take the lead in putting on plays in this school. It all derives from English culture and literature, which we will be learning together over the next few terms, for those of you who remain in Kongwa long enough, that is. We will put on one play at half term. What is of interest to me is finding out who of you respond with the greatest enthusiasm to acting. During your Senior year this will become a much more important factor. So think of this as a recruiting period, when you'll get the chance to show your mettle. Any questions so far?"

A girl put up her hand.

"Please, sir, is this for boys and girls, sir?"

"No... er, your name, girl?"

"Pam, sir, uh, Pamela Shaw."

"No, Miss Shaw, this does not include girls, I'm afraid. The fact is there are other activities more suited to girls. Your Senior Mistress, Miss Strong, will be advising you about that in due course. Needless to add we will not normally be taking up classroom time with play readings; they are strictly extra-curricular, after-class hours."

"Thank you, sir."

"Excuse me, sir." Morag Cormack put up her hand.

"Yes, Miss Cormack, you may speak."

"Please, sir, will the plays you put on only have boys in them, that is to say, parts for boys to play? I mean, you know, do the plays have girls in them, sir?"

"Well, it depends on the play," replied Mr. Ferguson. "The one I have in mind for this term, entitled *Any Body*, has boys' roles only. However, in the Senior years there will be plays with girls' roles."

"So I suppose, sir," went on Morag with a knowing smile, "boys will have to play girls' roles?"

There was a titter from the girls, which had been the point of the question; Morag knew the answer before she asked it.

"Yes, Miss Cormack," with a sigh, "boys may well play girls' roles. Now can we get along, please?"

Mr. Ferguson continued, "I want to assess your reading skills. We will have each of you, and that includes you girls – you can benefit from the reading exercise anyway – come to the front and read a passage from this book. I want you to read with as much feeling and projection as you can muster. Right then, we'll begin with you there, sitting next to Edwards, it's Westley, isn't it?"

"Yes, sir, Westley, sir."

"Yes, Westley. Come on up to the front and read your passage."

And so it began. Each of us took our turn but no matter how modest I wanted to be it was clear who best knew how to read.

"Edwards, I'm impressed with your reading. Where were you before you came to Kongwa?"

"I was at a prep school in England, sir. It's called Allan House."

"Hmm, well, clearly that accounts for it."

Actually I'd been a fluent reader by the time I got to Allan House from Cable House, my nursery school, but I didn't dare correct him.

"Tell me, Edwards, does the idea of acting in plays appeal to you?"

"Yes, sir, if you think I'd be any good, sir. I'd certainly like to give it a try, sir."

And so Fergie went through the list of boys, including among others Berry and Jenner, recruiting those who were interested. After we'd read our paragraphs, Fergie explained that *Any Body* is set in the lounge bar of a pub, hence no ladies.

"The publican – I have you in mind for that role, Edwards – is the bartender and takes the lead role from behind his bar. Then there are the customers and the detectives and, of course, there will be a dead body because of the murder. Notwithstanding the nature of the drama it is a comedy, so we won't be getting too gory."

"Ooooooh," the boys groaned. We'd anticipated high drama, blood and gore. Then the bell rang and it was end of class. As we looked up anticipating break, a girl called out: "Oh my gosh, look out the window, there's all those baboons."

We stood in one accord to stare out the window, then back to Mr. Ferguson, wondering what we should do.

"They'll scoot off as soon as you all go outside," Mr. Ferguson assured us. "So, hurry along now, break isn't that long."

The boys led the way – tentatively. Sure enough, the baboons loped off and disappeared in the direction of Church Hill.

Westley was a handsome boy, stocky, with a twinkle in his eye and a ready smile. He walked with me on the open ground to the north side of the classrooms, which is where we took our breaks. It was recognised by its open space of hard-baked, sun-drenched, shade-free, red sand, sprinkled with derelict, burning-hot vehicles like the old First Aid caravan with its washed-out red crosses. With that, the skeletal remains of a pre-fab building and the donga, we had all the makings of a natural playground boys could want. The girls were less well catered to but once in a while the tomboys were allowed to join with us so long as they agreed to be either a lady who was tied up as a prisoner and needed rescuing or maybe a nurse dressing our wounds. They obviously couldn't be doctors because, after all, they were girls. Most girls preferred to cluster in whatever meagre shade they could find, talking and laughing among themselves ninety to the dozen.

As we descended the steps Westley asked, "So what's your Christian name?"

"Tony. And yours?"

"Douglas, but my nickname's Pepsi. I've been coming here for two terms now but you're a new boy?"

"Yes, only recently from England.

"I heard you flew here in a plane. Most chaps I know came by ship."

"I know, but not us."

"S'pose it was a plane that landed on the ground?"

"Of course! What else do you expect it to land on?" I asked, amazed at the question.

"Could be water. You probably don't know Glynn Ford; he's our House prefect and Wilberforce House Captain. Anyway, he flew to Africa on a flying boat; it's amphibious and can land on water or land."

"I do know him, I saw him on the train. Where did he land, do you know?"

"Well," said Doug, "He came to Tanganyika three years ago, in 1949 when there were hardly any airports, mostly just grass landing strips that could take small planes but not big heavy ones. So they could only fly to cities that were by the sea, or lakes or maybe a river if it was big enough."

"Golly, that must have been exciting, eh? I wish we'd done that."

"Hmmm."

"Do you know which way he came?"

"Yes. He told us all about it one time when we were telling each other stories last term. He said he took off from Southampton and flew to Sicily where they refueled. You know where that is, eh?"

"Of course. The Mediterranean, near Italy."

And then they flew to Alexandria in Egypt where they landed in the harbour and stayed the night. Next day they flew over the Sahara to Khartoum in the Sudan where they landed on the River Nile and stayed the night there too."

"Crikey, imagine landing one of those big things on a river. Must be pretty dangerous what with hippos and crocodiles and all?

"I dunno. I think the Nile is pretty wide there."

"Why couldn't they fly at night? My plane did."

"The airport needs a flair path along the runway to land at night. If you're landing on water there's no flair path. So they have to land in daylight so the pilot can see where he's going. Anyhow, next day they flew to Lake Naivasha; that's in Kenya, you know? Even though Nairobi is the capital, they couldn't land there on account of the landing field. So, he said they were driven by bus to Nairobi and stayed the night there too. Next day they flew from Nairobi to Dar es Salaam in a Dakota."

"But you just said…"

"Yes, I know, but you see the Dakota is a small plane compared to a flying boat. It can land safely on hard ground or grass strips if it's not too wet. A plane as big as a flying boat needs a tarmac strip."

"Oh, I see."

"But that wasn't the end of it. In Dar es Salaam they changed planes again onto a Lockheed Lodestar for the final leg to Kongwa."

"Same as I flew in to get to Dar from Lindi."

I changed the conversation back to where we'd left off. "Why do they call you Pepsi?"

"I don't know," Doug replied pensively. "I forget why I got that name." Then he continued, "You read awfully well. Fergie'll like you in his drama class."

"He seems to think so, but I've never thought about acting. We'll see. How about you, why don't you join?"

"Neah, it's not me to do acting. Don't think I'd like it. But I tell you what you will like and that's the donga. Let's go there."

We strolled over to the tree-scrub and brush that lined the eastern ridge of the donga. "We haven't got time to climb down it now, break's too short, but maybe we'll go this afternoon and I'll show you a thing or two. There're some great hideouts down there; it would be mushee if you had a dame with you."

"A girl?" I asked incredulously. "You play with girls?"

"Not play, you know – have a girlfriend."

"Oh… well… I, er, don't know much about that. I've never had a girl-friend. Not sure I want one."

"Well I haven't got one either, yet, but I think I will one of these days."

I changed the subject. "So you're in Wilberforce, eh? I'm in Livingstone."

"Yes, I am. Our houses are not far from yours, maybe a bit closer to here. We don't have as far to walk as you."

"What's it like in Wilberforce?"

"It's pretty good. I like it. The prefects are nice enough. Glynn treats us well. Sometimes tells us stories of the early days in the school – you know – when it first opened."

"I know. Sheddy and I listened in to some on the train."

"I've heard it can be rough in Livingstone; it seems to have more bullies than any other house; is that true?

"I don't know much about Livingstone yet; I haven't been here long enough. I hope not. So where are you from?"

"Kigoma; it's at the opposite end of the line of rail from Dar. Not many people, less than a hundred Europeans, my dad says. But it's a neat enough town next to Lake Tanganyika."

"I didn't think I'd seen you on the train. So how do you get here? Does your train come to Kongwa like ours did?"

"Neah. We, that is my sister Susan and I, take the mail train from Kigoma and get off in Dodoma. It takes two days and two nights to get that far. My dad has business colleagues there so we stay with them overnight. Then, next day, we and other kids catch the buses specially chartered for the school."

Hmm, same as Clive, I thought.

Doug and I talked a little more as we peered through the brush into the donga but soon the bell rang and it was time to get back to class. I liked Doug;

I thought we'd get along. It was a pity though that he was in Wilberforce; that would make it harder to get together during free time.

Ten or twelve weeks later a new pupil joined our class. A girl arrived at half-term. She was a bit younger than us, not even yet nine, but was temporarily put in our class anyway. We couldn't miss her arrival. You could see by her face how unhappy she was. I think she'd been trying not to cry but then started sobbing her heart out. Mr. Ferguson, taking English at the time, had no time for her unhappiness.

"Oh do stop crying, child," he shouted, "you're going to upset the whole class and I won't have it. Now shut up or go and stand outside!"

I felt sorry for her and understood how she felt. At the break she kept the company of several sympathetic girls who clustered around her protectively and tried to cheer her up. As I found myself standing near Morag Cormack I asked about her.

"Her name's Valerie Hext," Morag told me. "She arrived with her mum on the train yesterday afternoon. As soon as she got here and her mum met with Miss Strong, Valerie was told to run along with her new house prefect and two other girls who had been told to come and welcome her. She didn't realise she wouldn't get a chance to say goodbye. She saw her mum again at a distance in the evening, sitting with the teachers at their dinner table. Well, as you know, we're not allowed to go near an adults' table at their mealtimes, so she wasn't allowed to talk to her mum again, not even to say goodbye. She was told to leave the mess with the other girls, and that was that. She's not in my house but I heard she cried most of the night."

CHAPTER FIVE

A GOODY-GOODY

B Y TORCH-LIGHT WE PEERED AT THE MORSE code message that one of us had found pinned to the kitchen wall. It was after lights-out, we were out of bounds, the hyraxes were shrieking and we would be in big trouble if caught. It wasn't scary enough with the noise of the night and the threat from the unseen in the pitch black. Now we were in a deserted house, reading a message that clearly proved we'd stumbled upon something we weren't supposed to know about. We looked around at each other in our new-found dilemma.

"Now what are we going to do?"

Aranky took the lead. "I can't understand from this what's going on so we can't tell any teachers, especially not with us being out-of-bounds and after lights-out an' all. I think we should put the message back up on the wall and leave it. We can come back again, tomorrow maybe, and find out if there're any replies, like with new messages. We can't tell teachers anything 'til we're sure there's crooks around and what they're up to."

"He's right," said Paton. "Let's get back to our houses before we get in any real trouble."

It had been less than a week since our arrival when someone had come up with the idea, enticing chaps like me, who were called goody goodies, to go along on a raid of deserted houses. Our house ran close to the donga, which must have been about fifteen feet deep and twenty feet wide. The depression provided endless opportunities for hiding during games of cowboys and Indians, or for hunting insects, snakes or lizards. The donga was the western boundary of the school. The other side of it, where the abandoned houses were, was out of bounds. The donga itself was not.

Using our penknives as screwdrivers, we robbed the houses of the electrical parts like switches, lamp holders and the contents of fuse boxes. There was not a lot you could do with the parts but, if you acquired enough of them, it was possible to build constructions that pleased us. Some pieces with moving parts were in high demand and made for good swopping currency.

I, like a few others, should have been more alert maybe, but we were taken in when someone 'discovered' the Morse code message on the kitchen wall. Led on by the Cubs, as we realised later, we returned the next night to investigate further. For several nights we went back, each time coming upon a new message in Morse, until finally we naïve ones began to suspect what was going on. The Cubs had been planting false messages, and no one was more pleased with himself than Aranky. It was a fun game of imagination though, and during the ensuing weeks the Cubs taught the rest of us Morse; Semaphore too.

These late night raids had involved close shaves with trouble. Clive said we were taking major risks. He knew from personal experience of Fergie's willingness to beat boys with a kiboko. He'd been on the receiving end many times and seemed to be learning, if not to give up mischief, then certainly to be better at avoiding being caught.

One night a new raid was planned that was even scarier than the Morse code expeditions. It involved the empty houses of phases 5 and 6. There were twenty-five or thirty of them deserted and pristine, with their electrics intact. Sheddy was enthusiastic. So were Gunston, Jenner, Rushby, Aranky, Priestly and Paton. Goggles and Berry were hesitant but I, seeking to fit in, cajoled them into it.

Matron had made her rounds, and before long others from Livingstone were gathering around Clive's house. It was central command.

Once everyone had arrived, Clive addressed us. "It's important that this raid be done carefully. Fergie's always looking for trouble. If he catches us we won't be able to sit for a week so be really quiet, okay? Have you got torches with you?"

There was a chorus of no's and yes's and pairing off.

"There's no moon tonight so, apart from your torches, all you've got is the stars. It's good for not being seen but it's bad for not being able to see where you're going. It's a helluva trek to phase 5 so I hope you're all wide awake. So follow me, okay? Dead quiet and don't use those torches unless you have to."

"Clive?" Sheddy asked in a hushed tone.

"What, Sheddy?"

"Maybe we should spread out a bit, I mean, one long line of us stands a greater chance of getting caught."

"You're right; however, not everyone knows how to get to phase 5, especially in the dark, so that's why I thought we should do it this way."

"I know how to get to phase 5, so does Edwards."

"Well, if you like, we'll split into two then. You lead half the chaps and I'll take the other half."

We followed the track by starlight, keeping close to the edge of a culvert so we could vanish into the bush in a second if discovery threatened. It led to the tarmac road that divided our present phase from the unoccupied phases. Here we paused. Clive's group had disappeared. There was no sight or sound of them. They must have made fast progress. On Sheddy's command, we dashed across the tarmac and melted into the bushes the other side. Now there was no road to follow, just hard-baked paths weaving through the dried out bushes. But they were good for keeping us out of the tall grasses, among which who knew what danger lurked.

After many minutes Sheddy paused, turned and bade everyone keep down in a crouch, finger to lips, "Ssssshhhhh."

After peering ahead Sheddy turned and whispered, "It seems clear. I can see the first of the houses. I don't know where Clive is; I can't see a sign of him or his group. He must've found another part of phase 5, or maybe he's at 6. So let's get to the closest buildings. Once inside, we shouldn't be spotted, so long as we don't use the torches too much."

Before long we arrived at the first house.

"Okay, you four, you can have this one. The rest follow me. This is the outside choo I told you about," said Sheddy as we moved along the line of houses. There were twin choos set between each house, maybe twenty-five yards from each. As we continued along, we passed the fourth house. With

THE SLOPE OF KONGWA HILL

everyone else accounted for, Sheddy and I went into it along with Ivey and
Gunston.

"Oh look, this is super," I said. "A fuse box. There's going to be all sorts
of stuff in here."

I set about dismantling it using my Swiss Army knife. Sheddy glanced at
it and said, "That's a good one, Tony, but I'm going into the loft." With that
he asked Gunston to help him up. The gypsum board that was the ceiling was
already damaged and had large holes.

"Gunny, let me sit on your shoulders. Maybe I can reach the cross beams
through the hole there. Now, try not to wobble, see?"

"Uh, huh, you're heavy, Sheddy. Grab those beams quickly. I dunno how
long I can hold you, man."

Sheddy gripped the beams and launched off Gunston's shoulders, swinging in the air, then hauled up his legs so he could get in place. Then he called
Gunston, "Wanna come up?"

"Yes, but how?"

"I'll lie on these beams and we'll grab wrists. I'll lift you high as I can
but soonest chance you get you must leave go and grab a beam. Then do the
same with a second one, okay?"

"Okay, Sheddy, I'm ready."

Gunston slipped his grip first time and dropped to the floor but after the
second try he made it. Soon the two were crawling the rafters looking for the
electrics.

I didn't see Gunston fall. I was too busy picking apart the fuse box, until
I heard the yell followed by a solid thud. I turned to see him as he rolled over.

"Ow, my arm!" wailed Gunston. "I may have broken it."

Sheddy swung down, pocketing his gains on the way and checked his
friend.

"You'll be fine," he decided in his authoritative way, after running his
hands all around Gunny's arm. "There's no break so it's probably a sprain.
It'll heal. No skin broken so Matron will never know. Seems like we've finished here. Let's scarper and meet at the baobab I showed you."

That night we returned safely, and the next day most of us swopped parts
with others who coveted what we had. They would come up with items such
as gob stoppers, an Eagle comic, a catapult or a penknife.

It was the third raid that brought this pastime to a painful end, at least for most of Livingstone's Juniors. Several weeks had passed so it was time for another foray. Clive was insistent we not go. He'd been caught on other things and been caned. He talked it over with prefects from the other houses but was unable to persuade them we'd gone far enough. And so it was that after having gathered at another house many of Livingstone's boys set out on a raiding party. We of Clive's house were not pleased.

"Come on, man," appealed Sheddy. "Let's go, man. We've been before and never been caught. What's the matter with you, man?"

"I said no," said Clive. "No one from this house is going."

"But why?" I whined. "Everyone else is. We've always gone before."

"No."

"Come on, Clive," said McLachlan. "Let those go who want to go. It's us'll be in trouble if we're caught, not you if you stay back."

"I said no, and I mean no."

"We know that not everyone else has gone," I carried on. "There's several houses where some chaps have gone and not others. Why can't you be like those prefects, and just let those of us who want to go, go?"

"Because I said so, and I'm not prepared to discuss it any more. Get back to your beds and shut up," he said irritably, "or I'll spank you myself."

Some hours later, we were woken by a kerfuffle outdoors. We scrambled to peer through the mosquito mesh to the black outside. We couldn't see much but we could hear urgent and muffled voices and running footsteps, mixed in with the noise of the insects and bullfrogs of the donga, and what sounded like an adult voice calling out from far in the distance but we couldn't be sure. Clive came through from his room and, after peering through a window, urged us to our beds.

"Go back to sleep right now, you hear me. No one is to be awake. Lie down and say nothing. Almost certainly Fergie will come around on inspection. I don't want anyone to even be awake when he walks in." And with that he retreated to his room.

It wasn't long before I heard our door handle turn. Someone entered, almost certainly Fergie, I could tell by the walk and beside which who else would it be? But the identity of the figure wasn't revealed because he was in deep darkness behind the brilliance of his lantern. It had an exceptionally strong light beam, and he shone it on the head of every boy in the room. I know because, as the one furthest from the door, I dared to keep an eye open as he entered. As the beam of light moved from head to head and approached me, I closed my eye and feigned restlessness as I turned to face the other way. I opened an eye at the wall and saw my shadow. The beam moved away, and then I heard the gentle click of the front door closing as Fergie withdrew. Moments later we were sitting up as Clive came through.

"Boy, that was a close shave. You lot are bloody lucky that we were all here and in bed. At least he knows none of us were on the raid."

The following day Fergie called a house meeting in the art classroom at four o'clock. We stood around the room facing the front, as he called our attention and launched into a tirade.

"As you know," he shouted, determined to sound angry, "we're here because of the boys who were outdoors, misbehaving after lights-out last night. You are nasty little thieves, despoilers of property and irresponsible in the extreme; especially you prefects who not only permitted this to happen, but participated. All prefects here, with the exception of Knight whose house was not involved, are hereby demoted from privileges until further notice. With the exception of Knight's house, you are all horrible, despicable little people who are to be severely punished. You may argue that while some among your number went on the raid, you personally did not. Well, that's tough. Just one boy missing from your house means that all from that house will be punished so I don't want to hear any protests."

I caught Paton's eye across the room, where he sat next to a boy named Jones. His house was one where some but not all had been missing from their beds. Paton hadn't gone on the raid. I gave him a weak smile in sympathy. With that Fergie picked up the six-foot-long blackboard ruler and called us by name.

"Jones."

"Yes, sir."

"Come forward. Now, bend over and touch your toes. No, straighten up again."

"Yes, sir?"

"Move the table out of the way; I need more space up here."

"Yes, sir."

"All right, now, stand here, bend over and touch your toes."

And with that instruction, Fergie gripped the blackboard ruler with both hands, swung it back over his shoulder like a golf club, and brought it down onto Jones's behind. Again he did it. Then again.

"Right."

Jones straightened up, red in the face and grimacing.

"Next, Paton."

I averted my eyes.

And so it went on until he reached each prefect. "Bend over. You're a prefect and should know better. You'll receive six."

Thirty-one backsides, and plus or minus ninety nine strokes later, Fergie had finished beating every boy in Livingstone, except the nine of Clive's house.

Later, I reflected that it would have been better had our house gone on the raid. Being let off the hook led to teasing and bullying of the goody goodies.

"Oh look, there's Edwards, he's a good boy."

"Yes and Goggles. What are you two, mummy's boys?"

"Scaredy-cats to go on the raid, eh? Scared of Fergie's kiboko?"

"We didn't go on the raid because Clive wouldn't let us, that's all. We're not goody goodies."

"Oh yes, you are," said Viljoen in his Afrikaner accent, as his best friend Potgieter and he came up close and gave me a push.

"Hey! Bloody well leave him alone," shouted Venables. "We're not doing anything to you."

"It's not what you're doing to us, jong," said Potgieter. "It's what we're going to do to you." And with that he punched me in the chest and sent me staggering.

"I said, leave him alone," cried Venables, his last words before being punched to the ground by Viljoen.

I came back and lashed out a punch at Potgieter but he fended it off and landed another on me sending me down. It would have got a lot worse but a couple of others who'd paused to watch spotted Matron coming, and hissed the warning code, "Cuss-cuss. Cuss-cuss."

Viljoen and Potgieter broke off the attack, with Viljoen warning, "You've got off lightly this time, jong. Next time I see you and there's no Matron around, then you'll know what I mean, my boy, you'll be sorry."

Moments later Sheddy appeared from our house. He hadn't seen the altercation but he sensed it.

"What happened, Edwards, Venables?" he asked glancing at Potgieter and Viljoen as they walked away. "Were those two giving you trouble?"

"They were starting to beat up Goggles and me, Sheddy." Then in a subdued voice because Matron was passing, "They stopped when they were warned Matron was coming but they've threatened to get me and Gogs another time when no one's around."

"Oh, they have, have they? Well, maybe I'd better let them know that if they want to get you they're going to have to get past me first."

"I don't want you in trouble too, Sheddy. I have to fight my own battles."

"If it's fair, yes. But it's not fair to pick on you when you've done nothing to them, especially when they know you're not a boxer and they both are. That's bullying and I don't let my friends get bullied. Don't worry, Viljoen knows me well; I beat him in the boxing tournament last term; he and I are going to have a talk later on."

"Thanks, Sheddy, I really mean it, but…"

"But what?"

"I can't let you fight my battles all my life. I wish I could defend myself."

"I can teach you to box or you could join classes."

"I don't think I'd be any good at boxing, Sheddy. I just don't think it's something I could ever do, and besides which I'd get asthma."

"Well, how about wrestling? I've seen you play wrestling with the others in the afternoons. You seem to do that without getting asthma."

"Yes, I'm okay, I s'pose, at least when it's for play. But you're right; maybe I should take it seriously. Could you show me more about wrestling?"

"I'm as good with wrestling as boxing. I'll give you lessons. Want to start now?"

"Have we got time?"

"Yes," he said glancing at his watch. "It's half an hour 'til bath time. Hmm, I think I'll make a wrestler out of you."

"But Sheddy," I asked, "if someone's boxing and you want to wrestle, aren't you supposed to fight the same way, you know, both do boxing?"

"Not unless that's what you've agreed to. Don't mix up looking after yourself with tournament rules. If you haven't set any rules for fighting and you're defending yourself, you use what you know. Why should it be boxing just because the other bloke wants it? Why can't you both wrestle?"

"The other bloke may not want to wrestle; maybe he's no good at it."

"And maybe you don't want to box, because you're no good at it. So what you have to do if you can't avoid a fight is to fight the way you know how."

Back indoors, Sheddy started by testing me. Although I'd play-wrestled with Berry and Venables and Ivey, I'd not done so with Sheddy. I suppose it was respect for the fact that I knew I wouldn't stand a chance with him.

"Come on, come at me. Let's friendly wrestle. Do what you know how to do. I want to find out how good you are."

I thought I gave a fair account of myself but secretly I knew it was because he was letting me do things, and use moves I'd picked up, just because he wanted to find out what I knew. Sheddy wasn't trying to beat me.

Some of the others returned to the house talking about bath time, and asking if anyone had bagged the bathroom yet. "We'll have to stop now," said Sheddy, "but we'll talk at dinner. We're off to a good start but truth is you don't know a whole lot. I'm right you've never had any lessons?"

"Yes. Whatever I do is what I've learned watching others."

I heard later from Aranky that he'd seen Sheddy corner Viljoen after dinner. He had him pinned against a wall, and warned him that he'd be in trouble if ever he beat up Edwards or Venables for no good reason. In the following weeks I had many wrestling lessons, sometimes in the dorm but more often in a quiet place not far from the donga where there was seclusion.

CHAPTER SIX

THE TREE WHERE
ARMS GOT BROKEN

T HE SCHOOL'S MILK GARI CAME BOUNCING ALONG the track, squeaking to
a halt in a red dust cloud. From out of the front jumped prefects Robin
Hoy and Glynn Ford, accompanied by three 'boys' in the back. They lowered
the gari's tail gate, and began shouting orders on how best to remove from the
pick-up the zebra they'd shot.

Goggles, I and a few others, eternally hungry, had drifted by the mess
to hang around the kitchen. It was said that sometimes there was food left
over from the staff tables, and the cooks would share it around with anyone
passing by. We weren't given any handouts but did catch the arrival of that
night's dinner. Zebra Stew. As a result of the famine and the difficulty ob-
taining sufficient meat, the school was expected to supplement its rations by
conducting hunts. Senior boys who could shoot were invited to bring home
the bacon, so's to speak. We idled around watching, as the zebra was manhandled onto the fifteen-foot-square, concrete slab that sloped inwards to a
soak-away drainage hole in the middle. The slab was designed, in a prescient
nod towards the future of multi-tasking, for the dual purpose of cutting up
game or a location to wash the dhobi (laundry). Soon, several African chefs
emerged from the kitchen, keening their blades against steels. They ignored

the miasma of the over-flowing, broiling and foetid dust-bins nearby as they descended upon the luckless creature. We watched, fascinated, as the zebra was slit open, the guts spilled out and all the flies of Africa relocated from the dust-bins and descended upon the carcass. After a while the prefects focussed on us, and shooed us away. "Voetsek, man! Bugger off, eh!"

Little did we know that before the day was out one of us would be spilling blood too.

As we drifted, we came across others taking the afternoon off. Aranky should have been at Cubs. "Akela had to cancel today's meet," he said, "I don't know why."

"What's it like being a Cub?" I asked. "I've never been one."

"It's super, man. You learn a heck of a lot, especially First Aid and stuff. Sometimes we camp away from school over a weekend. We learn how to survive in the wilderness; they teach you a lot. It'll be even better when I'm a scout. I'll be taking tests for that soon and hope I'll be promoted next term."

"Do you think I could join?" I asked again.

"You can put your name down. Trouble is there's only one Akela; you know what an Akela is?"

"No."

"Akela is the leader of our Cub troop. Anyway, there's only one who does it for Cubs all the time, Miss Hambleton. Mr. Brownlow does it for Scouts, although Shutty sometimes helps out. But I'll let her know to put your name on the list, for when the chance comes up, okay?"

"Thanks, Aranky."

I joined up with Sheddy who was also a Cub. As we walked, he asked, "Do you want a drink?" and suggested the duka.

The duka was a square shack of a building within school bounds, with heavily barricaded, shuttered and thickly-meshed windows that closed out most of the light. Its green, solid, double-door entry was kept closed to keep out the drifting hot sand, as well as the heat and the light. The outside walls were whitewashed and reflected a rusty tide mark around their base, the trademark of Kongwa buildings, resulting from the ever drifting red sand. The unwelcoming doors were unlocked, so we entered. No one was there except the proprietor. I mooched around the grubby shelves looking for lemonade, but they didn't have any.

"No, prease, we only 'ave Coca-Cola, don't you see?" the South Asian proprietor told Sheddy in his stilted English. "I can only sell you that one, man."

"Have a Coke," invited Sheddy. "Why not have a Coke – it's good, man?"

I resisted; after all I'd never drunk a Coke before. I might not like it. But now there was no choice and my best friend Sheddy was telling me how good it was.

"They haven't got a fridge here," he said, "so it's not the same as home when its cold, but still it'll be good, man."

"Well anyway, I haven't got any money, Sheddy," I argued my excuse, "so I'll have to wait 'til I get some."

"That's all right, I already told you I've got enough, and I never did pay you back for the biltong in Kilosa so I'll buy you one." Turning to the proprietor, he said, "Please get another Coke for my friend."

"That will be pifty cents, prease."

Sheddy paid the man but as we turned away I whispered, "Asians always seem to have trouble with their Fs. Why can't he say fifty?"

And so I tried Coke, and liked it. At a later time I learned the drink was better tasting chilled, than at 80 degrees Fahrenheit, but in Kongwa the drink was always warm. No fridges.

We ambled aimlessly, chatting and kicking stones. After a while we came by a huge baobab covered in boys, some from our house. It had a fat, bulbous and pot-marked trunk that was smooth as glass to the touch. With its lowest limbs on the horizontal three or four feet above my head, I couldn't see how you'd climb it.

"How do you get off the ground?" I asked.

"Oh, you get a leg up, or you can stand on my back."

We gazed upwards. That smooth surface was the same all over.

"It's not really a tree, you know?" said Sheddy as I peered into its branches.

"Come off it, of course it's a tree."

"No, really, it isn't; it's a vegetable."

"That tree's a vegetable?"

"Yes. Baobabs haven't got wood. It's vegetable. No wood, no bark like a real tree. Just an oversized vegetable."

"Crikey, if it's a vegetable it's bloody-well oversized all right. Imagine if they gave you one of those branches at dinner instead of cabbage!"

Sheddy smiled as he beckoned me under its lowest limb and said, "Here, hop on my back and you should be tall enough to climb off me. But first take your sandals off; you won't get a grip with them on; too slippery."

"What, climb in my feet?"

"Yes, see that's what the others are doing. Your skin will grip better at least."

With that, he bent over and grabbed his shins.

I slipped off my sandals, struggled onto Sheddy's back, reached around the limb and, gripping my own hands, swung my legs up until I was slung like a sloth while Sheddy moved away.

"Now what?" I called from upside down.

"Curl around the limb until you're lying flat on the upper side," yelled Sheddy. "Then you can sit up and you'll be ready to climb."

I struggled and slipped and heaved to the upside.

"That's great, man. Now climb!"

I thought, *This is high enough!* Nine feet looked darn high to me. This was the first time I'd ever climbed a tree in my life. I'd never before had an opportunity. It was easy for Sheddy; he'd done it hundreds of times.

Several squadrons of kasukus circled the baobab looking for a landing spot but on seeing us, with even louder squawking, veered off in search of somewhere less populated.

I looked to Sheddy for reassurance but he'd left. Then I heard him calling to another friend as he hoisted himself up the other side of the tree. Soon he was looking down at me, from his position some twenty feet up.

"Come on, Tony, you can't sit there forever. Climb up here, man."

I followed Sheddy's directions cautiously, and he waited while I slowly followed on those slippery surfaces, climbing ever higher. Soon we must have been thirty feet up. I tremulously looked ahead; didn't dare look down. We stopped for a breather.

"What's baobab fruit like?" I asked, trying to distract Sheddy from climbing any higher. "I saw Alder pick one. Is it any good?"

"I like it. Look, there's some near your head. Try it."

I plucked a greeny-brown, egg-shaped pod about the size of a maracas instrument, and discovered it to be a hard shell covered with a thin furry coating.

"Smack the pod against the tree trunk. The shell should splinter and crack open. Try it, hit hard."

"It's split," I said as I watched a chunk peel off and drop.

"Now pull the rest apart."

I needed both hands so I wedged myself, then reached in and exposed a thick, fibrous material that reminded me of raffia. As I pulled on it, I saw what looked like a half dozen multi-planed 'eggs' cloistered inside.

"That's the fruit," said Sheddy. "We call it crème of tartar. If you suck on one, the outside white will dissolve in your mouth. Spit out the seed."

I found it sour and pinched my cheeks. It was nothing I'd want much of. Then Sheddy called me to follow him even higher, when suddenly—

"—Oh no!"

"Watch out!"

"I'm slipping!"

I glanced to where the yells were coming from directly below, just in time to catch a glimpse of Jenner at the start of his fall. One foot had gone out to the side of the limb he was on and at first he fell into a sitting position, but only for a second. He had momentum and was off balance. He slipped sideways, flailing, grasping for branches, gripping one briefly. But his momentum was too great. His hand slipped down the stem, setting dried leaves fluttering and then he was tumbling again. He fell forward, hit another limb with his chest, which slowed him briefly, then slipped again, unable to grasp any support from the lowest limb and landed in a crumpled heap and a cloud of dust below.

"Oooooow, uh, uh, aaaah!" he yelled.

Jenner, in a lot of pain, was quickly surrounded by those on the ground. Sheddy squeezed around me and descended the tree as sure-footed as a monkey and was on the sand again in moments.

"Can you get up?" he asked taking charge. "Do you think you've broken anything, man?

"Yes," Jenner gasped. "Fetch a teacher, I can't move."

I slowly descended, until I reached the lowest limb.

Sheddy turned to Aranky, "Fergie's house is the closest. See if you can find him. I think Jenner's going to need hospital."

Aranky left at a sprint.

Jenner didn't look injured. There was no blood to be seen and his right arm and two legs looked normal. But we couldn't see his left arm.

"It's broken," said Jenner between sobs of pain. "I'm sure it's broken."

"Can you roll over a little?" asked Sheddy. "There may be something we can do, fix a splint or something."

"It hurts too much, my chest too. How do you know what to do anyway?"

"Well, we get First Aid lessons in Cubs; I might be able to help a bit. You'll have to get into the car when Fergie arrives. Do you think I could roll you over so we can see your arm?"

"I don't know, man. I can try."

Berry joined in. "Let me help," he said. "Sheddy, if you can move the other side and pull Mike over a bit, I may be able to move his arm out from under."

"Maybe we should leave him be 'til Fergie gets here," said Alder as he peered between the two.

"We should try something at least," Berry replied. "We can't just leave him. We don't know how long 'til we get help."

"You're right," said Sheddy. "I'll move around."

"Are you ready, Jenner?" asked Berry.

"I think so," he grunted. "Be careful, man, it hurts."

"Hold on, Jenner," Berry said. "Okay, Sheddy?"

At that Sheddy grasped Jenner across his chest and gently eased him into a quarter roll.

"Owwwwwwwwwwww!" yelled Jenner. "My chest!"

"Gosh, it's broken all right," said Berry, as we got sight of the left arm. "There's a bone here split in half sticking through his skin, and badly shattered."

"And maybe my ribs too," gasped Jenner breathlessly.

Now, I could see the blood oozing into the sand, especially from my higher view point.

"I'm going to ease your arm around from the shoulder," said Berry. "I don't want to touch the rest of it with the bone sticking out and all but if I can get your arm moved from under, I think it'll be less painful. You're going to need to do this anyway to get into Fergie's car."

"Talking of Fergie, where is he?" someone asked. "Can you see him coming, Edwards?"

I peered in the direction of his house. It was not in sight and I could no longer see Aranky.

"I can't see him coming," I called down, "or Aranky; maybe he's not at home."

"'Struth, e's takin bloody donkey's years," said Lister Hannah, an Australian with shock blond hair. He had unusually pale skin but was a handsome boy, also new to Kongwa.

Soon Jenner was lying flat, his broken arm to his side, the wound gunged with sand wet with blood. Sheddy had a whip round for clean handkerchiefs. He tied several together as he fashioned a tourniquet to staunch the bleeding and used others to mop the wound and clean away globs of sticky sand.

"That's a real beaut job you dun there, Sheddy," whistled Hannah.

"Hannah, will you help out?"

"Too right, cobber, what c'n oi do?"

"I don't think Aranky's found Fergie. Would you run to the office? You should be able to find a teacher there who could bring a car."

"No worries, Sheddy, she'll be rite, mate." And with that he took off at a sprint.

I swung from the limb I was on, and dropped to the ground. "I've got a clean hanky, Sheddy, if there's more blood to be mopped."

We took turns in reassuring Jenner that help was on the way; there'd be a master here soon and to hold on. He seemed to slip in and out of consciousness.

"Oh blimey, he's not dead, is he?"

"Don't be a clot, man – can't you see he's breathing? I think he's going between conscious and unconscious."

At last we heard the sound of a car coming at speed. Shutty arrived in his VW in a cloud of dust. It was the only car like it in Kongwa, maybe all East Africa. Shutty had bought it in Germany during an extended holiday on his way to Tanganyika. We thought it weird. It was such an ugly car; it looked like a beetle. It looked like it would fit in the boot of most American cars we'd seen on the flicks. Who'd even want one?

"Let me through boys, out of my way," said Shutty as he exited his car and strode towards us while Hannah climbed out the other side. "Let's see what we've got here." The garrulous Shutty moved in to take charge and assess the situation. "Hmm, nasty break. You've lost a lot of blood."

"My ribs may be broken, sir," croaked Jenner.

"Come, Shed, Hannah and you there, Edwards, help lift Jenner and get him into the front seat. It helps that this happened to his left arm. We can rest it on the ridge of the open window, come on now, give me a hand, take it easy... steady now."

It was a delicate operation moving Jenner to the car. He was in pain but being semi-conscious, what with the loss of blood and all, it served him well that way. Shutty declined our offers to accompany him.

"Between the doctors and the nurses at the hospital, I'm sure we'll manage once I get there. Now, no more tree climbing today, please. I don't want any more broken arms. I suggest you find something else to do until bath time."

Shutty left, and we stood and watched as his car bounced along the track, before vaporising into a red cloud. No sooner had he disappeared than Mr. Ferguson rolled up in his Austin, with Aranky in front. With Fergie giving chase to the hospital – Jenner was a Livingstone boy after all – we tree climbers disbursed to our houses.

Jenner returned to school three days later. He'd been patched up, his left arm in plaster-of-Paris from shoulder to hand and in a sling and, with cracked ribs, bound tight with bandages around his chest. He was soon comparing notes, or plaster-of-Paris signatures anyway, with Donald McLachlan who also had a broken arm. In McLachlan's case he hadn't fallen out of a tree. Don was a year younger than us and living in the flats – and the flats had a back room that was at a higher level than the front room. Perhaps he and friends had been reading too many World War II stories, I don't know, but McLachlan thought he'd try out this parachuting thing, using bed sheets. So, with sheet enthusiastically drawn around him, McLachlan launched off the higher level with the intention of floating gently down to the lower level. Unfortunately his chute failed to deploy, insufficient time between leaping and landing, I suppose. The result was he returned to concrete floor more in the style of a flying rock than a gentle touch down. For his troubles he suffered a broken arm and languished in hospital for three days. While he was there, and for their efforts in acting as ground crew in abetting McLachlan in his pursuit of flight, his five co-conspirators received a caning from Mr. Ferguson. Fergie never knew an issue with boys that wasn't resolved by a good caning.

✦ ✦ ✦

BY NOW, WE WERE SUPPOSED TO BE as ready as we'd ever be to display our talents in the play, *Any Body*. In a remarkable display of improvisation, Fergie made some last-minute changes to Jenner's role.

"Jenner," Fergie said, "I've adjusted the script slightly to make use of your bandaged arm. It will lead to your character coming under greater suspicion than before. Can you learn the extra lines in time?"

"I'll try, sir."

The drama took place in an old English pub, built lovingly by Mr. Brownlow who excelled in his design, carpentry and props, all erected in the girls' gym.

By the day of dress rehearsal we were having a great time, the only problem being we found it difficult not to laugh. The play was a comedy and we never ceased to find some of the better moments funny no matter how repetitive the rehearsals. Because we were not precocious, we laughed ourselves silly at our own acting.

The big night arrived. Made up to look like grown men with five o'clock shadows or sporting moustaches and beards, dressed in suits and ties – it all seemed hilarious. As the publican, my trousers were hitched with braces and I wore a striped shirt and an apron. Throughout the one-scene play, marked by brief intervals that represented changes of days and times, with lighting adjustments, I was to be found behind the bar most of the time leading much of the conversation with my regulars, or the police detectives as the case may be, all the while hand-drying a never-ending line of freshly washed glassware.

> *"There is a tavern in the town, in the town,*
> *And there my dear love sits him down, sits him down,*
> *And drinks his wine 'mid laughter free,*
> *And never, never thinks of me."*

So went our opening song as the curtains were drawn back. The play was a roaring success. I don't know if the audience was laughing at the comedy or laughing at us but we were mentioned in despatches to the school magazine, *The Georgian*, where our performance was recorded for all time.

CHAPTER SEVEN

RUNNING AWAY

T HE DAY AFTER GUY FAWKES WAS TO be D-Day for a serious plan that
Goggles and I had hatched. Guy Fawkes Night turned out to be great
fun and were it not for our bad states of mind from bullying, we might have
dropped our idea there and then.

Guy Fawkes fell on a Saturday, and that afternoon we'd joined in gathering of brush and dead trees from the donga. Boys from Nightingale had
built the 'Guy' and placed him atop the bonfire to await his fate. We'd even
helped prefects position Roman candles, along with some rockets and pin-
wheels. Then, after we'd enthusiastically helped, we were told to, "Get lost."
Crestfallen, Venables and I left, returning only after dinner along with the
others to sit around the fire, watch the 'Guy' burn, and be amazed at the
fireworks.

The best time was after the display. The bonfire was smaller now but still
crackling from the tinder-dry brush as it sent sparks into the air and emitted
too much heat. We'd been told to withdraw and form a larger circle round
the fire when Joe Grandcourt produced his mouth organ, bursting into his
favourite country music. Before long there was an impromptu gathering of
the choir, who joined in and sung along. I enjoyed that and got so relaxed
that I pondered calling off our plan. But the peace and warm feelings didn't
last. Even as we returned to our house there was harassment from older boys

towards Goggles, and when I joined in to tell them to leave him alone, they turned on me too. Luckily we were close to our house by this time so no fighting broke out.

It was later recalled that we'd asked Paton, because he seemed to know so much about finding the way in the bush, "Which way would you go, if you wanted to walk to Dar es Salaam?"

Venables and I had decided we would run away. By running away, maybe we'd get some attention that might end our misery. Well, anyway, the thinking went something like that, in our simplistic view. We decided we wouldn't follow the rail line. We'd heard stories of Seniors who'd done that, got caught, and were beaten with the kiboko.

On the Sunday, the first day we could get a start without being missed, we began our safari. Breakfast completed, we wandered nonchalantly back to our house calling to others as they left for church that we'd catch up. With no encounters on our way, we reached our house and ferreted out my large, floral dhobi bag, an item donated to the cause by mother, without thought as to how it might be viewed by a collective of boys in a boarding school. Still, we filled it with our needs for the journey. Biscuits and sweets, specially saved for the day, were the main item, two small Coca-Cola bottles filled with water and plugged with paper, some crispy toilet paper and a change of clothes. The last item was Goggles' torch; we'd need that at night.

We reached the short strip of tarmac and crossed it, heading towards the derelict houses of phases five and six. We weaved in and around them believing there was less chance of being seen. Even this early the sun was high overhead, burning down oppressively. The air shimmered, our eyes screwed up with the brilliance, and soon we were stinging with salty sweat.

It was strange with no one else around. There was no movement, no people, no cars; all was quiet except for flocks of kasukus flying overhead, and the scrunch of our shoes on sand.

Our direction led south-east, toward the Kiborianis that would block our path. After a while, we came across the track that marked Kongwa's south-east boundary. As we crossed it, a lorry driven by a European came bouncing towards us. Startled, my heart jumped; for one terrible moment I thought it was all over.

"Quick, Goggles, let's cross the road and hide," I urged, but even as I said it I knew it was too late. The driver couldn't miss seeing us. We glanced back from the other side of the road expecting him to stop and call out, asking what we were up to. But his rattling lorry, trailed by a thick cloud of dust, continued on its way. We paused as it went, the red dust drifting to reveal two African 'boys' in its back, who caught sight of us as the dust cleared, and watched us blankly as they clung for support.

"Thank goodness he's not interested in us," I commented, half to myself, half to Goggles. "Come on; let's move fast in case he comes back."

Between that track and Dar es Salaam we were faced with 200 miles of nothing. There may be a kijiji (village) on the other side of the mountains to the south, or we might come across the rail line well away from Kongwa, if we were lucky, but otherwise we'd be alone in the wild. We didn't wear hats, but then, we didn't own any. On our feet were sandals; the least suitable shoes for walking in the bush. The dhobi bag swinging from my shoulder was a nuisance with the weight of the coke bottles, until later when we'd swallowed the water and discarded them.

After a few hours we tired but struggled on with precious moments of shade as we crossed a donga or found a densely-branched Acacia, to pause in its shadow. Large and dirty flies, the bane of Africans and animals alike, accumulated, covering our sweaty shirts and attempting to settle on our faces. We slapped at them. As we progressed, we attracted horse flies. Still we walked, often being startled as yet another locust suddenly took fright at our approach, and whirred away to some safer location.

We came across a couple of dikdik. I've no idea who frightened who the most for we'd not seen them. They started up from behind a bush in an instant and fled, leaving us with hearts pounding. Not long after, we must have disturbed the green mamba, for, right in front of us, it suddenly slithered off at speed, headed for a msasa tree up which it sleekly wound its way to the top with amazing alacrity. There it paused and watched us. We skirted the tree.

By now it was the hottest time of day, early afternoon, when the air shimmers and teases with imaginary scenes. It sat like a layer of high grasses, tanned by the sun and broken only by the intrusion of acacias, msasas, the odd euphorbia thicket and giant aloe. Like a rainbow, try as you might, you can never catch up with it. There were few baobabs in this region and in their absence we no longer kept the company of the noisy kasukus. We came across a vlei with dense, knee-high and rank grasses, wading through them as if in shallow water, unconcerned for what we might tread on. There must have been an underground stream that came close to the surface. When we cleared it to harder ground we found our legs flecked with ticks. We paused to flick the blood suckers off before they could take hold.

The time dragged and the sun was lower in the sky. Our lips parched, terribly hungry and a gnawing concern that night was not far off, we began to doubt our ordeal was such a good idea. I, being the more stoic and much too proud for my own good, would not speak, just kept heading straight for the mountain, the base of which was now a hundred yards away.

We reached its foot and paused. We gazed up the mountain's eighteen hundred feet in the fading light, breathing heavily and looking first at it and then at each other. Venables found his voice.

"It looks so steep."

"Yes, a bit. The bush is thick, can't see very far."

"It'll be difficult to climb, especially in the dark."

"Perhaps we should wait here 'til morning?"

"I'm worried."

"Why."

"It'll be getting dark quickly now. Even if we wait 'til morning we have to climb these mountains sometime. We don't know what's on the other side, I'm scared and I want to go back."

"Oh come on, Goggles, don't be like that, man. We can't go back now."

"I'm frightened."

"Venables!"

"I don't think we should."

"But, man."

"My parents will worry."

At that I thought of my mother worrying too and my father furious.

"Well, I don't want to go back, Goggles, but if you want to then I suppose we'll have to because I'm not letting you go alone."

And so I allowed myself to be persuaded. Reluctantly we turned around.

As I found out later, it's as well we did. The mountain facing us was the first of many in the chain. There was no flat ground to descend to. We probably would never have emerged alive; most likely never been found.

In spite of our weariness, our pace picked up as the sun disappeared. Then it was dark and we had two hours of walking still ahead. Avoiding the thorn bushes was difficult in the light of a fading torch. The dongas we'd

crossed easily in sunlight were now scary in their inky blackness, their unseen insect occupants and the yellow eyes that blinked curiously at us in the
reflected light, threatening. We got scratches that itched and Venables fell at
least half the height of one donga. I scurried after him given that he'd been
holding the torch. It was now out and the glass face broken. He cried a little,
and was nursing a knee with a bad cut that would quickly turn septic. The
torch was broken, but the light of the stars gave dim visibility.

After an age, we recognized the boundary road we'd crossed so boldly
earlier in the day. We followed the track that would lead towards our phase.
When ten minutes passed and we'd not encountered anyone, Venables got the
idea we might sneak back in with no one having noticed.

"Perhaps we haven't been missed?" he said. "Let's try to avoid teachers
if we can."

At that moment, the night filled with headlights. We stepped back into
the shadows, but too late, the school gari roared by. Even as it did, the driver
braked hard, then reversed. The driver was Robin and we were the two he was
looking for. He called us by name, "Edwards, Venables, is that you?"

He was tentative because he wasn't certain he'd seen what he thought
he'd seen. Venables called back, and in moments we stepped from the bushes
and were in the front seat.

Robin didn't say much except, "You two are in trouble. What crazy thing
do you think you were doing?"

He did ask how long we'd been in the area and told us the town had been
alerted for two missing boys. One worker volunteered he'd seen two boys
while driving his lorry earlier in the day. He told the school we were heading
south-east. Robin was on his way to the area, when he came upon us.

We stood in silence; the time 9:30 p.m. The mess was deserted except
for a table of teachers, late in completing their evening meal. Perhaps they'd
been out searching for us? Robin had marched us in, stood us at attention by
their table, then left. Mr. Ferguson asked a couple of questions, but we didn't
have much to say.

"We'll talk tomorrow," he promised. "Go and be seated over there and
we'll have dinner brought through. When you've finished eating, go to your
house."

Next day there wasn't any talk. We were summoned to Fergie's house
where, after perfunctory comments in which he showed no interest in why

we had tried to run away, or even how far we'd got, he told us we'd receive a thrashing. It was my first time for a caning at his house. I glanced around his living room anticipating a thick, leathered arm chair of the type I would bend over at Allan House, but there wasn't one and we just stood there. Having retrieved what I thought looked like a kiboko because it certainly didn't look like any cane I knew, Ferguson irritably admonished me, "Well, come on then, stand over here and face that way, bend over and touch your toes."

I looked at him in horror. "Not the kiboko, sir," I pleaded. "I can under-stand a caning but not a kiboko?"

"Bend over or it'll be the worse for you."

"But the kiboko is for Seniors, sir?" I said desperately.

"Now!"

I heard the swish of the whip and almost instantly felt a white hot burn-ing on my behind as the kiboko made contact and wrapped around the side almost as far as my hip bone. The agony was excruciating. I felt my breath go, everything in my body screamed *get away from this!* Thwack! A second strike, close to the first. Searing pain, I let out a horrible sound, a breathless *aaaahhhhhhh!*

"No! No!" I cried.

The third strike, too high, caught me at the base of my spine; I felt the tip rip at the side, above my hip bone. I saw stars and stood up unable to bend down any longer; I couldn't see; the burn was torture. I took steps away; throwing my head back; mouth open; no sound came; I had no idea where to put myself. My arms were out; fingers extended; I couldn't touch or be touched. My skin was alive. To touch me would have been unbearable. *Oh, God, make it stop, make it go away!*

Goggles had watched as I was beaten. After seeing my reaction he wouldn't bend over. He resisted Ferguson's order, looking at me appealingly as though there was something I could do. I just stood there in my agony, try-ing to look stoic, not to cry. I dare say my face told Goggles the worst. After being threatened with an extra cut beyond the three Edwards had received, for every number Fergie counted if Goggles didn't bend over immediately, he finally did so. Goggles was in a standing position again and screaming by the time of the third strike.

Everyone knew we'd received the whipping. We were thought lucky it wasn't administered in front of the whole Senior school, girls included; the

Head tended to do things like that when he did the beating, although it was agreed he only did that with Seniors.

That evening at bath time, my friends wanted to see the welts. They were horrified. The kiboko delivers a murderous sight. My skin had broken and my khakis lined in blood which was congealing by now and stuck to the wound. I lay face down on my bed as Sheddy and Berry helped to peel them off without causing more agony and trying not to open up newly forming scabs. The long welts were a deep, ugly, purple-and-black combination and ran deep, creating steep undulations. I hadn't been able to sit down since, not without the greatest trepidation. I didn't know how I was going to manage at dinner.

"I think you've more of a problem than sitting down," said Sheddy. "You need to go to Matron with this, man, else it'll go septic."

"I can't go to Matron and show her my bum."

"Yes, you can, and you must. She's Matron, for Pete's sake, she's like your mum. You have to let her treat this or you'll have terrible trouble when it goes septic… and then it'll be more than Matron seeing your bum, it'll be nurses too."

Sheddy walked me to Matron's house.

"Please, Matron, I think Edwards needs treatment. He was whipped by Mr Ferguson…."

"Oh no, not bose ov you!" responded Matron. "Fenables iss already 'ere." With a sigh, she added, "Come on in, Edvards. Sank you, Shed, you may go back to your room ya."

Venables was standing up, he'd already been treated. "You vill return to your 'ouse now, Venables, and get ready for ze dinner ya?"

"Yes, Matron."

Goggles, looking distressed, gave me a pained look as he departed.

"Now zen, Edvards, I neet you to take off your shorts, please, and zen lie face down on ze settee ya?. Make sure you lie on ze towels I put down for Fenables – I don't vant any bloot on my furniture."

As I took off my khakis I turned away coyly lest Matron see my front view, then laid face down as she'd bid.

"Oh dear, oh dear," Matron muttered under her breath as she took a closer look. "Vy do they haf to beat you zo? Zis iss not right, it's just not right."

Then, out loud she said, "Zis is going to sting batly, I'm afraid. Zere's no choice mit ze size of ze cuts and ze length of time since you caning. I haf to put on ze iodine. I vant that you holt ze tennis balls in your 'ands and sqveeze zem as tight as you can ven I put the dawa on."

"Dawa, Matron?"

"Medicine. Now, are you ready? It vill sting but it's necessary. I'm sorry."

The pain was like being beaten again. I buried my face in the cushions and let out a stifled yell at each new dab of iodine and squeezed those tennis balls until I must have flattened them. After an eternity Matron was finished.

"Just lie zere and don't move. The sting vill subsite, zen you can get up."

As I walked gingerly back to my house, a schoolboy ditty played over and over in my head.

> *Glory, glory, Halleluiah*
> *Teacher hit me with a ruler,*
> *Another beat me with a walking stick*
> *And made me black and blue.*

Once inside the door, I got a reproachful look from Clive. He didn't say anything but I think he felt disappointed in me, took it almost personally; after all, I was from his house. Of course he wasn't the cause, quite the opposite, but I think he felt let down anyway.

WHEN CAME THE DAY TO GO HOME for the hols a few weeks later, the broken skin had healed but signs of the ugly purple bruising remained. I just hoped the school had not told my parents. That and the whipping was a matter of shame, so it was important that they not know. I didn't fear them chastising me; it was just my pride.

The last days of term were happier, with the anticipation of the train ride and the long holiday. I'd be met by the Kherers in Dar and spend overnight with them. Then I'd be put on the plane early and soon be home. I didn't hold a mental picture of our flat; I'd not seen it after all, but in a letter mother had said it was nice.

Teachers were relaxed and by the end-of-term dance, the day before we left, the excitement was palpable. The dance I could have done without. Although it was supposed to be fun, I didn't enjoy being a sissy and dancing with girls, but we were expected to. The dance was a school feature that heralded the holidays. The only floor space suitable was the tennis courts. The music came from a wind-up gramophone that played 78s and needed a needle change after every record. It was loud enough if you danced close to it, but with a hundred and fifty pairs on the floor at the evening's peak, you could barely hear the music otherwise.

I did my bit asking girls to dance, especially after being cajoled by teachers. There the girls sat on chairs opposite us. Boys stood; no chairs, eying them from across the dance floor, assessing who was pretty enough to select and where the courage would come from to go and ask. It was a strange feeling. In spite of my reluctance I had to confess inwardly that once I'd plucked up the courage, there was a weird pleasure in holding a girl's hand, putting an arm around her back and being so close, face to face, her frame so slight, her step so light. I found an inner excitement that I didn't understand but I knew better than to ask anybody about it. Maybe it was just because holding a girl would never happen at any other time. Normally, we never got near one... weren't allowed to.

For their part, the girls clearly loved dancing. Of course they were dressed to the nines, looked beautiful, some of them anyway, and benefitted enormously from the absence of school uniform. The girls I danced with probably would have preferred that I kept off their toes, but what's a boy to do when he doesn't know how.

CHAPTER EIGHT

FLIGHT HOME

IT WAS THRILLING FLYING HOME FOR THE long holiday. I saw Mum and Dad on the apron even before the DC-3 had rolled to a halt. The first thing Mother had commented on was that my skin rash had cleared up. No sign of it.

"Something about Kongwa must agree with you," she said. "You look so fit. Look at him, Les. He was never so healthy-looking in England."

Mother had been especially gratified because she'd felt guilty about bringing me to East Africa with my skin troubles on account of what the doctors had said.

"Africa's full of disease, few doctors, no skin specialists, terrible risk of septicaemia," they'd warbled on about the risks.

But Mum was committed, so she took the chance; after all, I could always be sent 'home' again if the doctors were proved right.

Mater and Pater were pleased to see me, that was clear, and during the dusty drive home there were no questions to do with my running away. When I saw the 'welcome home' gift, I felt sure they didn't know about it. The first thing I set eyes on was a large box containing a 'Trix' electric train set. It was surrounded by other boxes with additional rail lines, a level crossing, signals and a station building kit.

"Oh golly," I said, "is that for me? That's smashing." And with that I dropped to my knees and began pulling everything out.

"We thought you were old enough for a set," said Dad, "so we decided to welcome you home with one. Hope you like it."

"It's absolutely smashing, Dad, thank you so much, and you too, Mum. It's the best present I've ever had!"

"Come on now," said Mum. "You should meet the servants and then we'll show you your bedroom. You can unwrap your trains later."

It was good to discover our flat. Dad had parked among the jacaranda and flame trees in the sandy courtyard. We'd carried my cases up the two flights that led off. The flat didn't have a front door, or a gate. In England our house had a front door and we always locked it, yet here there was no door, everything was wide open, hot, sunny, breezy and free... no keys. We just climbed the steps and at the top was our balcony. Turn right and you found the kitchen and dining/lounge. Turn left for the bathroom and the two chumba cha kulala, the large one for the bwana and memsahib, the smaller for the toto. Where in Kongwa we had narrow beds and conical mosquito nets that tucked in, here I found a springy double bed with a squared off king size net that hung away from the bed, ceiling to floor.

The lounge was light and airy, with two sets of French doors leading to the balcony. The flat was spacious and I loved the long, open, L-shaped balcony on which I designated the corner for the permanent location of my new trains.

I was welcomed with beaming smiles by Mpishi, our mzee cook, followed by our 'boy,' Juma. Juma looked smart in his flowing white kanzu tied off with a bright, scarlet cummerbund and a red fez perched firmly atop his head.

"Jambo, bwana mdogo. Habari eeeeh. Habari yarko?"

I returned their cheerful smiles and greeted them, "Jambo, Mpishi. Jambo, Juma. Habari?"

"Mzuri, mzuri sana."

I peered into the living room, making sure I really was home. There on the sofa were the Siamese cats Mum had written of, Prince and Figaro. One of them stretched a leg, flexed her claws and yawned. The other slept on.

I woke late next morning. Wandering along the balcony in my pyjama bottoms, I found Juma, sitting side-saddle on the retaining wall, soaking in the morning sun and polishing the silver.

"Jambo, bwana mdogo," he addressed me. "Habari?

"Habari, yarko Juma," I said. "What's for chakula?"

"I can ask the Mpishi," Juma responded in his stilted English, "what you can have. I think maybe he can make for you the eggs and bacon, bwana mdogo."

"How about a slice of paw paw first, with lemon and sugar?"

"Of course, bwana mdogo. I will see to eet."

From this upstairs balcony we overlooked the flame tree that was no higher than our roof line. I noticed I was on the same level as the double-decker weaver bird nests and pondered the racket coming from their unseen nestlings. The sun streamed through the branches, backlighting the tree's blooms in a vivid display of orangey red that was startling. No sight or sound of Mum and Dad; they must be at work already. Another stretch and then Juma called me for breakfast.

What will I do today? I thought as I savoured the juicy paw paw. *Maybe I'll start with a walk around town like I did with Annelize and Egbert.*

After bacon and eggs swilled down with a cold Coca-Cola, I got dressed and, with the heat of the day building fast and the humidity drenching – something I was not used to in Kongwa – descended to our sandy courtyard and started my tour.

I'd met most of what were, for us, the main half-dozen store proprietors. We'd not had time to explore a whole lot more back in January. In a few days I would link up with my friends again but for now I preferred to be alone, and there was much to discover. Not only that, but a cyclone had blown through Lindi while I was at school, and the aftermath of devastation had been written about in letters from Mum, so I was curious to see the damage.

Dad had left me directions, so I walked first to the Twentsche Overseas Trading Co. godown where he kept his office. Here the company warehoused imported dry goods, hard goods, white goods, tinned groceries, alcoholic beverages like Amstel beer, the new Philips hi-fidelity gramophones and LPs, and Raleigh bicycles. The building also served as a clearing house for the export of commodities such as sorghum, maize, gum Arabic, groundnuts, cashew nuts, coconuts, beeswax and sisal among others. It was here that Dad shared his office with his secretary, Mum. I walked in.

"Hello, Tony." Mother's face lit up with pleasure. "How are you, darling?" She'd glanced up from taking shorthand where she was seated close to Father's desk. "Did you get a good night's sleep? Have you had a proper breakfast? Did you brush your teeth?"

Yes, I was home all right.

"Hello, chum," Dad greeted me. "We're a bit busy at the moment. What have you got on today?"

"Oh, I'm just out exploring; thought I'd say hello to you first."

I didn't linger. I knew Dad didn't want to be disturbed. He was busy so when he said, after a few moments, "Okay, chum, that's enough," I knew. That's all he had to say. It was an intuitive thing on my part. I'd never been in trouble with Dad, how could I? We were never together. Now, at age 10, was the first time in my life that things might be normal, at least for a few weeks. Yet, I knew.

I continued my walk, past the Standard Vacuum petrol station. I greeted the Asian and Goan shopkeepers, reminding some of our first meeting, as they reclined sedentarily in the shade of their wide open stores.

I examined the posters behind dirty and broken glass outside The Novelty Cinema. They announced nightly runs of Indian films from Bombay but 'coming soon' was *Tarzan's Savage Fury,* a must-see flick, I decided. It would play next Thursday night; Thursdays were set aside for European films. I made a mental note to get myself taken to it.

I nodded polite jambos to African employees in their white smocks and topes, seated at their Singer treadle sewing machines. They were set back under the overhang of second floor ledges on buildings such as Bachupira House or the Rashid Versi Building. Here garments of every type were manufactured or repaired. The Africans never failed to look up with a cheerful smile and gleaming white teeth.

Lindi boasted two grocery stores, both owned by Indians or they may have been Goans. The one was named The Lindi Store, and the other A.Q. Braganza's. It was there the parents bought provisions. These stores were the source of fresh produce if we were lucky enough for it to arrive on the plane when it made its call three times a week. Often the produce got bumped for something more important.

I said hello to the people in Couth's, the chemist, then strolled on to The Lindi Bookshop, run by Europeans, the only store other than Couth's that was. It was a source of Dinky toys and comics as well as *The Famous Five* Enid Blyton books, and other items varying from ornaments to cheap perfume.

"Why, hello, Tony. Home for the holidays, are we?" I was greeted by Mrs. Langham, a busty lady of jolly sorts, who managed to breeze around her shop at such an alarming rate it was a wonder anything remained on the shelves. What with the breeze in her wake and three large fans in the ceiling that were revolving as fast as a plane's propellers, it was definitely cooler in here.

"Have you got any comics?" I asked, hair blowing in the turbulence.

"Of course, of course, here you are, dear. We keep them around this side now, better display, don't you see. We've got *The Beano* in."

"Do you get *The Eagle*?" I sniffed.

"No, my dear, no call for that, I fear. Most children here aren't old enough, you know. But if *The Beano* is too young for you," she thought on reflection, "perhaps you might like something our office in Dar thought we should try, these *Comic Classics*."

I pricked up my ears at that, took a closer look and was quickly impressed. These comics were more like thick booklets. Their subjects were picture stories that represented history of hundreds of years before, and looked interesting. The current issues, recently arrived by sea, were three months' worth stacked together. They featured stories of the conquest of South America by the Spanish conquistadores. There were pictures of galleons as they crossed the Spanish Main, their sea battles with the English, and their exploits as they conquered those heathens in the mountains of South America, bringing civilisation and God to those savage people. Brave soldiers those Spaniards, definitely should make for good reading. I selected a fistful of copies, one for each week of issue for the last eight weeks but I didn't have enough to buy twelve.

"You can take all twelve if you like and come back with your money another day, deary," assured Mrs. Langham. "Don't you worry about a thing. I'm sure you'll get extra pocket money soon enough, so you can pay me then."

I told her I was out for a walk and I'd call back later.

"Just leave them on the counter, deary," I was counselled. "They'll be here for you when you come back."

I returned to the humid stillness. I strolled by a few other stores, more for general merchandise, my feet getting more heated by the moment as white-hot sand blew between my sandal thongs and deposited gritty residue among my toes, making for uncomfortable walking. No wonder adults wore socks with their sandals.

Compared with what I knew from London, these stores looked unkempt; run-down warehouses, piled high with boxes, crates, cheap goods and bric-a-brac. Reclining under layers of dust, showcases with or without glass (and if with glass then dirty and broken) housed the more precious items like cheap watches, sheath knives, ivory carvings, elephant hair bangles, cheap jewellery and other trinkets. Bicycles and spare parts vied for shelf or floor space with basketry and Asian brassware, or carvings of sandalwood and yellow-wood, or household furniture inlaid with ebony and ivory.

The stores were staffed by the owners – large, fat, wizened Asian men and their even larger wives, enveloped in beautiful saris. I found them seated, sometimes just inside their store to escape the direct sun, or on the edge of the dusty, sandy road under the overhang. These smiling merchants greeted me kindly, if in a formal British style, but with their strong, Indian sing-song accents.

"Greetings, Master Tony. I see you are home for the holidays. It is good to see you. Are you well? How is the Kongwa school?"

"Yes, thank you, Mr. Patel *(the entire community seemed to consist of Patels)*, I am home again. I'm sorry I haven't got any spare money so I cannot buy anything, but I thought I'd say hello anyway."

"That is fine, Master Tony," Mr. Patel continued. "It is velly nice to see you, man. How is your father, by the way?"

"Oh, he's well, Mother too. They're working, of course."

I glanced at Mrs. Patel politely so as not to leave her out of the conversation. She said nothing but summoned a polite smile. I had a question I was burning to ask. It was difficult because Mother had always counselled not to ask personal questions or pass personal remarks. "It is simply not done, Tony, in polite society."

But I couldn't resist.

"I don't mean to be rude or anything, really I don't, Mr. Patel, but I am curious. Most Indian ladies I see around town have a red dot in the middle of their foreheads. What's it for?"

Mr. Patel chuckled, "There's nothing wrong with that question, Master Tony. The red dot is called a bindi and indicates, if she is of the Hindu faith that the lady is married. This lady is my wife. Your mother wears a wedding ring on her left hand, I'm sure; our ladies wear a red bindi."

"Oh." But then on reflection, "But, Mr. Patel, sometimes the bindis are not red. Does that matter?"

"If they are not red then that girl is not married. Many Hindu girls like to wear a bindi like their mothers do, but it is for decorative purposes, like jewellery. It will only be red if the lady is married."

"Oh. Thank you for telling me that."

Mrs. Patel smiled.

"I like some of the sheath knives you have here, Mr. Patel. I wish I could afford one of these, with the ivory handle and gold inlay. Golly, it's beautiful."

"It is, is it not?" he replied. "I am sorry if the knife is a bit expensive for you. Perhaps you can save up your shillingies and we can do some business at a later time?"

"Perhaps, although I'm not sure my Mum and Dad would be keen on me buying it anyway," I said with a sigh. "They're a bit funny like that, especially Mum."

"Ah," said Mr. Patel knowingly, "mothers and fathers do not always understand a young boy, do they?"

We chatted a little longer and then, with a cheerful goodbye, and the assurance I would be back, I continued my walk.

Along these white-sanded streets I strolled in the oppressive heat. Torpid natives ambled by in this stifling climate where, it seemed, no one much wanted to work.

"Jambo, bwana mdogo, habari?"

"Jambo. Habari yarko?"

Watoto, wearing their vestigial rags, were the only ones with energy, often running with their hoops, or directing in the sand a home-made, large-scale, toy lorry beautifully carved out of balsa, with rotating wheels. It was attached to the end of a four-foot stick that was the steering column. At the top end of the stick was a steering wheel made with wire. The other end was attached, through a hole behind the cab, to the axle, so that the front wheels could be steered by its youthful driver.

I coveted one of these garis but my attempts to interest a toto into selling one never did bear fruit. The toto preferred his gari to any money I might have come up with. When I'd talked of these toys to my parents when I was first in Lindi, I'd been discouraged from acquiring one.

"You have more than enough toys of your own, which will be awaiting your return on your holidays," Mum had said. "But in any case, whatever would people say if they saw you walking around town playing with a native's toy?"

LINDI WAS A GRITTY LITTLE TOWN IN a pretty setting. The air was clean and clear and always bright, save for the welcome relief that came from a daily hour or two of rain, in the season. Gentle hills descended close to the water, along the edge of which the town nestled. The harbour inlet narrowed into the estuary of the Lukuledi, while a short way upstream, past the impenetrable mangrove swamps, lay the hamlet of Mkwaya.

The Lindi Club, on the beachfront an easy walk from town, was the main centre of activities for Europeans. The Club's white, sandy grounds were filled with the colours of frangipani, hibiscus, gladioli, canna lilies and bougainvillea. Flame trees and Jacarandas lined the narrow road, and made for months of blooms as spring gave way to summer.

The beach was lined with coconut palms, interspersed with the delicate, wispy, conifer-like casuarina trees, with their slender branches and pin-prick leaves. They were said to have seeded there after riding the wind across the ocean from India.

Inside the Club, the bar and the snooker room got most of my attention. The bar, empty during the day, was a source of Coca-Cola and Smith's Crisps. All I had to do was sign a chit for the African bartender, and the charge would go to my father's account. At a later time, I might get a pointed comment, to do with my level of consumption!

The snooker room provided some of my entertainment now and during future holidays when I was by myself, for it was here that I taught myself to play, practicing for hour after hour as I honed my skill. There was one full size table and all the scoring accoutrements, cues, etc. In the beginning I had to prevail on Dad to teach me. He didn't mind, so long as there was no one else wanting a game. The Club was for adults, so I wasn't supposed to be there at any time! In the early days we would vacate the table when someone else arrived, but with the passage of time, I became known for my prowess and would be encouraged to continue playing with Dad, while the new arrival watched. Before long the watcher would say, "I'll play the winner."

Opposite the Club, on the other side of the road, were the tennis courts where Dad got his exercise most evenings. To seaward was the patio with its collection of outdoor furniture under the breezy palms. The sea lapped lazily some twenty yards across the beach. Lindi Bay widened at this point, where the beautiful beach swept around in a crescent to the headland in the far distance. This was the popular walking beach. There was never a crowd, and for the most part you might have the beach to yourself, unless you chanced by while a half dozen fishermen were preparing to leave in their outriggers, or returning with the day's catch.

Half way along the crescent, I discovered the wreck of the dhow. It had blown ashore during the cyclone and not been re-floated. It was recognizable but disintegrating. A mile or two up the beach was a bar and resort at Rasbura. It seems to me it was quite exotic. Lost among the coconut and banana palms, casuarina, mango and avocado trees, the open air bar, being the base of an old dhow, would be lit by coloured lights slung from branch to branch. Light Latin and Calypso music, like Belafonte's *Island in the Sun* was played in the evenings with the insects providing harmony. It all made for an exotic mood.

There was plenty of excitement when the beach became a landing strip. Somewhere, not far away, a sisal farmer would take off in his WWI Sopwith Pup biplane. He'd fly a low pass over the water to make sure the beach was clear, perhaps assessing the tide, or the sand's firmness, then he'd plop down. It's at times like this that I was amazed at the population. There was no one around, and then suddenly there was, with watoto materialising as if from nowhere, curious and excited as they encircled his plane. The pilot put the tallest toto in charge for guarding it, with the promise of a few shillingie on his return. He might be picked up by a friend with a car or he'd walk into town a half mile away.

Along this same beach, I ferreted among the seaweed and rocks for shells on the warm, white, sand and savoured the unending off-shore breeze that brought coolness, as it rustled the leaves of the blue gums and the fiery blossoms of the flame trees. Tired of that, I would swim, naked and alone in the warm ocean waters, diving time and again into ocean rollers the second before they broke. Hour after hour I'd do this, all the while becoming more deeply tanned than ever. Later, with no towel, I'd dry off in the sun as, inspired by the Sopwith Pup, I ran, zooming and banking up and down the beach, arms out-spread, imagining myself as the WWI fighter ace, The Red Baron. The casual observer might have raised eyebrows, given that while he was the single most spectacular ace of WWI, he was, nonetheless, German. Some among my ancestors would have approved however.

By the end of the week, I'd built my railway layout in the corner of the balcony. I soon thought of additional items I needed to make the set-up more interesting. But, as Dad explained, new parts would need to be ordered from England, and would take months to arrive by sea. I did manage an oasis-like setting for the main centre. I obtained some lead camels, with riders, from the bookstore along with lead palm trees. Mother donated a circular make-up mirror for a small lake.

Sometimes, for a change, I would climb the flame tree in the courtyard, risking a fall and a broken arm or two as I tried for a close-up look of those bird nests, then negotiated the space between the end of a tree limb and our balcony, rather than climbing down and taking the stairs. As I did this I might be dive bombed by the weaver birds, or swallows or martins as they tried to steer me from their territory.

In this same courtyard was held the daily bargaining for fresh foods. African vendors would bring eggs for sale. I followed Mpishi one morning to watch the exchange. He was carrying a large saucepan of water, and, meeting with the egg seller, became seated comfortably in the sand. After much exchange in a Swahili that I had yet to learn, the two checked the eggs for freshness. Each egg was carefully lowered into the water. If it sank, Mpishi would set it aside. The first time one floated he rejected it.

"What was wrong with that one?" I asked.

Mpishi chuckled. "Bwana mdogo, that egg is no good. You would not want to eat that one."

"But how do you know?"

"If it floats it means the egg is old and will not taste nice. Only if the egg sinks will it be nice."

"Oh."

On other days the fish seller came by with his morning catch. Still others would wait patiently downstairs with offerings such as live lobsters, claws opening and shutting, feelers waving and their tails opening and clamping shut when picked out of the net. Vegetables were scrutinised for freshness, and live chickens were assessed for yield. Mpishi taught me to cook and, on many occasions, I'd spend hours in the kitchen assisting as he prepared the evening meal.

I loved our evenings the most. The living room was lit by table lamps which, together with the upholstery and colours of Mum's preference, provided a warm and welcoming glow. The geckos ran around the walls, feverishly scooping up their mosquito dinners and outside, the concert put on each evening by the insect population created its noisy wallpaper. At some point Dad would decide it was time for his evening bath. He would call out in a stentorian voice, "Boy!"

From halfway down the stairs where he and Mpishi had been sitting, smoking and talking, would come back the newly alerted response, "Yes, bwana," as Juma scurried back up the stairs to heed my dad's voice.

"Bathooo!"

"Ndyio, bwana." Juma would then draw the bath, and when it was time, come to the living room and let my dad know, "Bathooo is ready, bwana."

After his bath, Dad in silk dressing gown would sit there, he and Mum sipping on their sundowners of whisky and soda, the three of us reading – Dad his opera scores mostly while the music played loud, Mum her Agatha Christie, and me Biggles, The Saint or a WWII story. On and off over the years, Dad would take up or give up smoking. Presently it was cigarettes. As I sipped on my Coca-Cola and listened to the classical music on the HiFi – thanks to the newly-invented long-play records – I watched my parents and pondered who exactly they were.

It might be overstating it to say my Dad was austere, but on the other hand neither was he warm and friendly. Maybe taciturn was the best word, at least as far as family was concerned. He was one of three children, born on the wrong side of the tracks in South East London. His dad, a fitter and turner, had died, choked in the street, when my dad was ten, so he'd grown up with little influence of a father and under the guiding hand of a stern mother who hailed from Somerset. She'd worked in munitions factories during the war and at Paddington Railway Station bartending after that. Because his father was a Mason, it meant that with his dad's death, my dad would be admitted, free of charge, to their posh and upper class public school, the Royal Masonic School, at Bushey on the outskirts of North London. I suppose he went through the usual privations that marked British boarding school life. He was a good pupil though, and was known for his tremulous soprano voice in the chapel choir.

The result of that school was that Dad never appeared to be working class. Though he sported no pretensions or affectations, he nonetheless fitted in with the educated middle class. He spoke excellent English, with a wonderful vocabulary, and a memory that defied understanding. Unfortunately, Dad did not infuse me with any of his undoubted abilities. We never spent time talking on worldly subjects. I was offered few pearls of wisdom. He never once told me he loved me. But then, of course, in those days, an English father didn't show soppy sentimentalism of that nature to a son; that was girl talk. He called me 'chum' most of the time and my actual name was usually used in the context of a stern voice.

I never feared Dad in the sense of his hitting me – he never once did – and yet I feared him anyway, and jumped to attention the moment he asserted his role. We had what I call a professional relationship; he was the man, I was the boy, and we both played our respective and separate age-related roles. This meant minimal intermingling such as playing together, helping me with my holiday homework or anything like that. Well, except for the electric train set perhaps. He was impressed with the trouble I went to with that, and would join in once in a while, cleaning the rails of rust, or perhaps the collector shoes of an engine.

I liked watching Dad joking with friends when we visited others, or they came to us for drinks. People just dropped in. We might be having a quiet Sunday morning. I'd be playing with my trains, Mum would be reading, and Dad would have remained in his dressing gown as he sat close by his HiFi listening to opera. The arrivals would be readily welcomed, as they achieved the summit of our concrete stairs unannounced. Dad would remain in his dressing gown; neither party thought it unusual. It would be a casual gathering, drinks would be served and Mpishi would throw extra potatoes in the pot if they accepted an invitation to lunch. Sometimes visitors might depart after a drink or two, because they were on their way to drop in on someone else for a meal.

I enjoyed Dad's sense of humour, and how he would get them laughing. I giggled watching them too. I recall when long-play records had first become available. As the importer of Philips Electronics, he was ahead of the locals in knowing what was new in the record technology of the day. People were used to the fragile 78s that seemed to shatter if you even looked at them, never mind dropped one. So when friends would come by for drinks, Dad might ask, "Have you seen the newest thing out, long-play records?"

"No, never heard of them. What are they?" the visitor might ask.

Dad would have picked one up in its cover and, as he approached the visitor, he would lob the record at him, rather like pitching a low-powered Frisbee designed to fall short, saying, "Here take a look."

The knee-jerk reaction to catch the record in flight lest it drop and smash into a million pieces, was accompanied by a look of horror as the visitor, as was intended, fumbled and the record fell to the floor.

"Oh my gosh, I'm so sorry, Les," they would gasp. "I'm such a fumble fingers, I'm terribly sorry. Oh dear, it must be broken, I'll have to replace it for you."

Dad laughed as he stooped with his characteristic grunt to pick it up. "Don't worry, it's not broken." He'd then slide the record out of the sleeve and show it to them.

"Oh my gosh, isn't that wonderful!" Faces would light up in delight amid breathless exhalations. "Oh, you gave me such a fright. I nearly had a heart attack."

And so Dad would make a few more HiFi and record sales.

Mother was an affectionate sort, soft, gentle and kind. She loved having me at home and yet, strangely, I never witnessed any distress on her part when it was time for me to return to school. Perhaps she was being stoic, and didn't want me feeling worse than I already was? She could be possessive and over-protective, however. Mum had been raised in a Victorian-like household, where rules were strict. She had a strong sense for decorum, and a fixed opinion on what constituted the British way of doing things. Her mother was a direct descendent of the wealthy class, with ancestors from Germany where a great, great, great grandfather, a chap named Sumner, had been a high court judge. One of the Sumner daughters had married into the Oppenheimer family, of diamond fame.

Anyway, Mum, while loving and affectionate, was, on the other hand, not very good with children. She never played games with me; children's games were for children. She was of the view, especially when visitors were around that *children should be seen but not heard.* I seem to recall mostly being admonished to, "Come and sit quietly over here, dear."

Mother was the offspring of an unlikely mix. Where Granny was from wealthy stock, her choice of husband, Harold Plowman, was of farming stock, although he himself never got into that. But, he'd grown up on a small-holding in Histon, near Cambridge, and enjoyed a bucolic way of life, until it came time to earn his keep, when he got into tailoring. It was then he'd met Maud, my granny, but I was never told how. As young newly-weds, they moved to London, where he got out of tailoring, which he hated, and into invisible mending, opening up his own shop just off Piccadilly. When Mum was due to be born, they moved from the place they'd leased, and bought a brand new terraced house on Rosebank Avenue, in the newly-developed, post-WWI suburb of Sudbury Hill, between Harrow and Wembley.

At age fourteen, Mum was sent to La Pension de la Sagesse, a convent and finishing school run by nuns in Lille, France. While there, immersed in the French language, she was taught how to comport herself like a lady, finished high school, and studied shorthand and typing so as to equip her for the work that ladies may do when they achieved adulthood and that was to become typists or secretaries. She remained content with the idea that, as a woman, she should expect to be a secretary or a nurse perhaps, when she left school. After all, that was what respectable women did. As she didn't get on with blood, Mum became a secretary and remained so all her days.

She was a peaceful sort, carried herself with class inbred by her mother, and one who, by nature, was inclined to be delicate and reserved. She had been loyal, not to say courageous, in accompanying my dad to live in the wilds of Nigeria. I was amazed at the punitive conditions she'd endured in that country, and how extreme they were compared with life as she'd known it in Britain. Places like Kano on the edge of the Sahara and northern 'towns' (which were little more than native villages really) like Sokoto, Unguru and Zaria come to mind. She would find herself the only European woman within several hundred miles. She'd sit outdoors, sweating profusely in the extreme heat, eternally buzzed by mosquitoes and other insects, manual typewriter perched precariously on a rickety table, and type Dad's correspondence. Her homes in those northern regions had neither running water nor electricity, so light came from Tilly lamps, cooking was done on a wood stove and water came from the well. They did have paraffin refrigerators, but air conditioning was unheard of. The only way to cool off was to have the 'boy' fill a tin tub with muddy water from the well. She'd climb in and soak for a while, removing insect legs and frog body parts from the brown water while she did so. But of course, as soon as she emerged to dry off, she'd become dripping in sweat once more. It was a tough experience, but one to be soldiered through, until promotion finally landed you in Lagos.

I'd always been reproachful that I'd not been taken to Nigeria with my parents, and many was the time I'd challenge them on the subject. The answer was always the same. It had to do with the indescribable heat and humidity, the plethora of insects like mosquitoes and other creatures that could, directly or indirectly, affect a child's life. They talked of yellow fever, black water fever, jaundice, malaria, bilharzia, worms and 'The White Man's Grave.' This was a term coined in the 1800s to describe first Sierra Leone, then West Africa generally, as the most disease-ridden region of the 'dark continent.' And those were just some of the mortal threats to health, to which white children were especially susceptible. The parents described the few English children they ever saw in Nigeria, as wasted, unhealthy-looking and tormented with prickly heat.

"It just wasn't done to bring children to West Africa, dear. People would have been horrified. Besides which they didn't have schools there either."

The absence of schools I thought to be rather a good idea. However, I suppose I sort of understood their point. What I might have said but never did was, "You'd have sent me to boarding school in England once you moved to East Africa too, if I hadn't harped on so much about being taken to Tanganyika with you." Of course, being at boarding school in either country, I wouldn't have been with my parents, so perhaps it didn't change that aspect of my life all that much.

I only got to know my parents, to the extent I knew them at all, during my five years in Tanganyika. It was the only period when we were together – when I was on holiday that is. All in all I lived with them for give-or-take four months a year. It was kind of like being a part of the furniture. I didn't feel tolerated, never mind rejected. I just felt that this was where the parents lived, and I with them when I wasn't at school, and that was that. I didn't interfere with their social life. On their frequent evening sojourns for drinks, cocktails or dinner, I remained at home. One didn't take one's children to a 'grown-ups do.' They didn't appear to find this a problem, and neither did I.

It was just as well that I didn't need people around me because, at home, I was alone a lot. When I was younger, the 'boy' remained hanging around the flat until the parents returned home; as I grew older, that stopped, and I kept my own company, going to bed when I'd been told I should. I suppose in the end, this upbringing, together with my relationship with boys in Kongwa, inbred a self-reliance that stands with me to this day.

My parents did not show affection to each other that I ever noticed. Of course, arguably they'd not have done so in front of the child anyway, but I always felt there was more to it than that. I sensed, rather than knew, that the relationship was cool, although they never fought or anything, just a few well-chosen words from Dad from time to time if he was irritated over something, then Mum would clam up. If ever I made some provocative comment like: "how it would be good to have a brother, or possibly even a sister, although on second thoughts probably not a sister," my words were dismissed, with some humourless joke about the stork not journeying to Lindi much these days. It seemed that I was thought of as plenty enough where children were concerned. To be truthful, I only posed the question to get a rise out of them anyway. I never yearned for a sibling. Sometimes, when visitors from out of town would drop by, and they might have a young son of my age with them, I'd require prodding and nudging from the parents to show him my toys, or to go out and play together somewhere; I didn't want his company; I was content on my own. I did usually warm up after a while though, if I assessed the visitor as a decent sort.

There would be one incident during these years where our usual way of dealing with each other fell apart. It involved a car accident. Just beforehand, I'd been expecting my parents to make a rare visit to me at school. When the time approached, I'd sensed something was wrong, well before Mother finally wrote to me about it.

"Your father's had a bad road accident," she'd written, "and it's become obvious we're not going to make the visit, or at least he can't!"

The unexpected happened when I asked Dad for the whole story at home one evening, and instead of clamming up he warmed to the invitation.

Dad completed making a fresh siphon of soda water and disengaged the sparklet, then strolled with his cut-glass of whisky and soda to his chair next to the radiogram. Turning down the volume, he began: "I was about thirty miles out of town, when I lost control of the car in the black cotton soil," he said. "I found myself tumbling down an escarpment, which I later found out was more than a hundred feet. I was sure it was all over. I remember thinking; it was not an elegant way to go. Then I blacked out. When I came to, I knew I was injured – the pain was excruciating. I had broken bones and couldn't escape. I don't recall the time when it happened other than it was daylight, late afternoon, I think. From what I could see in the mirror, the car was enveloped in bush. I heard vehicles above but none of them stopped. Then night fell so I switched on the running lights."

"It must have been too terrible, Les," Mother interrupted. "To think what might have happened to you. You might never have been found, you know? And I was supposed to have gone with you that day. Had we not changed plans because of the extra typing you gave me, I could have been with you, trapped too, or even dead. Ugh, it's too terrible to think about."

"Anyway," Father continued, "as Mum says, I could have been there much longer, nor ever been found, but for the presence of mind of a Catholic nun – and the fact that it was dark. You see," he continued, "the nun was on her way to Lindi in her mission's lorry. She was running late, and planned to stay the night, before picking up provisions in the morning. She was seated in the front, gazing out the window at the endless bush, now lost to blackness. With her was the African driver, and there were two mission 'boys' in the back. As the lorry bounced by the area, her eyes focused on a red glow at the base of the escarpment. She told her driver to stop; they piled out, and stood at the edge, peering into eerie blackness. As I understand it, all they could see was a smouldering red colour; there was nothing to indicate what it was. The number plate lamp was off, and the outline of the car was not visible. To make matters worse it was a moonless night. The nun speculated the red glow was from a vehicle, but initially her Africans didn't believe her, never mind would they climb down to check. All they could see was bad juju. It took all her persuasive power, probably promising hell and damnation if they didn't, to get her 'boys' to clamber down the slope to find out.

"Fortunately, the lorry carried several coils of rope, something they needed, as the escarpment was too steep to climb down without being tied off. The 'boys' hacked away at the bush with pangas, as they were lowered. They made a lot of noise, I was told, as they wanted to scare away lurking spirits and, I suppose, give themselves extra courage. The two finally reached the glow, discovered that it was a car and that someone was still in it – me. I was asleep at the time, so they didn't know if I was alive or dead.

"The nun thought I was in such a bad way, from what she was hearing that I might not survive waiting for rescuers, so she decided to rescue me. Fortunately, cutting equipment wasn't needed, so the Africans manhandled me out of the car. The driver, who'd remained up top, threw down another rope, so they could truss me around and under my arms. Then the two 'boys' that had come down the slope, were hauled back up, so all three could drag me to the top. It was terribly painful. Can you imagine being dragged up the side of a steep incline of some hundred feet, bones broken, your hip pointing in the wrong direction, and nothing to shield you from grinding the sides, and dragging against the bushes and trees that were snagging me, all the way up? It would have been bad enough if I wasn't injured."

"Wow, Dad, I can't imagine," I said. "Don't want to imagine. It must have been terrible."

"They got me to the top, and then laid me out on the bed of the lorry. They spread some hessian sacks, for something a little softer to lie on. I'll leave you to imagine what the drive to town was like." Dad then added, "I think if I hadn't got so many bones already out of place, they would have been by the time we got here. An empty lorry has hard springs, you know? Anyhow, they got me to hospital where, to cut a long story short, the quacks diagnosed hip displacement. They concluded I'd have to be flown to Nairobi, because there were no orthopaedic wallahs in Tanganyika. A day or two later, the company chartered a light airplane, in which I could be laid out, and flew me there."

"It wasn't too long before Dad was up and hobbling around, partying with other patients and enjoying a good time," said Mum knowingly. "He and his new-found cronies were having a hilarious time with risqué jokes at the nurses' expense when I visited him. I must say, the nurses seemed to enjoy the fun well enough, and had plenty of insulting retorts of their own."

PART TWO

ONE OF THE BOYS

CHAPTER NINE

THE NAKED AND
THE NEAR-DEAD

THE ANNUAL DECEMBER 24TH LINDI CLUB CHILDREN'S party threatened to be a dull affair. I was nearly 11, home for my second holidays.
Because Christmas arrives in high summer, the party was held in blistering
heat. Mums organized games for the young ones but none provided any entertainment for me. Other than Annelize and Egbert, there were no children
older than five, and most of them were much younger than that. So, I and
my friends watched the party listlessly. Eventually, Father Christmas arrived.
Apparently his sleigh had broken down, "So," it was explained, "he'll come
by boat." In fact, he arrived in an outrigger complete with black elves. It
was all fun of a sort, but with Annelize, Egbert and I wishing we could find
something else to do.

It wasn't long before we found our chance to slip away. Most of the
adults were sitting around knocking back drinks during a Tombola contest,
while a few of the more devoted mums continued to find ways to entertain
their babes.

"Let's go," I suggested lethargically.

"Where to?" Egbert yawned.

"Well, we can start off at my flat with my trains," I sighed. "And then we'll find something else after that."

Annelize wasn't interested in trains but she didn't have any better ideas. We dragged our feet.

"It's sooo hot," she complained, as she surveyed my train layout. "I wish there was a way to cool down."

"Well, there isn't," I said.

"What I need is a cold bath," said Annelize. "That's what I do at home when I'm too hot. Maybe that's what I should do, go home."

"We have a bath," I replied, wiping my neck with a hanky. "You can have one here if you like."

We ambled down the corridor to the bathroom and peered inside. It was situated on the shady sign of the block, and got no direct sun through the window, so it was cooler.

"Oh, that feels better already," said Annelize. "Would you mind if I take a quick bath?"

"No. Help yourself."

Annelize stood there expectantly for Egbert and me to move along.

"Why don't you have a bath together, seeing as you're so hot?" laughed Egbert.

"What! Together?" asked Annelize, amazed at the suggestion.

"Why not?" asked Egbert. "You're both too hot; you both want to cool off, what's the harm?"

"Boys and girls don't bathe together," retorted Annelize. "It's just not done. Dad would be furious."

"But why would he know? He's not here. I won't tell him, I promise. Aren't you a little bit interested in seeing Tony in the nude?"

"Egbert, I don't think—" I began.

"—Oh come on, it's not that big a thing. Just a little ol' bath. No one's hurting anyone."

"Well, what do you say, Annelize? I'll do it if you will."

"Well, I don't know…."

"Come on, Annelize, don't be a wimp, man. You've told me before you'd like to see Tony naked."

"Egbert! I said no such thing. How could you?" Annelize blushed.

"Don't worry about him, Annelize; he's just your baby brother. But it is hot and a cold bath is a good idea. Here, I'll start running it. I'm going to get in. You can follow me if you wish, or not if you don't."

At that I unbuttoned my shirt and dropped my shorts. Annelize averted her eyes.

"Come on, Annelize, he won't bite you," laughed Egbert. "Don't be so prudish."

Then she looked back at me. The water was deepening as I stepped into the tub. Annelize watched as I sat down.

"Oh, this is wonderful," I gushed. "Oh, to feel so cool again."

I slid down and stretched out to cover my chest with cold water.

At that Annelize relented. "All right then, I'll come in too."

In moments she had slipped her dress over her head, revealing an unfilled bra and then dropped her knickers. She climbed in facing me, then followed my lead by lying down so as to get the cold water all over. Egbert burst out laughing. I don't think he expected that we'd really do it and now we had, laughed his head off. Wouldn't come in with us though!

IT WAS JANUARY 1954, THE LOCOMOTIVE AND water tender of our school train had a large sign bordered by flags strapped to its face. Imprinted thereon was the legend, *Kongwa School Special*. The *"Special"* was chartered because the school's population had grown too large for the mail train. It didn't carry other passengers and departed at 10 a.m. instead of 4 p.m. Boys' sleeping accommodation was improved, with four-berth compartments. Because the train was dedicated to the school, it got to Kongwa in six to eight hours less travel time, which is why we now arrived at two in the morning.

In inky blackness and bright headlights, we crowded onto the usual lorries at the rail siding and were brought to the mess, where a light snack awaited. No sooner were we tucking in, when the Head arrived. He rapped a spoon against a glass.

"The first and most important thing you need to know – everyone here present being a Senior – is that several things are changing. The first is that you will be residing in a new phase. The school has expanded considerably, so now we are housing Senior boys in phases 5 and 6."

Mr. Whitehead continued in his gravelly voice. "The girls who used to be in phases 1 and 2 are now moving to phase 3 and the Junior boys and girls will now take over phases 1 and 2. When you've finished your snack, we want you outside to be assembled by your Housemasters. You will be led by your prefects to your new house, so proceed in an orderly fashion. It's late and we want you in bed and asleep as soon as possible. Due to your late arrival and the fact that pupils from up-country won't be arriving until tomorrow, there'll not be classes until the day after. You may arise one hour later than usual, have breakfast and return to your dorms to unpack. The rest of the day you'll have free. The following morning will be your first class. Now then, any questions?"

There were none.

"Very well, finish your snack, then congregate outside."

We stood under the stars, the lights from the mess casting a yellow glow on the red sand making it look muddy. The Seniors' Housemasters announced themselves, including Mr. Moore who let us know he was Livingstone's.

I think Mr. Moore may have been the most 'proper' of teachers. He had an elevated air about him that seemed almost snooty, although he proved to be a fine Housemaster and not like that at all; perhaps it was his vertical head and short, dark hair in a not quite brush cut that did it. His white shirts and rather long shorts were indeed white and immaculately pressed. He wore long white stockings up to his calves, and white tennis shoes. For boys, this was the uniform for Sundays but Mr. Moore was dressed like this now. He would dress like this every day except for evening attire.

Facing us at the head of the line, Mr. Moore read our names and house prefect, and we stepped forward to group around the designate. The Senior prefect for my house was a chap named Pete Gemmell, and he was supported by Brian Marriott. I'd looked around for Clive when we'd arrived, hoping he'd still be our prefect, but I'd not found him. Now, I realised, he wasn't with us.

"Any idea where Clive is?" I whispered to Berry. "I haven't seen him."

"Well, firstly, anyone arriving from up-country won't get here 'til tomorrow is what I heard. Secondly, I believe Clive left Tanganyika anyway," said Berry. "His parents have moved to Uganda, but he's being sent to school in Nairobi, I think, leastways that's what I heard. So he won't be returning."

Well, that was a disappointment. "Geez, he didn't even say he was leaving."

"Maybe he didn't know 'til he got home for the hols."

The good news was that Sheddy and Berry were in my room, as well as Aranky, who'd also been in my house in Juniors. In the other room were Mike Jenner, Michael Gunston, Alan Alder and Don McLachlan. I commented that Ivey wasn't with us on the train.

"I suppose he must have left school like Clive?" I muttered.

"He's moved up-country from Dar," someone said. "He should be arriving with the others tomorrow. He'll be in the next house along."

With him would be Goggles, Graeme Maclean, Anthony Paton, Peter Taylor and a number of others who'd moved with us. We strolled languidly in the sultry air. It smelled like rain but who could be sure? "And so far," we'd heard, "the rains are late again."

Pete and Brian were leading with powerful lanterns. They were locked in close conversation, with occasional outbursts of raucous laughter, and took no notice of us. We recognised the red sanded pathways from our raids. Lining them was the coarse magugu grass with its sticky burrs. Ahead lay the rows of houses.

"Your beds have been designated, so look for your name," said Pete, as we stood around him and Brian in a torch-lit circle, outside house 1. "In that direction," he pointed east along the row that reached into the gloom where the others were walking, "is the rest of Livingstone; you can see the houses, they have their lights on. In that direction," he turned to face west, "are Matron's house and the one beyond that is the Housemaster's, Mr. Moore and his family. Okay, you can mess around for a few minutes and then I want you in bed."

I was glad my bed was in the larger of the two rooms, formerly the sitting room, and next to the glassless window frames enclosing diamond-shaped burglar bars and mosquito mesh. Glancing around, I noticed the ceilings had been repaired or replaced, and of course the electricity was working. They must have replaced the missing electrical parts. There was a ledge on which my radio could stand. I was concerned about receiving a good reception, so I'd brought lots of aerial wire with me. At the sound of noise outside, I ambled curiously through the French doors, to hear challenges being made for a pissing contest. I joined in with the others standing out there in a line, pissing as far as we could into the sand, a reliable measure as to who had won. Back indoors Pete ordered us into bed.

"What do we do for pyjams, Pete, seeing as our cases won't be delivered 'til morning?"

"You don't need pyjamas, Berry, it's warm enough for anyone."

"But what must we do, sleep naked like on the train?"

"Why not? You're all boys. Never seen another naked boy before?"

"But Matron might see us."

"Oooooooh, I'm sure Matron has never seen a naked boy."

There were a few snickers, as we inspected our beds. There was a sheet and a blanket. Wouldn't need the blanket.

Berry jumped on his bed, in exuberant anticipation of something soft to bounce on. Not being a new boy, he should have known better. There was the creaking of flat springs in lieu of bed boards but no bounce. The mattress was about an inch thick made with kapok.

"I'd forgotten how hard these beds are," he muttered.

I shed my clothes and climbed under the sheet. I was tired and wanted to get to sleep. It was irritating that the light remained on for as long as it did. We were told to wait for Matron. She'd probably got a lot to do having arrived on the train with us.

After a while, we sat up and started talking again, so were wide awake when our new Matron came by. Miss Richmond had a pleasantly pink face atop an amazingly long neck, but otherwise non-tanned skin, apparently not one who liked much sun, or maybe she was new out from England. She had a kindly smile behind her spectacles, and was dressed in her matronly whites, with a little cap perched precariously on top of her curly blonde hair. Because of her long neck the boys instantly nicknamed her Twiga (Swahili for giraffe).

"All right, who have we got here?" she asked with a Somerset slant. "Why don't you introduce yourselves? I may not remember everyone's name tomorrow but we have to start somewhere."

We each told Matron our name, and answered the brief questions she had of us.

"So, Edwards, your birthday in February is the first coming up?" she asked. "You'll be twelve?"

"Yes, Matron."

"Okay chaps, remember that," said Aranky. "February 12th Edwards gets the bumps."

To celebrate your birthday a sheet was stripped off the bed and your colleagues would grip it around the edges and at the corners after piling the unlucky birthday boy (or girl) into the sheet. In unison they'd toss you off the ground in the sheet in a rapid succession of lifts – and drops onto the concrete floor; one bounce for every year of your age!

"Now then," Matron continued with a smile, "I'm a bit of a stickler for tidiness and cleanliness, so be warned, I'll be watching. For example now, who do these khaki shorts belong to, lying on the floor here?"

"They're mine, Matron," confessed Berry.

"Well, pick them up and put them away then. I won't have clothes lying around on the floor, young man."

"I can't, Matron."

"You can't? What do you mean you can't? Are you without legs perhaps?"

"No, Matron."

Smirks from the rest of us.

"Then you will get up immediately, and put your trousers away, please."

Berry hesitated but didn't seem to know how to explain.

"Please, Matron," I said, "we haven't got any pyjamas on because our suitcases haven't arrived."

"Oh dear, oh dear, a shy boy. Well, I'm sorry, but I'm your Matron, and may well see you in your altogether from time to time, so I suggest we do away with this coyness right now. Come on, Berry, pick up your shorts and put them in a drawer."

So Berry climbed out of bed, under Matron's watchful gaze, picked up his trouser shorts and put them away.

"Thank you, Berry. Very well then, lights out now, sleep tight."

"Night, Matron," we chorused.

As soon as Matron had completed her inspection of the end room, and her footsteps receded, we sat up and laughed.

"Did you see the shocked look on Twiga's face, when she saw you naked, Berry?" teased Aranky. "I'm sure she's going to see if she can find some dawa to make it grow longer."

"Ha de ha ha ha – very funny, Aranky," Berry retorted with a sneer.

"Don't worry, Berry," I smiled. "I'm sure she was impressed."

Going to bed at three in the morning, with all the hubbub that had been going on, left little time to notice what our new house was like. However, now, in the early sunrise, as I looked around, I felt dismayed. The Spartan bedroom included the four basic cot beds, and nothing much else, except a four-drawer chest for clothes. One light bulb hung from the centre of the ceiling. The floor was of ochre painted concrete. At least in my room, we had French doors leading onto the stoep. The other bedroom was smaller with no direct access to the outdoors. In the tiny bathroom was a tub and a hand-sink, with cold running water and no toilet. This phase had the outdoor choos. I was first out of bed and needed to go, so, in the bright morning sun, I went for it. I paced it off at twenty-five steps. I wasn't surprised the choos had been built far from the houses given the awful smell coming from them in the early morning heat.

I took a deep breath, tugged on the rickety door, and made to step inside when, in one horrific, heart-stopping moment I froze, petrified at what faced me. My jaw dropped, muscles tensed and inside I felt fear like I'd never known. A black mamba, asleep on the ledge next to the toilet seat, reared at my intrusion. Its head on the same level as mine, it stared at me through unblinking and deadly cold eyes, forked tongue flicking, head swaying. My mind, racing against the horror a split second away, screamed at me, *Don't move! Don't move!*

Any kind of movement and the snake would strike, sinking its fangs into my face. I'd heard that mambas strike a second and a third time. Three bites were not necessary; I'd be dead in twenty minutes from one, but mambas like to make sure.

I was drenched in sweat, under my hair line, down my arms. My heart beat so loud, I thought the mamba would hear it, and lash out. My mouth was open, I thought to shout, but no sound came. We stared at each other for an eternity, me as unblinking as the snake. Finally, I suppose it sensed no further threat, because the mamba lowered its head and turned to slither off the seat, slinking through a hole in the wall. When only its tail was left, I found my voice and leapt backwards calling out, "S – S – Sn – Snake! There's a snaaaaake!"

Boys, in various states of undress, rushed outdoors, some pulling up their khaki shorts as they ran, others wrapped in only a bath towel. They tore in the direction I was pointing, as the snake wound its way, sleek and so fast, towards the thick manyara hedge. The hedge that marked the out-of-bounds border for our houses was twenty-five yards from where I watched, in a state of shivering horror, as that amazingly long snake, clearly visible on the short, yellowed grass, made its escape. Boys were running in hot pursuit shouting, "Snaaake!" at the tops of their lungs, as they anticipated catching up at the kill of the hapless creature.

Anthony Paton tore after them. "Don't hurt it," he yelled.

"Stop where you are, the lot of you!" Keith Jones, prefect in charge of the second house, bellowed over the excitement. "Leave that snake alone! It's extremely dangerous. That's a mamba. Those snakes are aggressive. If you get close, it'll turn on you. If you're bitten by a mamba, you'll suffer a painful and certain death. So stop where you are and freeze! Now, walk backwards... Now, return to your houses, and get ready for breakfast!"

It was thought important not to be late for breakfast.

Over bacon and eggs, my friends estimated the mamba's length at nine feet, and talked enthusiastically of my escape. I wasn't in a talking mood. I was shocked. True, snakes were an everyday event; I'd learned that quickly enough in my first term of Junior school. You could come across animals anywhere; this was the wilds of Africa after all. If our lives were ruled by fear we'd never go outdoors. But I'd never come so close to death before. We coped with the insects, the spiders, the scorpions and the iguanas. There was always a risk of being bitten or stung by something poisonous, especially in the choos where button spiders made their homes. And then there was the hazard of hyenas that patrolled our houses after dark. Hyenas in cackles may challenge lionesses for their kill; how would they see one or two young boys, walking alone in the middle of the night? Paton told us hyenas have jaws so powerful, they can halve a man's leg in a single bite.

Not far from here, game roamed free and lions stalked. Africa reminded me of this boarding school. It was savage, with everything hunting, killing and eating something else. This school was like that, at least for the boys; an Africa within Africa with its own culture of barely suppressed violence.

> Now this is the Law of the Jungle
> as old and as true as the sky;
> And the Wolf that shall keep it may prosper,
> but the Wolf that shall break it must die.
> As the creeper that girdles the tree-trunk the
> Law runneth forward and back

For the strength of the Pack is the Wolf,
and the strength of the Wolf is the Pack.
—From: *The Jungle Book* by Rudyard Kipling

As we left the mess to return to our houses to unpack, me still subdued, I became aware of laughing and giggling in the distance. I looked up and watched some of the girls emerging from their end of the mess. What a mixture of feelings! There I was in this rugged boarding school, in the wild of Africa, with all its potential dangers, yet there they were with their typical girlish ways, holding the promise of a gentler life.

✦ ✦ ✦

ONCE UNPACKED, AND WITH THE REST OF the day free, Sheddy, Berry and I wandered off to explore. I stared at the scenery; it was a different view from that of the Juniors' phase. The down slope stretched gently north until it reached the area where I gauged the rail line to be. Beyond that it flattened and the seemingly lifeless plains that had been cleared for the groundnut plantations stretched forever. To the north-east, in the mid distance, was another hill named Chimlata. It looked higher and longer than Kongwa Hill, but stood alone against the backdrop of the groundnut units. Stepping off the stoep, and walking around the outside of the house, I was struck by how close Kongwa Hill was. It was way more prominent in this phase. It must have been about a half mile, directly south. It brooded over us now, whereas in phase 3, Church Hill had dominated.

Between our row and Kongwa Hill lay several other rows of phase 6 houses on the up slope; the rows were about a hundred yards apart. With there being higher ground at the base of Kongwa hill, I could see the rooftops of the larger, former 'luxury' homes of Kongwa, in which the girls had been residing, but were now given over to the Junior school. I could also see the row of flats.

The rest of the day was eventful. Firstly, Kongwa had been buzzed by a low-flying plane, a LodeStar that belonged to Williamson's Diamond Mines. It was the pilot's way of saying, "We've arrived; come and fetch your students from the landing strip." The plane had brought children of mineworkers to join the school. It seemed to us that the pilot must have been a bit crazy with an excessive number of dives and zooms, didn't seem like all that was necessary to announce his arrival. But anyway, it was exciting and it landed safely.

Then, we'd unpacked and I'd found my radio. Sheddy wanted to get that working. Berry and Aranky had managed to help one another climb on the roof. Berry took the aerial wire with him, attached to his belt, while he clambered up. Soon the wire had been fixed to the thin vertical post that was the stay for the electric cable. It wasn't long after that we got the radio going with the fresh, new, car-size battery. My concern about a good reception was well-placed. The signal was so poor that we gave up on it. It was no surprise, but we'd hoped. Oh well, at least we should be able to receive the BBC in the evenings, when the signal was strong and the atmospherics reduced.

Sheddy tended the kasukus he'd bought from the Africans at the end of last term. Allan Alder was spotted with a chameleon. I'd never got to know chameleons, even though I'd seen a few in the hedges. We weren't allowed to keep pets as Juniors, so we didn't catch them.

Sheddy, Aranky and I got into a game of nyabs, on the out-of-bounds road the other side of the manyara hedge. Competition was keen; we were older now and more competitive, but more importantly, the winner kept the marbles in play. You didn't have to play for keeps, but few would play if you didn't. As we finished a game, we heard yells from further along towards the Wilberforce houses. We ran to the shouts, thinking maybe a luckless snake was being hunted.

As we got nearer, I recognised Pepsi in the distance, along with Rushby and Voutyrakis. They were throwing rocks at the ground.

"Hey, Peps! When did you arrive from Dodoma?" I yelled out to Doug as we approached.

"Hey, Tony – 'bout twenty minutes ago."

"What are you doing?" I called again as we drew close.

"We're dive bombing siafus (safari ants)," Doug shouted. "There's a helluva long column of them, come and see."

As we approached, we could hear the hum of the column, angry at being attacked. The column must have been at least six inches wide, "And probably about a mile long," said Sheddy.

Rushby and Voutyrakis told us they had walked 'miles' in both directions to find the beginning or end of the column, but had come to neither.

The direction the column is heading is straight through Wilberforce," said Rushby.

"Not in the houses, I hope," I said.

"Luckily it's missing our houses and going past the choos," said Voutyrakis, "but it's going in the direction of Nightingale. I don't know if they'll pass near their houses."

"Well, if they do, the chaps better keep out," said Sheddy. "There's nothing you can do but let them pass through."

The huge, black ants were packed tight, like soldiers in columns, so thick, there appeared to be no room between them; except in the places that our missiles had landed. There the larger column was interrupted, by the whirling in every direction of platoons of ants, despatched it seemed, to find the enemy and put a stop to the bombing and killing of their colleagues. As they spread out, the rear section of the column played catch-up with the front half and attempted to reform into their disciplined march, only to be bombed again, and more so as we joined in. Pepsi had taken his eye off the ants as we approached, and moments later was howling at the bites. A squad of ants had climbed his sandals and were swarming over his foot. Pepsi hopped about on the other, desperately brushing his skin to get them off.

"You don't want to let safari ants get a hold on you, Peps," said Sheddy. "Those things are deadly, man. Once they stick their mandibles into you they never let go, not even if you cut 'em off at the head. Witch doctors even use 'em like our doctors use stitches to sew up a wound. When they're on the march, there's nothing stops them. They don't let anything get in their way. Do you know that safari ants are the only insect known to have eaten a wounded human being? And they often will eat a large animal like a buck; I've heard tell they can strip an animal to its bones in a day."

"Really!" I was stunned. "How ghastly."

"Don't ever get in the way of a safari ant column," Sheddy repeated. "You got no chance, I'm telling you, man."

"I can't get 'em off properly," Doug yelled. "I brushed them off but it's like they're still there, look at my foot!"

"Yup," said Sheddy, "you brushed them off but they left their mandibles in you. You won't get 'em out now. You could try with an Acacia thorn but you'd best wait 'til your skin grows out."

"Agg no, man!"

"What about a concrete wall?" I turned to Sheddy to continue my line of questioning as I glanced warily at Doug's foot and stepped further away from the ant column.

"Straight up and over, no trouble. That's why you don't want them going into our houses, nothing'll keep them out."

"There must be something... I'll bet a river would stop them," I said.

"Neah, not even that," said Doug, as he executed the remaining ant on his foot.

"Depends how wide," Sheddy added. "I've seen where the leading ants form an ant bridge over a stream, then the column marches over them to dry ground the other side. It's amazing to watch I'm telling you."

"How do they form an ant bridge?" I asked.

"The leading ants dig in on dry ground. The next row in the column come up, walks over 'em and then the mandibles of the first ants grip the rear legs of the second row. Keeps going like that 'til they're in the water. Then the same thing. 'Nother row comes up, the front row grabs the rear legs of the next row and so it goes on 'til they reach the other side, with the bridge the same width as the column itself."

"Wow, that's amazing, eh?" I stared from Sheddy to Doug.

"What happens after the column has crossed?

"Some still survive but most of them drown. Anyhow, I gotta get back to the house," said Sheddy. "My bike should be delivered soon and I wanna be there when it arrives. Coming?"

When we got back, we found Ivey out looking for us.

"Hello, Ivey," I said. "Where've you been? I thought you'd left school when you weren't on the train. Then someone said you'd moved up-country?"

"Yeah, well, that's why I wasn't on it," he explained. "We moved from Dar, in the holidays. Now we're living in Tengeru, that's a game department camp not far from Arusha. So I came by bus from there and stayed overnight in the Dodoma Hotel. I arrived here with the others a little while ago. How about you, still in Lindi?"

Sheddy's bike was delivered after lunch. I was envious; I wanted one so much. Sheddy didn't know I'd never even ridden a bike, so when I told him, he said, "Come on, I'll teach you. Maybe your parents won't buy you one, but there's no reason why you shouldn't learn to ride."

I felt guilty. I was sure not being bought a bike meant that I should not be riding one either. I felt I was betraying a trust, to learn to ride when they were not around. But, with Sheddy's enthusiasm, I overcame my hesitation. I brought his bike up close to a rock that I could stand my left foot on as I got seated in the saddle. Then, with right foot on pedal and Sheddy behind holding on, he asked, "Are you ready?"

"Yes."

"Then push off!"

I cycled, handlebars steering erratically.

"Go a bit faster," Sheddy called. "You can't cycle too slowly. Come on, I've got the saddle, I'm running with you."

I pedalled faster, handle bars becoming steadier and Sheddy let go. A few more wobbly moments and then I found myself cycling. What a thrill! I was exhilarated.

BATH TIME WAS A RITUAL. THE BOILER was a forty-four-gallon drum, on its side over a fire pit. It was filled by hose. The 'boy' lit the fire daily, so the water would be hot by 5 p.m. This time of day brought a scramble for the tub, amid the hurry that comes with running late, because you didn't get back to your house until a quarter of an hour before inspection. Then there'd be naked boys scrambling to bathe, others running around with a towel round their bums until it was pulled off. Hot water was rushed from the boiler, to several chaps in the bath tub, sitting in water that had transformed into a viscous, rusty slurry. The scramble for the soap hidden in the murky depths, and the splashing in search of it, added to the urgency. All this was followed, while not yet quite dry, with the ritual dressing for dinner in blazer and tie. Then we'd march to the mess.

Over dinner. the conversation quickly became dominated by an amazing story. The plane that had brought the diamond mine students to school this morning had crash-landed shortly after take-off after leaving Kongwa. There was no radio contact, of course, so no one knew about it until a rather bedraggled pilot came limping into Kongwa after a ten-mile march through the bush. Speculation was rife about what had happened, with the diamond mine kids coming up with all manner of tales that had to do with the amount of brandy the pilot had been slugging while flying them to school.

Later, back at our houses, when it was 'lights-out,' Matron came bustling around.

"Well, let me see now, are we all present and correct in our pyjama bottoms? I want everyone into bed. Edwards, how are you feeling after your fright with the snake?"

"I'm fine, Matron, but what do we do, Miss, about going to the choo in the night? What if the snake comes back?"

"It's unlikely," she replied. "Snakes don't like people anymore than we like them. He was probably comfortable there, no humans having occupied these houses for a while. Now that we're back, he'll probably stay away. In any case, if you have to go, be sure to take a torch. There're no lights and you need to see what you're doing. Check carefully for scorpions as well as spiders when you first enter."

"Yes, Matron."

"You settled down, Shed?"

A quick nod.

"Berry?"

"Yes, Matron."

"I see you've put your clothes away tonight," she said with a smile.

"Yes, Matron," responded Berry coyly.

"Aranky?"

"Yes, Matron."

"Goodnight then," and with that Matron pushed her spectacles back up on the bridge of her nose, switched off the light and retreated to the other bedroom to check on those four. Soon she'd made her rounds and we heard the tramp of footsteps past our windows as she returned to her house.

CHAPTER TEN

HOSPITAL

I WOKE UP, STARTLED, AT THE CLANGING OF a bell. I glanced at my watch. That couldn't be the time surely – 4:30 a.m.?

I noticed the seconds hand was not moving. "Oh no, I forgot to wind it."

Others were stirring but no one was climbing out of bed. Moments later a sleepy Pete Gemmell walked into the room in his pyjamas. "Come on, up, everybody up. Into your gym shorts. It's 6 a.m. and time for PT."

"PT?" queried Berry. "Why do we have to do PT? We never had to do it in the old phase."

"You were Juniors then. Don't ask me why you didn't have to do PT before, but you do now, so up!"

I looked at Pete. "What's PT?" I asked.

"Physical training, nincompoop," he answered. "You never heard of PT?"

"I s'pose not. We called it gym back in England. And anyway I'm excused it."

"Well, it's not gym, that's different, it's PT and by the way, who excused you?"

"Well, because I get asthma, I'm not supposed to do anything too energetic. My mother's told the school. Mr. Ferguson and Matron in Juniors knew about it."

"Well, this is this year and Seniors and no one's told me," Pete replied, "so, until I'm told otherwise, you'll have to get up and do it like everybody else. Now come on all of you, I want you outside in two minutes."

I was alarmed. I knew what strong physical exercise could do, and didn't want an asthma attack. I appealed to Pete, "Please don't make me do it. I can't do it; I'll get asthma."

But Pete didn't know me from my previous years. I and my friends were new to him and clearly he'd not been told.

"Nonsense, man, I don't believe you," he responded. "If I listened to all the excuses I hear there'd never be any PT lessons. It's good for you, man – your asthma will get better if you're fit, man."

I joined our group in unusually hot, humid air, with Pete as instructor.

"Okay, first we're going to do warm-ups. Ready, legs slightly apart, arms out to your sides, right now, swing your right arm over and down to touch your left toes…."

And so it started. I was fine in the warm-ups but once we got into jumping jacks I felt the tightness coming on. I flagged.

"Come on, Edwards," said Pete, "put some life into it, man. Out and in and out and in. Let's keep it going, eh, come on, Edwards, what's the matter with you?"

"I told you," I began to gasp. "I can't do it."

My breathing was getting heavy; I was labouring and feeling dizzy. The sun was hot and streaming into my eyes. Sweat was running. Pete squinted at me as if trying to tell if I was malingering.

"All right," he said, "I'll excuse you the rest. I'm going to have to discuss this with Matron; we'll see what she says."

But too late. My chest was tightening fast, I was gasping desperately for air. I felt faint and swayed on my feet, my wheezing loud and rasping. Legs were giving way and I'd have fallen but Sheddy stepped in and held me.

"Shed, take Edwards to Matron right away, quickly now. The rest of you, put some life into it there. What are you looking at? Never seen anyone with a breathing problem? Come on now, up and out, and up and out and…."

Sheddy more or less dragged me to Matron's, and knocked loudly on her door. I was in a bad way and he knew it. The moment she set eyes on me, Matron ushered me into her house and set me down on a living room couch, telling Sheddy he could return to his house.

"What is it?" Matron asked. "Asthma?"

"Yes," I gasped. "Can't… breathe."

"Wait here," she said, "I'll be back in a moment."

With that, she rushed off to Mr. Moore's house and brought him back post haste.

"Oh my God," he said, "this is a fine start. Why did you do PT if you knew you couldn't do it?"

Ridiculous question I thought as I shrugged, *when prefects are in charge and no one from Juniors told Matron I'm excused PT or sports.* But I hadn't the breath to reply and would never have dared be so cheeky as to answer back anyway.

"Matron, I'll bring my car to your door, and take Edwards to hospital."

And so it was, the second day of the new term I spent in hospital, having been given an ephedrine pill and required to sit up, be quiet, read a book and not move. When my breathing had improved enough, to be able to talk to the new doctor around lunchtime, he came to see me along with Sister.

"I see you're improving, young man, but not fully recovered. I think we'll give him a second ephedrine, Sister. Tell me, what did the doctors do for you in England at a time like this?"

"They gave me adrenaline injections, Doctor."

"Uh huh, I thought they might but I didn't want to do so without knowing a little more of your history. They worked well for you, did they?"

"Oh yes, Doctor, they work within seconds, sir, not like the pills they give me here. They take hours and don't always work well."

"No, I read that in your chart. You were in Juniors last year, I believe?"

"Yes, Doctor. They also give me injections in the hospital in Lindi, sir."

"Very well then, we'll stay with the ephedrine this one more time, but we'll bear that in mind for future occasions." Turning to Sister, he said, "He's to remain here for the day, overnight if necessary. Give that second ephedrine a chance to work. If it doesn't, let me know. All right, young man, I must be off." And with that he and Sister disappeared, leaving me to get back to *Biggles.*

That evening, I was recovered and, having eaten in the hospital, Mr. Moore came to fetch me and take me back to my house, in time for lights-out.

"I'm sorry," Pete apologised. "No one told me. You must know, eh, I can't accept excuses not to do PT 'cos if I did no one would do it."

"I understand, Pete," I said. "It wasn't your fault."

The following morning, after washing and dressing, there was an almighty yell from the prefects' room. Brain Marriott emerged at the door, supporting Pete with scrunched up face, gripping a wrist by the other hand and clearly in great pain.

"Pete's been stung on the hand by a scorpion in his dhobi bag," said Marriott, "I'm taking him to Matron. You lot carry on until I get back."

After leaving Pete with Matron, Marriott returned, interrupting the buzz about Pete's sting and the wonder at how a scorpion could even get in his dhobi bag. He inspected our rooms, ensuring beds were made, dirty clothes had been placed in dhobi bags and stored away, although there wasn't much of that yet, as we were told to wear the same khakis for at least three days. The worst were our socks, which we did change daily. The excessive heat, the extensive amount of walking resulting in constant sweat and the accumulation of sand into our socks combined to make our feet hot and smelly. *Toe jam,* we called it, and it was horrible.

Once ready, we gathered outside, all talking at once and exchanging notes on our experiences with scorpions.

Matron came scurrying along after tending to Pete. "Calm down, all of you, please. Gemmell will be fine. Mr. Moore's taking him to the hospital for treatment. Now then, form a column, two by two ready for inspection, and no talking until it's complete."

Circling around impatient to set off, a number of boys were on bicycles, including Sheddy. It was five past seven and we were five minutes late starting out for the mess. Breakfast would start at a quarter past.

"We're all present and correct, Matron," said Michael Holiday, Senior prefect for Livingstone House.

"Thank you, Holiday. Good, then you may proceed and you'd better get a move on."

The boys with bikes cycled off.

"You'll stay in line for the walk to the mess," Matron called out. "I expect you prefects to maintain order. There'll not be any dawdling. When you reach the mess, line up in pairs where your prefect directs you. I don't want any shoddy drifting along any old how like some did yesterday; is that understood?"

A chorus of, "Yes, Matron," followed, and then Holiday barked, "Commence march."

It was ten past seven. The sun burned even at this hour, as we walked. It was amazing how short the shadows were already. The boys with bikes had long since disappeared, all except Neil who was cycling slowly, peeling around in circles so as not to get ahead, as he attempted to talk with prefect Keith Jones, who was walking and maintaining order. Berry and I walked as a pair and chatted.

"I didn't get a chance to ask, when you came back from hospital last night, how'd it go with Matron yesterday, you know, with your asthma and all?"

"Well, she called Mr. Moore, and agreed I'd have to go to hospital, so he took me there. The nurse gave me a pill and propped me up in bed. I just sat there all day, waiting 'til my breathing got back to normal."

"Now Pete's going down to the hospital," commented Berry. "I wonder who it'll be tomorrow."

"From what Sheddy told me there's always someone down there, mostly broken arms he said – at least with the boys."

Keith Jones interrupted, as he called out, "Get back in line, Aranky. You too, Ivey, what do you think you're doing? Anymore drifting out and you'll be writing lines, understood?"

"Yes, Keith."

I continued with Berry, "Anyway, the nurse brought me a few *Eagle* comics, they were old and I'd read them, but she also brought me a couple of *Biggles* books. I haven't read many of them so I easily found a new one."

"What one?"

"*Biggles on Mystery Island*," I replied. "They also had *Biggles Flies Again*, but I didn't have a chance to read it.

"I've got both those at home, they're good. Did they feed you?"

"Of course," I frowned. "They wouldn't leave me all day without food. Actually, I often don't want to eat when I get asthma, but I was feeling better by lunch time and the food smelled so good that I was hungry. Anyway, by evening, they changed their minds about me staying overnight, so Mr. Moore came to fetch me."

"Well, I suppose it worked out," said Berry, "but that's rotten luck. I wouldn't want to get asthma, even if I did get free days off in the hospital."

The two boys in the lead, Aranky and Paton, came to an instant halt with Aranky yelling, "Snake!"

The stop was so sudden that the rest of us concertina'd into the boys in front, resulting in stepped on ankles, loud exclamations of "Ooouuch man, what do you think you're doing, man?" "You clumsy idiot!" "Hey, watch it, eh!" and a number of indecipherables.

"Stay where you are, all of you," called Jones, running up to the head of the line, as we began straightening out. "Waar is die slang?" he broke into Afrikaans. "Waar is hy, man?"

Aranky said, "He's gone now, Keith. He went that way," pointing to the thick, yellow verge of tall grasses next to the pathway. "He's somewhere in there, man. He came right across our path in front of us, man, got a helluva fright, eh."

"I think it was harmless," said Paton.

"Well, it's gone then, so leave it, man. We all keep walking to the mess, eh? Straighten up the line all of you. Godverdomme, man, any excuse, eh."

As we resumed our walk there was a racket above. I looked up as flocks of kasukus flew low overhead, chirping their hearts out, drowning our conversation. Our line broke up again as, looking up at the birds as we walked, we strolled off at angles, out of line in some cases, bumping into other boys in others. I trod on Berry's toes.

"I say, have a care, old chap."

"Sorry. Those kasukus are so beautiful," I said. "I'd really like a pair to keep as pets, just like Sheddy has."

"Get back into line the lot of you," bellowed Jones. "That's 200 lines I want from all of you by this evening. I told you not to get out of line. You'll write, 'I will not get out of line without Keith's permission,' two hundred times, and if I don't get them by tonight it'll be double by tomorrow. Now get back into your places."

Berry continued, as we straightened up, "Some chaps have put the word out to the 'boys' to catch kasukus. They'll catch them for us for a shilling each."

After breakfast, it was only a quarter past eight, my colleagues strolled purposefully toward the Seniors classrooms. I hesitated because, being in hospital yesterday, I didn't know where to go. I asked Sheddy if he knew which classroom I should go to.

"You're in a different class from me. I'm in Seniors 1B and you're usually in the 'A' stream. Ask Stewart, he's an A."

Stewart confirmed that my name had been called yesterday, so he knew I was in his class, 1A.

"Follow me; we have history first, with Shutty."

Each of the Seniors classroom buildings was about twenty yards from the other, and each contained six classrooms within its L-shape. The outside walls, which were also the inside walls, were dark brown, creosoted wood. There were thirty desks in each. Desks included a receptacle under a lid where we kept our text and exercise books; a porcelain inkwell was set in the top right corner. Teachers sat at the front and behind them the blackboard.

We were joined by contingents of girls, dressed in their light tan blouses, brown below-the-knee-length skirts, white bobby socks and brown, buckle-up shoes. At the classroom door, Berry pointed out the one unoccupied desk reserved for me by Doug. I noticed the girls sat together on one side of the room, the centre aisle separating them from the boys. In Juniors we'd been mixed up.

"Hello, mate," greeted Doug. "I was hoping you'd be back today. I heard about the hospital, jolly bad luck that, although I bet you enjoyed the nurses, eh?" he said with a knowing wink. Doug was always one for the girls.

Mr. Shuttleworth brought the classroom to attention sharp at eight-thirty by thumping his desk with a paperweight. "Settle down, everybody. I want quiet, please. You, boy," looking directly at me, "I didn't see you yesterday, what's your name?"

"Please, sir, my name's Edwards, sir."

"Ah yes, Edwards. You were in hospital yesterday?"

Fifty-eight eyes turned to stare at me.

"Because you were absent, your desk has been filled with the text, exercise books and other accoutrements you'll need for term. You're a lucky man, are you not?"

"Yes, sir, very lucky, sir."

Smirks all round.

"You should thank Westley for that; he volunteered to help out. Now then, I want to know from you, Edwards – everybody else here yesterday keep quiet, please – why are we here, boy?"

"Um, er," I was caught off guard; what could I say that wouldn't sound foolish?

"Because I was sent to school here by my parents, sir?" was the best I could come up with.

The class, knowing the correct answer, tittered at my ignorance.

"Wrong answer, young man! The reason we're all here is W – O – R – K," he spelled the word out one letter at a time. "WORK! Now then, class, why are we all here?"

The class enthusiastically intoned, "W – O – R – K. WORK."

"Good, now I want you all to remember that, you too, Edwards. We're not here to play; nor are we here to stare out of the window, are we, Berry?"

Stewart turned sharply from the window.

"No, sir, we're here to work, sir."

"Good, now you can all get out your history text and exercise books."

We lifted our desk lids in search of them.

"Please, sir," said a girl, as she put her arm up, "we haven't got any ink in our inkwells so we'll not be able to write."

"What's your name, girl?"

"Tessa, sir, Tessa Maure."

"Ah, yes. Well, Tessa Maure, firstly, if you wish to speak, you will raise an arm. When I acknowledge you, you will speak and not before. Am I making myself clear?"

"Oh yes, sir."

Smirks from the girls.

"Good. Now then, how would you like to see to it that we get that ink? Take a colleague, go to the office; you know which building it's in by now, I presume?"

"Yes, sir."

"And ask one of the good ladies for a quantity of ink powder. You may take this jug with you. Upon your return, you will divert to the ablution block where you will obtain water and mix the ink for us. Now tell me, Tessa Maure, do you think that is within your power so to do?"

"Oh yes, sir."

More smirks from the girls.

"Excellent Miss Maure, right then, off you run… Oh and don't take too long about it," Shutty added as he contemplated the distance to the office and back via the ablution block.

Meantime, the history class got under way. As Shutty proceeded with his dissertation to do with the Roman occupation of England, with emphasis on the fact that the Romans built *fortified* towns, not *forty-five* towns as some among our number believed to be the case, I hastily scrawled down, for writing up later, the class schedule, still on the blackboard from yesterday. It included mathematics, English language, English literature, French, history, biology, science, chemistry, geography, technical drawing, art, and a choice of woodwork or metalwork. Class began at 8:30 a.m. and continued in forty-five minute intervals until lunchtime at 1 p.m., with a twenty-minute break mid-morning. There was another ninety minutes of class after lunch that might include 'prep,' followed by sports on some days or extra curricular activities on others.

During break, Sheddy beckoned to join him. We were looking for shade but there was none. The baobabs nearby were too small and with the sun high overhead, shadows cast by buildings were non-existent, save for an inch or two. We were joined by 'Angel-face' Berry who was christened with that nickname on day one by Miss Currie, the art teacher, as well as Goggles, Gunston and Paton.

Sheddy announced he wanted to take a raiding party after sports.

"Raiding party?" I asked, thinking of the abandoned vehicle dump that he'd told me about on the train. "What are we going to raid?"

"One of the Shambas," Sheddy responded, "is just the other side of the manyara hedge that the mamba slithered into, you know, where we played nyabs yesterday and saw the ants?"

"Oh, yes."

"The Africans have mahindi growing there. It would be smashing if we could swipe some and cook it ourselves, you know, after dinner."

"Mahindi?" I asked, "What's mahindi?"

"You know, maize, corn on the cob."

Actually I didn't know and said so. "I don't believe I've had corn on the cob, er mahindi, before," I said. "I don't think we get that in England and I haven't ever had it here."

"You must know corn. Everyone knows corn."

"Well, I don't know about corn on the cob."

"You know, they make corn flakes from it."

"Oh. Does it look like corn flakes?"

"Don't be a clot, Edwards, of course not."

"Well, what does it look like?"

"You'll find out when we go on the raid."

"In any case how would we cook it?"

"You know the hot water drum for our bathwater? By the time we get back after dinner the ashes will still be pretty hot and we can stir the fire up again, then we'll be able to cook the maize, you know, on the ashes."

"Won't we get into trouble for stealing the maize?" asked the more-aware-of-corn Goggles.

"I won't be joining in, Sheddy," said Paton. "I have Cubs."

"Of course not," said Sheddy, with a nod to Paton. "We're not going to get caught. Here's my plan...."

As it happened, sports were cancelled, so we had the afternoon off. Sheddy rustled up Ivey, Aranky and a few more conspirators to join in.

"Stay behind me," cautioned Sheddy as we approached the shamba. "Keep your head down and be quiet. We'll slip in here," he said after looking around furtively to make sure no teachers or Africans were watching. We pushed into the mahindi forest where the plants were higher than we were, and would have been instantly out of sight had there been observers.

"How will we know what to pick?" I asked.

Jenner, who was close by, said, "Look for the fat cobs, see, like this one. Then check the silk hair sprouting from the top. If the hair is dark brown, you know it's ripe. You just bend the cob down and it'll snap off."

"No more than two each," Sheddy stage-whispered with urgency. "We mustn't take too many in case it gets noticed, and we can't keep them anyway, they must be scoffed tonight, eh. So just two and hurry up, man, 'cos I want to get outa here before we're found out, man."

"This reminds me of when I went scrumping in England," said Ivey.

Just as we'd each collected our rations, Jenner called out, "Oh bloody hell, look! We've been spotted."

We turned in alarm to look down the row of corn. Three red-sanded watoto, each about five years of age, had appeared and were watching us. They were unusually well dressed, in khaki shorts and colourful shirts, even if they were a bit grubby. But they stood there, watching us innocently, their noses running as always, little unshod feet, staring in our direction.

"Quick, let's scarper," said Sheddy. "We'll be in trouble if they run and tell their parents."

When we approached the road, our ill-gotten gains secreted between our shirts and our belly, Sheddy signalled silence and went into a crouch at the shamba's edge. He peered through the final line of stalks looking for approaching adults, then whispered, "It's clear, but we must get across the road, through the hedge and back into school bounds as fast as possible. When you get to your room, hide your corn between your sheets – we don't want Twiga discovering them."

After lights-out we enjoyed a tasty feast. By the light of the stars, Sheddy stoked the smouldering embers under the water drum, adding dried grass and tinder to rekindle the flame.

"See, Tony," he said, "place your cob on the coals like this. You'll need a stick for a poker."

"Hey, don't hog the space, chaps," Aranky nuzzled in a place quickly followed by Gunston. The rekindled embers were soon glowing brightly, and I felt their heat on my face. Flames started flickering.

"What's that smell?" I asked. "I can smell perfume, I'm sure."

"That's not perfume, that's some of the corn burning," said Aranky.

"No, not that, I understand about that, this is different."

"Maybe you can detect the aroma of acacia," said Sheddy. "If the 'boy' put any acacia wood in with the firewood, then you might be smelling that; it has quite a sweet smell, they can even make perfume out of it."

"Oh."

"I need to turn mine. Mind out, Edwards," from Ivey.

"I think mine's ready," said Gunston. "Here, let me get at it before it burns."

"Yours needs turning, Tony," said Sheddy.

I reached in with the poker and managed to flip the cob over a bit. Some of the kernels looked black.

"Don't mind that," Sheddy said, "It'll taste good anyway but try to turn it over in time if you can. Actually you'd best get it out now – here I'll help you."

Sheddy hooked my cob from the ashes and caught it before it fell to the ground. He quickly lobbed it from hand to hand, because it was too hot to hold. "Jeesh, owe," then said, "Here, you take it."

"Yikes, it's hot, man. Owe!" I said as I too shuffled it from hand to hand, brushing off red sparks and ash.

"That's right, brush the ash off, see," Gunston demonstrated with his advice before he took a bite out of his.

"Mmm, that's sooo good," murmured Aranky as he chewed.

"Great scoff, eh?" said Gunston.

I bit into mine. It was hot, burning, but so tasty. I could hardly believe the flavour – burned kernels, ash residue, it didn't matter. "Wow, this is really mushee," I said smiling.

Raids like this caught on, and the poor Africans found their shambas unusually reduced of corn. But they recognised the telltale markings on the stalks, listened to the counsel of their watoto, no doubt, and soon were complaining to the Head.

Livingstone and Wilberforce houses were summoned one afternoon. Atop a dais, at a lectern, stood the Head in his standard white shirt and shorts. He was short and stocky with bowed legs and a freckled skin with lightly covering ginger hair. He was frowning and as stern as thunder under his mortar board, eyes in deep shadow from the high sun. Clutched in his right hand was a kiboko. He swished it around almost nervously and stroked the lethal end through the palm of his left hand.

"It has come to my attention," he bellowed his address, "that there are a number of nasty little boys, horrible little thieves, among your number who have been stealing mahindi." He suddenly got even louder, "This is not to happen again! I will not have this kind of behaviour! I will not tolerate theft in my school! That's what it is, you know. Theft! Just because it belongs to the Africans doesn't mean you're allowed to steal it. You're not! Is there anyone here who would like to own up to this enterprise of misappropriation? … No, I thought not," he answered his own question. "Well, understand this. If there's any more theft that comes to my attention, I will find out who is involved and they will be severely punished."

With this he flicked his wrist and the flex end of the kiboko curved around the guard rail of the dais before unwrapping again and returning to the straight. His point was well made. No one wanted to be on the receiving end of that, least of all me.

"Dismissed."

Midnight feasts came to a prudent stop for a while. What was called for was more cunning, pinching from a larger shamba where losses were less noticeable. Eventually the excitement resumed and remained with us in the seasons.

CHAPTER ELEVEN

TORTURE

W<small>E WERE CLIMBING</small> S<small>NAKE</small> R<small>OCK, OUT-OF-BOUNDS THOUGH</small> it currently was. Sheddy and Ivey had left the sports field because they'd not been included in teams today and didn't want to mooch around in the heat watching. Berry and I joined with them to go out of bounds and have some fun. Berry slipped while trying to reach the summit of the rock, fell and hurt himself badly, especially around a shoulder. I said I'd walk him to Matron. Sheddy and Ivey would hang around a little longer.

Matron was entertaining several other of the school's matrons for afternoon tea when I knocked. Seeing the bruised and battered Berry at her door, Matron exclaimed, "Oh my goodness, what have you done to yourself this time? Come in and let me take a look."

I hovered inside the doorway as Berry slipped off his torn and scuffed shirt and showed Matron his colourful shoulder. The other matrons peered over inquisitively.

"A broken collar bone seems like," she said glancing at her colleagues with a sigh, after Berry winced at being touched. "You boys will be the death of me, if it's not one thing it's another."

"Oh I don't know," interrupted one of the visiting matrons cheerily. "Black eye here, broken arm there; with boys that's nothing. If you think they're a lot of trouble, change places with me anytime and look after girls. Then you'll know what real drama is."

She smiled at her joke.

Matron returned the smile, rolling her eyes.

Meanwhile I'd spotted the cake and jam tarts and was hoping I'd be offered a reward for escorting Berry, but she didn't catch my appealing look.

"Thank you, Edwards, you may return to your house."

Turning to her visitors, she asked to be excused while she took Berry to Mr. Moore for the drive to hospital.

I found myself alone with not much on. I lay on my bed, sweating. I'd let Sheddy's kasukus hop about. Now I watched my baby chameleon, found in the manyara hedge weeks earlier, as he took a half hour to walk from one side of my chest to the other.

He ought to be hungry, I thought. *After all he's been in his cage all day.*

As always dozens of flies zigzagged about, settling on skin, needing to be swatted. Some were climbing the thin mosquito mesh. I stood on my bed, chammy in hand, getting as close to the flies as possible so that he could flick his tongue and catch dinner. But the chameleon was reluctant, or way too slow, I don't know which. As I held him up to within striking range, he'd swivel both eyes in all directions, instead of focusing on dinner walking up and down the screen and doing what chameleons are supposed to do. I sighed. *Perhaps I should just put him back in the hedge and let him get on with life.* For now I returned him to his cage and lay on my bed to keep cool.

Then I remembered the geraniums. Our houses had token flower beds in the form of whitewashed rocks making borders. There wasn't any special soil and certainly nothing growing in them. But I'd noticed that Mrs. Moore and Matron had cultivated their 'beds.' Some flowers and bushes would grow, if they were watered.

I asked Matron one day, "Matron, I was looking at your flower beds with those beautiful red flowers. Do you think I could grow some like that for our flower beds? I would have the time to look after them while the others are at sports."

"They're called geraniums," replied Matron, "and, certainly, I think that's a good idea, Edwards."

"But where will I get geraniums like you have?" I asked hopefully.

"They'll grow from cuttings, you know. I'll give you some and show you how if you like."

"Gee, thank you, Matron, that would be mushee."

I'd taken a fistful of cuttings and planted them according to instructions. Over recent weeks they'd been growing well, except in house 3 where, mysteriously, they seemed to keep getting broken. Now it was time for another watering.

I was walking the line with the bucket when I heard muffled conversation. Shouldn't have been any, all boys were out playing sports unless they were excused like me, and I didn't know of any who were, not in Livingstone. At the moment no one was in sight, but whoever was there was around the corner, and getting closer. I caught their conversation.

"They're at sports, man. No one's going to catch us," the voice whispered. "Come on, follow me."

I couldn't believe it. Somebody – and if I recognized the voices it was Viljoen, and others from Livingstone's house 3 – were about to invade my house to cause trouble, and here I was about to discover them, or them me and then what? It was even more alarming knowing that, bull terrier-like Viljoen had disliked me since my first day in Juniors, and bullied me every chance he got. I kept silent. Perhaps they wouldn't round the corner. Perhaps they'd go away.

In moments, Viljoen, Potgieter, Turner and Clark, the latter two being boys I rarely had anything to do with, had rounded the corner, and stopped in surprise at seeing me.

"Oh no, look, it's Edwards," sneered Viljoen.

"What are you doing here?" asked Potgieter, frowning, as though he had some rights around my house that I had not.

"Oh look, he's watering his littal fwowers. Isn't that cutsi wootsi?"

"They're so pwitty, Edwards, you can put some in a vase for me," said Potgieter. "I'll share them with Viljoen."

That brought a sneering laughter.

"When I first saw the fwowers I thought there must be a girl around," said Turner. "Now I know there is and she's called Edwards."

"Oh my gosh, look," said Viljoen. "I accidentally on purpose trod on some. Those poor pwitty fwowers are all broken down. Oh dear, oh dear, what shall we do, Edwards?"

"This is my house, just leave me alone. You're not supposed to be here. What are you going to do?"

"We'll show you if you like," responded Potgieter.

"But he'll see us," said Clark. "We can't do this when he knows what's going on, and who did it."

"Oh, I think we can," sneered Viljoen. "He wouldn't dare sneak."

"You wouldn't dare sneak, would you, Edwards?" asked Turner.

I didn't respond. I was in trouble and didn't want to help it along.

"Come," said Viljoen. "Bring Edwards inside while we have fun, then we'll take him outside and torture him."

"Leave me alone, Viljoen. Just leave me alone. You know I won't sneak. Just get out and leave me alone."

But they were looking for trouble, and not going to leave me be. I sat curled on my bed where I'd been shoved and told to keep quiet. Seconds later, Viljoen took a running leap at Sheddy's mosquito net, folded and dangling from a hook in the ceiling, caught it in mid-flight and landed on the bed with the net wrapping around him and the protesting springs, such as they were, squeaking their dismay. Turner did the same to Berry's net, and Clark took the third by tearing Aranky's from its hook.

"Come on, Edwards, off your bed, yours is next," said Potgieter

"I won't get off, this is my bed, just leave me alone. What do you think Twiga will say when she finds out? You're going to be in trouble."

"Except she won't know it's us that did it… will she, Edwards?" Viljoen asked pointedly, pushing his face up close to mine. "She won't know it was us, will she?"

"I s'pose not if she doesn't catch you," I agreed.

"It's not our house, we were never here, why would she suspect us?"

"That's a good point," added Clark. "Maybe we should leave Edwards' net alone, and then she'll think he did it. All the nets down but his. What else is she going to think?"

"I don't trust him not to sneak," said Viljoen. "We have to make the point he's in big trouble if he does. Clark, go haul down the rope from the 'boys' washing line. Potgieter, take that chair outside and put it in the sun. Come on, Edwards. Up, I said, come on up."

I was no match for Viljoen even less with the other three, so he hauled me to my feet, clasped my hands behind my back and forced me outdoors.

"All right, now sit on the chair. Come on, sit. Where's that rope? Okay, tie him up. Hands behind the chair, tie him all around, by the chest, his legs, everywhere, I don't want him escaping."

This was way beyond a joke. How was it going to end? I became more nervous by the moment. The sun scorched. Were they going to leave me tied to this chair, baking? Were they crazy?

"Why are you doing this to me? What have I done to you? What have you got against me?"

"You're just such a wimp, Edwards. You never play sports and you're excused PT. We have to do cross country running, but do you? No, you poor little mama's boy, you get out of everything, don't you? While we have to do everything."

"It's not my fault I get asthma," I argued. "I don't want to have it. I'd rather run than have asthma. I don't know why you think that's a feeble excuse, it's very real."

"Oh, you poor littal boy. Where's your mummy then? Maybe she can come and rescue you, you little wimp. Just because of a little asthma, which you're probably shamming anyway, you get excused everything. Well, you're not getting excused this."

While Viljoen was verbally berating me, Turner and Clark were tying me to the chair. I felt bad about Clark. It's not that we were close friends, but neither did we ever quarrel.

I was becoming incensed at what they were doing, my chest tightening and I could feel asthma not far off. If I got an attack I'd be in serious trouble. I breathlessly asked, "Please don't do this to me. I won't tell anyone you were here. I just don't want to get an attack. You don't understand, it's dangerous, man."

"Oh, is it welly dangerous, you poor littal boy? Oh dearsy wearsy, are we going to cry? Are we going to start acting like a little girl? Oh, you poor little fing."

With that the final knots were tied. After standing back to admire their handiwork they tired of that and went back inside to pull down the nets in the other rooms, rip the beds apart, throw the bedding all over the place and ransack clothes and shoes they pulled out of the drawer chests.

I faced the afternoon sun. My eyes streaming; my chest tightening. All the same I'd seen enough cowboy films to know that those tied up always work to untie themselves. At the pictures, cowboys would find a loose strand or a slack bit so they could loosen the rope and escape. Surely I could do that too? I began working on it.

The problem was that real life was different from the flicks. I found a slack bit. I even loosened the rope. Given time I'd free myself. But where in the pictures, when the bad men came back to check on the bloke they'd tied up, they usually think he's still tied, and then leave him again; in my case they didn't do just that. When they came to check on me, saying they'd better do a bunk now and get out before the others came back, Viljoen said, "Check the ropes and knots first. I don't want him escaping."

Potgieter came round the back where the knots were, and saw where I'd loosened the rope. "He's loosened it," he called out. "This needs to be re-tied."

"That's what I mean," said Viljoen. "That's why we check."

The three of them went back inside the house telling Clark to do the tying.

"And tie it properly this time, Clark."

As he worked at it, Clark whispered in my ear, "I'm sorry, Edwards, really I am. I didn't think things were going to get this out of hand. Listen, I'm going to leave the rope loose again so you can work your way free... like I did the first time. But wait 'til we're gone before you do it, see?"

The others returned.

"All right," said Viljoen. "Now kick the chair over, Clark, I want him on his side."

"That's going too far, Viljoen," Clark objected. "Look at him; he really is breathing hard."

"I don't bloody care. Let him know we'll be ruthless if he sneaks on us; that's all that matters, man. Now do it."

Turner walked over. "You don't have to really kick him over, Clark. Just lower him down on his side, man; I think that'll keep Arend happy."

Clark and Turner then lowered the chair until I was lying on my side, with all my weight on the one arm that had been tied around the chair back.

"No, don't do it," I pleaded. "It's hurting, man. Please don't leave me like this."

"All right, now gag him," said Viljoen. "I don't want him calling for help."

Potgieter stuffed a hanky into my mouth, using one of Aranky's Scout kerchiefs he'd found, to tie it in place. Now my breathing was harder than ever. You can't breathe through your nose with an asthma attack. You breathe through your mouth or you stop breathing.

Viljoen and Potgieter laughed, Turner and Clark gave half-hearted chuckles like they didn't really mean it, then they were gone. Walking around the end of the house, they glanced back to make sure I was still there, and then disappeared.

I struggled for air. I didn't yet have an attack and was still able to inhale using all my strength, just barely, through my nose.

Soon it would be over, I thought. *What did I do to deserve this? Surely Viljoen didn't really want me dead. He was just so irresponsible; he just didn't believe me. Didn't want to believe me.*

I wrestled with the knots, tears of frustration welling in my eyes; Clark had said he'd leave them loose, but he didn't know I'd be on my side. I couldn't move around at all and the weight of my body on my arm was becoming more painful by the second. Soon I could feel the arm going to sleep; my blood had been cut off from circulation. I was struggling to breathe through my nose and was burning in the heat as the sweat ran down my head, getting into my eyes and stinging. *If someone doesn't come soon, I'll die.*

I remained aware of other things. A flock of kasukus flew overhead chirping their hearts out and this set off Sheddy's two who became excited, hopping from perch to perch at the rate of knots. Next to their cage was the smaller one for the chameleon. He, or she maybe, sat there as ever, eyes rotating through 360°. As the minutes passed, I watched an armoured spider emerge from a hole under the stoep. It began walking towards me and I wondered what would happen if it got on me, but it changed its mind and direction, disappearing out of my sight.

Then the ants arrived. Not safari ants but common ones, thank goodness, and the leading scouts began their investigation, crawling over my face and down my neck, where most of the moisture from sweat was accumulating. I felt their pinching bites. *God damn Viljoen and the others.* How I hated them. The idea that he and his friends could be in big trouble if something bad happened was no consolation. I was sure Clark or Turner would admit to what they did, so it would come out. And in any case it would be obvious that someone had done something terrible. Mr. Moore would find out.

But, it didn't come to that. I was burning up, my head swimming, eyes rolling, beginning to lose consciousness as my nose became all but blocked, when I became aware of the animated conversation of Sheddy and Ivey returning to the house. They arrived through the front door and went to our bedroom, without at first looking outdoors. From the direction I was facing, I sensed the shadow of their movement through the corner of a barely open eye, but I couldn't call out. I made grunting sounds as loud as I could summon. Either my grunts, or perhaps as a result of focusing on the devastation around the bedroom, something caused Ivey to look out the window.

"Bloody hell!" he exclaimed. "Look, Sheddy, look what someone's done to Edwards."

Even as he said it he came rushing out of the house, jumped off the stoep and over to me. Sheddy was right behind. They lifted the chair to the vertical then quickly undid the gag and took the hanky out. I gasped deeply, shaking my head, stretching my neck, struggling for air, desperate to breathe even through my mouth.

"What the hell happened, Tony?" Ivey asked.

"Who did this to you?" yelled Sheddy. "Who the bloody hell did this to you?" Sheddy rarely swore but he was angry as hell. I had no breath to answer.

He noticed my arm turning blue and the indentations in my skin, and started rubbing it with both hands to stimulate circulation.

I continued gasping, trying to get out a few words, "Can't breathe... need medicine... must go... Ma....."

Both friends grabbed an arm each and hustled me, unable to stand, the fifty yards to Matron's house.

"Let's just pray she's in," said Ivey.

Matron came to her door. "Oh my goodness, not another attack, Edwards? Bring him in, boys; set him in the chair over there, it has a tall back. He needs to sit upright. Stay there now while I get his dawa."

Moments later Matron spotted a number of ants crawling over me. "Good heavens, child, where'd the ants come from? How on earth did you get them crawling over you? Why don't you brush them off? And why's your skin so red. What were you doing sitting in the sun, foolish boy? Come on, let's take this shirt off."

"I was sitting on the stoep," I gasped. "And could barely breathe," I said as I struggled for breath. "Perhaps that's when... *(gasp)*... they must have crawled on me."

Between receiving the medicine and being able to breathe through my mouth again, I slowly returned to a more relaxed state. The ants had been brushed off, with the help of Sheddy and Ivey. Matron addressed them.

"I'll send Edwards home when his breathing gets back to normal. You two might as well get an early start on your baths."

She left me for a while, busying about her laundry.

"How's Berry?" I breathlessly coughed at Matron later. "Is he *(cough)* coming home today?"

"Berry's at the hospital. He has a nasty collar bone break. Now don't try to talk, wait 'til your breathing's back to normal. I don't understand how he managed to do that, falling off a small flowerbed rock. I could understand a sprained ankle or something, but a broken collar bone? I don't suppose you saw exactly what happened, did you?"

"I was looking away at the time *(gasp)*, Matron," I lied. "So I didn't see his actual fall."

"Hmm, well, anyway, I believe the hospital will keep him overnight and check on him in the morning. I expect he'll return tomorrow."

It was a little over an hour later I told Matron I felt better and could return to my house. I arrived to find the chaps had tidied up and most had bathed and were ready for dinner so, as there was no time left, I didn't bathe but got dressed.

With Sigurd back at his house, Sheddy had told the others, while they'd cleaned up the mess, what they'd discovered when they got home. But now, everyone wanted to know more from me, especially who had done this.

Not sneaking meant not telling adults or Seniors like prefects. It did not apply to talking to your friends or a prefect if he was also a victim of the outcome, or so I was told. It became clear, when I wouldn't tell them anything, that my friends were not going to let this go.

"Let's just forget it," I said. "Best not create any more trouble than there's already been."

"No, Edwards, man, you have to tell us, see," said Gemmell. "All that happened to you is way too serious, man. We cannot ignore it, eh?"

"But, Pete, you know I can't sneak."

"This isn't sneaking," said Sheddy. "What they did to you, whoever it was, is way too serious. And anyway, we were kind of victims like you, man, what with the mess and the mosquito nets and all. Same for the prefects, man."

"I agree," added Jenner. "You have to tell us, man."

"And Twiga's going to find out about the nets," said Aranky. "If I'm going to be punished for that, I want to know who I'm going to be getting back."

Marriott looked around at all present, everyone except Berry from our house. "Are we all agreed, Edwards will not be sneaking if he tells us what happened?"

"Yes," they chorused.

"What about Berry?"

"He'll agree with us," said Sheddy. "When he gets back from the hospital we'll tell him what happened. There's not a chance he wouldn't."

"No one's against it, right? Okay, there you go, Edwards; no one will treat you as a sneak. We're all agreed; so tell us, man."

And so I did.

After dinner Viljoen and Potgieter got beaten to a pulp by persons un- known. Turner and Clark were shoved against a wall and warned that if they did anything like that again, they'd wish they'd never been born. When Matron came around for lights-out the only thing she noticed out of the ordinary were the mosquito nets. To start with she hadn't. She was more intent on satisfying herself I was recovered and no attack had developed. As she left our room to walk down to the other end, she popped her head back in again, looking over the top of her spectacles, knowing something was missing.

"Where are the nets?" she asked. "Where are your mosquito nets?"

Sheddy went over to a drawer and pulled them out. "They're here, Matron, they've lost their loops."

"So I see. And how did they come to lose their loops?"

"I don't know, Matron."

"Aranky?"

"I don't know, Matron."

"Edwards. You were here most of the afternoon, were you not, before your asthma? Your net is still in place, the only one that is, I see. You must know what happened?"

"I don't know, Matron."

"So, it's to be like that, is it? Is this the same story in the other bedroom?" she asked as she left our room and walked down the end.

"I see you've all lost your mosquito nets too?"

She made enquiries of those boys, of course, none of whom knew what had happened.

"Gemmell, Marriott, what do you know of this? Oh no. Your nets are down too?"

"Sorry, Matron, we don't know how this came to be."

"We'll see about that."

When Matron checked the other houses for lights-out she was pleased to note there'd been no bad behaviour there and equally glad to note that Potgieter and Viljoen were already fast asleep in their beds, heads buried in their pillows. If she'd have thought about it, Matron would have found it unusual; however for now she was too preoccupied with the mosquito net debacle in house number one, and the sewing repairs that entailed.

The following afternoon I was sent by Matron to see Mr. Moore over the mosquito net issue.

Judi answered the door with Steve peeking around.

"Is your dad home?"

Mr. Moore was right behind. He told his girls to run along and play outside and then asked me to follow through to his sitting room.

"You were the only one present all or much of the afternoon, as I understand it. In your house everybody's mosquito net had been pulled down but yours. You must know what happened. Either you know who did it, or you did it. After all, who else would have? There was no one there. Why is your net still in place?"

"I don't know, sir."

"Very well. As you know, ten days from now there is to be a fête put on by the Kongwa Club. It's primarily for the benefit of the school. It should be a lot of fun. As punishment for the destruction of the mosquito net loops you are forbidden to attend it. On that day you will be restricted to your room, where you will write a thousand times, 'I must not pull down mosquito nets and break their loops because Matron has to sew them again, and does not enjoy doing so.' That same afternoon you will deliver those lines to Matron at bath time. Is that clearly understood?"

"Yes, sir."

"You may go."

That night tears welled as I tried to sleep. It was so unfair, so terribly unfair after the torture I'd gone through. Neither Matron nor Mr. Moore knew anything about that, nor about the mess the house had been left in. Now I was being punished for the mosquito nets too.

I hate this place, I consoled myself. *I hate school; I hate Kongwa; I hate the injustice and I hate everything to do with it. One of these days I'm going to run away again, and this time I'll stay away, and won't ever come back. That'll show 'em.*

CHAPTER TWELVE

TRENCH WARFARE, KONGWA STYLE

A N OUTBREAK OF CHICKEN POX HAD CREATED the scare of an epidemic. Staff had moved fast to contain the contagious ones in the hospital so that, in the end, only about fifteen boys and seven girls actually caught it.

While that excitement was going on, I'd not had any teacher trouble, or been bullied, so life was good. For me, a peaceful period of several days was as good as a holiday. I'd even won a prize for reading in a school-wide competition. So I groaned when I heard that Livingstone prefects wanted to raid Curie, in a catapult fight. It could mean big trouble just as things had been going well; and catties were bloody dangerous. But, I had no choice.

That night, after lights-out, we were nodding off from boredom of the wait, when the word went out. Suddenly our room filled with older boys, including our own Pete Gemmell and Brian Marriott. They were in camouflage gear, mudded faces, ears, blackened clothes, bristling with catapults and slings, and looking terrifying.

"Up, up, up, everybody," they urged. "Come on, everybody up and out."

We were given moments to dress and camouflage ourselves, then, grabbing our catapults and with sheath knives hanging from our belts, we joined the milling throng gathering a couple of houses away, in the dim light of the quarter moon. General instructions were given. Selected squads were directed to attack specified Curie houses.

The orders went like this: "Move under cover to within twenty yards of target. When you hear an opening volley of rocks clattering off tin roofs that will signal the attack. You're to release a warning volley off the roof of your target house. Re-load on the run, and then let loose a second volley at the windows of the house you're attacking. Your range should be about ten yards; your objective: create as many holes in the mosquito mesh as possible and startle Curie into retreat. You then rush the front or rear doors, whichever is closest, again re-loading on the run, burst into the house, threaten occupants and demand surrender. 'Let loose' on anyone who doesn't give up."

The night was ideal. There was enough light to see, not so light that everything was brightly lit for defenders. It was warm. The sky was brilliantly clear, the stars stood out in relief. There the Southern Cross, easy to detect and provide a bearing. It was, as ever, noisy from the insects. Unseen rustles signalled movement of a snake, an iguana, or one of a hundred little lizards in the grass. The distinctive huuuu-rumphs of the hyena were never far away, perhaps just the other side of the hedge? The rock-hard red soil was softened from the rain. The tracks linking the houses were rutted, divided by rivulets, and small dongas created by the rushing water that followed torrential downpours. There wasn't much rain to be had these days, but when it was our turn, we knew all about it.

This was the time for maximum cover for a catapult raid. The tall magugu grass was fresh and new, though it wouldn't remain that way for long. Soon the P.W.D. would be out with the African workers and their slashing mundus, cutting it short around the houses. It was a dangerous time in the grasses, where the slow-moving puff adders would hide from exposure to the circling hawks during the day or the owls at night. The flat-topped acacias were temporarily green, branches covered with tiny leaves among the thorns with their murderous white points.

Stage one of the raid went off without a hitch. We moved to within twenty yards give or take. The first rock clattered off a tin roof, creating a kelele. The insects stopped chirruping at once, and my heart started beating fast. We stood up from our cover, in a thin broad line covering a couple of hundred yards to let loose our opening volley. But before we could, the whiz of rocks propelled at high speed tearing by our ears, and in two cases making contact with Livingstone boys, resulting in high-pitched yells, sent us ducking for cover with the realization that we'd been expected. Our cover was blown. Some bastard had talked! Before I could gather my wits, new orders were being shouted.

"Come on, Livingstone, they're waiting for us but we go in anyway, reload, shoot at will, let's get em!"

Kongwa's version of WWI trench warfare was under way.

We ran at Curie in a half crouch, re-loading our 'catties' on the run, firing at anything that moved. As I closed on the house I'd been told to attack, apparently alone because I was not aware of any friends around, I stopped, panting, to take a breather and assess the situation. I dropped to a crouch, hidden by the grasses and listened intently. Surprise was gone... that was certain, and who knew what defences lay in wait.

The centre of battle, with considerable noise, had shifted in the direction of the older Seniors' houses, which were the prizes, and I wondered why I was supposed to attack a house single-handed or what I'd done to find myself in the wrong place. Then I heard strained whispers. Two or three of the enemy were lying in wait.

"There's at least one out there, I'm sure, maybe two," I heard.

"I can't see anyone, are you sure?" came the response.

"Well, I think so."

And then the voices became muffled and I couldn't make out what was being said.

My heart beat faster, I felt sure I was alone and wouldn't get any mercy. At the least they would fire at me and a catapult rock at this range was bloody dangerous. Worse than that might happen if I was taken prisoner. From my crouch, I couldn't see anything other than the roof outline of the target house ten yards away.

Then I heard them. Several pairs of feet were leaping through the grass and getting louder! Coming in my direction! I decided to go down fighting. I sprung to my feet, and saw three boys converging rapidly towards me. The one in the centre loosed his rock; it whizzed close by my head for I heard its flight. I fired back on reflex without aiming and my rock caught him in the stomach. He staggered, then slumped to his knees winded and gasping. The other two were in point blank range. They had slowed to a walk, both catapults trained on me, and I had no chance to re-load.

"Oh, look, it's Edwards," sneered the one in exaggerated comment, coming to a halt and raising his catapult at my head. "You got Snelling in the stomach, didja? Where do you think we should get him?" he asked in an aside to Oliver.

"Don't move an inch either of you or you'll get this load in your head!" Sheddy emerged out of nowhere, and levelled his catapult directly at Wessels, the nearest one threatening me.

"Damn," said Wessels to Oliver, "I told you there was another one around."

Oliver half shrugged as he stared in amazement.

I was in equal disbelief. I had no idea Sheddy was there. Was it coincidence? Or was he looking out for me?

"The way I see it," said Sheddy, "is this. You can both let Edwards have it if you want. But then I get you, Wessels, and after that, that leaves you and me, Oliver. Of course, we won't need catties!" Sheddy's wrestling and boxing prowess were legendary.

The reply was deafening in its silence as the two pondered their situation.

"Of course there's another option," he followed up. "You could relax your catties and drop the rocks. You do that and I'll do the same, then Edwards and I'll get out of here. How about it?"

There was a pause as the two looked at each other but then the decision was taken out of their and our hands. Beams from the headlights of a car a hundred yards away, otherwise black and invisible in the darkness, flashed, as the vehicle twisted and turned along the rutted track that led to Curie's houses. At the same moment, three torches could be seen swinging from the hands of adults walking the path through the high grasses in the same direction.

"Cuss-cuss! Cuss-cuss!" came the warning cry. It was time to scarper. From the point of view of our five, the confrontation was over and all were saved face. The general enemy was on the way, and it was every boy for himself. Wessels and Oliver fled in the direction of their house. Snelling, still clutching his stomach, staggered after them. For our part we had a little more time. The noise and action was around Curie where teachers were heading. But we must retreat. It was certain we'd be checked on.

The thin, blue line of Livingstone boys, two hundred yards wide, beat a fast withdrawal. Some in open ground made good progress but Sheddy and

I, in long grasses, blustered into thorn bushes, impossible to see in the dark. Disentangling was a nightmare, those thorns hurt badly. Add to that our anxiety, when we were in a hurry!

Scratched and bleeding, we finally hit the clearing at the second house in the Livingstone row. Our house was the first, 50 yards to our left. No other boys were in sight, it seemed like we were the last.

"Good, we're almost home."

Then my heart missed a beat. We caught the flash of torches of the alerted Mr. Moore and Matron just leaving Matron's house. Obviously the two were on their way to check on their boys. If we continued to our front door, we'd arrive at the same time they would. If we stayed away, they'd see our empty beds.

"Quick, follow me," said Sheddy.

He and I slipped across the beaten path and ran like the wind on the rear side of the second house. We crossed the open ground between the houses, pausing briefly at the choo to make sure we were out of sight from the approaching adults. Running on tip toes, we arrived at our rear-entry French doors, seconds before Mr. Moore and Matron turned the knob of our front door. Lucky our beds were in this same room. We eased through the partially open doors quickly but quietly, pushed them to behind us, slipped our catapults under our pillows and slid ourselves between the sheets, glancing at Berry and Aranky who were sitting up and motioning frantically.

"Quick, quick," they whispered urgently, having heard the scrunch of feet on sand outside, "someone's coming."

We pulled our sheets up as the front door squeaked, and the adults entered.

"It appears that whatever that trouble is up at Curie, doesn't involve our boys," said Matron to Mr. Moore as they left the furthest bedroom and walked the corridor toward our end.

"Hmmm," grunted a suspicious Mr. Moore.

Fully clothed and shod still, we pulled the sheets high on our heads and faced away from where Mr. Moore and Matron would be standing when they surveyed our bedroom. Their footsteps fell lightly down the corridor as they paused to glance into the prefects' room.

"All present and correct here."

Satisfying themselves on those two they arrived at our room. Mr.

Moore's powerful lantern was shone from head to head. It paused on each as the adults' eyes adjusted and they were satisfied there were heads in those beds. Mr. Moore and Matron withdrew, to continue their inspection down the line. A few moments later we were sitting up; torches hauled out as we talked of the fight and the close-cut withdrawal. The biggest relief was that Sheddy and I had made it to our beds in time.

"Let's hope it's the same for the rest of Livingstone," someone said.

Sheddy and I were heroes, especially with Gemmell and Marriott, for having got under our sheets with seconds to spare as we must have been the closest to giving the game away. Just one out of place and Mr. Moore would have had everyone up, when the sight of us, camouflaged and fully dressed would have shocked him and Matron.

The warning call came again, "Cuss-cuss!"

Mr. Moore and Matron were on their way back from the furthest houses. We cut the torches and zipped under our sheets but no problem; the Housemaster and Matron were returning to their houses, satisfied that Livingstone had not been involved in the fracas.

Next day, Curie had the book thrown at them. There were mass canings and deprivation of privileges, in addition to the bandaging of bruised and bleeding bodies. Though the teachers must have thought that Curie would not fight itself, they were unable to finger another party. No one at Curie sneaked, so never a word was breathed; but Curie did let us know that revenge would be wrought! In the meantime, in Livingstone, a rash of bike collisions and slammed doors explained to Matron how some of her boys sustained their injuries.

A week later, Matron found herself treating Sheddy's and my septic scratches. We'd gone the usual route of popping the yellow bubbles with acacia thorns and squeezing the pus ourselves but, as it kept reforming, we went to her for some dawa. Eventually the pus would go and the scratches would heal but this was the way it was.

"Where on Earth did you two get all these scratches anyway?"

CHAPTER THIRTEEN

HAVING IT OUT

T HERE WAS RARELY A DAY WHEN WE didn't hear of blokes squabbling over some insult, true or imagined. But fights, frequent though they were, tended to be short-lived and not too serious. I'd watched a few more serious ones between older Seniors; some horrific I thought. Didn't think I'd get into one myself.

It was rare for a teacher to intervene. Fights would be pre-arranged at a location where teachers didn't go, like along the walks to classrooms or the mess. Teachers drove their cars. The fights would be held away from girls, because they were known to telltale if they knew one to be in progress. It was understood we'd be punished if we were caught fighting, but I never knew of anyone who was. The visible signs of fights were not punished, because the boys had not been caught in the act and you couldn't punish them because they'd walked into a tree or had a door slammed in their face. And besides which, "Boys will be boys. Toughens 'em up, you know, breeds character."

After a fight, the House Matron would dutifully bandage their charges, having doused them in either Dettol, Gentian Violets or sometimes iodine. Septicaemia was the main concern when skin was cut. Even the slightest pin prick or paper cut would go septic, if not cleaned and treated.

It was a warm evening, the stars twinkled and a full moon was rising. I was in the queue outside the mess waiting for dinner. Someone had snuck up behind me, slapped his hands around my eyes and called out, "Guess who?"

I didn't guess who because I didn't know his voice. Because I couldn't guess his name he wouldn't let go, and all the while his fingers were digging into my eyes. It was sore so I implored him to relax his grip a bit. He wouldn't do it.

I said, "You don't have to let go, I'll still try to guess, just don't press your fingers in my eyes."

"Come on, Edwards, guess, guess, guess," he urged. "Tell me who I am and I'll let go."

"I can't, you're hurting my eyes, man, don't squeeze my eyes, man, let go."

"Guess, guess, guess."

I became angered, clenched my fist, brought my left arm forward then rammed my elbow backwards into my assailant's solar plexus. He let go with a grunt, then started to half laugh, slightly winded and said, "What's the matter, Edwards; you're not a sport, man. Can't you take a little game, man? What you have to hit me for, man?"

I turned and recognised Boris Ustinov from Nightingale, a boy I barely knew or had anything to do with. I yelled at him, "Because you were pressing too hard on my eyes. I don't mind playing a game but you were hurting my eyes. You shouldn't do that to someone, you know?"

"Oh poor little Edwards, can't take a bit of fun, worried about his little eyesie wisies. What sort of a bloke are you anyway? Why don't you go down the end there and stand in the queue for the girls' mess? That's where you belong."

"Oh shut up, Ustinov. If you can't play a game properly then don't play at all. You're just stupid to go on like that."

"Stupid? Who are you calling stupid?"

"I'm calling you stupid because of what you did."

"Oh yeah, well, you wanna make something of it? You wanna have it out? You wanna see which one of us is the most stupid?"

Suddenly, Ustinov almost tripped into me, after being shoved by someone. Ustinov wasn't expecting it so didn't follow through but just yelled even louder, nose to nose, "Come on, you wanna make something of it? You wanna hit me?"

Then I stumbled into him, after I too was shoved. Boys were bunching in on both sides, egging on the belligerents, trying to ensure a fight got started.

"Pack it in, you two." Neil Thomson, prefect on duty, investigated the noise and the anger and came forward to keep us apart. "Get back into your own line, Ustinov, and you lot, straighten up and pair off if you want dinner."

The lines moved into the mess but by now, having smelled blood, the crowd were energized to ensure a scrap took place. Everyone liked a good fight.

During dinner my anger cooled and I think Ustinov did too. But that would not be the end of the story. The boys were not going to let a good fight go un-fought. Throughout dinner, my colleagues at the table, other than Sheddy, encouraged me to teach Ustinov a lesson. Viljoen, at other times my nemesis, assured me, "You can't let him get away with it, Edwards, sticking his fingers in your eyes like that. That's dangerous, man; you shouldn't let him off that easily. If it was me I'd knock him into next week, man."

I'd had enough trouble with Viljoen myself, so it was no surprise to get this advice from him, although, given our history, his being on my side didn't ring true.

"Yeah," said Gunston. "Arend's right, man, you shouldn't let him get away with that."

Potgieter joined in, "You need to beat him up, man, right after dinner, we'll get him, man. He can't do that to you. Don't worry, man, we'll support you. He's trouble that Ustinov, from one of those 'commie' countries or something. He's always creating trouble. You gotta teach him a lesson, man."

Sheddy remained quiet as we ate but then advised, "Leave Ustinov alone, Tony. He and his brother are tough. I'm not saying you can't win but it could be a really rough fight. You should drop it, unless he starts it and comes after you."

The fight protagonists didn't argue with Sheddy. He was a relentless fighter if he had to be and no one in the same age and weight range stood a chance against him. So his opinion was respected, at least well enough not to argue at the table.

I whispered to Sheddy, "Well, you said I've become good at wrestling; I've got that going for me."

"Maybe," said Sheddy. "Maybe, but I'm not sure you'd get a chance to use it against a good boxer. And Ustinov is a good boxer."

Meanwhile, Ustinov, at his dinner table, was under the same pressure to fight me after dinner, and it became obvious on the walk home in the dark.

We left the mess. Fifty or more boys from Livingstone and Nightingale were by now alerted, had taken sides according to house and were now surrounding their fighters in two large and milling groups, urging us to action. No one was going to let this go.

The moon was full, lighting the soil, glistening off the denuded branches of the msasas and the acacias, turning the white thorn tips into a spectacle like star dust. Everyone was talking at once, urging Ustinov and me to get on with it, to have it out and to settle this thing. I found myself carried by the throng, with urgent calls to action. I was aware of Ustinov, surrounded by an equally noisy crowd, trailing a few yards behind. I tried to explain to my supporters I was not angry. I had no wish to beat up Ustinov, that it was over. But no one except Sheddy would hear of it.

"He's a boxer, you know?" Sheddy reminded me. "It's his favourite sport. You're not a boxer, Tony. You'll be in trouble if you take him on."

"Nah, man, you must beat him up, man," urged Viljoen. "He'll never learn if you let him get away with it, man. Ustinov needs teaching a lesson, that's what he needs. Go give it him, Edwards. Go beat him up, man."

As this was all happening, out of the gloom, we became aware of the gentle sound of an mbira, a sort of thumb piano, a native musical instrument that gives a delightful, gong-like music and something Africans like to play as they walk. Realising we were being approached by adults in deep shadow, everything came to a stop.

Good, I thought. *This should break it up and we can forget it. I just want to get back to my room and be with my friends. To heck with Ustinov.*

As we peered into the shadows, several men stepped out into the moonlight. An unusual sight of three older Masai warriors approached, draped in their loose-slung, red kikois. They wore strings of beads around their necks, hair was pasted with red ochre mud and stretched earlobes enclosed huge ear rings. Two of them supported their mkukis resting on their shoulders. They almost loped by in their wide, springy step yet somehow relaxed fashion to the accompaniment of the mbira being played by the third. In an ironic way for colonial Africa, we showed deference to the fact that they were adults (and by extension might interfere).

The music came to a stop as the obligatory salutations were exchanged: "Hamjambo, vijana, habari."

"Jambo mzee, habari yarko?"

"Kwaheri, vijana."

"Kwaheri mzee."

The three Masai returned to the shadows as they passed by, and the music resumed once more before fading into the distance. The hiatus now came to an end with renewed calls to get on with it. Now the two throngs forced the mingling of the crowd into closed ranks in one large circle, the protagonists in the middle, in the tradition of the prize fight.

I had mixed emotions. On the one hand I didn't want to fight, had no anger for Ustinov and wished the problem would go away. On the other, there was a strong argument for an apology, failing which Ustinov would be delivered a clout to teach him a lesson. It was clear there was so much raw emotion aroused among the crowd; there wasn't a chance we'd get to bed without something happening. The boys wouldn't accept no for an answer.

I was nose to nose with Ustinov. I asked him to apologize so we could shake hands and forget it… but he would not. He said nothing, just shook his head. The jeering and shouting, the taunting and the encouragement were ringing loud in my ears.

I delivered the clout. A ringing slap with the flat of my hand across his left cheek drew a roar of approval. I turned, glad it was over, and walked to the edge of the circle that broke ranks for me. I was closely followed by Sheddy and a couple of others.

Sheddy was saying, "Well done," to me for leaving it at that when there was a heightened roar from the crowd. Ustinov was not going to leave things be. He came running at me, rammed me hard from behind, setting me staggering forward trying not to fall, before I could recover and turn.

He beckoned, "Come on and fight," then threw a couple of punches into my chest to get things going.

"Let me take your blazer," said Sheddy. "You can't fight with your blazer on.

I slipped out of it as Ustinov did the same and the crowd roared. At last it was starting.

I attempted to retaliate, trying to return blow for blow. But I had no training in boxing. I found myself reeling backwards. Ustinov had landed a full force fist into my left eye. There was a muffled sound, blackness and stars as I staggered almost losing my balance. He followed through with more body punches and then another to the side of my head. I went down on my knees. Ustinov came skipping up, circling me, calling me to get up, he wasn't finished.

"Come on, get up, you bastard, if you dare," he yelled. He was circling me as he skipped, coming in ever closer. In my daze, I wiped blood from my nose and cheek, amazed at the amount of sticky substance that came away on my hands. I shook my head, trying to clear the numbness, trying to think, searching for what I must do. It came to me.

Ustinov skipped in ever closer until suddenly, with great speed I like to think, I let out from my crouch, arms outstretched and encircled his legs in a tackle. He yelled in surprise as he lost his balance and fell, there was a deafening cheer from the crowd as I was all over him. Astride this squirming enemy underneath, lashing out as he was trying to throw me off, I laid into him in a blistering action of punches, using all the strength I had. But Ustinov was strong and threw me off. Squirming away from underneath he was on his side, blood gushing from his lips and nose, kicking out in an effort to back away, to get up on his feet, where he would be in control again.

I thought, *I have to keep him on the ground. I can't win by boxing, wrestling is my only hope.*

I scrambled after him, clawing at his tie to hold him. It tore away from his neck, and I reached for his shirt. As Ustinov lashed out in his struggle to get back on his feet his kick connected with my groin putting me in untold pain. I let go. He staggered up, stumbling around as in some drunken lurch, then recovered, coming back to circle me. In my agony I couldn't get up before he moved in again, this time kicking me in my stomach. At that, Sheddy and Ivey moved in and grabbed Ustinov, hauling him back, almost into the ring of spectators. This brought a howl of protest from Ustinov's supporters.

"You fight clean," Sheddy roared at Ustinov, "or we'll take over."

They let him go to resume his skipping and circling motion, me still curled up in torment. Now I got up on all fours and reached out to steady myself as I rose. But Ustinov came roaring in at me, yelling and lashing out a hail of punches that sent me to the ground again.

I heard Sheddy yelling out to Ustinov above the roar of the crowd, "You let Edwards get up properly next time, if he gets up, or I'll lay into you right now."

I got back onto my knees and hands again, staring through the mists of two eyes blocked with rapidly congealing blood and sand. My body was in anguish; it would be easier to stay down and let him win. But I couldn't, I just couldn't, I had to get up. I wiped more blood from around my eyes as I straightened. I could see vaguely through the haze. It was the moment Ustinov had seen coming. Now he would finish me off.

But, a split second before his fists made contact I ducked low, my arms went out once more in a claw as I wrapped them around his body. I intended to bowl him over backwards, get astride and try again to end it with my fists. However, he had been charging me and had the momentum. As my arms wrapped round him, my feet went from under and I was carried on to my back with him all over me. Sheer luck had me in the ideal position as Sheddy's wrestling training cut in. I instantly wrapped my legs around him. In a flash my ankles locked as I tensed to hold him in a scissor grip. At the same moment I wrapped my left arm around his neck and had him in a neck lock.

I squeezed my legs and arms like I've never squeezed before. My back arched off the ground as I put all the force I could muster into both grips. As I did this, all I was aware of was the agony of pain, of the noise from cheering, of insects; of blood thumping in my veins, of a vision so blurred I could see little but colours and stars. I was being punched by Ustinov, as he lashed out with his fists at my un-giving grips. I knew his legs were thrashing around as he tried to get some purchase where he could force himself free, so that I would let go.

I don't know when or even if I would have let him go. The crowd roared approval, yet through it all I was vaguely aware of Sheddy's voice shouting, "Let him go, Tony, he's trying to give in. He can't breathe. You'll kill him, man; he can't breathe."

But I would not. Even though Ustinov's flailing gradually stopped and he was no longer punching me, never was I going to let go so he could start up again and finish me.

And then I was shocked to feel my legs being unlocked, torn apart from the ankle lock. My one hand gripping my other wrist as I held the neck lock, was being undone! What sort of super human strength did Ustinov have? How could he do this?

As my limbs were prized apart, I realised it was not Ustinov doing it. I was giving ground to arms much stronger than mine. Prefects Neil Thomson and Pete Gemmell had happened on the scene and intervened. With their greater strength, they undid my grip on Ustinov and pulled us apart.

"You crazy fools!" yelled Neil. "What'n hell do you think you're doing? Are you trying to kill each other?"

I struggled to get at Ustinov, but Neil held me like a vice and wouldn't let go.

"It's over," he shouted into my face, then at Ustinov as he, badly winded and being supported from total collapse by Gemmel, gasped for breath, wheezing noisily through his wind pipe. We glowered at each other.

"It's over, do you hear me! Get back to your house at once; Shed, make sure he cleans up. It looks like I'll have to take you to Matron, Edwards, but get the worst of the blood off you first. I don't know what she's going to say. You'd better expect big trouble when Mr. Moore comes to hear of this.

Turning to Ustinov's now subdued crowd, he yelled, "You lot from Nightingale, get this idiot back to your Matron straight away; go on, get out of here!"

They sullenly slinked off.

I cleaned up the worst of the blood before Neil came to my room and took me to Matron's house. She was shocked at the sight of me.

"Oh my God, not another fight?"

I could barely see her through my swollen eyes. By now I was having repercussions from the exertion. My chest was heaving. An asthma attack seemed imminent. Matron went to her bathroom cabinet and reached for the dawa, while Neil called out telling her the story. I swallowed a pill and sat back as Matron fussed around, dabbing at my wounds with cotton wool and Dettol, muttering about stupid boys and their stupid fights. Then she said, "Thomson, go over to Mr. Moore's house and ask him to come over right away, please."

Mr. Moore, returning from staff dinner, was just parking his Jeep when Neil arrived. He accompanied Neil, walking in that stilted way that was his manner, dressed in evening grey flannels, cream shirt, light navy blazer and silk cravat, clasping his box of thirty cigarettes and a lighter in hand, listening as he went to the version of the fight according to Neil.

"What's this all about, Edwards?" he asked airily, after entering Matron's living room and lighting a State Express with his Dunhill as he did so. "I hear you've been fighting... who was it?"

"Ustinov, sir."

"Yes, Ustinov." Mr. Moore exhaled a cloud of smoky air. "What was that all about? You know I don't allow fighting in my house."

"He's in Nightingale, sir."

"I know he's in Nightingale, wretched boy, but you aren't. You're in Livingstone!"

"Yes, sir."

"So, what was it all about then?"

"Please, sir, I didn't want to fight, sir."

I went on to explain what had happened and why the fight had started which, in spite of my clout, wasn't really initiated by me or Ustinov but by the crowd, at least in my view.

"Hmmm, well, you seem to have given a good account of yourself, Edwards, I must say. He's tough and among the school's best boxers. From what Thomson tells me it appears as though he was trying to surrender, and you were at the point of winning, isn't that so?"

"I don't know, sir."

"Yees, well, anyway, what do you say, Matron, will he be all right? Doesn't need hospital, does he?"

"No, Mr. Moore, I don't think hospital's necessary, there's nothing broken. He'll heal all right."

"Hmmm. By rights I should ban you from attending the flick tomorrow night, but, I think we'll leave it at that. You've received punishment enough. Glad you beat him though. As long as Livingstone beats Nightingale, that's the main thing, what? Wouldn't you say so, Matron?"

With a disapproving harrumph forthcoming from Matron, Mr. Moore added, "Right then. I'll leave him in your most capable hands, Matron. I should keep him with you until his chest and breathing settle down again. Goodnight."

The flick that Mr. Moore referred to was *The Day the Earth Stood Still*, a winning science fiction film, starring Michael Rennie and Patricia Neal. It had completed the cinema circuit in Britain in 1951 or '52. There was no cinema building in Kongwa anymore. There had been one, open to the stars that had existed near the club, back in the day of the Groundnut Scheme. Somehow it had burned down and never been replaced. In fact Doug told me about it once. He'd heard about it from Glynn Ford. The cinema was surrounded by some form of corrugated, solid fencing that blocked the view from ground level to anyone who hadn't paid. But the cinema was right next to a baobab tree. Glynn and friends would climb the tree from which they could overlook the screen and enjoy films, especially those supposedly banned to children. In any event, the school did, once or twice a term, put on a movie evening, with a sixteen-millimetre version of a feature that could be projected on the school's Bell & Howell. The buzz was that this picture was not to be missed.

Like most others I'd been on my best behaviour, at least until this fight, as it was known teachers would use a film show or a fête to impose the punishment of not being allowed to attend. We'd rather be caned than miss a great bioscope and from time to time, when we were given the choice, we always elected the caning. I had already missed one flick on a previous occasion, when I hadn't been given the choice – *Shayne*, a super cowboy film I was told. My friends talked about it for weeks afterwards.

The Day the Earth Stood Still held us spellbound, even if I was watching it through partially closed eyes, and no more so than when the film broke at a crucial moment, followed by a collective groan.

Our film evenings were also held under the stars. A huge screen was erected earlier in the day, attached outdoors to a classroom building. It seemed like it might comprise a dozen or more bed sheets strung taught between the four sides of a frame. The entire thing was lashed to the veranda posts. During the afternoon, prefects directed boys into carting classroom chairs outside and setting them in rows; the boys one side of a central aisle, the girls the other. During the progress of the flick that night, the aisle would take on a life of its own. Its width became narrower and narrower as the boys on one side and the girls on the other edged their chairs towards each other. Whenever there was a film break and the lights went on and of course at the end of the film, there was a frantic scraping of chairs back to their former locations lest any teachers should happen to spot any errant would-be lovers holding hands.

Doug often managed to be the 'Lights Operator.' What that meant was that he would be posted at classroom light switches all evening, to operate them, their spill being the only light available for the outside. So, during a film break, the call would go out for, "Lights! Lights, please, someone turn on the lights."

At a later time, Doug would have his girlfriend along with him. She was not a boarder because she lived with her teacher parents and therefore not subject to keeping the company of other girls after school hours. By keeping it discreet, he got away with this, although he nearly gave the game away on one occasion by not being responsive when the call for "Lights!" was made!

✦ ✦ ✦

ALTHOUGH I ALWAYS WANTED A KASUKU, I never seemed to find the materials to build a cage, or maybe I didn't know how. Finding materials, and nailing them together, using retrieved bent nails from Kongwa's dust and using a rock as a hammer, both to straighten out the nails and then to hammer the cage together, required a talent that was not mine. That's why the best I could have, was to enjoy Sheddy's birds. It turned out though that fate had a plan.

It was a week before the end of term when Sheddy announced he would not be returning to school. I was stunned. He was my best friend. I couldn't believe he was leaving to move back to England and he would not be returning to Africa.

"Oh no, Sheddy, that's terrible. You're my best friend, man."

"Me too, Tony, I'm sorry. But there's one good thing. I'm not allowed to take my kasukus to England because of six months quarantine. That's expensive and my dad won't pay for it, so there's no point in taking them home to Dar either. I know you've always wanted parakeets, so if you like, you can have my two."

"Wow, Sheddy, that's super. I mean, I really don't want you to go and all; I'd much rather you stayed here, but if you have to go then I'd be really glad to look after them for you. But what will I do for a cage?"

"You'll have mine, of course. What will I do with the cage and no birds in it? You get the birds, the cage and the nesting box. It'll all be yours. You can take them home to Lindi, can't you, I mean, on the plane and all?"

"I don't know. I s'pose so. They'll jolly well have to let me. I can't leave them in the airport. I'm sure they can find a spot somewhere on the plane, behind the passengers at the back near the bathroom maybe. Oh I don't know, we'll see. Golly, Sheddy, thanks a lot, man."

Wow. Not only was I soon to be the owner of Sheddy's kasukus but his cage too. Everyone knew Sheddy's cage was the best.

In future terms I would sometimes take these kasukus to class with me. We weren't supposed to of course but, as long as they didn't chirp we could get away with it by keeping the birds tucked into our shirts. Although my birds never cheeped in class, I did run into a bit of trouble with the chaplain once. Because the school had expanded so much, we no longer traipsed up Church Hill for Sunday service but congregated in the school gym instead, boys one side of the aisle, girls the other. I had my head bowed, praying for forgiveness for a whole raft of new transgressions, when one of my kasukus took advantage of a buttonhole in my shirt having come undone. Before I realised what was happening, the flightless kasuku hopped from his hiding place and landed with a thump and a squeak on the floor between my feet. Even as I hastily reached down to catch him, he ran off ahead of me under the thickly-packed pews so that I was powerless to retrieve him. For a few moments I did nothing, hoping he would remain under the pews and I would catch him after the service. But no. Firstly, a huge flock of wild kasukus flew overhead, as ever chirping their little hearts out. This set off mine who instantly began chirping back. The chaplain, in the middle of his sermon, paused; not knowing if he'd heard - inside his church - what he thought he'd heard. Moments later, my kasuku cleared the front pew and was now in the open, running as fast as his little legs would carry him, towards the chaplain and the alter beyond, chirping all the while. As the chaplain gazed down, eyes fixed on the journey of the small kasuku, it ran between his legs and up to the alter under which it stopped and chirped all the louder. The pupils of the school were all looking at each other, exchanging glances and smirks, and wondering whose kasuku had escaped and therefore who was going to be in trouble. The sermon came to a pause. The chaplain looked over his flock, mainly the boys' part of the flock, and wanted to know to whom the errant kasuku belonged. After a pause, with nudges from colleagues left and right to own up, I tentatively got to my feet, looking suitably ashamed and said, "He's mine, sir."

The chaplain gave me the curling finger, come hither routine. As I squeezed past my colleagues and approached him the chaplain uttered, "Retrieve same."

A moment later I was on hands and knees, grovelling under the alter chasing a kasuku trying not to be caught. But I out-foxed him. Hand high over his head, finger pointed at the kasuku, I swivelled my hand rapidly on its wristly axis, so that the kasuku would not know which direction I was coming from, and therefore which way to run. As I did this I dropped my hand in a pounce. Gathering up the little creature cupped in two hands I returned to my feet and looked at the chaplain for instructions.

"You may leave the church," he said, "and wait outside until the end of the service."

I hadn't been enjoying his sermon anyway.

CHAPTER FOURTEEN

FIGHTING ON

M Y LONG HOLIDAY HOME DURING THE COOLER months of 1955 had been marred by thoughts of returning to Kongwa. What with fights, teasing, bullying, canings and being made a fool of, my self confidence was at an all-time low. To me, school was little better than torture and it was no surprise that my marks, which had been so high when I arrived from England, were dropping and my ranking lower. I wanted to persuade Mum and Dad that I would be better off staying in Lindi, and getting educated some other way, but this would have involved revealing too much about Kongwa that I couldn't do. It would have amounted to sneaking, and if they took up issues with the school it would get out and be the worse for me. I knew too that Sheddy would not be returning.

Then there was the issue of our house prefect. We'd known there would be changes, because some chaps had left, parents moving back to England, the Rhodesias or Southern Africa, as well as new boys. I guessed Koos Groenberg would be our house prefect and I dreaded it. Last term, Pete Gemmell had departed school early and for good. At that time, shortly before the end of term, Koos had moved into our house in promotion as the relief prefect. Koos was a cruel bastard, who had somehow achieved prefect status, no one knew why. He was not even liked by his own age group. His cruelty we'd been warned about was soon evident, although it was tempered by there being a Senior prefect already in place, Brian Marriott and the fact that there'd been only two weeks of term left.

We arrived on the *Kongwa Special* at 2 a.m. We were taken directly to our houses and told to get to sleep. No midnight snack. My worst fear was confirmed. Koos was our only house prefect this term, with no second, because Marriott had been moved. That meant there would be no one to cool down the mood when he got rough.

Within a day of our return, Koos picked on Alan Alder who became his first fag. Perhaps he selected Alder, who was an assertive if non-aggressive sort, because he was a tough and determined little bugger. Maybe Koos had ideas about knocking him into shape.

"Alder," he bellowed from his prefects' room, "come 'ere!"

But Alder resisted, pretending not to hear and slipped out the door before Koos could see him. When there was no response Koos went roaring down the corridor to Alder's bed, bellowing his name and roughly pushing others aside if they were in his way. When Alder was eventually caught up with, Koos dragged him back to his prefects' room, firmly grasping him by the ear and shove him.

"Polish my fuckin' shoes!" he shouted. "I want to see my face in them like a fuckin' mirror."

On some occasions, Alder, not always known for his better judgment on matters like this, would protest. "I already polished your shoes yesterday, man. There's no need to polish them again today. I can just dust them off, man."

From both ends of the corridor we'd hear the ringing clout across his face, usually followed by an equally loud back hand across the other cheek. "Polish my fuckin shoes!"

Sooner or later it would be my turn to be his fag, and it wasn't long coming.

"Edwards!"

"Yes, Koos."

"Where the fuck are you?"

"I'm here, Koos," I said, as I appeared nervously at his doorway.

"Is there anyone in the bath?"

"Yes, Koos," I said. "Gunston is in the bath with Priestly."

"Tell them to get the fuck out. I want a bath now; you go fetch the hot

water, and make sure it's hot. I want at least three pail-fulls brought through...
tell me when the bath's ready."

"Yes, Koos."

I told Gunston and Priestly they'd better get out in the next few seconds,
then I went to the boiler. *Thank goodness*, I thought, *at least the water's hot.*

I filled the pail, carried it indoors and poured it into the quickly emptied
tub, then went back for a second pail. As I approached the bathroom the
third time, Priestley, who'd been helping himself to a drink from the filter
in the corridor, turned as I staggered in and we bumped each other causing
a small splash. At the same moment, Koos emerged from his room calling,
"Edwards, what's happening with my fuckin' bath?"

He set eyes on me and Priestley as we straightened from our collision,
and saw the splashed water on the floor.

"What the hell's wrong with you two? You can't walk straight without
bumping into each other? Look at the mess you've made. Get into my room
the both of you and wait until I've had my bath."

Priestley and I stood for a while looking at each other helplessly, then sat
on the spare bed, then stood up again, not knowing what to do with ourselves
and speculating about the fuss he was going to make. We guessed we were
going to be hit. No chap hung around Koos's room unless he was going to be
hit. Koos finished bathing and came strutting down the corridor, towel around
his waist. He came to his room, us both standing there, undid his towel and
stood naked as he finished drying himself.

"What am I gonna to do with you two squirts?" he asked. "Spilling water
and making a mess. Why didn't you clean it up!?"

"Because you told us to wait in your room, Koos."

"Don't give me any of your lip," he yelled as he pulled on his khaki
shorts with cuffs upturned to make them even shorter. "Wait here!"

Koos strutted back down the corridor, folding his wet towel into a tight
cone with the material at an angle so that it ended up as a thick handle on one
end and a pointed tip on the other. He wetted the tip under the tap in the basin,
squeezed it, and then returned to his room.

"Okay, Priestley, drop your towel and bend over."

Priestley did as he was told and bent over, exposing his bum to Koos
while touching his toes. Koos then used a toweled whiplash that he was all
too proficient at, to create a burning sting on Priestley's behind as he flicked

the wet tip like a whip. It could be agonizing when he caught the flick just right and exceptionally sore afterwards, much more so than when he used his slops to beat us. The skin of Priestley's bum went bleach white. For a moment, I swear I could see a deep skin indentation, then a burning, purple red replaced the white as Koos brought the towel back once more in another deft flick of his wrist.

"Uhh…" Priestley stifled a yell. Then a third snap from the towel caused him to straighten halfway. He dared not fully straighten or it would be the worse for him and he knew it. So somehow he returned to the bent over position.

"Okay, now you, Edwards. Priestley, you stand over here and watch Edwards just like he watched you."

And so I was 'whipped' with the towel too, all for the accidental splash of water on the concrete floor that we wiped up while our bums were still burning.

It may have been a week later, when I was having a squabble with Aranky in the corridor. I don't know if Koos had been trying to nap, or was reading or what but he came storming out his room, "What the fuck's all the noise about?"

He laid eyes on Aranky and me, "Oh, beating up Edwards, are you, Aranky, is that what's going on? Well, carry on then, don't let me stop you," he said, his lips curling in his cruel smirk.

But the squabble was over and neither of us wanted to go further.

"What's the matter, Aranky, can't you beat up Edwards? I'm waiting. I want to see this, Aranky… Now!"

"It's over, Koos. It was just an argument, we weren't really fighting."

"It's over when I say it's over, Aranky. Edwards, beat him up. That's what you were doing, wasn't it? Finish it off."

"But Aranky's right, Koos. It's over, it was nothing."

"Listen, you two little fucks," he spat. "I'll tell you when it's over. Now here's what you're gonna do. Aranky, you're going to hit Edwards about the head. And Edwards, you're going to hit him back. Every time one of you hits the other, you're going to retaliate. I'll tell you when it's over! And if you don't do it right now, you little pricks," Koos hissed, "I'll do it for you. Do I make myself clear? You hit each other or I'll hit you both and it will be a lot harder, I promise you."

After further hesitation Aranky clouted me across the face.

"Harder than that, jong! Edwards, hit him back."

So I clouted Aranky back, harder, to satisfy Koos and get it over with. But that upset Aranky because he now clouted me back, much harder than the first time.

Now I was upset. Why'd he have to hit me that hard?

So I hit Aranky again, even harder. The sting brought tears to his eyes.

I thought, *Now I'm going to get it.*

But suddenly it was over. "Okay, you little fucks, get outa here, get outa my way. I don't want to hear another squeak from either of you again this afternoon or you'll be getting it from me. Are we clear?"

I WAS AT THE HOUSE WHILE MOST were at sports. It was a relief to know there'd be no trouble from Koos 'til bath time. All the same I was deeply depressed. I wandered out to inspect the geraniums; they hadn't been watered while I was on hols, and were now recovering. But even as I poured water around them, I began blubbing, to be startled with the unexpected arrival of Mrs. Moore, our Matron this year.

"Whatever is the matter, Edwards?" she asked in her kindly way. "Have you hurt yourself?"

"No, Matron," I replied as I turned away, attempting to wipe away tears before she saw them.

"Well, something seems to be wrong. Whatever can it be?"

"It's school, Matron."

"What about school?"

The voice in my head screamed: *Tell her about Koos!*

"This school... I hate it."

"Oh dear," said Matron. "I'm sorry to hear that. What don't you like?"

"Everything!"

Tell her about Koos! the voice screamed again.

"I just hate it," I said. "You just don't understand how much I hate it. I hate it here, I don't want to be here, I want to live at home, not in this terrible place."

"Well, it can't be all that bad," said Matron. "What about your friends and the fun times you have?"

Realising I was talking to a grown-up who just didn't understand, and to whom I was forbidden to confess because of schoolboy lore, my emotions rose to a crescendo. I don't know what triggered it exactly, but I was spitting venom.

"I just hate this school," I yelled at her, fixing my narrowed eyes on hers as though it was her fault. "I loathe this school. I haven't got any friends. I don't want to be here. No one will ever make me like this terrible place!" I shouted, tears welling and building to a climax. I screamed, "No one! It's ghastly, it's horrible and I hate it! I hate it! I hate it!"

My passion was so incensed that Matron must have decided that she didn't know how to handle this, saying only, "Well, I'm sorry to hear that, Edwards, but I'm sure you'll feel better later on," and then hurried along, leaving me to my misery.

✦ ✦ ✦

RELIEF COULD COME IN STRANGE FORMS. ONE evening as we returned from dinner wondering what sort of misery Koos would inflict this evening, and on whom, as we approached our back doors, Berry and I came to a startled halt. The light had been left on and was flooding the stoep through the open doors. There on the concrete was a carpet of bugs, each about twice the size of a ladybird.

"Oh jeepers, look at that," cried Berry. "Stink bugs. Squash just one of them and you'll make a terrible stink."

I stared, awestruck, at a stink bug carpet; there were no spaces between them; they covered every inch of the floor indoors, under our beds, everywhere.

"Stink bugs?" I exclaimed, not having seen them before. "Those are stink bugs?"

"Yes, they are. And you'd better not squash any," Berry repeated, "if you don't want to stink us out. Look – the bedroom floor is covered with them."

From around the front, we heard shouts from others who'd found the same thing, except in their case, they'd not the chance to see them before they entered.

Lister Hannah had been walking with Coen Compaan. Hearing the news from the boys at the front, they'd come round to see if things were as bad on our side.

"Y'se got bugs in ya room like they've got in the front?" he asked.

"They're all over the place," I responded. "There's not a spare bit of space between them. It's impossible to go in without squashing dozens, maybe hundreds."

"Better grab Matron," Hannah suggested. "Struth, this ain't sumthin y'd clean up by y'self. Back home this happened to us once in me ol' man's humpy up in the hills and we had to sweep the flamin' joint out with a bloody broom 'n' a shovel."

By now there were dozens of squashed stink bugs, and the odour was wafting about. We withdrew, as did the others, and someone ran off to fetch Matron.

Minutes later Mrs. Moore arrived. "Stand back all of you," she called as she approached. She was clutching two brooms with a mop tucked under an arm. We could see Mr. Moore not far behind bearing similar weapons. Most of the clean-up took place from the rear stoep, because we could see what we were doing. Also, we could clean off the stoep before moving indoors.

"Starve the flamin' lizards, mate, what a bloody pong," said Hannah. "Y'se'll never get rida that flamin' mob in a helluva hurry."

No matter the drama at hand, Matron was not one to let anyone get away with speaking poor English.

"I've told you before, Hannah, we expect you to speak properly in this school. They may talk like that in Australia but we are not in Australia. While you are here you will speak the Queen's English, please."

"Yair, righto, Matron, woteva ya reckon's a fair thing."

Matron rolled her eyes.

"Edwards, take this broom and work your way from the side. Don't squash them, whatever you do, just gently sweep them sideways from the stoep onto the ground. Once the stoep is clear, you can repeat the action from the indoors. After you've done some, let Berry help. Now, I must check on the rest of the houses."

As I swept, Koos returned. I glanced up when he first arrived, and saw his mouth open to ask what the fuck was going on, just looking for trouble. But, for a change, he closed it again without saying anything. He seemed to take in the scene and thought on it.

"Do Matron and Mr. Moore know about this?" he asked.

"Yes, Koos, they brought brooms and a mop. I think she's sharing them across the houses, because she said she was going off to check on the others."

"Hmm, well, keep sweeping, man, and don't squash any more of those fuckers than you have to. When you get indoors, I want you, Edwards, to make it your personal responsibility to see to it that there's no bugs, not one, left in my room, is that understood?"

"Yes, Koos."

"Good. I'm going to find Matron."

And with that he disappeared off towards the second house.

When I'd finished the stoep Berry said, "Here let me have a turn." He deftly continued the sweeping of bugs, now from the bedroom onto the stoep, so, gradually space was opened up for us to step indoors, without squashing them. Even so, the bugs emitted their awful stink. It was rank and nauseating and we were supposed to be getting ready for bed.

It took two hours to clear every last bug out of our house, so it was gone eleven before we got to bed with the rank odour still wafting around.

Berry thought it a good time, seeing as we were so wide awake, to ask me to tell a story. I forget how it started, but a term or two back someone found out I was a good storyteller. Since then, my roommates would, from time-to-time, ask me to tell them a tale when we went to bed. I suppose my stories helped them sleep, so that wasn't encouraging. But still, I enjoyed doing it and was happy to give it a whirl. It was a hazardous pastime though. With Koos as our prefect, there'd be severe punishment for talking after lights-out if I was caught, so I would speak in subdued tones.

The stories were always dramatic, action adventures. The heroes were me and my bedroom friends, as well as others from Livingstone but occasionally included boys from other houses, like Pepsi. We were usually holed up in a jungle fortress modelled after one of those of US cavalry fame. The impenetrable jungle made for Tarzan-style transport to get us around. The enemy was adults, who would find our fortress to be a threat to life and liberty as they knew it. The result was, they were constantly attacking us to put an end to our breakaway regime. By happenstance we were better fighters than they so that, bleeding and bloodied, we invariably triumphed.

CHAPTER FIFTEEN

BATTERED HERO

PEPSI AND I WERE CLOSE THESE DAYS, especially with Sheddy gone. In fact, Doug became my new best friend who, although I didn't know it then, would remain so for long after school days. We spent a lot of time together, especially since he'd brought his bike and was more mobile. It was a wartime paratrooper's. Its claim to fame, aside from being painted in army camouflage, was that it unbolted at the crossbar and at the head tube on the frame so that, by loosening two fly nuts, in one deft movement the bike could be folded in half. It was an uncomfortable crossbar to ride, due to the butter-fly nut located at a tactically inopportune place, but still, riding crossbar was faster than walking, if you didn't have a bike of your own.

Doug seemed to enjoy a charmed life, compared to me. Not only did he have a bike but the house he was in, Wilberforce, was, by all accounts, a happier environment. No bullying. He had me amazed at some of what he got away with. His parents had groomed him on how to get what you want from the world. In this case it involved being given money quite regularly. Perhaps they shouldn't have; we were not supposed to carry any more money than our one shilling a week pocket money allowance provided for, but for him, that's the way it was. So he was able to bribe their 'house boy' into ensuring there was always plenty of hot water for his bath and to perform other duties that might be asked for. The 'boys' that served the food in the mess were reliably tipped resulting in any number of extra treats for both Doug and his immediate table mates. Life for him was easier.

And for us, breaking bounds to disappear for an hour or two of freedom was something we just did. Exploring in the bush, with no adults around and no one knowing where we were, was exhilarating. When we had less time to spare, we might cycle to Kongwa village to buy sweets or a drink. True, there was tuck day. We queued at our Housemaster's house to collect our weekly one-shilling allowance, then made the trek to the classrooms, where was set up the tuck shop. It was an ad hoc assembly in the reading library on Thursday afternoons when a variety of sweets were laid out on tables. Depending upon how early or late you were in the queue, there was more or less to choose from by the time you got indoors. Which is why the village became our recourse for additional rations. The Indian shopkeepers were happy for our patronage and, we bet, would never report us. After all, we made for extra sales. We would approach the village with great caution as teachers and other European adults who might be shopping, knowing it was out of bounds, would have reported us and that would have resulted in four cuts. I was never caught doing this; however, on one particular occasion on my way there, I was to get more cuts, if of a different kind, than I would have bargained for.

Doug was supposed to be playing cricket, but he'd sloughed off and, arriving on his bike, found me not too far from the large baobab tree, practicing nyabs by myself. I had lost too many marbles to others, especially Alder and Russell who never seemed to mind playing with me. I gradually worked out why and decided I needed to improve my game.

"Hey, Pepsi, shouldn't you be at cricket?" I greeted him as he dismounted.

"Oh, they never put me in to bat," he said, leaning his bike against the baobab. "All I do is sit around the table, mostly told to keep score. Well, they can get someone else for that. How about you, I thought you were at Scouts this afternoon?"

"I should be," I replied, "but we had to cancel because Mr. Brownlow had a bit of an emergency or something and rushed off to Dodoma."

"How's the Scouting anyway? Is it fun?"

"Yes, it is. It's a pity you're not in it, Peps. With your know-how you'd probably be the chief Scout."

"Neah, that's not me. It's too organised."

"I've learned a helluva lot, you know. My tracking is pretty good and

I'm okay with knots and all that. The best part is the field trips. Camping and getting into the bush is great. I'm working to become a troop leader. That'll be really mushee."

"Uh huh."

"And Mr. Brownlow treats us like grown-ups. He says Scouts are that responsible, so why would he treat us any other way. So what shall we do then? Want to climb the tree?" I asked.

"Neah."

"How about Snake Rock?"

"Neah, I'd rather go to the village."

"The village? That's miles away, we haven't got time," I responded, frowning at my watch. "It's late now; close to bath time."

"We can make it if we hurry."

"But I haven't got any money."

"I have. I've got enough for a couple of Cokes. Let's go?"

"But we haven't got long enough, man. To get to the village and back in time will mean cycling at top speed. We won't have a chance to approach slowly and make sure there're no teachers there. If we're caught it'll mean four cuts."

"I know," said Doug, "but my bet is there won't be. It's late now and they'll also be getting ready for dinner. I'm sure if they wanted to shop, they'll have done it by now. You'll see; there'll only be Africans and Indians."

"Well, all right," I sighed resignedly. "I hope you're right."

I turned my bum to the crossbar, making sure to miss the butterfly nut. Then Doug swung up behind and kicked off.

Kongwa Hill's slope appeared gentle enough until you were riding a bike, or worse its crossbar – then you knew how uneven the ground was. Doug peddled hard, straining to cycle his gearless bike with double the load. The handlebars wavered as he sought to balance and pick up speed. Before long, we descended into a small, dry rivulet at great speed in order to get momentum for the other side without dismounting. Soon we met the road to the village and stayed on that for a while, in spite of my cautions that a car could come along at any moment. In fact, the road proved worse than the paths, with its corrugations deep enough to shake a tank apart.

Then Doug steered onto a pathway through the high and dried-out yellow grasses. I watched as the front tyre spun over this hard-baked surface, mesmerised briefly by the red sand rushing underneath, the twisting and turn-ing as the front wheel steered to avoid rocks or clusters of acacia thorns or around the msasa trees. The increasing wind in my face, warm though it was, carried sand specks that were getting into the eyes.

It was taking too long.

"We're going to run out of time, Peps. The village will close and we'll never get back for our baths."

"Neah, we'll do it." And with that, letting caution to the winds, Doug peddled faster than ever as we raced for the village, ahead in the shimmering haze. The path weaved and wound, the curves really too steep for our speed. We'd swerve to avoid a large rock, yet another rivulet, down an incline, up the other side that turned in the middle of the rise. Faster Doug peddled, faster, faster.

Normally I never got nervous riding the bike with Doug. No one had the need to cycle this fast, and certainly Doug never did. And then I felt this premonition of disaster.

"Pepsi, we're going too fast. Ease off, man, or we're going to crash."

"Neah, we're fine, we'll soon be there."

I muttered to myself, "We're not going to make it, I can just feel it, we're not going to make it – Pepsi, please!"

Doug sloughed off my warning. "The dukas will close if we don't get there soon."

Even with the high grasses I could see the turn ahead would be too tight. If we didn't make it we'd be off into those grasses and then you couldn't see the surface and who knows what we'd hit. I gritted my teeth and clung on.

We reached the curve and Doug steered hard, leaning us far over to the right as we attempted to follow the path. As we rounded the corner the grasses gave way to an open space of rock-hard sand, covered with a wide-spread collection of loose boulders and large rocks. Too late – we couldn't avoid a collision.

We'll never be able to steer around them! flashed through my mind.

Instead Doug tried to avoid the rocks by going into a controlled, rear wheel skid that would alter our direction. As we completed the corner on the thin, loose sand, Doug lost control, probably because of my extra weight. We spun wildly, collided with a pile of boulders, and came a right cropper, with me thrown through the air before landing on my face.

I was disappointed at first. I didn't hurt and hadn't been knocked out. What was I going to say to the chaps? It would never make as good a story if I couldn't tell them I'd been knocked out. I lay there in a daze, slowly becoming conscious of the sun shining in my eyes and swearing coming from Doug's mouth. Maybe I'd been knocked out after all and was just coming to?

And then the pain set in.

"#!+**&% Christ! Tony, are you all right? Oh my God, Tony, say something! Wake up! Wake up! Say something! Wake up, man! God, you're a mess, get up, c'mon, wake up, man. C'mon, get up, we gotta get back. C'mon, quick! God, you look terrible."

I began to focus but my next thoughts were only of the trouble we'd be in if it was known we were out of bounds.

"We mustn't say where this happened, Pepsi, all right?" I groaned. "We'll just say we were out riding near the houses, if anyone asks."

"Okay, Tony, don't worry about that right now."

"Maybe we can clean up, so there won't be any awkward questions."

We retraced our journey, limping, tripping and me nearly collapsing with Doug supporting me in case I did. His one knee was hurt badly, but he showed no concern for himself, being much more concerned about me. I didn't know why. I couldn't see myself, although I was aware of the dripping blood from my face and the rough and raw soreness that I didn't dare touch. We arrived back on the road at the edge of bounds, the wrong side of the manyara hedge, before we saw a soul. As we drew level with the Wilberforce houses, two boys on the road, chasing a nyoka in the fading light, looked up as we approached. As they caught sight of me, the one exclaimed, "Jeez, Edwards, what happened? You have an accident?"

Brilliant question.

"You'd better get to Matron, man."

Darkness descended fast. We were becoming enveloped in its shroud, being dive bombed by bats and aware of the aroma coming from the open cooking fires of a close-by kijiji.

The first Matron, the one for Wilberforce house, was not at home when we knocked, so we kept moving another fifty yards. Then we knocked on the door of Doug's Housemaster. He opened the door and stared at me, mouth agape and shock in his eyes. We could see behind him that he was entertaining. He and his guests, who approached to take a closer look at this apparition after his exclamation of shock, were horrified at the sight of my wounds. But they did not take us in. Instead we were ordered to my Housemaster.

"I'm off duty now," Mr. Hobbs explained. "You both need to go along to Mr. Moore's house. He's on duty today."

Another several hundred yards to walk! I felt dismayed we would be sent on our way because the adults were having guests. We returned to the road, skipping by Livingstone so we wouldn't be gaped at. Many houses further on, we passed by the unused Matron's house, leaving another fifty yards to Mr. Moore's driveway. I felt my legs giving way as shock set in. I slowed to little more than a stumble of one foot ahead of another. The last glimmer of light had gone. Darkness had descended.

"C'mon," urged Doug, his arm around my shoulder, encouraging me along, "C'mon, man."

I felt faint and nauseous, my head swimming.

Mr. Moore opened the door in response to Doug's urgent knock. He and his wife, our Matron, also had company. As he opened his door, the brilliant light from his living room fell on us standing there against the black backdrop of the night. He took one look and exclaimed aloud, "Oh - my - God!"

Mrs. Moore and house guests started up from their chairs in fearful response, and huddled around Mr. Moore in the doorway, to find out what had drawn his exclamation. As they did so, they drew deep breaths of shock as they set eyes on me, the ladies with hands to mouths.

"Mummy, Mummy! Judi's taken Puffy and won't give her back," little Stephanie cried as she came trotting round the corner from the other end.

Mrs. Moore turned to her youngest, "Please return to your room, Steve. I'll be back to sort it out in a minute, now go, please!"

"What's wrong with him?" Steve asked pointing at me.

"Did you hear me, young lady?" rebuked Mrs. Moore. "Go to your room."

"Come on in," she said, turning back to us. "Let's take a closer look and see what we can do to clean you up. Come on inside."

"How did you do this?" from the lady guest.

"Bike accident, miss," Doug replied.

"Where?"

"Just along the road a little way."

"Edwards looks in a terrible state, I'm not sure we can do this," said one.

"You're quite right," said Mrs. Moore. "Maurice, I think you should take Edwards to the hospital immediately, do you agree?"

"Yes, my dear, I do. Come, Edwards, follow me to the car. Can you manage? Here, let me help you."

"Now, what about you, Westley. You've cut your knee?"

"Yes, miss, it's pretty sore."

"I think we can fix you up here. Come into the bathroom. Excuse me," she said to her guests, "while I attend to Westley. So sorry about this. If you don't mind entertaining yourselves for a bit until I've looked after him and Maurice returns."

Mr. Moore rushed me to hospital in his Jeep, and drew to a quick halt outside reception. An African nurse, in white cap and apron, came running out at the sound of urgency, referring us hastily to three doors along. There we found three European nurses on duty, relaxing in their common room, enjoying a smoke and a chinwag when we walked in. They stubbed out their cigarettes as they came bustling forward.

"Oh my goodness, what have we here?" exclaimed Sister, the Senior Nurse, who put her arm around my shoulder, saying, "Come with me," as she escorted me along the corridor to the infirmary, leaving Mr. Moore standing.

"Nurse Pierce," she called over her shoulder, "call the Doctor on duty, who is it? Doctor Fallworth," she answered her own question, "and ask him to come to the hospital immediately."

"Yes, Sister."

"And stress this is an emergency."

"Yes, Sister."

"Nurse Roberts."

"Yes, Sister."

"Let's start cleaning him up right away. I want him ready by the time Doctor Fallworth arrives."

"Yes, Sister."

Taking directions from Sister, Nurse Roberts bustled away, leaving me staring at the Iron Lung machine, and thinking how horrible it would be to live in it. She quickly returned with a stainless kidney bowl containing cleaning swabs, and moved in on me.

"We want to clean you up, dear, while we're waiting for the Doctor. What's your name by the way?"

I looked at her through my swollen eyes and feeling of faintness, but still managed to be amazed at how lovely she looked.

"Edwards, nurse."

"And your Christian name?"

"Tony, miss."

"That's a good name; I suppose you're an Anthony, really? Called Tony for short, are you?"

"Yes, miss."

"Well, Tony, we'll soon have you looking better. This may hurt just a little. I'll be as gentle as I can, but the Doctor has to be able to see what he's dealing with all right, that's why we need to clean you up before he arrives." She started dabbing at my face with her swab.

"Uh, Ow…" I tried not to make a noise; I wanted to show this beautiful nurse I was tough.

"I'm sorry, sweetheart. Oops. Am I allowed to call you sweetheart, a strapping boy like you? Probably not, eh?"

"I don't mind, miss."

"There, that's looking better already. Now a little bit more here above this eye."

"Owwww…" And to myself, *Bloody hell, you idiot, keep quiet.*

While Nurse Roberts was attending me, Sister and Nurse Pierce hovered nearby, talking in hushed tones with Mr. Moore.

"What happened anyway? How did he come by this?"

"Bike accident, you know. Probably riding too fast, I shouldn't wonder. You know what boys are. Can't tell them anything. What do you think?"

"We can't say," said Sister. "It looks rough but it'll be up to the Doctor when he gets here. It may just look worse than it actually is."

Nurse Pierce said. "I think I know him. He's been here before, gets asthma, doesn't he?"

"You're quite right, Nurse," said Mr. Moore. "He has and he does. Doesn't seem to be any sign of it so far though, eh what?"

"No," responded Sister, "but we'd better be alert to that, just in case."

"What do we do for the asthma?"

"He gets adrenalin injections," replied Nurse Pierce.

Then Sister decided they shouldn't be discussing me within earshot, so she escorted Mr. Moore and Nurse Pierce outdoors.

I felt faintness coming over me and tumbled forward from my seat, but Nurse Roberts caught me before I could fall, and set me back in the chair.

"Here, I think it's better if you lie down on the bed, rather than sit in the chair, don't you?" she asked with her gorgeous smile as she patted the pillow and drew back the white sheet. She stood me up, arms around to support me, and guided me to lie down on the bed.

"Sister," she called over her shoulder, "he's quite weak and almost fainted again. Complaining of nausea. I've laid him on the bed. Do you think we should check for other injuries?"

"Yes, we should. He hasn't complained of anything specific, has he?"

"Only that he hurts all over, Sister, but no one thing."

"No? Well, check him anyway. Get his shirt and trousers off and do an inspection. Doctor will prefer that we've looked him over."

With that Nurse Roberts sat me up briefly then undid my shirt buttons as Sister helped slide it off.

"No vest?" asked Sister.

"No, we never wear underwear," I croaked. "Too hot."

I was laid down again, and then Nurse Roberts undid my fly buttons. I gazed intently through my haze at the ceiling, pretending nervously not to notice as I felt a slight stirring, and focussed on watching geckos playing catch-me-if-you-can with the mosquitoes that unwisely landed near them.

It had been happening to me and other boys in our house, this stirring in the nether regions. I'd be dreaming furiously and then wake suddenly in the night, finding myself wet. It wasn't just at night either, it would happen during the day, not all the time but enough that it could become embarrassing. A chap didn't want to walk around in front of all those dames with a bulge in his trousers. And yet, it happened and I couldn't stop it. Now I became more aware of the pungent, antiseptic smell that pervaded the room; it was almost like a perfume for me, with Nurse Roberts there.

"I'm just going to briefly slip down your khakis, Tony, all right? We can't afford to risk missing anything for the Doctor."

I grunted.

"Lift your bottom," she said.

I nodded vaguely, and then she pulled them down around my thighs.

I was stirring more! *Oh golly,* I thought, *how could this happen? I'm injured – this shouldn't be happening.* I stared harder than ever at the ceiling wishing the problem away.

"Hmm," said Nurse Roberts, with a knowing tone to her voice. "It seems there's nothing much wrong with this young man. I think he'll live, Sister."

"Indeed he will," confirmed Sister who had returned to the bedside to check on me. "There's no sign of any injury there, so that's good. He appears not to have suffered beyond scrapes and abrasions on his waist or legs either. Let's roll him over and check his back. Careful now, I'll hold his head so his face doesn't touch the pillow."

As I was rolled over, Nurse Roberts exclaimed, "What's this!? What are these lines on your back and your behind, Tony? They're not fresh, not from the accident?" she asked with concern in her voice.

Sister responded for me. "Looks like he received a caning not long ago."

"Oh you poor thing," said Nurse Roberts. "I can't imagine what terrible thing you did would justify leaving marks like that."

"It's not for us to comment on school discipline, Nurse," Sister asserted primly.

"It's not right. I don't believe he could have done anything to deserve this treatment."

"Nurse, did you hear me?"

Nurse Roberts did not respond.

"Nurse!" Sister insisted, "Did you hear me?"

"Yes, Sister, I heard you," she grumbled.

"Then we'll hear no more of it. Now, let's see, hmm… a few scrapes, bit of ruffled skin, but not much. Seems you really did, quite literally, land on your face, Edwards. I'm not sure if that improves you or not," she added with the suggestion of a chuckle, as she tried to get the tone back onto a lighter note.

"Come on, Nurse, let's roll him back again, and get his khakis back up, so he can recover his modesty."

I heard the sound of a car engine. The vehicle's headlights briefly lit the infirmary before being switched off.

"That'll be the Doctor now, Mr. Moore," said Sister who had returned to the veranda. "Do you want to wait for his prognosis or may we ring you?"

"I'll wait a little longer," said Mr. Moore. "He's one of my boys, you know. Need to know what state he's in. The Head is going to want to know as well. Is this something we need to telegram the parents about, that sort of thing."

"Very well," said Sister. "Perhaps now that the Doctor has arrived, you wouldn't mind being seated in the visitor's room. I know there's a newspaper there, arrived from Britain on the mail ship only a couple of months ago, so it's pretty current. We'll be out to let you know the Doctor's opinion, soon as we have news for you."

"Thank you very much, Sister. Thank you indeed."

The Doctor decided I'd live. "A break in your nose and some nasty deep cuts," he said. "Scratches and abrasions all over your face, and elbows, and such. We have a lot more cleaning up to do, Nurse, before we give him stitches. We're going to need to get in deeper. Edwards, Nurse Roberts will give you an injection in a moment. It's a sedative. I need to do a lot more cleaning and we don't want you to be in pain, see?"

I nodded.

"Oh, he's used to injections," chipped in Nurse Pierce, who had returned. "We've had him in here before, haven't we, Tony? He's pretty brave with adrenalin injections."

"Adrenalin? He's an asthmatic?"

"Yes, Doctor?"

"Now, I recognise you. I thought I'd seen you before. Bit difficult to tell with your current face, Edwards, ha ha...."

We've already had that joke, I thought.

"—Ahem, yes, well, all right, we must watch for that, Nurse. We don't want any asthma attacks on top of all this, do we?"

"No, Doctor."

After what seemed an age of cleaning the wounds and receiving thousands of stitches, the giving of anti-tetanus injections and jabs against septicaemia, and with, by now, most of my face covered in bandage but for one eye, I was given a further sedative and put to bed in the European ward.

When I awoke it was to familiar surroundings. After breakfast had been cleared and I with my head buried in a book, I became aware of a car arriving, followed by the chatter of people down the corridor. I thought I heard Douglas's voice but couldn't be sure. I got back to my reading. Later, the welcome sound of the lunch trolley being wheeled down the open concrete walkway came to my ears.

"Oh good, I'm so hungry."

As the kitchen assistant prepared to enter the ward with my lunch tray, she nearly collided with Douglas.

"I beg your pardon," he said politely, and held back to let the lady enter. She set the tray down on the table over my bed.

"There you go, dear," she said. "Hungry, are we?"

"Oh yes, miss, I can't wait for lunch. I'm famished."

"Hello, Tony," called Douglas. "How're you doing, man?"

I looked up in surprise.

"Who are you?" the lunch lady asked Doug inquisitively. "Are you a patient?" she asked, seeing him limp, and noticing the huge bandaging around one knee.

"Sort of. You see, we were both in this bike accident yesterday. My friend Tony was brought to the hospital last night, but I wasn't until this morning. They didn't know how serious my injury was to start with, so it's only today that I came down. I won't be staying overnight though."

"Would you like some lunch, dear? I have one or two spare plates just in case. You can sit here and eat with your friend, if you like."

"You should have some, Peps – the food's super."

"No, thanks, miss. My Housemaster brought me down so the Doctor could examine my knee. Now he wants to get back to school, so we can have lunch there. He let me call in for a quick visit with Tony, but I can't stop. Thanks all the same."

"All right, dear," and she was gone.

"How are you, man? What all happened? That is you under all those bandages?"

"Very funny, Peps. Yes, it's me, and I'm doing all right. Not too much pain now, thank goodness, but it was pretty rough last night, I can tell you."

I went on to tell Doug everything I could recall from the evening admission.

"The nurse undressed you?" he asked incredulously, this being Doug's area of greatest interest. "Wow, Tony, you lucky bastard."

"Shush, Peps, they'll hear you."

"And when the nurse was cleaning you up, did you, 'you-know'?"

"Yes, I did 'you-know'," I assured him. "It was very embarrassing actually. I'm supposed to be badly injured and that had to happen."

"Cor, Tony, you lucky sod. I hope you didn't leave her disappointed," he laughed.

"You should have seen her, Peps. She's off duty 'til tonight so you won't see her now, but she's a stunner."

"Some chaps get all the luck. Anyway, so what are you reading?"

The Colditz Story. I'm nearly halfway through it already. It's a great book about P.O.W.s escaping from Germany. They have more WWII books in the store room, if I want them. But anyway, why are you here? How's your knee, what happened?"

"It was pretty bad actually," replied Doug. "Mrs. Moore cleaned it up last night, but this morning my Matron took a look; she said it was worse than first thought, and needed looking at by a Doctor. So, anyway, the Doctor's examined it, cleaned it up even more, did some stitches, gave me an injection and some other dawa; I don't know what. He said my knee-cap was exposed to the bone! He thinks that, while we were crashing, the bike, and me and you were all spinning, sorta like a top, on my knee. The Doctor told Mr. Hobbs to tell Matron that it must be looked after very carefully, kept clean and all that stuff, because if we weren't careful I'd have trouble with it for the rest of my life."

"Wow, Peps, that sounds worse than me."

"Could be, I dunno, but listen, I have to get back, Mr. Hobbs is waiting. But we'll see you soon, eh? And leave nurse Roberts alone, all right, I want her." And with that he laughed as he limped from the ward and was gone.

Three days later, back at school, I was the hero for a while, for having survived such a bad accident. Wild stories had spread, about what exactly was supposed to have happened, including the weirdest version which had me with an iron bar through my nose. I was relieved to note however that no one even hinted that we might have been out of bounds.

CHAPTER SIXTEEN

SERIOUS CRICKET

"ANYONE WANT TO PLAY NYABS?" ASKED IVEY.

It was shortly after breakfast, on Saturday. We'd returned to change into cricket togs, and were off to the pitch. Constantinides, a new boy this term who occupied the bed next to me, replied for both of us, as I reached for the score book. "We don't have time, Ivey. Edwards's scoring for the match against Dodoma that's starting in half an hour, so we have to get going. It's too far to walk and play nyabs. Do you want to bring your camera, Edwards?"

"Oh, I didn't know they got you scoring, Edwards. Isn't that boring?" asked Ivey.

"No, I like scoring. I'm not often asked to do it for a big game, so it should be fun. And Graeme Maclean's captain of the school team."

"Well, it's about time Livingstone had something to do with the school team," Ivey smirked. "I'll come along with you. I've nothing on. I might watch the match, some of it anyway, don't know about all day."

"Let's go," said Constantinides

"I don't think I'll bring the camera now," I answered the earlier question. "I haven't got enough film to take pictures of cricket. I'd like you to take a photo of me dressed in uniform later on – or tomorrow maybe and p'raps one or two photos of the houses."

"Hey, chaps, may I join you? Where are you going?" Berry called after us.

"To watch Dodoma lick Kongwa at cricket," Ivey yelled back.

"Watch it, Ivey," I said with a smile. "We're one game each in the best of three. We're doing all right."

"I'll come with you – wait for me."

"That win of ours was luck and you know it," Ivey retorted. "Dodoma nearly always wins."

"We won one game, we can win another," Constantinides jumped in with support. "Don't count Kongwa out yet. I don't know much about cricket, but they say our team's a lot stronger this year."

As we walked, kicking stones and hunching ourselves against the swirling, sand-filled dust devils, we saw ahead several younger Seniors lobbing rocks up into a baobab tree. Its lowest limbs were spread just above the boys' heads. As we drew close, we saw them peering up, and others scouring the ground.

"What are you doing?" called Berry.

"Bees," one of them shouted back. "We're going to clobber that nest."

We glanced at the huge bee nest ten feet above their heads.

"Wembembe!" I exclaimed.

"Wembembe? What's wembembe?" asked Constantinides.

"Killer bees," I replied in alarm as, along with Berry and, without stopping to think, the two of us started running towards the boys.

"Are you crazy?" Berry shouted at them. "Don't touch the nest! Leave them alone! They'll kill you!"

"Come away from there!" I yelled. "Those bees are super dangerous."

But the first couple of boys hadn't heard the warning cry and had lobbed more rocks up at the nest, one of them missing by less than an inch it looked like. As Berry and I caught up with them I knocked one aside, just as he was on the point of throwing another rock.

"You mad idiots," shouted Berry. "If you hit that nest, thousands of bees'll swarm and attack you and you'll be killed. Don't you know what you're doing, man? Didn't anyone ever tell you about killer bees?"

"We didn't know, Berry. No one ever told us. Is that really true?"

"Are they really killer bees?" asked the one I'd knocked down, as he scrambled to his feet. "Would they really kill us?"

"Yes, they would," I added with a shout. "In fact killer bees might attack you in a swarm just for walking too close to their nests. Ask McLachlan if you don't believe me. He had to run like hell, swatting at them like crazy and was lucky to get away with only a few stings. So get out of here and leave them alone if you don't want to be stung to death."

The chastened boys followed Berry and me, as we rushed from the area before the bees could get ideas. Back at the track we'd been walking along, Ivey and Constantinides had been standing, watching.

"You chaps must be nuts to get that close," Ivey greeted Berry and me. "I've seen those things attack a man, and it's terrible. I wouldn't go near it."

"I couldn't just leave them to it," said Berry. "If they'd hit that nest it would've been all over for them, man."

I just shrugged.

With the would-be nest-bashers running off to find something else to do, we continued our walk to the cricket pitch.

THERE WAS A HOLLOW *CLAP* THAT CARRIED in the still air across the hard-baked sand, and reached the ears of observers in the pavilion. The batsman had made contact with the ball on the willow wood's sweet spot and was rewarded by his fans with a polite hand clap. The small, rock-hard, red-leathered ball soared, reaching high over the heads of the fielders, and landed just within bounds, before rolling over the white-washed boundary line. It looked like Maclean had hit a 4. I looked for the umpire, and noted his horizontal outstretched arm that he waved briefly from side to side.

"Yes, that's a four, all right," confirmed Constantinides.

I filled in the number in the score book, then reached into my pocket for a hanky to wipe the sweat. A temporary pavilion had been erected, so the scorekeepers and coach could have some shelter, as we sat for hour after hour in the blazing sun watching this day-long match, but still and all, it was scorching today.

"What do you think, Tony?" asked Constantinides. "Do you think we'll pull it off?"

It was cause for concern among the school's cricket fans, not to say Mr. Ferguson who laboured tirelessly to create a winning team, because we'd had little success playing the Government Indian School in Dodoma. In fact, in the past, we'd even had to team up with the best from the Mpwapwa Indian School in an alliance against Dodoma because of our shortage of talent. That hadn't worked either. But this year it could be different. There'd been great enthusiasm in the inter-house rivalry among our own four houses.

"The standard of play is measurably improved," especially from Curie, the teams had been told. Now the best of the best had been selected, to fashion an away team to represent the school. Today, it was the final game, a home game, seeing as we'd won the toss for choice of location for two of the best-of-three and now the score was one game each.

"I don't know," I responded. "Dodoma did pretty-well this morning, 238 all out. We're now 153 for 6, with two hours left of play. We have a chance, but at the rate we're going it's not good. Their bowler's keeping our score down. Maclean's 4 were the first runs in a while."

"Their bowlers doing more than that," Constantinides worried. "Gunston and Willman were out for ducks, and they're among our stronger players. The others didn't run up much of a score. Vutriakis scored six, didn't he?"

"Seven."

"Well, seven then, that wasn't much, and he's out."

"Who've we got left who could change things?"

"HOWZAT!?" came the yell from the Dodoma team.

I looked up, distracted by Constantinides' questions and narrowed my eyes into the sun to see the umpire. Yes, there was his arm straight up, finger pointing.

"Damn, he's out – who was it? Oh, it's Martin. Well, better him than Maclean. Who's going in now?"

"Oliver's on his way."

Martin passed Oliver, on his way out to the crease, and approached the pavilion with bat under arm, pulling off his cricket gloves. He sat down to remove his leg pads.

"Bugger me, it's hot out there."

Mr. Ferguson looked over his shoulder, eyebrows raised at the sound of the words, 'Bugger me.'

"Sorry, sir," said Martin.

"What happened, Martin?" I asked.

"LBW. That bowler's so fast, man. You can't see the bloody ball, er, I mean the, uh, ball. He's good."

"But you hit a four a few minutes back."

"Yeah, probably luck."

"Oh come on, you're a good batter."

"Thanks, but not anymore. I'm out. Is there anything to drink around here?"

"There're some Cokes in a tub of water round the back."

Martin went to find a Coke, and Constantinides picked up where he'd left off.

"Problem is, how long will Maclean last in this heat? He was the opening batter and we've lost six. We'd better hope we have a dark horse left among the last two."

"I don't know about a dark horse. We've got Hannah, he's good."

CLAP! The ball soared towards the boundary.

"Yeeeeeeesssss. Run, chaps, run!"

"Is it going to be a four?"

"Yesss, looks like."

"No, the fielder got it – where are they?"

"They're on their third."

"Run, chaps, run!"

"The ball's coming back."

"Freeeeze! Don't go for a fourth, you'll be run out."

"No!" yelled Maclean at Oliver, putting up his hand. "Stay!"

Oliver stayed. If he'd run he'd surely have got Maclean run out.

"Yish, that was close. If Maclean was out it'd be all over."

And so the game progressed with both batters slowly running up the score, a run here, two runs there and the occasional four. As we watched, and as I recorded the score, Constantinides, who was the only one left keeping me company after Berry and Ivey had drifted off, continued to chatter. He'd been in Kongwa less than a term, and was forever discovering something new.

"You know," he said, in his grown-up way of speaking, "this is my first ever cricket match to watch, I mean, you know, a serious one. It's amazing really just how many different sports and activities this school organises." He was counting them off as he wrote them down on a piece of paper. "I make it at least twenty-seven different sports or activities. Seems sometimes like there's so much going on, I'm surprised anyone has any free time."

"Yes, well," I replied, glancing at his list, "most activities have only a few people interested. Or you have an extra curricular class with only one teacher and she or he can take maybe ten to be practical, or like Scouts for example that has a max of twenty-five. So, there's never a chance that you could get into too many things. But you're right, there's a lot of choice."

"Schools don't provide all this in Greece, I can tell you," said Constantinides. "Over here, in Kongwa at least, they provide tons of things."

"Sports are essential to British tradition," I said. "Go to any English school, well, boarding school anyway, and school sports are a big thing, very big. What's got you so excited anyway? Do you want to sign up for everything?" I laughed.

"No, of course not. Most I'd never touch, except the music. I just adore classical music. My favourite opera is *Aida*! Do you like opera?"

"Love it."

"No, it's just that I'm so surprised. Put it down to this being my first time in an English school. It's impressive."

"And don't forget the girls," I added, glancing at his list. "They do some of the things we do but not everything."

"I don't think they play cricket, do they?"

I laughed. "No, of course not, nor football or rugby although they do play hockey and net ball. But I expect they have other things that only girls do."

"Like what, for instance?"

"I've no idea; I'm not a girl, but they must do something."

"I'm sure not all schools offer this much, not even in England," Constantinides reflected.

"I don't know, you may be right," I replied, pointing to his list. "Don't forget to add Shinty – the Juniors also play Shinty; that makes twenty-eight."

"They do? What's Shinty?"

"It's a Scottish game, kind of like field hockey in a way but different rules. Don't know much about it; I've never played. But anyway, tell me something, how is it you speak such good English? You've never been to England, or an English school and you've only been in Tanganyika a few months?"

"HOWZAT!"

"Oh no, not Maclean," I frowned into the sun.

"How?"

"LBW?"

"Not out. The umpire ruled not out."

"Jeesh."

"That's my parents," Constantinides continued. "They wanted me to learn it from when I was very young. In Athens I went to an expensive private school. It had a Headmaster who was an Oxford University professor. He, and the other teachers, taught us everything in English! Can you believe that? No Greek at all except the Greek language lessons, of course. It was speak English or nothing."

"Wow."

CLAP!

"Yesss! What a great hit," someone called out. "That's got to be a six."

"Yes, it's a six. Well done. Who was it?"

Enthusiastic clapping broke out from the crowd.

"Maclean. You can't stop him, man. Boy, I hope he keeps it up."

"What's the score, Edwards?"

"With that six, 197."

"How much time left?"

"Little over an hour."

Time passed. Flies attacked. Necks were slapped. Noisy kasukus swarmed overhead. Boys and girls watching the match circled listlessly around the pavilion, trying for a little shade before being encouraged out. This was not a tent for the crowd.

"HOWZAT?"

"Oh, no."

"Umpire agrees, who is it?"

"Oliver."

"Foxton's going in."

"What happened?"

"Caught by silly mid-off. You should have seen it; just glanced off his bat."

I heard the familiar voice of a new arrival, seeking shade.

"Hey, Tony, how's it going?" asked Doug, coming up behind me.

"Pepsi, good to see you, man. How'd it go?" I turned with a knowing smile.

"Pam's knock-out, man," he spoke quietly over my shoulder, in deference to Fergie being in earshot. "She's a fine girl."

"So you finally got her to be your girlfriend, huh?"

"Yeah. I don't know what took her so long," said Doug in mock superiority, heaving his chest with a self-indulgent smile. "I'd have thought she'd snap me up."

I chuckled. "Maybe she's not ready for you, Peps," I said, in hushed tones. "She's very pretty, could have any boy she wants. She'd probably prefer to have someone good looking."

"Watch it, Edwards," Doug quietly chuckled, lifting his fists in a mock threat. "If she wants good looking she should never have hesitated."

"I'm not sure what you see in having a girlfriend, but anyway. Where'd you go?" I whispered sideways.

"The donga," he leaned in close to my ear.

"And did you kiss her?" I mouthed, intrigued.

Doug looked a bit sheepish. "Well, I wanted to, I did try, but just when I tried she turned her head away."

CLAP!

"Yes, another four, maybe? Run chaps, ruuuuuun!"

"The fielder's got it," I said.

"You've got time for a run! Ruuuun!" Mr. Ferguson yelled.

"Run!" yelled Maclean.

"No, stay!"

Foxton hesitated.

"Run!" yelled Maclean again. He was committed and on his way to the other crease.

Foxton finally broke into a run, but it was too late. He tore down the pitch and was within inches of the crease when the wicket keeper caught an incredible throw from the fielder at deep square leg, and in a continuing pivot from the catch, knocked the bails off the stumps.

"HOWZAT?"

The umpire signalled Foxton out.

"Okay, Hannah, you're last man in. It's all on you and Maclean now," said Mr. Ferguson. "What's the score, Edwards?"

"221, sir."

"All you need is 17 runs," yelled Fergie after Hannah, "and it's ours. Work with Maclean, follow his lead."

"How many minutes, Edwards?"

"By my watch, 28, sir."

"Why'd she turn her head away from kissing a handsome bloke like you, Peps?" I picked up the conversation in a whisper again.

"I dunno," he breathed back. "She said something about it being too soon. Hey, Foxton," Doug turned as Foxton arrived at the pavilion. "Sorry you were run out, man."

"My fault. I should have listened to Maclean. If I had, I'd still be out there. Oh well."

Fergie shook his head. "You know what to do, why don't you do it?"

"Sorry, sir."

"Never mind. It's not over yet. We can still win.. Hannah's a strong batter, been doing well in the nets. Who knows? Between him and Maclean, we'll yet pull this off."

CLAP!

"Watch that ball go; it's going to be a four… yeeees, it's over the line."

There was a round of enthusiastic clapping.

"Who hit that four?" I asked.

"Hannah, didn't you see?"

"No, Pepsi's in my way."

"Sorry, mate."

The minutes were ticking. Both batters were scoring ones and twos.

"You know what?" said Mr. Ferguson. "Their bowler's tired. He doesn't have the same oomph he had earlier. The batters are connecting more often. If they could just get a few more big ones this would be all over. How much longer?"

"Sixteen minutes, sir."

CLAP!

"Yes, yes, yes, he's hit another six! Maclean hit another six."

"What's the score?"

"236, sir," I said, in barely contained excitement.

"Minutes?"

"Ten, sir."

"Their bowler's tired, sir. No doubt. After all he's been on all afternoon."

"Who's batting?"

"Maclean."

"Yes! Good hit. Careful, boys," Mr. Ferguson muttered to himself. "Only two runs to win. Don't get run out now whatever you do!"

We watched as the fielders changed for the next over and Hannah stood in the batsman's crease.

"That bowler's still pretty fast," I continued. "I hope Hannah's watching carefully. One slip now and it's all over for the sake of a couple of runs."

CLAP!

"Oh my gosh, look, he's done it. Hannah's hit another 4. Look, it's way over the line!"

"We've won!"

The sixty or so boys and girls milling around the pavilion, who were the game's sometime enthusiastic audience, broke into enthusiastic clapping. There were even a few cheers and a couple of the girls threw their hats in the air, in an untoward display of excitement not normally encouraged in this sober sport.

CHAPTER SEVENTEEN

SERIOUS LOCUSTS

FERGIE'S ENTHUSIASM FOR CRICKET WAS AS CONSTANT as it was for school plays and I continued to be given first option for leading roles. Berry was another favourite. He became the star of the moment when he was asked to play Hermia in *A Midsummer's Night Dream*.

Stew didn't want to play a girl's role, but as Fergie explained, "With that angel face of yours, Berry, you're the closest I can get to a girl, and besides which actors have to be prepared to play any role."

"But, sir," Berry protested in class, with the girls chuckling and enjoying the exchange, "we have plenty of real girls in the school, sir. Why don't we use one of them?"

The titters from the girls rose in volume to outright laughter, when Pat Kerswell's arm shot up, volunteering to play the part.

"Now you know very well that we don't mix the boys and the girls out-side classrooms. The boys put on plays for the boys, and girls put on plays for the girls, and that's the way it is. So I don't want to hear any more complaints, Berry, unless you'd rather drop out of the theatre group."

"No, sir," said Berry, with a reluctant sigh.

"I'll teach him how to be a girl, sir," Pat Kerswell volunteered, followed by a renewed outbreak of laughter.

"No, you can't have him – I want to teach him," called Wilma Milne with a pout.

"I'm older than you two so I get first dibs," Avril Jenner joined in.

Berry was by now cowering, wishing he wasn't being noticed.

"Well, you have several offers for education on how to be a girl, Berry," said Fergie, as he, unusually for him, rose to the humour of the occasion. "Tell me, Berry, which one of the girls' offers will you accept?" he asked with a pleasant smile.

To everyone's surprise, because Stewart was thought of as a shy type where girls were concerned, "All of them," he blurted out, in one, huge, en-lightened moment.

The class convulsed in laughter, with some within reach slapping Berry on the back. "Go get 'em, tiger."

Stew broke into a broad grin. He was pleased with himself.

Before the laughter died away Silvia Papini called out, "I bags being a boy in our next school play. I always wanted to be a boy anyway, they have all the fun."

"Yes, let's all be boys," the girls chorused.

"All right, quiet down," said Fergie, sensing the moment might be getting out of hand. "That's enough."

We clammed up.

"Now, Berry, notwithstanding your apparent acceptability to the oppo-site gender, are you to be in the theatre group or not?"

"Yes, sir, I am, sir. Thank you, sir."

Berry was a good egg to me and gave a lot of help. He'd been top of the class more than once and was always in the top three. During afternoons off we would spend time at the house, lying on our beds and going through maths problems. He was always patient, and I never understood why. I sup-pose I was his friend and for his friend he found it to be no trouble.

I did return the favour though. I'd had my grounding in Latin at Allan House and was way ahead in the subject when it was introduced into the cur-riculum. So I was popular as the 'go to' for help in prep. It was the one time I was able to return the favour to Stewart who, unusually, found something he was not so good at.

✦ ✦ ✦

IN AN EARLY AFTERNOON CLASS, MR. SIMMS walked in to take biology.

"As you know I'm not your biology teacher, I usually keep to what I call the laboratory sciences. However, as I have a smattering of knowledge on the subject, I'm filling in for Miss Bayliss, who's been delayed returning from long leave. Now then, we have an interesting time ahead," he continued, having brought the attention of the class to focus. "We will be having a diversion from your scheduled subject to do with birds, to learn about locusts instead. Anyone with any ideas why we'd do that?"

"Yes, sir." Avril Jenner's hand shot up.

"Ah yes, er, Miss Jenner?"

"Yes, sir." ˙

"Why, pray tell, do you imagine we might prefer to talk locusts, rather than birds, in today's lesson?"

"Well, sir, I heard Matron talking with Miss Hurley at breakfast. Miss Hurley was telling Matron she heard on the radio that there's a locust swarm on its way to the Mpwapwa region, sir, so I suppose that would include Kongwa, sir."

"You are correct, Miss Jenner, you heard right, that is the reason indeed. Very attuned of you, young lady. Now tell me, class, have any of you experienced a locust swarm?"

No arms shot up. We looked around at each other expecting at least one of us would have experienced a swarm, but no one had, not even Paton who knew most stuff to do with animals and creatures. After a pause, Addie Schneeman slowly put his arm up and, when nodded to by Mr. Simms, asked, "Please, sir, what's a locust?"

"Anyone want to tell Schneeman what a locust is?"

"Yes, sir." Anthony Paton's hand shot up.

"Yes, sir," my hand shot up too, much to the surprise of fellow pupils who didn't know I knew anything about biology.

"I know you know, Paton, but I'd like Edwards to answer this one. So, Edwards, what, pray tell, is a locust?"

"A grasshopper, sir."

"So far so good. What else can you tell Schneeman there? Are all grasshoppers locusts perhaps?"

"No, sir. The locust migrates, sir. It is what certain types of grasshopper are called when they are ready to swarm, sir."

"Excellent, Edwards. Anyone else want to add to that? No? Tell me, Edwards, do we know the name of the type of grasshopper in this region that becomes a locust and swarms?"

"No, sir, I'm afraid not, sir."

"Hmm. Anyone else?"

"Yes, sir."

"Very well, Paton, what's the answer?

"The Red Locust of Rukwa, sir."

"You're quite right, boy. Let us learn a little more about them, shall we? I'd like you to pull out your text books if you've not already done so, turn to page 133 and thereon you will find commencement of a chapter on grasshoppers and locusts, together with a photograph. How are we all doing? Berry?"

"Er, yes, sir, I can't find my text book, sir; someone must have borrowed it, sir."

"Berry?"

"Yes, sir."

"There's no such word as *can't*."

"Yes, sir. What I mean is, I am unable to find my book, sir."

"Now tell me, Berry, why would someone want to borrow your biology text book? It is inscribed with your name and form number, is it not?"

"Yes, sir."

"And it is true, wouldn't you say, that all present were issued with biology text books?"

"Yes, sir."

"So then, if anyone had removed your book and kept it for themselves, we would instantly know who the culprit is, would we not?"

"Yes, sir, we would, sir."

"Very well. Everyone will place their text book on the top of their desks opened to the inside cover, wherein we should expect to see your respective names."

With that, Mr. Simms prowled the aisles examining closely the name inscribed as being the owner of the book, and matching that name with the pupil before him.

"It would seem," said Mr. Simms, after completing his examination, "that each book on each desk matches the owner. Therefore, Berry, no one has borrowed your book, at least, no one from this class. What did you do with your book after your last prep, Berry? Could it be that you mislaid it?"

"Now you mention it, sir, that is possible. I had the book at my house, sir. Perhaps I forgot to bring it back, sir."

"Indeed, Berry, indeed. I expect to see that book returned to your desk by the time we meet again. Do I make myself clear?"

"Yes, sir."

"In the meantime you may share with your neighbour, assuming of course that your neighbour is prepared to let you share his book. Tell me, Edwards, are you prepared to let Berry share your text book?"

"Yes, sir, I'd be glad to help out, sir."

"Excellent, perhaps now we can get some work done. Are you ready, Berry?"

"Yes, sir."

Titters all around.

And with that, we launched into an examination of the red locust of Lake Rukwa and learned all that had found its way into our biology text books. But the more interesting part was to follow.

"Now that we know what a locust is, Schneeman, and the red locust in particular, we will discuss the swarm we are told is forthcoming. I shall share with you what we know, and offer a little advice. However, you may expect to hear more on this from your Housemasters and Housemistresses should it be determined that we will indeed be inundated and that the swarm has not veered elsewhere – something the locusts would be wise to do heading, as they are, for a school full of children."

We thought that funny, except perhaps for Stewart who had become distracted again.

The wooden-backed blackboard duster thrown by Mr. Simms landed squarely on Berry's desk in front of him and continued its momentum onto his lap. Berry jerked around in fright.

"Berry!" called Mr. Simms. "You have a propensity for staring out of the window that is becoming irksome. Am I going to have to give you lines or extra prep perhaps in order to regain your most esteemed attention?"

"Oh no, sir," Berry quickly flicked his head forward, amid the chuckles from the girls at Mr. Simms' sarcasm. "I'm very sorry, sir. I am listening to what you say, really I am, sir."

"Is that so?" asked Mr. Simms who moved to Berry's desk to retrieve his duster. "Then perhaps you would be pleased to refresh our memories on what it was we were most recently discussing."

"Of course, sir, ahem, well, I, er...."

But Berry had been day-dreaming, missed his cue and for a moment was dumfounded.

"Birds," whispered Doug, from across the aisle, as Mr. Simms returned to head of class, "This class was supposed to be about birds."

"Birds, sir," said Berry, "we were about to get into the biology of birds."

At that the class burst out laughing, with Douglas the loudest. I found it funny too, but being empathetic with Berry's plight I did my best to restrain laughter so he wouldn't think everyone was laughing at him.

"That's a dirty trick, Pepsi, man," I whispered behind a cupped hand. And then to Berry, head low, hand to mouth, "We changed the subject to locusts, the red locust, remember?"

Berry focussed and recalled the lesson.

"Actually, what I meant to say, sir, is that we *were* to have discussed the biology of birds but due to the impending locust swarm, you switched today's subject to the red locust of Rukwa instead, sir."

"Excellent, Berry, we are full of surprises," said Mr. Simms from his teacher's desk as he swivelled to face the class once more.

Berry looked sheepish and busied himself with the text book.

Mr. Simms continued, "These locusts will consume every leaf, every blade of grass, every bit of vegetation they can find if we give them the chance. It will become our purpose to deny them that chance, at least as much as we can. Locusts are large and each one eats voluminous quantities. There will be millions of them; there could be as many as twenty, thirty, forty million of them, per square mile, so think about that."

The girls, who already knew they disliked locusts from seeing just the odd one here or there in the grass, stared at Mr. Simms, wide-eyed, jaws dropped, ashen faces.

"Forty million?" gasped Carola Sorenson on their behalf.

"Yes, young lady, quite easily, but do not concern yourself overmuch, Miss Sorenson, they will not all land on your shoulders at the same time," smiled Mr. Simms.

Laughter from the boys followed that witty comment, but the straight-faced girls were not in the slightest bit amused.

"They may be quite scary," Mr. Simms continued, "as they look horrible in close up and if they are swarming about your face and eyes and ears, you may become even a little scared, especially you girls who don't much like any insect, I believe it is true to say."

The girls were regarding Mr. Simms in alarm. Locusts in their faces, locusts in their hair? Forty million of them? …in a square mile? The prospect was horrific.

"How many square miles of them, sir?" I asked mischievously, with the girls in mind.

"Could be anywhere from fifty to one hundred, Edwards."

"Fifty to one hundred square miles of locusts sir, with forty million per square mile? Wow."

Even the boys stopped laughing at that.

"Of course, you'll be spending most of the time indoors when, or if, the swarm arrives. It's not something you would want to be out in. However, you boys will doubtless be expected to do your bit in discouraging the swarm from remaining in our proximity. Fires will be lit and noise will be made. Does the prospect of making a lot of noise inspire you, Westley?" enquired Mr. Simms.

"Oh, yes, sir, I'm sure I'll be able to help out, sir," Doug responded enthusiastically.

"Excellent, because that is what will be expected of you boys. Now, I've no doubt the fire lighting and smoke creation will be something prefects will do under supervision from teachers or Housemasters. But, during the next few days, until the swarm arrives, you should think about what you can do to make as much noise as possible once the swarm hits. Locusts don't like noise, we're told, so my expectation would be that a school full of boys should provide quite some discouragement to their hanging around for long."

The girls thought that funny and giggled.

"Please, sir, we've all seen individual locusts in flight, there's plenty around."

"That is true, Paton."

"Well, sir, I was wondering, as we always see locusts alone, what would make them get together in their millions and swarm, sir?"

"An excellent question, Paton. Locusts are indeed solitary creatures. Alas, science has yet to answer your question. I think though, you can safely take it that it will, one day, provide resolution."

"Thank you, sir. Oh, and er one more thing, sir."

"Yes, Paton."

"Well, sir, one locust by itself seems to make quite a lot of noise. If just one is flying around, you easily hear its clacks and the whirring of its wings."

"Paton, your powers of observation never cease to astound me. Pray continue your thoughts."

"Well, sir, if one locust can make that much noise, I ask myself, what sort of noise would forty million make, sir?"

"Indeed, Paton, indeed. How would the noise of forty million sound?"

"It seems to me, sir, that not even Westley could make sufficient noise to overcome that lot, sir."

The class burst out in laughter, not least Paton who enjoyed his joke.

Westley smiled around, taking some bows.

"We will have to see, Paton, we will have to see; perhaps you're right at that."

The dying down of laughter was punctuated with hoots from the train whistle. It was a familiar sound when the engine with a baggage car and occasionally a passenger coach attached arrived three times a week. The whistle shrilled as we tuned to the warming chuffs of the engine reverberating in the foothills.

"There's the train," I whispered to Doug. "I hope it's bringing a letter from Mum."

"Me too. I haven't heard from my folks for about three weeks, I don't know why. Isn't it about time you received another *Eagle*?"

"Yes, it is. My Uncle Arthur back in England buys it every week and then posts several to me. I usually get three at a time."

The lesson progressed.

Over the next few days the school was abuzz with talk of the coming locust swarm. The anticipated drama led to endless gazing at the horizon, in the hope of spotting the dark grey cloud of their approach. And the promised arrival of the swarm gave the boys yet another opportunity to annoy the girls. It was found to be hilarious if a boy could sneak up behind a dame quickly, tickle the back of her neck and yell, "Locust!" The resulting female jump, amid squeals or shrieks, punctuated the days of waiting, as the girls never seemed to get used to this new trick in the boys' torture arsenal. Having un-failingly leaped in fright, the girl would then round on her tormentor: "Ooooh, you pathetic little boy, Edwards, I suppose you think you're soooooo *(with a vigorous shake of the head)* funny."

Three days later, the swarm was spotted on the horizon, looking like an angry tropical storm. We'd finished afternoon classes and were leaving the area. Teachers ran around barking orders at prefects to man the bonfires. The rest of us were admonished to, "Get back to your houses quickly, before they arrive. Stay indoors and remain there for the duration."

From the brooding grey cloud in the west, as they drew closer, the lo-custs' gossamer wings were rim-lit by the late afternoon sun, so they became, for some minutes, a beautiful frosty-looking sky, like star dust. Then they were upon us and it became apparent that to create noise was not the answer. We'd have been no challenge. Few would have wanted to be out among that lot. Those that were, teachers and prefects, were manning their smoky bon-fires, made so by a combination of old tyres and liberal splashing of water onto flame.

From our indoor view, thousands of locusts landed on a collision course with our window mosquito meshing, and found themselves crawling the net-ting in search of food. Some found the same holes that were popular with mosquitoes for making their way indoors. Then we snuck up on large, red individuals, thumb and finger at the ready, so when we got close enough to pounce as they crawled on our mosquito nets, our walls, our beds or our clothing, we gripped their wings and hind legs from behind and they were powerless to move. Then we escorted them outdoors.

At first the locust arrival had been awaited with curiosity, even excite-ment. But soon enough we wanted them gone. We didn't have long to wait. The larger number of them had flown by next day, while quite a few re-mained behind to join the local population. We learned that good can come of all things. Although they ate every bit of greenery Kongwa had, the locusts themselves made a good meal for the African diet, a generous addition of protein. Some said it's much like eating white ants, which swarm from their nests on the one day a year that they possess wings. They were known to be delicious when fried in butter and the appropriate seasonings. For my part I could do without them.

According to *The Georgian*, a surge of interest in natural history followed the event. It caused a number of female teachers to recoil in horror at the variety of live specimens presented to them in biology class.

CHAPTER EIGHTEEN

OUT OF HERE

IVEY AND I WERE ON OUR WAY to climb the baobab and join the others. We played marbles as we went.

"What do you think of the news about Metcalf?" he asked.

"What did he do?"

"You don't know?" he looked surprised.

"I s'pose not. You mean that new Livingstone boy, Philip Metcalf in house four?"

"Yes, of course."

"What did he do?"

"You didn't hear? He ran away again."

"Again?"

"Yes, but not before trying to blow up the school."

"What!? How could he blow up the school?"

"Well, you know how on Quarry Hill there's that storage cache where the Groundnut Scheme kept dynamite and other explosives?"

"Yes, well, I've heard of it but I don't think I've seen it, well, maybe once I did. It's in between Church Hill and Kongwa Hill, isn't it?"

"Yes, sort of; it's the place where the girls like to go instead of snake rock. Well anyway, you know how he hates school and how unhappy he is. I heard that he managed to break into that dynamite cache and steal some of it. They say he planned to blow up the school."

"Crikey! You must be joking."

"Uh uh. That's what they say."

"Actually, I feel sorry for him. I remember what it was like to hate school so much and he has good reason, he gets bullied a lot."

"I know. But running away is one thing, planning to blow the school up is pretty serious."

"He'd have a difficult time doing that, I should think. There must be over sixty buildings for the school. Unless he could make a big enough explosion to blow up all of Kongwa."

"I don't know about that, but anyway, that's what I heard."

"And so where is he now? I'll bet he's in trouble."

"They don't know exactly on account of he ran away. But the teachers think he may be following the railway spur so they've gone after him there."

"Hmm. How'd they expect to catch him up? If he's got a good start on them I doubt they'll be able to."

"Well, that's it, you see. According to Neil, Mr. Moore and Mr. Shuttleworth drove down to the station and borrowed the rail trolley, you know, the thing railway workers use to ride the rails, when they're looking to make repairs or check up on damage. So with the two of them pumping away on that, they'll probably catch up quite quickly."

"Wow. That's amazing. Poor old Metcalf. I wouldn't want to be him when they get him back to school."

"He'll be expelled; no doubt about it."

"I s'pose."

We continued walking and playing marbles, pretty much in silence for a while, as we thought on how daring Metcalf had been and how rough it was for him. Then we passed by Mr. Moore's house at the bottom of his drive, when a new thought popped up.

"Did you hear about Mr. Moore's puff adder collection?" I asked.

"Uh huh," Ivey responded vaguely as he moved into position for his next shot. "You already told me the other day."

"It makes you realise just how many of those snakes are around," I said, straightening up, "with Mr. Moore collecting their skins like he does."

"How did you find out about it?" asked Ivey as he went into a crouch for his next shot.

"I had to go to Mr. Moore's because he called for me. He said he'd heard from my parents that I might need to leave school early to go to England, but nothing's firmed up. His older daughter, Judi, came to the door when I knocked. She called him and came back to say he'd be along in a minute. I asked her about the toy furry snake she had in her hand. Oh, it's not mine," she said, "it's Steve's. You know they call the younger one Steve, eh?

"I thought her name was Stephanie," said Ivey.

"It was, I mean is, but they call her that. Anyway, she told me Steve calls her toy snake 'Puffy,' on account of all the puff adders her dad catches. But here's the thing, apparently Mr. Moore catches the snakes very carefully so as not to damage them. When it's dead, he skins them. He gives the body to the dogs but keeps the skins. Judi says he plans to make a handbag out of them for her mum, when he's caught enough.

"If I was him, I'd be worried about those girls running around like they do with so many snakes about. Those two run wild seems to me."

"Well, it's the same for all of us if you think about it. Remember my black mamba incident? So far no deaths for school kids. I expect they'll survive like the rest of us."

I finally won a game. "Want to play for keeps?" I asked, feeling cocky.

"Talking of girls, what do you think about dames?" Ivey asked, ignoring my question.

"I don't know, not much really, I don't think. They seem to be the reason I get in trouble mostly. A girl will always sneak on you if they spot you doing something they think the teacher won't like."

"Yeah, I know about stuff like that, but, you know, they say we'll grow up and like dames, even want one of our own, that's why people get married, you know, like mums and dads. No one forces them into it."

"I know, you're right, that's what they say. Heck, Pepsi and Pam get on fine. Did you see them together manning the light switches for the flick last night? Pepsi's lucky to get away with that, he couldn't if she was a boarder. But I don't know. Sometimes when I look at them, especially a pretty one, I can imagine getting to like her, maybe, but I don't think they'd be as much fun as boys are. We have some good times… at least when we can get away from prefects. Do you ever see dames climbing baobabs? When was the last time you saw a dame trying to dive bomb a snake? They just run and scream if they see one, although I must say Mr. Moore's little girls are the exception. Do you ever see girls sneaking out of bounds to the village? You know, they don't seem to like the same stuff as us."

"I know, but you know what, we change, we all change... by the way that one closest to the hole was mine you know, not yours... and we'll change and like to do new things, maybe not always the same old things. I mean, you know, you don't see grown-up men running around dive bombing snakes or safari ants, eh?"

"Well anyway, what are you trying to tell me? Are you suddenly getting keen on a dame? Who is she, who are you after?"

"No, it's not that," replied Ivey. "It's more like a thought that leads from one thing to another."

"Oh?"

"Like, you know what they say about sex, eh?"

"I don't know much actually, not sure I want to."

"Well, you know how they say babies are made right?"

"The birds and the bees and all that stuff," I said. "You're talking about mums and dads making love?"

"Yes, I suppose, something like that."

"Well, I don't really know how that's done. I've heard stories that sound pretty weird. I can't imagine wanting to do it."

"Well, that's the thing you see – when you're older you will, at least I think you will. My older brother, you've never met him, he's quite a bit older and works now although he still lives near us in Arusha, anyway, he chases girls like crazy. He told me he was just like us when he was our age. But, he said, we all change as we grow up and we're going to end up liking girls too."

"Well, you may be right; I can't say you're not. But anyway, what made you start on this?"

"You remember when I had to leave school at half term to go to Europe?"

"Yes, you got a lift with Graham Muddle to Dodoma, didn't you?"

"With his dad, yes. I was lucky with that because otherwise I don't know what I'd have done, there's no transport except at beginning or end of term. Anyway, they dropped me off at the Dodoma Hotel. I had to stay the night because the bus to Arusha wasn't 'til morning."

"Uh huh. I've never been to Dodoma, what's it like?"

"Oh, it's just like any other little town, you know, but here's the point of the story."

"Hang on; it's my shot, isn't it? Gotcha! That's you out of it."

"That's your first lucky shot today," said Ivey, as he moved into position to try to make a comeback. It looked like I might just win this round too.

"Anyway, it was late when we got to Dodoma. I was just in time for dinner before they closed the restaurant. After that, I walked around town, but there was nothing to do, no radio, nothing, so I went to bed. Next thing you know, I woke up, and it was dark although the room was lit from a street light... Darn, too hard, can I have that again?"

"No!"

"Oh, come on! Well, anyway, I heard this talking. Now you know how it is in these hotels, when they're busy you have to share your room unless you're a married couple. So I realised there must be someone there, although there'd been no suitcase, no nothing when I went to bed."

"So did they wake you up with their noise?" I asked.

"Must've. Anyway, I opened an eye and saw this man, built like a rugby player, standing at the bedroom door. He was undressed 'cept for a towel around his waist and he was talking to someone. Next thing you know this woman came in the room, she couldn't have been his wife because she was African and he was European. I mean, I s'pose she could have been but she almost certainly wasn't because, well, you know."

"Go on." I stood looking at Ivey as he talked, the game of marbles temporarily suspended.

"They closed the door and before you could look around she was getting undressed. Right there in front of me she was naked. She had her back to me so I had this view of her behind."

I laughed. "Must have been quite a view, Siggy. Did you see sights on the front side too?"

"Well, yes, later when she was getting dressed again. See, she didn't know I was there, and while she was undressing they were talking in Swahili. My Swahili's not good, eh, so I don't know what all they said, but anyway she was about to sit down on my head. There was this big black bottom and I almost yelled out."

At that I broke up. "That must have been so funny, Siggy! I bet you got a fright; think of it, a big black bottom sitting on your head!"

"Yeah, yeah, I know, very funny. Anyway, luckily, just as I was about to yell, the rugby player called in a loud whisper, 'Don't sit there; there's a kid in that bed.'

"She jumped forward in a helluva fright and as she turned around to look at me, I closed my eye and made like I was fast asleep. But I heard her whisper back to him, 'Why didn't you tell me there was a kid in your room? I could have sat on him.'

"The rugby player replied, 'Don't mind that, he's a little chap and fast asleep – come on over here.'"

"Oh boy," I said, staring at Ivey.

"Well," said Ivey, "you know what happened next. She went over to his bed, naked and all, and lay down on it. I saw her because I opened my eye again and watched. Then he dropped his towel on the floor and now there was this big white bum. But he climbed right on top of her."

"Really?" I asked, frowning in serious doubt. "He climbed on top of her? Wouldn't he squash her?"

"Well, I s'pose not, she didn't yell out or anything. Anyway after some sort of fiddling around he, well, you know."

"No, I don't know. What did he do?"

"Well, I suppose he must have been making love to her. I mean I haven't seen anyone do it before but what else would they be doing? I mean, what they did was the same as what some chaps have told me they've seen their parents do."

"Wow, right in front of you." And then I asked, "And what did you think after that?"

"I didn't know what to think. They sure made a lot of noises, especially her, and they didn't sound like happy noises, more like when someone hurts you or something, but she seemed happy enough after, wasn't crying or anything. After he'd got off her she got up and got dressed and he paid her money; and they were nice to each other, she even chuckled at something he said, so I s'pose he must have been happy too."

"Wow."

"But do you know the funniest part? Next day our bus got stuck in the mud about thirty miles out of Arusha. You know how it is, that's not the first time I've helped dig out the bus. Anyway, there we were, heaving and pushing and digging, when this pick-up drove up and stopped beside us. The driver asked if any of the first class passengers, that was us, wanted a ride into Arusha. The adults decided children first, so he took us there where our folks were waiting at the bus station. But here's the funny bit. I thought I'd seen the bloke somewhere before but couldn't think where; then I remembered. He was the chap who'd shared my room. Turned out he *was* a rugby player too; he was with Southern Highlands Rugby Eleven travelling to catch up with his team in a match against Northern Province. Lucky he didn't recognise me, eh?"

I THOUGHT ABOUT IVEY'S DODOMA STORY. IT was strange really. In its telling he'd stimulated my evolving interest in girls. He'd got me thinking, and not a little intrigued. I suppose it came at a time of increasing pressure to have a girlfriend; some boys seemed to think it was the thing to do. I wasn't there yet, but I had a sneaky feeling I was going to be, especially seeing as how much Pepsi liked Pam. Then there was the time the story of my bath with Annelize had got out. I never did find out which of Annelize or Egbert spilled the beans. I'd denied it when the story was doing the rounds and I was being teased. *Perhaps I wouldn't be so quick to deny it now,* I thought.

Before an opportunity to chase a girl would arise however, other events came to pass. Mr. Moore sent for me to appear at his house again after I'd bathed and dressed for dinner. Judi peered inquisitively through a doorway, with young Stephanie trying to squeeze between her and the door frame, the two checking on which boy was in their house this time. I didn't see Mrs. Moore, but could hear the crying of their newborn, Alan.

Mr. Moore said, "I have a letter here from your parents. The plans have been firmed up. You'll be leaving school before the end of term. You'll be going to England to visit your grandfather and, for reasons that are not clear to me, it is necessary for you to depart Kongwa two weeks before everyone else. You will be leaving on the train from Gulwe at two o'clock Thursday morning. Here's what you need to do. Tomorrow afternoon you will pack your trunk, it'll have been left on your bed during the morning while you're in class, and then bring it here and leave it on the stoep. Tomorrow evening at lights-out, you'll have remained dressed, of course; you'll walk here and await the school's milk gari with Mrs. Moore and myself. The gari will be

making its milk run to Mpwapwa, but tomorrow it will leave earlier in order
to take you to Gulwe before it picks up the milk. You will need to depart by
eleven p.m. Although it's only twenty miles or so to Gulwe, the roads are
such that it will take a long time to get there, plus leave a little time in hand.
Is that all understood?

"Yes, sir."

I caught the smiles and titters from Judi and her sister.

"Any questions?"

I looked from them back to Mr. Moore.

"How about my kasukus, sir?"

"You will not be able to take them. I understand your mother will meet
you in Dar es Salaam and that you will be flying to London, either the same
or the following day. I suggest you give them away, or entrust their care to
one of your friends."

"Yes, sir."

"Anything else, Edwards?"

"No, sir."

"Then you may go."

I stuck my tongue out at the girls as I left.

AT ABOUT 10:45 P.M. THE FOLLOWING EVENING, after being treated by Mrs.
Moore to a Coca-Cola and a number of chocolate digestive biscuits (why she
couldn't do this all the time I didn't understand), the pick-up, driven by its
African driver, Jonah, pulled up. Jonah dumped my trunk in the back and I
took my seat in the front.

"Goodbye, have a nice holiday," said Mrs. Moore who had disappeared
to tend to a gripey Alan but returned, with him in arms, in time for my departure. Mr. Moore hovered but didn't say anything. He disapproved of my
leaving school before the end of term.

The road to Msagali, off which we would turn for Gulwe, was rough,
little more than a rocky track, through 20 to 25 miles and about an hour and
a half's drive of unpopulated bush. The night was pitch black; headlights
flashed and weaved to the bouncing of our gari, the only vehicle out. Deep
shadows lurked in the corrugated pits as we bounced over the rutted surface,

our headlights picking out the eyes of a thousand night-jars. Francolins, mesmerized by our headlights, would wait until we were upon them before darting out, half-heartedly trying to fly, directly into our headlights or radiator and occasionally the wind-screen where they left a viscous smudge from their broken bodies. Hyenas slunk in the shadows and somewhere far off a lion roared. Progress was slow. We might have a smooth patch for a moment only to be shaken seconds later as I fell out of my seat. The windows were open, too hot to have them closed, dust or no dust. The sound was of bedlam.

Jonah started to talk soon after we'd cleared the boundary of Kongwa's township, asking if it was true I was going to fly in an ndege to England. I told him that it was true, that I would be flying very high in the sky; way above the clouds and that the ndege would travel very very fast.

"Much faster than this gari," I said. "Maybe ten times faster."

"How much is ten times faster, bwana mdogo?"

"Well, how can I explain? We are driving at maybe twenty miles an hour?" It was difficult to know what speed we were doing because the needle was jumping between zero and forty no matter what our speed. "If this needle was still, like it's supposed to be, it would probably be on the twenty," I said.

"Maybe, bwana mdogo... maybe thety."

"All right, let's say thirty on this flat patch. So let's imagine this needle could go past forty and fifty; past a hundred even, past one hundred and fifty, past two hundred, past two hundred and fifty, up to two hundred and seventy. That's how fast that aeroplane can fly."

"Thet's too much, bwana mdogo. Velly fust. Velly fust. I don't e know how something can go that e fust. Are you suar?"

"I went in the cockpit when I came to Africa; that's the place the driver sits, he's called a pilot. He showed me the instruments that told us we were flying at 270 miles per hour, so that's how I know. It has strong engines with much nguvu and much dawa to make them go."

"Must be very strong. And how does it stay in the sky?"

I was leaning against the door, my arm resting on the open window. I looked at Jonah. How was I going to explain – I wasn't sure myself. I stretched my arm out the window. Not very wise with trees up to the roadside, I could have hit one with my hand and had my arm snapped off. But as I thought on it, I turned my hand forward and let the wind push it up; in fact it was quite difficult to keep the hand level as the wind tried to lift it or push it down.

I said to Jonah, "See my hand riding the wind here. The wind wants to push my hand into the sky. An airplane works like that. The engines pull the plane along; the wind gets under the wings and pushes the plane up like my hand."

"Oh, I see, bwana mdogo. This is very clever."

Jonah was satisfied and I thought I'd got it about right.

"Mebee one day my chilen can fly in an ndege," he said.

"Mebee one day your children could pilot an ndege," I responded.

"Oh, bwana mdogo, I don't e know about e that."

After a pause to reflect, I asked, "Where do you live, Jonah?"

"I live in e the kijiji, bwana. On the side of Kongwa Hill we have a kijiji where many Africans are living now. My wife, she is there and we have three chilen."

"Is it nice? Are you happy there?"

"Yes, bwana mdogo, it is good. I come here for the groundnuts, you know, when the Europeans they were planting many groundnuts. But e they didn't e grow much, bwana mdogo."

"I know, I heard about the Groundnut Scheme. The buildings we use now for the school are left behind by the people who came to work it."

"It's too bad, bwana mdogo. No rain, no rain."

We pondered the lack of rain.

Jonah and I talked for a while longer and then lapsed into silence as our common interest dried up. Truth was, it probably had more to do with me being tired. It was late and my friends would have got to sleep long since. I dozed.

And then it happened.

There was a rough jolt when, without warning, the door I was leaning against flew wide open. I found myself lying outward, suspended over the road rushing beneath my head, my left hand having instinctively grabbed at the door's empty window frame as I fell, my right arm flailing. I had slipped onto the floor and my back was overhanging the road. Jonah braked as he reached to grab the belt of my khakis. Before we ground to a halt, his other hand let go the wheel, grasping the neck of my shirt at the same moment I lost my grip.

"Oh, bwana mdogo, are you all right? That was terrible, too terrible, are you all right?"

I straightened as Jonah hauled me up into my seat but this time more to the centre of the bench, away from the door.

"Yes, Jonah, I'm all right. Don't worry about it," I said, as I brushed myself of dust and took a few, deep breaths. "It was not your fault. I won't tell anyone what happened, all right? I don't want you to get into trouble."

"Thenk you, bwana mdogo, as long as you are all right, thet is the main thing."

Our slow progress and the near calamity combined to slow us down, so that we arrived at Gulwe with only minutes to spare. Amazingly, the train was on time. Out of the pitch black it came, spotlight penetrating the night and lighting up the track ahead. Huffing, puffing and wheezing, led by its enormous locomotive, with much sneezing and exhaling of steam, it squeaked to a halt, causing a displacement of chickens and renewed enthusiasm from the insects. We walked alongside the carriages searching for my name. To my surprise the conductor came hurrying up and, after quick farewells to Jonah, escorted me to the train's rear, where we climbed aboard and he pointed out my coupé.

Sixteen hours later, at 6 p.m., we steamed into Dar es Salaam. Mother was at the station to greet me, after which we hailed a taxi and drove to the New Africa Hotel.

That evening, we had dinner on the hotel's patio. The air was sultry as we overlooked Dar es Salaam's beautiful, natural harbour and tucked in to the most deliciously prepared guinea-fowl for dinner. Coloured lights, strung through the patio's pergola, twinkled against the backdrop of harbour lights and the ships' reflections in the calm waters. Insects were chirruping and bats swooped. African vendors at the restaurant's perimeter tried to catch the eyes of diners and interest them in a purchase of posies of dried flowers, sea shells or home-made jewellery. The atmosphere was exotic, and I loved it. It was now I learned of a change of plan. As I devoured a huge and colourful banana split Mother explained how the 'Suez Imbroglio' was consuming the world's headlines. Egypt had nationalised the Suez Canal, a property owned by Britain and France. Israel was somehow involved but I didn't really understand much about that.

Mother explained, "This villain in Egypt, a chap named Nasser, apparently the one in charge there these days, has ousted Britain and France from operating the Suez Canal… which we and France own, mind you… and taken it over. There's a threat of war in Egypt because of this, and now, Cairo airport is closed to international flights. So that affects our flying to England."

"So what's going to happen, Mum – won't we go now?"

"Your father's made alternate arrangements. We're flying on another airline…."

"Not B.O.A.C.?"

"No, not B.O.A.C. It's called Hunting Clan, and it flies different routes to avoid Egypt, well, most of it anyway."

"So we won't be going there?"

"Well, not to Cairo. As I understand it, flights are permitted to land in Mersa Matruh, near Egypt's border with Libya, but other than that, no, we'll be steering clear and flying by way of Kenya, The sudan, Malta, Italy and Southern france. It should be interesting."

"But why so many days, Mum? When we fly B.O.A.C. it takes less than two days and we fly all night. Now we'll be flying for three days and staying over for two nights? Why can't we fly at night?"

"I don't really know, dear. You'll have to ask your father when you see him. Something about instruments, or the lack thereof, but I'm not really clear. It's not so much that they can't fly at night, as they can't find their way at night."

"Oh," I said, as I considered flying over the desert at night, trying to find one's way by gazing out the windows.

"Do you know what sort of plane, Mum?"

"I knew you'd ask that, oh dear, your father told me, what was it? Oh, a Viking, he said it's a Viking, does that help?

"A Vickers Viking? That's not very big; only two props, not much different from a Dakota. I liked the Hermes we came on to Africa."

"Now, let me see. Somewhere in my handbag I've got the schedule with the route marked, if you want to see it."

"Yes, please."

She rummaged around then handed it over.

I read it out. "Our first stop will be Nairobi, then we fly to Entebbe in Uganda and Juba in The sudan before arriving in Khartoum for our first night's stop. Then, the next morning, we'll fly to Wadi Halfa which is also in the Sahara on the border of Northern Sudan and Egypt according to the map, on to Mersah Matruh which is on the Mediterranean coastline but is actually in Egypt still, and then our second night stop is in Malta. On the third day we'll fly to Rome, then Nice in the south of France and finally London. Boy, I hope we get there, and don't get captured and made prisoners of war in Egypt."

"Please don't talk like that, Tony. I have quite enough to be worried about without you speculating on things which I'm sure will never happen."

BY THE TIME WE LANDED IN KHARTOUM the following late afternoon I was ill.

"Sorry about the bumps, ladies and gentlemen," our captain had crackled over the plane's dubious speaker system. "It's the desert, don't you know. We're unable to fly very high – not pressurised, I'm afraid, the plane has a ceiling of ten thousand feet. When one flies over the Sahara at this height, I rather fear conditions can be turbulent. We're trying our best to level things out, but there really isn't much we can do. Be sure to keep your air-sick bags close to hand."

When we'd finished taxiing, the plane's door was opened and we were hit by the torrid heat. "It's 118 degrees F, in the shade," the captain had told us.

We descended the short steps and walked across the sticky, melting apron to the brilliant adobe building, glaring in the shimmering heat. No refreshments were brought; there were no fans, no relief for our thirst or nausea. And there we sweated for what seemed like an eternity.

The Arabs were solid black. White dishdashas were the sole garment, complete with sandaled feet. I ambled outside, where I found steps that led to the flat roof. I climbed them, narrowing my eyes at the top in the unimaginable glare. I strained to recognise objects. I thought I could see a row of palms toward the horizon. Perhaps it was the lining of the Nile? Perhaps it was a mirage? Aside from that there was nothing. Sand, sand and more sand.

After a while I was called back to the stifling room where passengers were attempting to fan themselves with airplane schedule brochures. Passports were being examined. More time passed, and then we heard a motor. With much rattling, and squeaking, a bus drew up. After yet another age, our stewardess announced it was time to leave.

"The bus will take us to our hotel. When in the city you may move around within the general area but you are not to wander too far. Take off tomorrow morning will be at 9 a.m. sharp. The bus will be at the hotel at eight, so don't be late."

We piled aboard. It was quite the most dejected bus. There wasn't any glass. The seats just about hung together – and some didn't. The groaning engine made dying noises and should have been buried long since. We set off with a jolt, and rattled squeakily along the tracks that passed for a road. After a long drive through arid terrain, we came upon an outcrop of buildings; adobe huts with Sudanese, goats and indolent mules standing there as still as the heat. Further on we detected signs of movement. More mules, these ones reluctantly towing flat carts, heavily laden and being beaten by their masters. Then there were the camels. Now the road widened into a broad, sandy main road, with traffic in both directions.

We bumped onto paved road, and soon were driving a cultivated boulevard, in which stately palms rose tall out of a central median with a luxuriant verdure. It ran between a row of buildings to our left and the Blue Nile to our right. Among the buildings was our rambling, colonial hotel. High ceilings, large verandas, concrete floors. Windows were shuttered to keep out the heat. A fan rotated languidly. Residents took turns to freshen up in the bathroom down the corridor. Later, Mum and I found a table on the veranda near the saloon bar, where we were served drinks. Sipping our tall and well-fruited iced teas we surveyed the contrasting beauty of the florid plant life, and the scorched sand through which flowed the refreshing Blue Nile. Our hotel was situated at a point, maybe a half mile from where the Blue Nile merged into the River Nile proper, but we didn't go to look. Much too hot. Instead, I watched, entranced, the occasional dahabieh sailing sedately by, as they sniffed in their superiority at the myriad felucca boats with their lateen sails weaving among them in their commercial enthusiasm, charging and feinting.

The coolest option for us was to not move, stay in the shade and drink cold drinks. There was nothing to do, and it was too hot even if there was. After dinner, we went to bed. I stripped and lay under the ineffectual fan. The heat was dry but I was sweating cascades. Eventually I slept.

We continued our bumpy flight across the desert, but I was not ill this time. I was invited into the cockpit, now almost routine. Wadi Halfa, in the Sudan but on the border with Egypt, was a welcome stop for lunch. We were taken on a bus, in better shape than the one in Khartoum, to a hotel. It was set among palms and colourful gardens, with verdant green lawns, watered luxuriantly from the River Nile. There we enjoyed a refreshing break and a tasty lunch.

Then on to Mersah Matruh, which is linked by road west of El Alamein. It's a pretty little harbour town, with gorgeous, azure, Mediterranean waters and soft, white beaches. It boasts an interesting history from the Second World War, when it was the headquarters for Field Marshall Rommel during the desert campaign. Alas, we were not given time to explore.

That evening we landed in Malta, where accommodation at the classy Phoenicia Hotel was delightful. While touring Valletta, we learned how the island was awarded the George Cross during the Second World War, in recognition of the stoic invincibility of its people, in withstanding the worst air attacks from the Luftwaffe.

On the third day, our first stop was Rome.

"I'm sorry," the air hostess explained, as we sipped from our glasses of juice in the 'in-transit' area of Rome's airport, "but we have a little engine trouble. The captain noticed it on the way in, and has concluded that the plane will have to wait here for repairs and spare parts from London. The good news is: we have managed to book you all, well, most of you, on a B.O.A.C. flight that will soon be landing here, en route from Bombay to London, so the delay will not be long. For those of you who were due to depart our flight in Nice, we'll be arranging a local Alitalia flight to get you there."

Hours later I gazed out the window of the four-engined Argonaut, a plane much like the Hermes I'd flown to Africa in, peering at the Alps a little more than four thousand feet below. The air was crystal clear, the sky a vivid cerulean blue, and the white-peaked mountain caps so close we could almost touch them. I picked out tiny hamlets nestled in the valleys. I thought how I'd never have seen this if we hadn't switched planes. There's not a chance a Viking could fly this high.

The captain told us we were experiencing a strong tail wind. "In fact," he said, "we're ahead of schedule. Soon we'll be flying over Mont Blanc when we should get a wonderful view." Moments later he came on the speaker again. "I think it would be rather jolly," he allowed, "seeing as we're flying ahead of schedule, if we make a little scenic diversion. I'm going to descend a couple of thousand feet, which will put us, give or take, at two thousand feet higher than the tip of Mont Blanc. We'll spend a few minutes circling it, first on our port side then to our starboard. With the weather as clear as it is, you should be able to take beautiful, close-up photographs of the mountain. So, get your cameras ready, hold on to your hats, and we'll take a peek."

We banked hard to port as we circled the mountain, which rose so close; I thought I could see skiers at its crest. We completed a full circuit and then, as promised, the captain brought the plane about and banked hard to starboard and did the same again, for the benefit of those seated on the other side of the cabin.

"That's it, folks. Show's over, now we'll head for home."

OUR HOLIDAY IN ENGLAND RUSHED BY. FIRST off, Mum and I had taken a continental bus tour; eleven days driving through France, Switzerland and Italy. Like the rest of Europe, the South of England was bathed in a gorgeous summer. Staying with Grandfather, Mum persuaded him to have a telephone installed. This had been hard work, for Pop was not a man to waste money.

"I don't know anyone with a telephone," he argued, "so who on Earth do you think I'm going to keep ringing-up? I haven't even got one at my business. Not only that, but I don't know anyone with a telephone who'd want to ring me."

"It's the modern thing to do," argued Mum. "And it's for your safety. You don't have to keep using it, but just have it there for in case you have an emergency; then you can call for help, without struggling to get down the street and find a phone box."

"I don't want to be buggered with it," Pop had argued, not wanting all these new-fangled ideas. "Next thing is you'll want me to buy a television too."

"As a matter of fact…" responded Mum.

By the time we returned to Africa, a telephone had been installed in Pop's hallway, and a television was set in place opposite his favourite chair. Mum was content. Meanwhile our booking was re-arranged to an Airwork flight that flew Viscounts and could fly at night. We landed in Dar the day before the *Kongwa Special* would depart for the second term of the year that would take us through to Christmas. It was the one time a parent put me on the train.

The new school year brought the arrival of a new teacher by name of Jim Sweeney. He brought his wife and three children who became day boarders of course. Frank was the closest in age to me. They lived up along the area known as Millionaires Row.

PART THREE

GROWING UP

CHAPTER NINETEEN

LION COUNTRY

W E WERE SHORT OF MEAT AGAIN, AND it was Livingstone's turn to do something about it. Mr. Moore called upon three of his prefects, inviting them on a hunt. They'd been given permission to ship their rifles to school, to remain under lock and key with the Head, until needed. The prefects were encouraged to bring their fags along. I was Neil's, so, as he was selected to join the hunt, he let me know I'd be going with him and the others on safari.

It was Saturday when Walter Fantino, who was Head Boy, together with Neil Thomson and Claus Meyer, with their fags, Aranky, Ivey and me, left the mess after breakfast. We clambered into the open back of a Bedford lorry, with its disintegrating, wooden side slats and hand-cranked winch bolted to the floor behind the cab. The three Seniors had retrieved their guns from Mr. Moore's car, and these were handed to us to hold, as gun bearers.

"It's a Holland & Holland .375," Neil explained to me. "Here, I'd better show you the basics. First, the safety catch. Most important part of the gun. Make sure that's on at all times, see?" He flicked the catch on and off to demonstrate. "Now, you probably won't have to load it, I'll do that, but you need to know just in case, so watch…"

Walter Fantino possessed a BRNO .30-06, and spent a few minutes showing Ivey, who knew a bit about guns from his dad. Claus Meyer owned a Mauser 93 Magnum that, he said, was heavy duty enough to bring down an elephant. Aranky didn't claim to know any more about guns than I did, so he was shown the basics.

"Let's go," called Mr. Moore. "Fantino, you can drive, I'll sit beside you and navigate. The rest, in the back."

In half an hour we were beyond Kongwa, bouncing along a corrugated track, heading past the twin mountains known as Sheba's Breasts (and to us boys as *Two Tits*), in the general direction of Kiboriani. This was my first hunt. I had mixed feelings about being here but as I had no say, I kept my thoughts to myself. It's not that I was scared. I just don't like killing things. I like eating meat; I just don't want to have anything to do with the animal's destruction. On the other hand, this was an elitist thing to do. There were few who got the chance to spend the day hunting for the school's dinner. Most of my friends would have changed places in a heartbeat.

We headed east initially to miss the void of the Units, later turning southeast in the general direction of Sagara. We reached the foothills at the easterly limit of the Kiboriani Range. Here the track wound into the extreme south of the Masai Steppe, where the landscape changes to Savannah. Baobabs, acacias and msasa dot the landscape, and elephant and predators were said to roam with a prolific range of other game. It was a long drive from Kongwa given that we were out for only a day. But the animals of the region had continued their drift away from humans, so we had to travel further than in earlier years.

"Wow, it certainly looks different here." I commented to Ivey and Aranky. "I'll bet we'll see animals around here pretty soon."

"Let's hope so," Aranky said. "Nothing much so far."

The improved vegetation was an eye opener. Ahead of us, countless square miles of savannah reflected no landmarks to distinguish these one hundred from the next. The track we'd followed petered out to where a variety of shallow tracks had distributed in several directions. Now even they were gone as we jogged over untraveled land, bundu bashing. In and out we weaved between the bush, skirting acacias here and baobabs there, keeping a close eye out for rocks, ant hills and dongas, large and small. If we hit one at speed, we could break an axle and be stuck. We had no way to contact the school if we broke down. Obviously if we didn't return when expected, a search party would be despatched but whose to say they would find us, never mind when.

As ever, the sun burned. Except for the two in the front, the rest of us were in the open bed of the lorry without shade. The wind cooled a little. We didn't wear hats; school hats for boys were not available. The lorry bounced and weaved; the fine dust kicking up behind swirled around us, for we could not outpace it. Soon we were coated in a powdery film, darkening our skin and leaving the insets to our eyes pale white. Later, the rock-hard earth gave way to tall grasses in burnt gold, providing a relief to the view, but additional hazards in not being able to see what danger lurked. Suddenly we came across small game.

"Pass me my gun," Thomson urged reaching for the Holland & Holland that I hastily handed over.

"It's only Dik-dik," said Ivey. "You'd need a lot of those to feed the school," he chuckled.

Although Thomson and Meyer raised their guns in anticipation of a shoot anyway, the small antelopes, letting out their shrill whistle alarm, were too fast and long gone, or hidden in the tall grass, before a shot could be got off.

One moment we were bouncing around, bored with the lack of action, the next moment we were catching our breaths in excitement. The acacias were more clumped than usual, the small spaces between them filled by dense thorn bush, making the area impenetrable. But not so for the water buffalo herd that had been quietly browsing.

"Buffalo!" exclaimed Aranky.

Fifty yards to our right, we could see they were as startled as we were. I did a quick count. "There are nine including the babies," I called in excitement.

"They're one of Africa's most dangerous animals," said Aranky. "We'd better watch out."

"Shall we take a crack at a buffalo?" Thomson leaned down towards the cab window and addressed Mr. Moore.

"No, leave them alone. We can't afford to take chances in just wounding one. They're exceptionally dangerous creatures. Let's hold on until we find something more suitable."

The male was reacting with alarm, throwing up his head and stomping the ground with a hoof after he turned to face us.

"Oh my gosh," Ivey blurted. "I think he's coming for us."

"Don't worry, man," said Meyer. "We're already passing by. We can out-run him, man."

But even as he said that the buffalo began trotting towards us.

Luckily Meyer was right. Fantino put his foot down and we were faster, even with the uneven ground. Soon the buffalo aborted the chase, pleased with himself no doubt that he'd seen us off.

Another hour passed and we'd found nothing of substance, until Meyer spotted a wisp of smoke curling languidly in the shimmering heat. It was difficult to make out – we didn't all agree there was smoke but Meyer was certain – so what with that and the lack of anything else to interest us, we veered in that direction. Soon the smoke from an open fire was readily seen, and in the near distance a cluster of small, red-roofed buildings. Fantino stopped the lorry not sure whether to continue into the compound ahead, or steer clear in our continuing search. We hopped out the back and stood around, stretching legs and kicking stones as Mr. Moore surveyed with his field glasses.

"I wonder what…" began Mr. Moore, and then, "…oh yes, that must be the Roman Catholic mission I've heard about. Can't imagine what else it could be. Let's pay them a visit."

We resumed our drive towards the mission. As we approached, we passed a grove, alive with bright, yellow lemon trees. A little further on stood a whitewashed chapel, adorned with a cross perched above its front doors. On the other side of the compound was another low building, this time with a Red Cross sign on its side, an indicator of an infirmary. There was a cluster of low buildings off to our left – looked like our houses in Kongwa – and behind them lay several kayas. As we squeaked to a halt, two nuns, dressed in habits and scapulas, approached curiously, and we greeted them as we jumped down from the tail board.

As he brushed the dust off, Mr. Moore addressed the nuns first, calling out, "Good day, Sisters. I hope you won't mind us stopping by to say hello."

The cheerful nuns greeted Mr. Moore enthusiastically – the more so, it seemed, when they spotted us chaps bringing up the rear and strolling hesitantly toward them.

"What brings you so far out here, to be sure?" asked the first nun, in an Irish brogue.

"Oh, we're a hunting party, Sister," said Mr. Moore, in his immaculate tone. "Meat is in short supply at Kongwa, I'm afraid, so we're on a mission

– if you'll forgive the pun – to redress the situation. Having spotted your smoke, we thought it an idea to call by and enquire if you have knowledge of any game hereabouts."

"Well, to be sure we don't know," replied the other nun, "but I've no doubt Patrick, our foreman, may steer you in the right direction. But first, won't you come in and meet Father Doherty? I know he'll be delighted to greet you. Your boys look thirsty; no doubt you could all do with a nice glass of fresh lemon juice."

"Well, they have their own water bottles with them so I—"

"—Oh nonsense, of course they'd like lemon juice to be sure – isn't that so, boys? We'd be delighted to share with you. Do come this way."

Before long we'd been greeted by Father Doherty and shaken hands, as he eyed us with surprise, doubtless pondering increasing the size of his flock. Alas for him, the school was too far to contemplate that, and in any case, we were already parishioners of St Andrew's Anglican.

"Well, to be sure this is a surprise indeed," said Father Doherty. "We do not receive many visitors out this far, I fear, but content ourselves with our congregation from the local Gogo kijijis. We do know of Kongwa, of course; pop into the village once in a while actually, but not often, as we purchase most of our supplies in Dodoma. So, how may we be of service?"

As we thirstily downed our incredibly delicious, fresh-squeezed juice, Mr. Moore told Father Doherty of our search for game. "The only sign we've seen of any was a herd of water buffalo some way back," he said, "and I wasn't going to let the boys take any shots at them. Those animals are far too dangerous, particularly if wounded and I didn't want to let a wounded buffalo be wandering around the bush. I must say, I'm surprised to see any in this neck of the woods."

"It's because we have a good water supply I expect," replied Father Doherty. "The water Kongwa gets from Sagara is believed to be fed by an underground river which runs close to the surface not far to the south-east of here. There's a large region of swampy ground."

By this time the one nun who'd disappeared reappeared with Patrick. He told us there was game in the area, but as he'd not been hunting for several days he couldn't be sure exactly where.

"I can tell you, bwana," he assured Mr. Moore in his strong Gogo accent in speaking English, "they are not-e very far away. But eh I just don't-e know exactly where they may be. I mean to say, I can guess the area but I cannot-e be suar."

"That's no problem, Patrick," responded Mr. Moore. "If you'll point us in the general direction, with any luck we'll happen upon them, or we'll spot their dust and take it from there."

Before we were allowed to leave, Father Doherty insisted on giving us a tour of the mission, and the Red Cross infirmary with which they enjoyed a cooperative agreement. The two nuns fussed around as an advance party, making sure inhabitants cleaned them up quickly ahead of our inspection. We were shown the classroom in which the Watotos were taught, but they were away tending cattle as it was the weekend, and their teacher had gone home to his village.

We'd not been aware of the mission's kijiji initially, but set back behind the buildings was a modest one that housed about forty people, complete with boma (thorn brush enclosure) for the cows and goats. At this time of day the boma was empty as the animals were out grazing, tended by the watoto. The women were hard at work however, babes lashed to their backs, pounding millet in tall kinoos as they prepared their pombe for drinking when their men came home. The smell of dry wood smoke, cow dung and blood lay heavy.

"You may come across our watoto, with our ng'ombe, when you leave here, bwana," continued Patrick. "Please be careful not-e to disteb them too much because-e we have to keep them all together. We cannot-e have them wander off due to the simbas, bwana."

"Simbas?" said Mr. Moore in surprise, suddenly catching our ears. "There's lion around?"

"Yes, bwana, there are simbas, eeeh. They caught-e some of our ng'ombe one time so now we have to be extra careful. They don't-e give us too much trouble because there is lots of game, but sometimes they do."

"All right then, we'll watch out for the simbas too. Hear that, boys? Eyes peeled for lion."

Back on track we'd still not spotted anything remarkable, no shots had been fired and the hunt was looking bleak. Then we came across the small cow and goat herds from the mission. We'd slowed down to circumvent a fallen tree and avoid a huge boulder, when we heard the sound of cowbells. It was strange. We could hear the cowbells but not see anything with the animals and the children melded into the trees and scrub. But then they materialised and we stopped to greet them. A pungent smell wafted over from these magnificent long horned ng'ombe with their dangling dewlaps, and bleating goats. The curious watoto herders eyed us cautiously. Meyer, who spoke the best mix of Cigogo and Swahili, greeted them from our stationary lorry.

"Hamjambo watoto. Tumetoka hivi sasa misheni tunapokaa. Tunatafuta nyama ya kuwinda. Patrick, mtumishi mkubwa ametuambia tutapata hapa pamoja na ng'ombe na mbuzi wako. Umeona wanyama wa porini hapa karibu?"

"I told them we have just come from the mission where we met with Patrick," said Meyer. "I asked them if they've come across any game."

The older children, about ten years of age, approached with their spears over their naked shoulders, wearing European shorts, no shoes, just large, flat, dust-covered feet, and got into an animated conversation with Meyer that was so fast talking that they left me bewildered.

"The watoto say there are signs of lion in the area. That often signifies game as the lion tend to follow the herd. However, they've not seen any today so they couldn't be sure how far. Maybe one day travel, maybe two, they said. But then of course, they're walking."

Well, we were not out on a several days hunt – we were supposed to find something today, so we thanked them, gave them a ten-cent coin each and drove on. We were by now a long way from Kongwa. If we did bag anything, there would be no time for preparing it for tonight's dinner. Well, the cooks at school knew this might be the case. They had their instructions on what to prep if we didn't return by 3 p.m. Around 1 p.m. we came across a cluster of shady acacias, so Walter turned in that direction and brought the gari to a halt. Mr. Moore jumped out, saying he thought this a good place to take a rest and eat our lunches. We noticed the grass around the trees had been flattened. It was good that we wouldn't have to prep the ground before we set to with our food. On the other hand, as Walter questioned, "How did this grass get to be so flattened?" immediately answering himself with, "Quite possibly a lion pride."

Mr. Moore looked at him and then at us. "Be very aware, very alert, boys. Clearly if Fantino is right the lions are not here now but that's not to say they're far away. We must be extra careful. Now, you're all Boy Scouts, aren't you?"

"Yes, sir!" we chorused. "Except for Ivey."

"And your motto is?"

"Be prepared, sir!"

"Right you are then. I know this is not a Boy Scout weekend but let's keep to their best traditions, shall we? You too, Ivey."

We gun bearers, having loaded then checked the guns were ready for use, handed them to our prefects, who in turn double-checked them and took up a defensive position. With the thick cluster of trees at their back, Fantino faced in one direction, his .30-06 at the ready, Neil took a position at 180 degrees to him, facing the other and checked his Holland & Holland yet again. Meyer took up position at ninety degrees to each, his impressive looking Mauser resting on his shoulder, his right hand supporting the gun around the trigger. We fags were located close to our prefects, to provide ammunition and supply drinking water or other support.

We sat to eat, but Mr. Moore remained standing. As the tallest he was keeping a wary eye out over the high grasses swaying gently in an early afternoon breeze. He was probably concerned about how things would go were a lion to come strolling nonchalantly toward our redoubt. I know I was. During the conversation that followed, when we found ourselves listless and dreamy in the midday heat, it being unusually humid, Aranky announced that his dad was teaching him to shoot.

"Really? You didn't mention that when we were loading up. Aren't you a bit young?" Mr. Moore responded casually, as he brushed at the flies around his face.

"I'm fourteen, sir!" Aranky replied indignantly. "My dad says you're never too young to start, well, almost. He just thinks that living in Africa... it's an essential part of being prepared for the bush, sir."

"So how's the training coming along?" Claus followed up, through a wide yawn. "Are you ready to replace me, so I can get some sleep?"

"No, Claus," Aranky smiled back, "I only just started last hols. But my dad says I'm pretty good. We'll see."

We were weary. Our lacklustre conversation petered out as we dozed and not even Mr. Moore noticed Aranky's actions; neither did anyone observe the Black-Tailed scorpion that strayed into our clearing. Suddenly there was an almighty yell; we turned wide-eyed in alarm towards Aranky, who'd stood to stretch. That's when we saw that he'd committed the greatest no-no. He'd removed his boots and socks to give his hot and sweaty, toe-jammy feet a breather. On his one heel, a huge Black-Tailed scorpion clung by a pincer. As Aranky shook his foot to shake the creature off, it delivered, what he told us later was, his second sting.

We responded fast, no more so than Ivey who'd been wiping the sweat from his brow with a saturated hanky. In a second he lashed out at the scorpion. The damp hanky snagged the second pincer and ripped the scorpion off Aranky's foot. Meyer, who had whirled around at the yell, quickly stamped on it with his boot.

The immediate danger was gone. But Aranky was hopping around in gritty silence, grasping the foot with both hands, face screwed up in pain.

"We need to cool that sting fast," said Fantino.

Mr. Moore took control, "Quick, go to the lorry, there's our last flask of water in there. That's the only cool thing we've got. Soak a rag with the water and apply a compress immediately."

In no time we had it applied to the sting, using one of my hankies to tie it on.

"Damn," said Mr. Moore. "What on Earth did you take your boots off for, you foolish boy? Now look at the trouble we've got. I thought you were an experienced Scout! We'll have to get you back to school as fast as possible and that'll mean no game shot today. Honestly I'd have thought you'd know better than to do that."

"I'm sorry, sir," said Aranky, his face scrunched. "My feet felt so bad with all that toe-jam, sir, I didn't think it would do any harm, sir."

"As a Boy Scout you should have known. If I was your troop leader I'd reduce you in rank. Oh dear, oh dear."

As soon as we'd done everything we could for Aranky, we piled him into the front of the lorry. Mr. Moore decided to drive, as the rest of us scrambled up the sides to stand in the back. He then eased the vehicle into a tight turn, following our own tyre tracks in the direction from which we had come.

CHAPTER TWENTY

CLOSE ENCOUNTERS

W E'D DRIVEN ONLY A SHORT WHILE, WHEN Claus knocked on the roof and, leaning over to the driver's window, called Mr. Moore. "There's a dust cloud ahead, sir. It may be a sand storm or it may be animals, I can't tell."

Mr. Moore brought the gari to a halt. "Where away?" he called – he was fond of nautical terms; perhaps he'd been in the navy, I never did find out.

"On the forward bow, sir, dead ahead."

Mr. Moore climbed out the cab and onto the back to join Meyer and Fantino, peering into the distance.

"The dust isn't moving much, sir. I mean, I don't think it's a sand storm, I think it may be game."

Mr. Moore stared through his field glasses.

"It's game all right. Zebra, wildebeest and maybe Tommies, can't be sure. But there're plenty of them. It's unfortunate we can't continue the hunt."

Aranky had climbed out of the cab and was looking up at us. "If that's game, sir, let's go after it. I'm feeling better, sir, the pain's not too bad and I'm not having bad effects from the venom, sir."

"Hmmm, I don't know Aranky... Are you sure?"

"I'm not so bad, sir, bit like a bee sting. I can handle it, sir."

I stared at Aranky and decided he was putting on a brave face. He was in pain all right, but, like the tough little bugger he was, trying not to show it.

He wasn't going to be responsible for us returning to school empty-handed. He may not be suffering as bad as some would, but he was definitely hurting.

"Good lad. It seems you're a fortunate one," said Mr. Moore, as he took a close look at the location of the stings. "Some people would be laid up for days but you're either not so allergic, or maybe the scorpion's venom was of a milder variety. Very well, let's proceed with care; with that game ahead I want to bag something. We don't want to return home with Livingstone being unsuccessful, do we?"

"No, sir!" we chorused.

"We're going to have to be clever about this. I'd like to drive closer before we intercept them. Fantino, check the wind."

Walter jumped to the ground, and threw a handful of dust into the air. The wind was blowing to our right, it was a westerly. The animals had the wind at their backs, what luck!

"We shouldn't approach from this angle, sir; they'll pick up our scent. I think we should make a wide arc around to the east so we can head them off and be in their path as they move downwind."

"Good thinking, Fantino. Right then, we'll veer east now, then turn north again at a point where we'll come out ahead of them. Here, take my field glasses, take turns with Meyer to keep an eye on them and let me know how I should steer so we end up in the right place. Thomson, you go over everything with your fags, double check those guns, make sure safety catches are on, and get ready for anything. If we are spotted by the herd and they make a break for it, we might need to give chase. You three may have to take your best shots from a moving vehicle. Let's hope it doesn't come to that."

Our gari bounced over the uneven terrain. In places, rusty sand billowed behind in an elongated cloud, giving concern lest the game spot it and sense danger. But we were still some distance away, so, if they did see it, they were not alarmed apparently for they did not change direction.

Unexpectedly, Fantino called out, "Watch out! Donga ahead."

Mr. Moore slowed the vehicle, and then came to a halt just short of the donga's sides.

"Oh, no," he said. "This looks long and it's running north/south. If we turn north to follow it now, depending on how long it is, we may not be able to come at the game from downwind."

"The donga's shallow, sir," said Fantino, "and there're no mountains close by so it's a good bet it'll remain like this its entire length. Let's turn south again, sir, and see if we can find a point where the sides are shallow enough that we can drive across. If we do, after that we can continue east and eventually north again at the right point, sir."

"I was thinking along similar lines, Fantino. Good for you. All right, let's do it."

We turned south, keeping within a few yards of the donga's edge, so we could see its sides without stopping. The donga was lined with trees and scrub that were thin and scraggy. Clearly it carried little run-off and infrequently at that.

Thomson had now joined his friends, leaning on the roof of the cab. He was to the left and closest to the donga side of the gari.

"There! There's a place I think might work, sir." He rapped on the roof.

"Where away?" Mr. Moore called back.

"On our aft port beam, sir, about thirty yards back."

Mr. Moore brought the lorry to a stop. We jumped off to peer through the scrub as we walked back along the donga's side.

"Go carefully, boys," called Mr. Moore. "Watch out for snakes!"

The words were barely out of his mouth when Neil, who was leading the way, stopped suddenly shouting, "Halt! Snake! —It's a puff adder!"

There in front of him, in a sunny gap between the grasses, was a thick and full-grown puff adder, perhaps four feet in length, with a huge girth, lying there, apparently not interested in moving out of our way. Mr. Moore came up and, out of strike range, peered at it.

"Time for a quick field lesson," he said. "That's a puff adder, all right. It has long fangs, potent venom and excellent camouflage even though you can see this chap clearly enough on the open ground. Anyway, as you know, it's extremely dangerous. Unlike most snakes, puff adders won't get out of your way, like this one, just lying there. Their habit of sunning themselves by footpaths, and lying quietly when approached, waiting for their next meal, like a mouse, to come too close, is why they're responsible for the most snake bite fatalities in Africa. It's good you spotted this one, Thomson, before taking one more step. It's a slow-moving snake but has a lightning-fast strike. To be bitten by this little devil would mean certain death. I doubt we'd get back to hospital in time if this one sunk its fangs into any of you. Now steer clear and leave it."

"Shall we kill it, sir?" Aranky asked.

"No," I interjected, so quickly I even surprised myself.

Aranky frowned at me with a 'What's the matter with you?' look.

"No, leave it alone," said Mr. Moore. "Normally I would, I'm collecting puff adder skins, but we have no time to spare. We can easily avoid it, just walk around and follow Neil 'til he finds the place where he thinks we can cross."

I shrugged at Aranky. "I don't like killing anything needlessly."

"You've been listening to Paton too much," he retorted.

We watched the puff adder over our shoulders as we walked by, giving it a wide berth. Neil soon found what he judged to be the shallow-enough sides to the donga at a point where the surrounding terrain was on a slight up slope. We stood and stared at what looked more like a defined undulation than a donga, noting that the other side of it was similar. Finally, Mr. Moore, after pacing the donga bed and checking the depth of the sand, made his decision.

"I think it'll work," he said. "The loose sand appears not too deep. We'll drive over as light as possible. You'll stay off the gari until I've driven across and up the other side. We'll unload everything that's loose in the back, so the weight is reduced to the minimum. All right, let's go."

We returned to the lorry, removed everything, and set it aside. On our return I'd noticed that the puff adder had disappeared. I wondered where it had gone and resolved to be even more careful. Then Mr. Moore climbed into the cab and drove the vehicle in a wide arc so as to come back to the crossing point, facing it broadside. He stopped about thirty yards short, revved a little, then, in low gear, accelerated as fast as the gari would pick up speed, crested the inclined edge of the donga and descended into it at a pace. It looked at first as though he might make it, travelling at the speed he was, loose sand spinning from the wheels in a ballooning cloud. But, a little over half way across, it was as though he had deliberately brought the vehicle to a stop. The lorry simply lost momentum and slowed to a halt, rear wheels spinning.

"Oh, no," I thought. "Now what?"

Mr. Moore didn't spin the wheels for long. He knew that would be pointless and, I suspect, probably expected this might happen. He climbed out the cab, walked back up the incline to where we were staring, disappointed, and started barking orders.

"All right, Fantino, we need to dig ourselves out. Take your party of boys, everyone except Thomson, and collect brushwood to stick under the wheels. Thomson, follow me, we need to start digging the sand away from the wheels. There are two spades over there – get them and bring them to the gari."

In relay after relay we collected brush, branches, fallen limbs, anything of any substance that we could stick in front of the rear wheels and some for the front too, to get them over the loose sand. It took twenty-five minutes but we were sweating like pigs by the time Mr. Moore said we'd done enough. We'd created two woody tracks an axle width apart, in front of both sets of wheels, leading most of the way up the incline to the opposite side.

"Now for the finale," said Mr. Moore. "We need to dig tighter around the base of the rear wheels, as far underneath as possible so that the wheels will grip on the brush instantly. I don't want them digging us any deeper into the sand."

Once he and Neil had completed that we received our last instruction. "It's now or never. I want three of you at the rear right-hand corner and the other three at the left, ready to push hard. On my command, get ready to take the strain and then heave with all your might, all right?"

"Yes, sir," replied Fantino. "Okay, Thomson, Meyer and Aranky, you take the right. I'll take the left with Ivy and Edwards. Do you think you can handle this, Aranky?"

"Ja, man, Walter, I'll do my bit – my foot's not hurting too bad, I can do it."

"Right then," said Mr. Moore, as he climbed into the cab. Quickly he engaged gear, yelled out, "Now!" and let the clutch out.

The lorry lurched, tyres biting into the brush and the dead tree limbs. Trouble was, it was too successful. None of us thought the tyres would grip quite so readily and were straining against the lorry's rear. Before you knew it, we were grovelling in the sandy river bed, having fallen forward as the lorry roared away and up the slope, kicking splinters of wood and a flurry of dried leaves behind it. Although a couple of us received sharp stings as shards glanced off our arms or legs, no one was injured, and we were laughing as we clambered back to our feet and brushed away the sand. Mr. Moore brought the lorry to a stop, climbed out to check on us and stood at the top of the incline, arms akimbo.

"Good job, boys," he laughed. "I think you've learned a couple of tricks today, and it's not over yet. Now, quickly, gather everything up and reload the gari, we have some hunting to do."

We continued our bush-bashing further east, until the prefects judged that if we turned north now, we would be far enough ahead of the herd to line ourselves up in their path. The terrain became thicker with grasses and trees, which helped muffle our engine noise and disguise our presence. We had just driven past a denuded hillock, rising strangely and alone out of the bushy terrain. I thought I detected movement near the top, some animals – were those lionesses? – but I couldn't be sure. Then, Mr. Moore brought us to a halt.

"All right, this is where we'll make our stand. I want dead quiet from everyone. Mostly use sign language or very quiet whispers. Fantino, you wait here with the gari and I'll remain with you. You can use the roof as your rifle support and maintain this position facing west if the herd continues to come toward us. The wind is behind them so that'll be a great help.

"Meyer, I want you to pace three hundred yards further north, find a good spot with plenty of cover and lie in wait facing west. Thomson, same thing. Pace three hundred yards south, more or less back on our tracks, maybe more in the general direction of that denuded hill over there. This way we have a six-hundred-yard line with three firing locations. One of you should be able to down something. My preference would be zebra; they make the best meat. But if you have a wildebeest, or a kudu or something of that nature in your sights, and an easy kill, then do it. Remember, I don't want any wounded animals running around the veld. I want a straight, clean kill, so hold your fire until you're certain of your shot. You fags, go with your prefects and obey their instructions. No noise now!"

With that, Neil and I began our pace towards the hillock as Mr. Moore, with Fantino and Ivey, climbed onto the lorry's back. As we walked, I told Neil what I thought I'd seen on the hillock. We stopped to peer up at it but there were no animals to be seen.

"You were seeing things, Edwards. There's nothing there."

Then we were startled by a troop of noisy vervets as they began leaping around in the trees, creating a hullabaloo, warning everything that cared to listen, of dangerous humans in the vicinity. I wondered if the herd would pay attention to monkeys.

I carried the Holland & Holland, plus everything else it seemed, but that was all right, that was my job. I was feeling hotter than ever, and my heart was pounding. The excitement was building, and whether or not I liked it, I was an essential part of the plan and possibly an important player in our success. Who knew what the herd was going to do?

We groped through the thick grass, stepping deftly and at half a crouch to keep our heads below the grass line so we'd not be seen. Msasa trees were prolific, causing Neil to mutter about getting a clear shot. He was looking for a tree with a fork in it where he could rest the barrel. Then he saw what he could use, an especially large ant hill, some eight feet high and maybe six feet wide at its base. Question was, was it occupied? Neil walked around it peering intently, then beckoned me to hand over the rifle. He dug and poked at it with the rifle butt. The vervets got even more excited. Red soil fell away exposing myriad corridors within the nest, but no ants; the former occupants had abandoned their high rise. This was a lucky break. Neil turned and signalled to move in.

The herd had moved closer to our line. I wasn't sure, but I sensed by their noise that it may have veered south-east a bit... and, if it had, that would mean the centre of lead animals would be heading straight for us, rather than Walter in the lorry. Neil nuzzled himself into a comfortable position against the ant hill after carving with his huge sheath knife a spot to rest the rifle. I stood away from the gun and its noise and its potential recoil, and a little off to his right. We remained motionless and dead quiet. The vervets fell silent too, as they peered at us in fearful anticipation of what was coming next. I looked over my shoulder towards the hillock to try again to see if there were any animals there, but I didn't see anything.

The smell of game thickened the air, the musky odour of hundreds of animals carried before them on the breeze. Now there was a new disquiet. Snorts and grumbles, the snapping of twigs or cracking of branches, all resonated invisible through the trees giving a sense for a heavy wall of life rolling relentlessly towards us. Flocks of birds began flying away, squawking noisily as they did. The vervets remained silent; they'd warned everybody. If you didn't leave now, it wasn't their fault. Soon we'd be approached by thousands of zebra, wildebeest, and Thomson's gazelle... and they'd panic as soon as Neil got a shot off. My heart beat faster than ever.

We were crouched in the heat, swatting flies and mosquitoes, wiping our sweat as we peered through the trees trying to spot the first animals. Neither of us was expecting the commotion when it came. There was a flash of moving brown in the grasses, then several flashes.

"Oh my God, simbas!" I said. "There are simbas and they're attacking the herd!"

"Shit!" exclaimed Neil. "They're going to mess everything up."

"I told you I thought I saw them."

Before you could blink, the herd had been aroused. The alarm was sounded, the stampede was on and it was coming directly at us. That wasn't in the plan. The herd should have scattered away from us, in response to a shot being fired.

"Close in behind me," Neil yelled. "Use the anthill for protection, it's our only chance."

Heart vibrating with the heavy thumps of a gong, I closed tight into a crouch behind Neil, making myself as small as possible, pulled out my other hanky and held it over my nose and mouth.

"They're coming this way," yelled Neil. "Don't move, Edwards, no matter what. They'll be all around us in moments, hold tight!"

Then my world was filled with stampede, the noise, the thundering of hooves, the sand and dust so thick I could scarcely breathe. *If it was not for my hanky, I'd probably suffocate,* I thought, my eyes closed tight.

A shot fired from right above me, then another but almost before the hollow sound of the blast had softened, the roar of the stampede became overwhelming. It seemed as if there would be no end, as hundreds if not thousands of animals tore past us, filling my every consciousness so that nothing else was happening in the world. Just one foot either side from where we were pressed to this hill of sand, death by stampede waited.

Will the hill hold against this stampede if any of the animals crashes into it? I thought. *Will it never end?*

I thought I heard other rifle shots in the distance, but I couldn't be certain; they didn't come from Neil's gun. The stampede lasted an eternity. Hours later, actually minutes, its noise diminished rapidly, one or two late stragglers ran by and then there was nothing but the receding sound of hooves and the swirling cloud of dust and turmoil, and then silence... almost. The cicadas were the first to let out a few tentative squeaks and then the vervets joined in, screaming once more as we moved out from our hide.

Neil and I staggered out from behind the nest, coughing, spluttering and rubbing our eyes that had filled with dust, closed or not. The swirling sand thinned as we beat our clothes to eject the layer that now caked us. Now what?

"Did you *(cough)* get anything *(cough)*, Neil? I heard you *(cough)* fire at least a couple of *(cough)* shots."

For long moments there was no response from Neil; he was coughing and retching far worse than I; he'd not been able to cover his eyes, nose and mouth like me. As the sandy fog dissipated and our coughing eased, he said, "I think I may have bagged *(cough)* one. I thought I hit a punda *(cough, cough)* after my second shot but my view was so clouded *(cough)* I can't be absolutely certain. Let's *(cough)* go and look."

We walked in the direction the animals had come from as the haze cleared, but didn't find any dead zebra.

"Ahoy there," from Mr. Moore, still a hundred yards away but yelling at the top of his voice. "Are you two all right, Thomson, Edwards?"

"Yes, sir," Neil shouted back. "I *(cough, cough)* think we *(cough)* got one."

"I hope so," Mr. Moore bellowed. "The whole herd turned in your direction. What caused them to stampede anyway? They seemed to run even before you got off a shot?"

"Lions," Neil shouted back. "The herd was attacked by one, maybe two lionesses."

"My God, is that true, Thomson? No wonder. Thank goodness you're both all right. Anyway, Fantino got off a couple of shots but missed. I don't know about Meyer, I think the herd missed him altogether, so it's all on you."

As Mr. Moore closed on our location, along with Fantino and Ivey, Meyer came running up behind them telling us that Aranky was following but was slower on account of his foot. "He'll catch up just now, man."

"Gosh, what happened, you two look as though you were in the middle of a stampede," said Meyer, only half jokingly.

"Thanks to two lionesses stampeding the herd, we were, literally, *(cough)* right in the middle of it," Neil told him.

"The anthill saved us. It was pretty damn *(cough, cough)* scary, I can tell you. I'm impressed with Edwards, how he kept *(cough)* calm and all. That was great, Edwards."

"Thanks, Neil."

"Yes, well done, Edwards," said Mr. Moore. "That's worthwhile praise coming from Neil."

We were gazing around in every direction, not having found any sign of a shot zebra, when we saw Aranky in the distance. He had Meyer's field glasses and when he was about a hundred yards away put them to his eyes and scanned something that had caught his attention.

"Lionesses!" he yelled as he approached. "With a zebra kill."

"That's my kill," said Thomson indignantly. "They can't have it."

"That remains to be seen," said Mr. Moore. "Do you fancy taking a kill away from even one lioness, never mind two or more?"

"There're six of us with three guns," said Neil. "I vote we at least find out whose kill it is."

"Yes," we chorused. "We can't just let the simbas have our kill."

"We don't know it was ours," Ivey said. "After all the simbas were out hunting too. Maybe we missed and they got the punda milia."

"I didn't miss," said Neil, "not on my second shot anyway."

"All right," said Mr. Moore, "back to the gari. Let's get into the safety of the lorry and we'll try driving close by and see what gives. Hurry now; we don't want the simbas to get too far with the meal before we get to it."

By the time we got to the lorry and had driven over to where Aranky had spotted the lionesses, we confirmed there were two of them, busy pulling the zebra apart. As we stopped close by, the one lioness stopped ripping at the hide and looked up. I suppose it was just my imagination but I felt mesmerised; she seemed to be staring at *me* with those huge, round eyes, locked on me, and me on hers! It was as though she was saying, "This is our kill, not yours! Think yourself lucky this is not you. Go find your own dinner!"

I shrunk back from the side of the lorry, at the same time trying to shake myself from the stare.

"There's no way we can use that meat now anyway," said Mr. Moore. "It looks as though we're out of luck."

"Darn, I can't believe it," said Fantino.

"So close, man. Why'd they have to mess everything up?" grumbled Neil.

I blinked away to re-focus, when a new thought came to mind. I spoke up. "You know what I think?"

"What do you think, Edwards?" Meyer asked indulgently.

"I think that kill with the simbas is theirs; it's not Neil's. If you think about it and where it is in relation to our anthill, there wasn't a clean shot from there to here and this animal was too far away anyway. I think it's possible those simbas did bring down that punda milia and it's not ours to take."

"Oh, is that what you think?" responded Neil. "Let me tell you, I'd swear I hit a zebra. It sort of shook its neck even as it was running, just like I'd hit it, but I must admit I didn't see it actually fall."

"Then let's turn around and follow the herd," I suggested. "Perhaps you did hit one, Neil, and it was wounded; just not the one the lions have. We don't want to leave wounded animals lying around, isn't that so, sir?"

"Yes, Edwards, that is so. Actually that's a good idea. Let's trek back for your anthill. Then we'll follow the herd's tracks and see if we can find blood or any other sign of an injured or dead animal."

We drove to our anthill, then jumped down to walk following the direction of the stampede. It was a few minutes before we came across anything. Then Aranky spotted it with those eagle eyes of his. As we came close by an acacia he detected what looked like blood on the trunk. We closed in to take a look. Aranky stuck his finger into the gooey substance and identified deep, red, sticky blood.

"Hmmm, wasn't a clean kill if this is your zebra, Thomson," said Mr. Moore, "but then I can hardly blame you in all that excitement. Looks like blood from an artery anyway. Let's press on a little longer and see what we find."

It had been my thought, so I was anxious to be first to spot the zebra if it was down. And it was. Focused far ahead of me as we all walked in a wide sweep, I could make out the rump of a creature lying in the grass and the suggestion of black and white stripes, even from one hundred yards away.

"It's ahead up there," I yelled. "I can see the punda, I'm sure I can."

We broke into a run, with our line tightening as we got closer and could see an animal in trouble. It was amazing that no other creatures appeared to have reached it, although marabou storks and vultures were circling. We reached the zebra, more or less all at the same time. It was not dead but was dying. On its side, it was breathing hard, nostrils flaring, eyes wide and terrified and foamy blood oozing from its mouth.

"Look," said Fantino, "you can see where the bullet went in at the left shoulder. It may have reached the lungs, certainly seems like it."

Neil walked up. "Damn, damn, damn, damn," he said. "I never do this to an animal … Damn it!" And then he brought his rifle up suddenly and without warning aimed and shot the zebra in the head. It was now out of its misery but the gun shot left the vervets screeching louder than ever.

We stood there, stunned, for a few moments. None of us liked the idea of the animal suffering, but we were shocked at Neil's sudden despatch. Mr. Moore seemed to understand his distress.

"Ahem," he said. "Well, that was an amazing hunt, Thomson; an incredible shot in the middle of a stampede like that, even if you didn't hit exactly where you needed to. Still it was amazing shooting, and I don't mind who knows it."

After that we took Mr. Moore's lead and confirmed what a great shot Neil was, that he'd done a fine job, reminded him that the whole school would eat meat tomorrow, and that he should not blame himself for his imperfection. Then we snapped back to attention.

"Okay, boys," said Mr. Moore, "we must be going. It's getting late and I don't want to be driving in the bundu after dark. Fantino, take Thomson with you, run as fast as you can and fetch the gari. The rest of us will guard the kill."

It wasn't long before the two returned. Neil jumped out laughing over his shoulder at some joke as Mr. Moore called out, "Reverse the lorry up close to the zebra, Fantino. Right then. One of you drop the tailboard and fetch the two long planks that are the ramp. Edwards, uncoil the rope and tie a section around the zebra's neck. Aranky, take the second rope and circle its front legs. I don't expect any trouble with you using the wrong knots!" he added knowingly. "Meyer, let's fasten the ropes to the winch, then between the two of us, we should be able to crank it and drag the zebra into the back. Ivey, you help Meyer."

Time was catching up as we closed the tailgate and jumped aboard, Mr. Moore getting comfortable for the drive and Aranky hauling himself onto the running board as he prepared to get seated in the cab alongside him. The last of the setting sun was disappearing, leaving spears of orange and red streaking the hazy horizon, reaching for a darkening sky. We needed to move, and fast, or we would find ourselves driving at night. You can't do that in this terrain and keep your vehicle in one piece. Instead, we might find ourselves sleeping in the open back of the lorry, under the stars, with a dead and increasingly smelly animal that would attract leopards from hell 'n' gone.

The engine had been started as Aranky bent to enter the cab. We were smiling and laughing, expecting the gari to move out any moment when Aranky, who had glanced back as movement caught his eye yelled, "Simbas! Two of them!"

We whirled to where he was pointing over our heads towards the rear. They were coming at us at a sprint.

They can't be the same two, I thought. *There's not a chance they'd be chasing down another kill.*

Mr. Moore saw them in the wing mirror. He engaged gear and let the clutch out so suddenly it jerked us off our feet, with Sigurd and me falling on our behinds. We groped for the slatted sides and held on tight, as Mr. Moore spun the bouncing vehicle on the sandy surface and put his foot down.

The lionesses were closing. They were hidden by our dust for precious moments when we thought maybe they'd given up the chase, but then they came bursting through, adjusting direction for the angle of the lorry, sprinting fast, eyes wide and intent. They leapt as they closed, causing us to recoil and duck below the height of the lorry's side planks in the same split second, terrified they would clear the sides and land on us and the zebra.

First one and then the other collided in mid-flight with the sides of the gari, those life-saving planks holding firm. I was inches from the nose and eyes of one of them. I stared through the gap in the planks as the lioness's claws held her paws to our side. I saw her feverish eyes, wide open mouth and huge white fangs; I felt the heat of her breath with its foul smell.

It seemed to happen in slow motion. I couldn't believe how long this lasted before she and her companion fell off, back into the tall grasses. Both lionesses scrambled to their feet but didn't give chase. Perhaps they were stunned. Perhaps they understood this one was not for them, I don't know, but they stood and watched as we disappeared, bouncing and bucking, travelling into an orange glow, all that was left of the day.

> Wimoweh
> *"In the jungle, the mighty jungle*
> *The lion sleeps tonight*
> *In the jungle, the mighty jungle*
> *The lion sleeps tonight."*
> — Solomon Linda, 1939

CHAPTER TWENTY-ONE

IN THE CROSSHAIRS
OF A DAME

THE STORY OF THE HUNT WAS ALL over the school, so we were heroes. I don't know how much that had to do with it, but it was not long before I became more aware of Hazel Miller. Now, I have to confess that, being fourteen, I may, in the view of some, have been a little late where an interest in dames was concerned. Some boys already had girlfriends, Pepsi being the one I knew of best. The risk he ran, it seemed to me, was that aside from the fact we were not supposed to socialise with girls other than on approved occasions, like classroom breaks, Pamela was also the daughter of a maths teacher. *High risk,* I thought. Doug told me he thought Pamela's parents didn't mind, even encouraged the romance by sometimes inviting him to join the family at the pool in Sagara on a weekend.

I'd talked to Hazel from time to time; she was best friends with Annelize. On our flights between Lindi and Dar we might chat and in Kongwa we exchanged a few words if our paths crossed during breaks. Hazel was older, so I was surprised when she approached me. I was hanging around with friends near the recently constructed flagpole from which the Union Jack drooped. Berry was telling us that we wouldn't be seeing him on the school train anymore because, in a letter from home, he'd been told the family would be moving to Mwanza at the end of term. That meant he'd come to school by bus from Dodoma.

As we contemplated that, Susan, Doug's sister, a girl for whom I had a secret admiration but didn't dare say anything, walked up to me bold as brass, in front of her brother, Ivey and Berry and handed me a note, wrapped around a gob stopper. Without a word she turned and retreated to the corner of a second block, where Hazel and Nadia Aranky were waiting. I watched in amazement as the three disappeared around the corner out of sight.

"What's it say?" my three friends chorused. "Come on, open up the note, Edwards, what's it say?"

I unpeeled the sellotape fastening, revealed the gob stopper that I popped into my mouth and read aloud, with plum-in-mouth pronunciation. "Dear Tony, would you like to be my boyfriend? I think you are very nice… and brave… *(the flattery was duly noted)* and I'd like to be your girlfriend, if you'll have me. Please tell me or Susan if you'd like to, then we can plan to get together and talk. From Hazel Miller."

"Aha, you old devil, Edwards, you've got the dames chasing you now…. Boy, what a man!"

"Thanks, Pepsi," with a slight sneer of indifference.

"I didn't know she was that good friends with my sister," he followed up.

"But she's so much older than you… there must be something wrong with her," said Berry, frowning sagely.

"What do you say, Tony? What do you think of Hazel? She's a looker, eh?" asked Ivey.

"She's not bad actually," ventured Pepsi. "You know, not film star beautiful, but not bad at all, pretty attractive in fact. You could do worse, man. And so what if she's older than him, Stewie – she can teach him a thing or two!" he chuckled.

"I think she's a good looker," I said.

"And well-developed," added Doug, giving me a flashing eyebrows smile along with an elbow nudge.

"Big bazoomas," Ivey followed up, sticking out his chest and making their shape with his hands.

"At least one and a half BSH's each," chuckled Doug, with a twinkle in his eye.

"BSH's?" I frowned, unsure.

"Oh, come on, Tony, you know what that means," said Doug. "British Standard Handfuls!"

More flashing eyebrows and chuckling from the other two.

I frowned disapprovingly. "That's not nice, chaps."

"Gosh, you're not defending her already, are you?" asked a smiling Berry. "You haven't even accepted her yet."

"No, it's just that…" I hesitated. "Well, I already know her, you know, she lives in Nachingwea so we've talked on the plane sometimes; she's quite a nice girl actually. The thing is, I'm not sure I even want a girlfriend."

"Oh, come on," said Ivey. "You must have given her the eye, Edwards," he nudged me with a knowing smile. "You must have given her some sign you're interested, right? I mean, what do you do on the plane? You know, dames don't just go around proposing to chaps; especially not when they're older than the bloke."

"That's what I'm saying," said Berry, in his enlightened way. "She must be two years older. She can't possibly be interested in you."

"I had to chat up Pam Chambers for ages before I got her to be my girl-friend," said Doug ruefully, "and here you are with the girls chasing you."

"*A* girl," I said to Doug, "Not *girls*, and also, Stewie, how is it that I got this note then, huh, if she's not interested? How is it I got this note and the gob stopper?"

"Maybe it was a mistake," asserted Berry. "Maybe Susan got the wrong chap and they're back there now and Hazel's upset with Susan for getting the wrong one."

"How many Tony's do you know in this school?" I asked, flashing the note in front of him. "See the name on the note, 'Dear Tony'!"

"Hmm, there aren't any other Tony's. Gosh, I s'pose it must be you."

"There is one other… Tony Smeed," Ivey reminded us.

"Well," said Pepsi, "I don't think my sister would mistake Tony Edwards for Tony Smeed. And besides which, Hazel was over there with Nadia, watching, so she could see which Tony was in our group."

"That's another thing," I said. "I didn't know she was friends with Nadia; you know Neil's sweet on Nadia, eh?"

"Neil Thomson?" asked Ivey in surprise.

"Yes, Neil," said Berry on my behalf. "Tony's Neil's fag, so, he has to keep watch when Neil goes to visit Nadia late at night, isn't that so, Tony?"

"Yes, it is, and some pretty strange noises they make too!"

That had everyone flashing their eyebrows and smiling.

"It must be you," said Westley. "What are you going to do? Will you reply?"

"I don't know. Maybe, but not right away. I need to think about it. What do you think I should do, Peps?"

"I think you should accept. I have a smashing time with Pam, wouldn't want to lose her. It's jolly good having a girlfriend actually, you know, girls are so different, and you don't have to see her the whole time or anything, just when it suits you."

"Dames get all attached and jealous," asserted Berry wisely. "You won't have the freedom you have now. She'll want to spend time with you every chance she gets and then you won't be spending much time with us."

"Esperer is probably right," chipped in Ivey, using Stewart's other nickname. "I had a girlfriend back home and she was possessive, I mean, you know, they want to be with you all the time...."

"...And sometimes they want to snogg and all that sloppy stuff," added Berry.

"Snogg? You think Hazel will want to kiss?" I asked in alarm, envisioning Hazel rushing off to give birth right afterwards.

"Well, she might," Berry postulated with a wrinkle in his nose. "Girls like stuff like that."

"It's true," said Doug, "she probably will. Pam does. It's fun, man. I love kissing her; I'm telling you – you should try it – not with Pam, of course."

"You let Pam kiss you?" asked Ivey in surprise.

"Yuk," said Stewart.

"And Hazel is older than you, Edwards," reminded Ivey. "She'll want to do that snogging stuff even more. You know, dames are like that when they get older, I've seen it in the flicks."

"That's true," said Berry. "And you just know that Hazel is going to want to snogg. You can see it in her eyes. She's the romantic sort of girl," he smiled conspiratorially.

"You don't know what you're missing," said Doug with a laugh. "I see Pam every chance I get. Truth is, I don't get to see her enough. But I'm going to see more of her soon."

"How do you mean?" asked Berry. "What chances are there to see more of her?"

"Well, there're two. One is after lights-out. We can meet at a place we'll agree on when everyone's asleep... you know, like Neil does."

"You'll what?" exclaimed Ivey. "You'll get expelled if you're caught—"

"—Or get six of the best and then expelled," added Berry.

"And the other chance," added Doug, ignoring the punishment warnings, "is on Sundays when we go for walks. There's no control over where we go or who we go with, so we could be together all day."

"There may be no actual controls but everyone knows we're only supposed to go out with other boys," Berry added authoritatively. "If you're seen with Pam, especially if it's just the two of you alone, you'll be in a lot of trouble."

"Anyway, we won't be obvious about it, but we'll find a way, you'll see."

My head had been turning from one to the other as I listened to the merits or otherwise of having a girlfriend. But I have to confess, I found excitement in Hazel's invitation and, with the things Pepsi was saying about Pam, it seemed to be a good idea. Perhaps I should. Some instinct suggested I not reply immediately. It wouldn't be good to look too keen. Besides which, I needed to think it over. It was a big commitment after all. We'd heard stories of big dramas when girlfriends and boyfriends broke up. That was mostly something that seemed to happen with the older Seniors, but still, it happened. We were stuck here in school after all. If I wanted to break up with Hazel... and if she didn't want to, well, it could be difficult.

I had a restless night as I thought on the Hazel thing and about girls in general. As I was usually out like a light I found it strange to be awake for so long. And that's why I still wasn't asleep when Gunston, from the other bedroom, having failed to get any of his roommates to go to the dub with him, tiptoed down the corridor and stage-whispered from the doorway, "Edwards, are you awake?"

I knew what was coming and pretended to be asleep.

After a few moments an urgent and slightly louder, "Edwards, are you awake, man?"

Again no answer.

Then my shoulder was shaken. Gunston was standing there, peering through the pinkie-white gauze of the mosquito net. "Edwards, are you awake – will you come to the dub with me?"

Well, I couldn't pretend sleep now, so I rolled over and whispered, "What's the matter, man? Can't you go by yourself?"

"I'm scared, man," said Gunston. "There's hyenas outside, that's why I'm nervous. Also because there may be lions as well."

"Have you seen or heard any?"

"No. But you know Frank Sweeney, the day boy, well he and his dad saw a lion in their garden just a few days ago... so, you never know, eh?"

"Frank told me that too, although his dad told him to keep it hushed up; they don't want everyone getting scared. But that's unusual, you got to admit," I whispered.

"Still and all. It only takes one."

"All right, I'll come with you. Have you got your torch?"

"No, the batteries died. I'm going to get some at the tuck shop on Saturday."

"I'll bring mine."

I swung out from under my net and reached for my shoes.

"And in any case there are hyenas outside right now, that's especially why I'm nervous," Gunston continued.

"Where are they?" I questioned in a whisper.

"See through the mesh there, look down towards the manyara, there's several around. I don't know if there's any up near the choo."

"How'd you come to spot them?" I whispered, watching the sniffing animals.

"Well, I heard them. They've stopped their harrumphing right now but when I woke up I heard them, so I looked out and there they were. I saw them easily because of the moon. Sorry to wake you, but that's why."

"Hmm, well, let's go out the front door rather than here. We don't want to try scaring them off this way because we might wake the others. Follow me."

We tiptoed the length of the corridor. As we passed their door the two prefects were asleep, breathing deeply. At the end, past the drinking water filter, the door to Gunston's bedroom was ajar. We eased it closed so as not to disturb anyone. Gently I nudged the front door open a crack, half expecting to see a pack of rabid hyenas cunningly lying in wait for us on our midnight excursions, but there were none.

It was good the moon was so bright amid a clear night sky. It made things easier. There was the 'boy's' kaya, moonlight glinting off the tin roof. Straight ahead was the hot water drum. It cast a deep shadow to its side from the angle of the moon. The fire coals were cold; there was no sign of smoke, no crackling of embers.

Far to my left, bathed in moonlight, was the two unit choo. I'd never forgotten that day with the mamba, and always approached the door carefully. Now, it was night, moonlit though it was, with a cackle of hyenas around the corner and who knew what else once we approached. We stepped tentatively and tiptoed to the first corner of the house. The dub was straight ahead now, but to our left, around the next corner, set against the manyara, were the hyenas. We'd be in their view when we approached the dub, so there was only one thing to do, frighten them off before they could get ideas. I eased slowly and flat along the edge of the end wall until I reached the second corner. Gunston was behind. I peered carefully around until I set eyes on the animals, sniffing, pawing at the ground and occasionally snarling at each other. First one and then another gave their unique *mmmm-uh* sound.

Without thinking more about it, I darted from cover, straight towards the hyenas, stamping as I ran, waving my arms in the air and letting out a loud, "Waaaaaaagh!" The hyenas nearly leapt out of their skins, kind of like a herd of gazelle being disturbed by a pouncing lion, and squealing, ran for their lives, through the hedge and disappeared. I came to a stop and looked back. Gunston was watching, amazed and fascinated at the same time.

"Why'd you do that? What if they'd turned on you? How'd you know they'd run?"

"Hyenas are timid," I replied. "Taken by surprise without a moment to size up the danger, they'll run; leastways, that's what Paton told me."

After we'd brushed away and squashed several huge and ugly, white armoured spiders from around the toilet seat and wiped away their milk white innards, checked for snakes and chased away a scorpion, pushing it along with my torch, Gunston performed his task while I stood outside, keeping the door ajar just in case, staring intensely at the moon, massive in the night sky. Stars are not as bright on full moon nights, I noted, but that moon was so very large and beautiful.

I glanced over to where we'd seen the hyenas; pondering their possible return. Paton was right, *They are nervous creatures. Heck, the whole school should know that.* Even Pat Lane had chased away a pack of hyenas. We'd heard about it in class from a girl in her house, while we were waiting for Mr. Moore to take Latin.

"Tricia was walking back to our houses alone after night prep," Silvia Papini told us. "She had her torch on, thank goodness. Anyway, here's the thing. She'd got near to Matron's house when she heard all this noise and barking and kelele going on. Then she saw a pack of hyena's attacking Matron's dog, Mif – a German Shepherd if you boys don't know. Tricia was so angry they were trying to kill Mif, she didn't give it a second thought about running at them. She had an orange with her from dinner and threw it at one, screaming to let Mif go. The hyenas broke off the attack and ran away squealing. Although they dropped Mif, they'd broken her jaw so Matron had to have her put down."

That was pretty brave, I thought, *especially with her being a girl and all.*

And then my mind drifted to thoughts about Hazel, wondering if this girlfriend thing was a good idea. I decided Pepsi was right. I should give it a try; I enjoyed the teasing from my friends in a strange sort of way. *I shall have to let Hazel know, through Susan, of course, that I would accept her as my girlfriend.* After all, there might be more gob stoppers where the first came from.

SUSAN LET ME KNOW THE TIME AND location for my first meeting with Hazel. It was to be on Saturday afternoon, behind the derelict Red Cross caravan, close by the donga. No one hung around there much anymore.

When I arrived, there was no sign of Hazel. I looked around hardly believing it. Surely we couldn't have set this up and then she not arrive. What would I tell my friends? I circled the caravan slowly, just in case she was waiting around the other side and then – in case she too was circling looking for me – quickly reversed myself and stole around in the opposite direction. But it was no good. Whichever way I went, she wasn't there.

Hmmm, I wonder if she's hiding in the donga, I thought. *I'll take a dekko.*

I couldn't see its base through the bush so I scrambled down the donga's sides. I wanted to be sure I'd left no stone unturned, but Hazel wasn't hiding there either. I clambered back up, digging my feet into the donga's sandy sides and grasping at tufts of grass or spindly bushes. As I came to the top, there in front of me were two, what I took to be a girl's, shins, bobby socks and brown shoes. I gazed up the legs that soon disappeared behind a long brown skirt, a tan blouse and reached the smiling face of Hazel.

"What are you doing down there, silly boy?" was Hazel's opening remark. "I thought we said we'd meet behind the Red Cross caravan. Is it in the donga perhaps?"

"Gosh, I mean, oh, hello, that is, no, I just didn't know where you were. I did look behind the caravan, but you weren't there. I was just checking to see—"

"—Never mind. I was a bit late," she told me as I scrambled over the edge. "Do you know Biddy Goodricke?" asked Hazel. "She's Head Girl now; anyway, she had me sewing badges on her Girl Guide's blouse and it took longer than I thought. Anyway, well, here we are, what do you want to do?"

I straightened myself out, brushed the sand off my clothes and asked, "Do you have much trouble with prefects?"

"Yes, they always give us a hard time, well, except for Nadia – do you know her? – especially Biddy. I'm always slaving for her like sewing her clothes, you know, repairing tears or sewing badges on her uniform like I was today. She works hard at keeping us busy, doesn't let us get much freedom, unless you can get away for an hour or two… like now. I think boys get much more freedom than we do."

"Wow, why do you have to do sewing?"

"Because girls are expected to be good at stuff like that. What do boys do? Just go without buttons and put up with tears in your clothes, I suppose?"

"No, Matron does ours. She repairs anything badly torn. I just take my Scouts shirt to her when I get a new badge and she sews it on for me; does it for all of us. Why is Nadia an exception?"

"An exception?"

"Well, just now you said the prefects give the younger girls a hard time, all except for Nadia."

"Did I? I think it's just because Nadia's so talented, you know. She's liked a lot by the teachers and the girls. She doesn't suck up or anything, she's just so natural, great at music. Simply loves this school, can't think why. You know she passed the tests at the Royal School of Music, with distinction?"

"No, I didn't know. I do know Neil Thomson's sweet on her though!"

"How'd you know that?" gasped Hazel, with raised eyebrows and clearly surprised. "That's supposed to be a secret!"

"I'm his fag. He doesn't have secrets from me, and anyway, you know too."

"Gosh, I can't wait to tell Nadia her secret's out."

"Just don't get me into trouble, all right?"

"Promise."

"What are your prefects like?" Hazel shifted the subject. "Do they give you a hard time?"

"Some prefects are nice enough like Neil; he treats me well. Robert Compaan's nice too, everyone likes him. Then there're others, like one we used to have, his name was Koos, who're beastly and hit us around a lot. Do you get hit?"

"No, girls don't usually hit each other, well, not often anyway. More like scratching and clawing if it does happen, but that's not often…. And teachers don't, they're not allowed to physically punish us, like with a cane or anything, like they do with boys. What's it like, I mean, you know, being caned? It must be jolly sore."

"It's more than sore," I responded. "It depends what you're being hit with, you know. Like Fergie, sometimes he uses a blackboard ruler on us."

"Really! How horrible."

"Well, actually, the funny part is, it's not so sore, not compared with other things he uses. The ruler is wide and flat and doesn't hurt nearly as much as a cane, or even worse a kiboko. Mostly Fergie uses a cane or his kiboko…. What do girls get for punishments?"

"Demerit points. You know, they keep a record and add them to our end-of-term report. That tells our parents."

"Oh. Doesn't sound so bad… not like being caned."

"You know, they used to cane girls too," Hazel added, "now I come to think of it."

"Really, I've never heard that."

"Well, girls weren't caned severely on the behind like boys are, but they used to cane us on the hands. There was a girl I knew before, Beryl Lloyd, she's left the school now, but she was here from the very beginning. Anyway, in the first year or two of the school when it was smaller than it is now, the Head caned her and other girls on their hands."

"I really hate when anyone hits girls," I said, angrily, "I..."

"And now I come to think of it, there's at least one girl here now, I won't tell you her name, well, she got tackied on her bare bum by Matron."

"So they do punish you like that sometimes?"

"I don't think they're supposed to. But anyway, let's talk about something else," Hazel changed the subject. "Let's keep this cheerful. I don't like the things they do to you boys either. How about we go for a walk?"

"All right, where would you like to go?"

"Well, I know you chaps like to play in the donga. There shouldn't be anyone there this afternoon because they're mostly at sports, so we could go down there."

"All right, follow me," I said.

As we stepped towards the donga, I held out a hand for Hazel. I didn't think about it, didn't know I was going to do it, in fact it even came as a surprise to me, but I held out a hand, I suppose like a man does for a lady in the flicks, and Hazel readily grasped it as we approached the edge and steadied for the descent. It was so exciting holding her hand; in fact it was exhilarating. I was aware my heart was beating faster; thumping within my chest. I'd never held hands with a girl before, not anyway in the sense as with a girlfriend.

It didn't last long. Hazel needed to use both hands to grasp tree branches and tufts of long, coarse, dead grasses, as did I to climb down without falling, so, with me leading the way, we scrambled down the steep side to the sandy base, fifteen feet below. When I reached the base I looked up to see what progress Hazel was making. Realizing I was looking a little way up the underside of her skirt I was immediately embarrassed and turned away. I saw only a little way above the back of her knees, but I felt it the wrong thing to do, even though it was unintentional.

At the base we looked at each other, maybe slightly coyly on my part, because I'd sort of seen up her skirt a bit and because we'd held hands, if briefly. It was a first for me. It was nice though. I felt sort of protective somehow, couldn't explain it really. But I was happy to do it again. I put out a hand to hers and she clasped mine. Who would believe the excitement, the thrill in holding hands with a girl? We began our walk along the sandy donga floor. I was so excited I was lost for words, couldn't think what to talk about.

Hazel took the lead. "Tell me about the hunting trip, Tony, you know, when you and the others came back with the zebra. I think that was amazing what you did, all of you what with the drama you had with those lionesses and all. That must have been *so* scary."

As we walked, I told Hazel our story, including our discovery of the Catholic mission and later on the near disaster crossing that other donga, shallow compared with this one, of course, but with the lorry getting stuck all the same. Hazel looked horrified when I told her of the puff adder and how close Neil had come to treading on it.

"One more step and Nadia would have been looking for a new boyfriend."

"I hate those vile creatures," she said. "They give me the willies. Just wait 'til I tell Nadia that little story."

"I don't mind them. I mean, you know, I don't want them as pets or anything, but they're interesting to watch and most snakes don't attack you, you know, they try to get away from humans."

"Well I've heard stories that they do attack. There was a friend of my parents visiting once and he told them a story of a snake, I forget which type it was but anyway, this snake, how it grasps its tail in its mouth and then rolls like a hoop when it's chasing you and that's why they're so fast and you can't out-run them."

"Your friend was having your dad on, trust me, Hazel," I laughed. "No snakes anywhere in the world can do anything like that; it's all old wives' tales, or old hunters' tales, maybe."

"Well, that's what I heard."

"As a matter of fact, Haze, there are very few snakes anywhere that would actually go out of their way to attack you. I've read this, you know, from explorers and naturalists who know these things. Now, it is said that the King Cobra of Hyderabad, that's in India you know—"

"—I know where Hyderabad is."

"Oh, well, anyway, it'll attack someone who isn't threatening it, but that's there, in India. In Africa, the black mamba, like the one I saw in the dub, might attack if chased or cornered but as a general rule they don't go out of their way to. That one in the choo didn't strike at me even though I'd frightened it."

"Hmm… well, tell me, Mr. Know-it-all, why is it that there are as many snake bites that happen as there are? It's very common to hear stories about snake bites, isn't it?"

"Yes, it is, but it's not because they attack people. The snakes are defending themselves, at least in their minds, like the one that nearly bit me. If you get too close, even though you haven't seen the snake and have no intention of hurting it, the snake doesn't know that, it just thinks you're very dangerous and lashes out. It can only get you if you're within striking distance and that means you must be pretty close. I mean, that's the way it would have been with Neil if he'd stepped any closer to the puff adder. He would just about have stepped on it before the puff adder would actually have struck."

"Hmm, well, I still don't like them."

"Don't you get snakes in the girls' phase?" I asked. "We see snakes around the boys phase all the time."

"Yes, there have been one or two, but not many, thank God."

"Our Housemaster collects snake skins, you know?"

"Yes, I heard. Wants to make Mrs. Moore a handbag," Hazel chuckled.

"We watched him with one the other day. We'd been playing nyabs near the end of his drive. We missed the kill but walked by his place just as he was taking a photograph of his latest puff adder catch. He got his oldest daughter, Judi, to hold it up by the tail. I was amazed; she wasn't at all scared. Steve – that's the younger sister – stood next to it too."

"Well, you wouldn't catch me doing that," Hazel assured me.

After we'd exhausted snakes, I told Hazel in much detail, perhaps with a little embellishment, of the actual hunt and the stampede and the subsequent looking for what Neil had assured us should be a dead zebra.

It wasn't long before we reached the baobab tree root that crossed the donga like a bridge above us. "We don't know which came first," I said. "Was the tree there before the donga so that gradually the donga formed under the root and exposed it? If so that tree must have been around a very long time. Or, was the donga there and somehow or other this one particular root kept growing and pushing out like some sideways stalactite, reaching through the air for more soil to hide in, and kept going until it reached the other side of the donga, where it become buried again? What do you think?"

"I have no idea," said Hazel with an indifference that surprised me. "Such things don't really interest me, I must say."

"What does interest you?" I asked. "You're pretty bright for a girl, I mean, in class and all from what they say. I hear you're good at science and maths and you're very good at English. So why wouldn't this unusual root interest you?"

"I have other things on my mind right now, that's why."

"Like what, for example?"

"You."

"Me?"

"Yes, you."

"What's so interesting about me? Why do you even like me? I'm younger than you; I thought girls preferred boys older than them?"

"Yes, usually they do, but not necessarily. It depends on the boy. Quite honestly I haven't met any boys of my age at this school who I like... or who like me," she added ruefully.

"I can't believe that."

"Well, it's true. My friends say boys don't like girls who are brainier than them. They say that's why I don't get on with the older boys, or at least they don't get on with me."

"I don't know," I said. "Maybe. I'm not frightened of you being cleverer than me... I don't think...."

"I don't believe I am cleverer than you. Well, maybe at school work, on account of I'm older, but you have a maturity about you that is different from other boys of your age, or even of most of the ones of my age as far as I'm concerned."

"Maturity? I've never even had a girlfriend."

"No, not that sort of maturity. I mean the maturity of being more grown-up. Not so little-boy-ish. You're always listening to the B.B.C., I've heard, and they say you know about stuff that most boys don't. That may be something to do with it, you know, more grown-up."

"How do you know that?" I asked inquisitively, with narrowed eyes.

Hazel ignored the question. "I thought you might not have a girlfriend. Annelize says she's not your girlfriend and there's no other European girl in Lindi who's old enough to be. So, as you haven't got one here either, or at least hadn't until now," she added with a coy smile, "I thought it would be fun to be your girlfriend and maybe teach you a thing or two."

"Teach me what?"

"Oh, about girls."

Hazel edged to the donga wall below the tree root, turned around and leaned against its sandy sides as she talked, starting off a number of gritty landslides in the process. A couple of geckos, irritated with the interruption from their sunny sojourns, scuttled off to find more peaceful hideouts. Because we'd let go for a while she now stretched out an arm in invitation for me to hold her hand again.

Hazel was looking into my eyes intently. There was a slight pull on my arm; she was drawing me towards her… and now we were close, hands still held, arms down at sides, nearly nose to nose. My mind was racing and excited.

Does this girl want to be kissed? I wondered. *If not, and I try it, she might be cross and slap me.* I'd seen that happen at the pictures, and besides which other boys had told me girls did things like that. *But she isn't talking or acting like she'd be cross. She seems expectant.*

I noted the shape of her breasts under her thin cotton blouse. Hazel was well developed and under other circumstances, probably with a group of other boys, might have been the object of teasing. Certainly her development had been noticed by my friends. One and a half BSH's, Doug had said. I definitely liked what I saw. No teasing from me.

Her chest heaved as she breathed hard. A flush of excitement washed over me. I realised I was short of breath, breathing heavily like her as I stared into those hazel eyes after which, I decided, she must have been named. She drew me closer, my lips almost touching hers. I thought she must push me away, she would think me too bold wanting to kiss when we'd only just become boy and girlfriend, but she made no move to do so.

We touched. Tentatively, slowly; her lips were so soft, so tenderly soft; I had never known such sweet softness. Her eyes closed. And then, as at some signal my arms lifted her gentle frame away from the donga wall so that I could wrap them around her. One of her hands came up and clasped me behind my head, pulling me tight, our bodies in contact. Her lips parted. *What do I do now?* I thought lips were supposed to kiss lips, that's not so easy with her mouth open— *Oh my gosh, that's her tongue; she's stroking my lips with her tongue!*

I followed her lead. This girl was older than me. She knew what to do. She kissed my top lip, then the bottom one. I kissed her back, then suddenly feverishly, our tongues found each other. This was ecstasy, this was unimaginable beauty, this was happiness beyond my wildest dreams, until I became aware that I was stirring down in my nether region.

Oh no! I thought. *Oh my God, what an embarrassment. She must be feeling me through her skirt; that's terrible.* I'd been having so much trouble with this recently, waking up in the night, worried that people, especially the girls in class would notice the bulge in my trousers. I would try to hide myself, or hold myself with hands in pockets until some prefect or teacher yelled out, "Hands out of pockets, Edwards!" (It was low class to have hands in pockets.) Why did this have to happen? And why did prefects and teachers have to yell like that. They were boys; they should understand!

I moved to break off our embrace. I needed to shift around, I edged sideways so I would lean into the side of the donga wall and be at Hazel's side, kissing her but protected from embarrassing myself.

"What's the matter?" murmured a smoky Hazel with a coy smile as she came up for air and our heads parted.

"Oh nothing, nothing's the matter. I'm very happy."

"Why did you move sideways?"

"Oh, oh nothing, just getting comfortable."

"Silly boy," she smiled knowingly, and then we kissed again.

CHAPTER TWENTY-TWO

MUM, DAD, HAZE
AND THE SNAKE MAN

L IFE AT SCHOOL WAS IMPROVING. I WAS almost beginning to quite like it. Things had first changed after that fight with Ustinov. I was rarely picked on anymore and I found standing up for myself usually resulted in the other chap backing off. Then again, I'd found new respect after the stories of the hunt had done the rounds. The tale became exaggerated, of course, but it didn't hurt. Then there was my girlfriend. Aside from my friends being impressed, it generated respect from others. Not only did I have a girlfriend but a bright one at that and somehow, even though I was younger, I held on to her.

Hazel and I had talked of getting together in the hols. Nachingwea was not too far from Lindi. But it was far enough that unless we could arrange a ride through our families' travels, we would have to go the entire hols without a visit. Hazel had written to her mum about me and, she said, her mum had shown interest. I wasn't sure about mine. I suspected she would not approve a relationship with a girl at my age, especially one older than me. Mum would probably be terrified that she'd 'get her claws into me.'

I'd returned to Lindi for the long winter holiday at the beginning of June. My first surprise was in learning of Dad's achievement. He'd been elected mayor. I knew Dad was involved as a businessman with many others in this small town, especially the Asians, because they bought imported merchandise off T.O.M. for their retail stores. He was an active member of the Chamber and one or two other societies too; it seemed to be something he liked to do. At a later time he would even consider a run for a seat in the legislative council. But for now he was the mayor, and could thank his Asian colleagues for their vote of confidence; normally they voted for another Asian. Mum hadn't mentioned it in her letters although she was proud enough when I discovered his new portrait, posed in mayoral regalia, framed and placed on a shelf. So there was that. Then I'd found him cleaning a gun one day.

"Gee, Dad, why do you have a gun? I didn't know you liked guns. I've never seen it before. What is it, may I hold it?"

"It's a Beretta pistol, chum. You may hold it while it's emptied of the clip but never otherwise, is that understood?"

"Yes, Dad. But why did you get a gun?"

"Well, you know about the troubles in Kenya with the Mau Mau and the emergency up there?"

"Uh huh."

"It seems our authorities are worried that the Kenyan insurgency is spreading to Tanganyika. There have been several cross-border incursions already. Personally I can't see it catching on with the locals. Britain is in negotiations for eventual independence with an African leader here by name of Julius Nyerere, so I don't know why they'd revolt, but either way Europeans have been encouraged to acquire guns, just in case. So I sent for it, mail order from Italy. Now give it back as I want to put it away."

I changed the subject. With a visit to Hazel in mind I asked, "Dad, when you next go on safari to Songea may I come with you?"

Dad was not encouraging.

"You've seen how it is when I return from safari, chum. That's because the travelling on these roads is hellish. It really is, and with you and your asthma attacks, God help us if you were to get one when we were out in the bush."

"But, Dad, I don't have attacks as often now, what with adrenalin injections and my puffer. It's much less likely to happen than used to be. It's worth the risk."

"You might think so but I don't. When I go on safari it's for work. I don't play around, have a great time, go for fun visits. I can't afford for you to get an attack, which would divert me, possibly for days, while I sorted you out."

I had to concede that whenever he returned from Songea, Dad looked utterly exhausted. Every bone in his body jarred and knocked; his arm muscles exhausted from gripping the wheel; his body dehydrated from searing heat and humidity that cloaked him in a permanent film of moisture. To complete that drive in a day meant a 6 a.m. departure and arrival some twelve to fourteen hours later, even longer in the rainy season when the black cotton soil turned tracks to swamp. When reports from travellers indicated the roads were worse than usual, impassable even, Dad would stop the night at one of the rare bush outposts to be found along the way.

After dinner I tried it on him again. "Dad, I understand why a trip to Songea may be a bit much. But a trip to Nachingwea is less than half way. How about that? I have a school friend there who I'd really like to visit and could probably stay with. (I avoided use of gender for now.) I mean, you could go on to Songea and then pick me up on your way home."

"Oh I don't know, what do you think, Vera?"

"Nachingwea being closer; he'd probably be all right that far. But I don't know where he'd stay. You would stay with the McNeils. I assume if you stopped at all, but they don't have another spare bedroom, they'd be putting him up on a couch."

"I'm sure my friend in Nachingwea has a room," I repeated. "I could write and ask the family, see what they say."

Eventually the parents relented and over the next week or so and an exchange of letters with Hazel, it was agreed I could go with Dad as far as Nachingwea on the next trip.

Mother had visibly winced when she asked to know my friend's name and I confessed to 'Hazel.' On discovering my friend was a girl she hesitated, considered withdrawing her approval. However, Father must have persuaded her when they talked alone that a fourteen-year-old boy was not going to get up to any hanky panky. If anything it was a puppy romance at most and nothing to be concerned about.

✦ ✦ ✦

THE 150-MILE DRIVE TO NACHINGWEA TOOK OVER six hours in the Land

Rover. There was a threat of unseasonal rain which could turn the road into a quagmire, so Dad muttered about that, wondering whether it would hold off until we'd returned. By mid-afternoon we found the turn off the Songea road to Nachingwea and not long after that the start of the long, twisted and barely passable track that led to the Millers. The one-level farmhouse was perched on concrete stilts about two feet above ground, with unenclosed space underneath. Hazel, in cotton frock and no shoes, came running down the steps, Mum and Dad trailing, and with great enthusiasm, threw her arms around me and gave me a hug. Fortunately, she held back on the kisses in deference to watching parents. I'm sure, for a moment, Father must have been wondering.

Good thing Mother didn't come, I thought.

As they descended the steps to greet us, Hazel's parents got me quite surprised. Mr. Miller was tall and slim with a continuing grin, teddy bear ears and a tanned complexion. He stood taller than his wife by almost a full head, wore typical khaki shorts and shirt with long socks stretching from his sandals to his calves. He held out his arm to my dad in a warm greeting, introducing himself as Miller, Harry Miller. With his tall head and beaming face he didn't, I thought, look like an engineer; although I was soon to learn after examining his re-built Morris Oxford that if a vehicle couldn't be taken apart and put together again, with a dash of grease perhaps, then it probably wasn't worth bothering with. I wasn't sure about his selection of British Racing Green for a Morris Oxford. Bit odd.

Mrs. Miller had a sparkly smile. Her curled brown hair peeked out from a wide brimmed gardening hat. She wore appropriate clothes for tending her flora in which her garden abounded. Mum was evidently pleased to see us, as she greeted us enthusiastically in her broad Liverpuddlyan accent. She introduced herself as Hazel Miller. Seeing a little surprise she added in her high voice, "Yes, my dear, I know, same name as my oldest. Not very creative with her name really, couldn't seem to come up with anything else at the time… you know how it is?"

And then, chuckling at her joke, she enquired, "Mr. Edwards, would you like to stay a while and have afternoon tea with Dusty and me, that's Harry here," she gave him a sideways smile, "but we call him Dusty, don't we, dear? Or maybe you'd like something a little stronger?"

"Leslie, the name's Leslie, please. I really ought to be getting along.

Well, what the hell, a quick one for the road maybe. The McNeils aren't expecting me just yet."

Father became engrossed and before long Dusty and he were laughing hilariously as they chugged their ales, clearly opposites but getting on well. Mrs. Hazel excused herself to buzz around chasing up the cook and the houseboy into continuing their chores. Miss Hazel and I wandered off for a tour of their grounds, mainly so we could find a hidey hole and greet each other properly.

"Where's Rose?" I asked, expecting to meet her younger sister.

"She and I have an understanding," Hazel smiled, "so she's gone visiting her own friends for a few days. You'll be sleeping in her room."

We peeked into the kitchen, a building apart from the main house, where the shamba boy had installed the fuel for the Dover stove. It was a fifteen-foot tree, one end shoved into the firebox, then continuing across the kitchen floor and out through the door into the yard. It took a high step across the tree to get from one side of the kitchen to the other.

"When the tree burns down a bit, the Mpishi will push the tree in a little further," Hazel explained, as though this was perfectly normal. "But let's go round the back here...."

"But why is the kitchen separate from the house?" I asked as we walked. "Seems weird to go to all that extra trouble."

"Farms like this were built a long time ago you know, between the wars in fact, probably 1920s or thereabouts. The people then didn't have all the protections we have now against insects and cockroaches so they built the kitchen separately to try to focus the insects on the kitchen and keep them away from the main house. Seems strange, hey?"

"What do you use this for?" I asked, as I came to a stop, gazing up at a 12-foot-high corrugated iron container.

"Oh, the water butt – that's our water supply, it catches rain water," said Hazel. "But don't worry about that now, I'll show you the white tree frogs that live in it later. Follow me, no, not that way, that leads to the choo, yes, big drop, same as you boys have in Kongwa, I'm afraid."

"We'd still have indoor toilets if you girls hadn't taken over our houses," I said reproachfully.

Hazel laughed. "Well, that's another benefit of being a girl."

"Gosh you've got enough banana palms and orange trees here to feed half the country!" I said, as we pushed through the undergrowth.

"Well, this is a farm, you know?" Hazel replied.

"Where does that path lead?"

"The 'boy's' quarters. Come; here you are; da daahh!"

"Wow, what sort is it?"

"It's a cashew nut tree, isn't it beautiful? This way," she said and slid around the back to where we were out of sight of the house and everything else. "It's even nicer round the back here."

Suddenly I was pulled in tight and we were kissing frantically.

Later, after Dad had left to find the McNeils – he was now running late for his arrival – Mrs. Miller presented her apologies, explaining to her daughter, "Your dad and I are due at the club for a few sets of tennis doubles, bit late already actually. Do you want to join us or will you remain here? I expect we'll be home at around, oh, eight o-clock-ish."

"We'll stay here," said Hazel quickly. "Tony's had a long journey and probably should rest. They prefer only grown-ups at the club anyway and there's really nothing for us to do there, Mum, especially if it rains. We'll rather stay home. And besides which," she added as an afterthought, "I know your eight o-clock-ish. I expect it'll be nearer ten or eleven and we won't have eaten. So we'll just stay here, then I can cook Tony dinner when we're ready."

"Sounds pretty nice to me," I added. "You enjoy yourselves, Mrs. Miller, we'll be fine."

"Okay, please yourselves. Be good, you two," said Hazel senior, smiling at her daughter with a chuckle and a twinkle in her eye, a female connection that I didn't miss. And with that she slipped her arm into her husband's and they left. No sooner had their Ford pick-up rounded the corner than we were once more in each other's arms, kissing with pent-up enthusiasm.

When we came up for air, Hazel said, "Oh golly, I'm so terribly happy you could visit. I've missed you so much. I never thought they would go, you know, my parents. I could hardly wait for them to go to tennis."

"Me too, Haze. I'm so happy too." And with that I kissed her with renewed fervour. After a while we sat down on the edge of the stoep, legs dangling and chucking the peels of fresh-picked oranges and bananas underneath as we ate, and talked of our holiday.

"Why are you living on a farm?" I asked.

"Well, my Dad had to do something. We'd been transferred first from Kongwa to Mkwaya, then from Mkwaya to Nach. Then the Groundnut Scheme collapsed, as you know. So Dad was given the choice. He could have his family and himself shipped back to England, or he could remain in Tanganyika; his choice.

"But farming's so different from being an engineer?"

"Well, he wanted to try – so here we are. It's fun. I like it. But anyway, what have *you* been doing?" Hazel asked changing the subject. "Had any fun?"

"Well, actually, I don't know about fun. Had a bit of a scare a week ago. I nearly didn't make it here, Haze."

"Why, what did you do?" she responded with a frown. "What happened?"

"Well, you know, well, maybe you don't know, but anyway, the Royal Navy Frigate *HMS Liverpool* paid Lindi a visit last week...." I paused.

"Yes," Hazel was staring into my eyes, "and then...?"

"Well, it's a bit of a long story. You see it was because three sailors from the frigate were out strolling the beach. They got Mum into conversation and before long were into chit-chat and certainly kept her attention. That was why I nearly copped it. See, I decided I'd swim out to the lighters in mid-channel."

"You did what? From what I remember of Lindi, they'd be far out in the middle of that huge bay. That's dangerous." Hazel tore orange segments from the peel with her teeth.

"Well, I didn't think so. The lighters were moored to a buoy but they didn't seem too far away. I even thought about swimming as far as the frigate but it was much further. I could decide about it once I reached the lighters."

"You're crazy," said Hazel. "They're sooo far from the beach from what I remember. I can't believe your mum would let you. I hope you didn't swim all the way out in that dangerous water, what with sharks and all."

"Well, here's the thing. Mum didn't know, she was too busy listening to the sailors. So, I waded in and began the swim. I swam a long way before realising that the lighters were much further than I'd thought. For a while I trod water and looked back. It seemed miles from the beach and I could only just see the figures of mother and the sailors. I thought about turning back, really I did...."

I took another bite of banana.

"I should hope so," chipped in Hazel.

"Mmm, well, yes," I said with mouth full, "but I only thought about it."

Hazel brought her hand to her lips as she thought of where this was going.

"Neither the sailors nor mother had noticed me gone, I was sure of that." I swallowed. "So I swam further out but got a bit nervous, you know how you feel when danger threatens. I'm sure you've had that?"

"You bet I have… with lions in Kenya when we went camping."

"You never told me about that. You'll have to tell me after. But anyway, I was in deep water and remembered that sharks were often seen in Lindi Bay. A Catholic priest had been taken by one when he was out swimming, and he wasn't even in deep water, his friends saw it all from the beach. I s'pose he didn't say enough Hail Marys."

Hazel gave a weak chuckle as she threw more orange peel under the stoep. "That's not nice."

"No, I s'pose. Well anyway, I knew about the Man O' War jelly fish and swam by several. I missed them only because I was watching out for them but they kept close to the surface. I was kind of worried about Barracuda too; I don't think they're dangerous but I didn't know. And then there was the current that could carry me out to sea if I got caught in a rip tide."

"So what did you do?" Hazel interjected. "Don't tell me you went on anyway?" She picked out another banana.

"Well, yes, actually."

Hazel's jaw dropped. "I knew I'd picked a crazy one." She began peeling.

"You see," I ignored her witticism, "I looked at the lighters again. They were so near and yet so far. I wasn't sure what to do. I'd kind of challenged myself and would be irritated later if I chickened out. So, overcoming common sense, as I'm sure you would say, I kept going. Besides which, I could rest a bit by climbing the lighter once I got there. If I got too tired I would wait until someone rescued me. Mother would be looking for me and soon she or the sailors would spot me."

Hazel was about to take a bite of banana, but paused. "Maybe," she said, "maybe not. They wouldn't be looking for you that far out. And anyway, if you could barely see them on land they probably couldn't see little old you standing on a lighter, miles away. If they saw you at all, a tiny spec in the distance, they'd assume you were a sailor… I would."

"I didn't think of that."

"And anyway, even if they did spot you, they didn't have a boat, did they?"

"Well, no," I paused. "Anyway, let me tell you the rest. It was another fifteen to twenty minutes of swimming before I reached the closest lighter, way further than I thought it would be, and I got two shocks. When I glanced around I could no longer see the beach or the club, just the swell of the sea and the tips of the palms on shore when I was at the peak of a swell."

Hazel gasped.

"And as for resting on the lighter, well, I couldn't climb on it. When there's just you in the water looking up, those lighters look as massive as the frigate. And they are large too; I don't know, ten or twelve feet of steel stretching from the water to the deck. There was no way at all for a man, never mind me, to climb up those sheer sides out of the sea, unless there was a rope or a ladder. And there was no one on board to help."

"I know exactly what you're saying," confirmed Hazel knowledgeably. "I could hardly climb into a rowing boat once when my dad was trying to haul me in, so I can see how you couldn't have climbed onto the lighter."

"Well, that's it, you see. Unlike your rowing boat where you had the side of the boat and your dad's hand to hold, there was nothing at all for me to hang on to; so now I got worried. I had to face the swim back, no other choice. It was amazing how aware I became of danger. I admit I got quite worried."

"I should say so." Hazel stared at me in astonishment, almost lost for words as she frowned and took a fierce bite of banana.

"Anyway, I nudged around the side of the lighter looking for something, like a ladder, but it turned out the only thing was the rudder. At least it was a break in the wall of steel. But that's all it was. It was massive man, I'm telling you. I couldn't grip the rudder never mind climb on to it. Not only was it huge but it was covered with razor sharp barnacles, like the entire surface of the lighter below the water line, and that was several feet above my head. This made holding it impossible. My skin was soft and crinkly too. I knew it would bleed at the slightest scrape."

"Yikes. Were there no other boats, a fisherman you could have called to?"

"Believe me I looked, there was no one. But anyway, I pushed myself away from the lighter's side so I wouldn't be brushed against it by the swell.

If that had happened I'd have been cut by the barnacles and the blood would have brought sharks."

"Wow, this is *so* scary, Tony. I'm so glad I wasn't there. I'd have just died."

"Anyway, I realized the longer I stayed, the more I trod water, the more tired I'd get. So, I decided to leave and swim back."

"Oh my gosh, all that way."

"At the start, I had only a general idea where safety was. I couldn't see the beach. At the peak of a swell, I set course by the palm tips and began swimming. I could only swim breast stroke on account of my asthma. Actually Haze, I was quite surprised. The closer I got, the more I realized I wasn't about to conk out. I really did have energy."

"Yes, well, obviously you got back all right."

"I was maybe two-thirds of the way when I could see the figures standing at the water's edge staring out. Mother and the sailors had missed me at last. But, then suddenly there was all at once a huge splash and a surge by me and the feel of something creasing my side. It made me jump out of my skin I can tell you."

"Oh my God!" Hazel brought her hand to her mouth in alarm almost choking in the process.

"I have no idea what it was beyond the obvious that it was a fish. But why it would jump just there or come in that close to me I don't know. If it was Barracuda or small shark it wasn't a man eater, I s'pose. Anyway, it gave me a heckuva fright so my pace picked up. As I got closer I could see the sailors and Mother standing there peering, hands shielding eyes from the sun and I sensed the drama. So, in order to seem a toughie who made the shore no matter what, I pretended to be exhausted. I put on a dying look. I tried a few strokes of the crawl with languid arms. I trod water for periods, making no headway."

"Shame on you, Tony Edwards... your poor mum."

"Then the ocean rollers carried me to shallow water. The sailors waded out to haul me in where I was berated by Mum who thought it was my last day on Earth."

"I don't blame her. I'd have bashed you one if it'd been me."

I pouted.

"Mother told me I looked utterly exhausted. She said the sailors were on the point of swimming out cos I wasn't going to make it. Oh, Mother, I said, don't fuss so. I'm quite a good swimmer and wasn't a bit tired!"

"Your poor mum. Don't you ever do anything like that again… and especially not with me. I don't want to be identifying your dead body. Anyway, I must say, I'm proud of you. That took courage and determination; even if you were stupid. What with your hunting and your swimming, you're quite the catch, aren't you?"

And with that I received another tight hug as Hazel shoved one end of a newly peeled banana into my mouth with her taking the other end. We bit our way through the fruit giggling and nearly choking ourselves until our lips met at the centre, ending up with a long and enthusiastic banana-flavoured kiss broken up by irrepressible giggles.

Evening arrived and I realised there was no electricity. Hazel walked around lighting Tilly lamps. Knowing that there would be no sign of her mum and dad returning for a long time yet and feeling hungry, Hazel announced she would cook dinner.

"Mum's taught me a lot so I should be able to rustle up something you'll like. Now let's see what have we here," Hazel muttered as she peered into the paraffin-powered fridge. "Do you like fish?"

"I eat anything, Haze," I replied, "and I'm certain that anything you cook will be delicious. How will you cook it though?"

"I've told Mpishi he doesn't need to cook tonight but I got him to light the stove. He's pushed the tree in a bit more," Hazel smiled, "so I'll be in and out a bit."

"Mind if I turn on your radio? I should be able to catch the World News from London."

"Help yourself. That small set next to you doesn't work well but the larger one in the corner is powerful and should, especially as Dad just connected a new battery."

I waited while the radio warmed and then checked the dial was set on the shortwave station of the B.B.C. The set greeted me with the usual howls, whistles and atmospherics but I caught the signature music that heralded the news half hour.

"Good Evening from London. This is the B.B.C. World Service. Here is the news."

I listened closely as always but this evening was especially interesting.

"Oh my gosh, Haze, can you believe that?"

"Believe what?" called Haze; from where she was laying the table. "I didn't hear what they were saying."

I raised my voice, "The B.B.C. says the Yanks have this new airplane that's really a spy plane and that it's flown as high as 100,000 feet over the Soviet Union."

"Oh really?"

"Yes, and it's called a U2. It's made by Lockheed."

"Uh huh."

"But that's amazing, don't you think, Haze? I mean, 100,000 feet, just think of it. The Hermes I flew to Africa in flew at 20,000 feet, but this is 100,000 feet!"

"Oh."

"Boy, I bet that'll upset the Soviets. They're not going to like that."

"No?"

"Definitely not. Would you want the Soviets spying on us from 100,000 feet?"

Silence.

I looked up as I asked, "Would you want…?"

Then I realised Hazel must have gone out to the kitchen.

"Oh never mind," I muttered. I was learning there were some things girls were just not interested in and small airplanes flying at 100,000 feet was one of them.

I sat engrossed by that until the news and related stories ended and a programme followed called *Desert Island Discs*. I didn't expect to pay much attention to this, so I left the chair to peruse the many books that surrounded me; Hazel senior was an avid reader. As I did so, snippets of the B.B.C. programme caught my ear.

"Tonight's guest," the interviewer enthused, "is well-known author, historian, former employee of the B.B.C. and now a person whose singular energy was perhaps the most responsible for the establishment of the East African Literature Bureau, Mrs. Elspeth Huxley."

I wandered back to the chair. This was about East Africa and this lady, Elspeth Huxley, had spent many years of her childhood in Kenya. As a part of Britain's East African colonies, this brought her story close to home, so I thought I'd listen for a while.

The format of the programme was that the interviewing of a well-known personality would be interrupted periodically by that person's selection of music, supposedly of what she or he would most want to have with them, along with a gramophone, if they were unfortunate enough to be marooned on a desert island. They made eight choices during the show. Towards the end of the first half hour, Huxley was quizzed about her youth in Kenya, in particular her life as a young girl on a farm.

"Why is it?" the interviewer enquired, "that in spite of your many and various fine writings, you appear not to have written a book about your life in Kenya. Your parents' farm was in Thika, wasn't it, quite some way from Nairobi?"

"Aha, young man," Huxley chuckled to the interviewer, "you're anticipating me. Don't you worry, I shall be writing about it in time. I've had rather a full plate, don't you know, what with the war years and my many and various commitments. But, my parents continue to live and work their farm in Thika. You're quite right; it is some distance from Nairobi, a long way when you're travelling by ox wagon as they did, but not too far now thanks to the automobile. I visit at least once a year actually. Of course, it's worrying at present with the Mau Mau. One certainly hopes these troubles will soon be over. We must understand that it's the Africans' country and we must not withhold their birthright indefinitely. Sometime, not too long hence, I hope, once the troubles are over, I will pay Kenya and my parents a much longer visit, spend a good many months in the region doing my research and then I'll write a beautiful book about that place and those times. Why, I even have a title for it."

"Will you share it with us?" asked the interviewer.

"You know," Elspeth replied, "normally I wouldn't because titles can change a lot between the time you start a book and the time it's ready for publication. But, I have a feeling this one will not change so I will share it with you. It will be called *The Flame Trees of Thika*."

Hazel came back into the house from the kitchen, two plates of hot food in her mitten-covered hands. "Dinner's ready."

✦ ✦ ✦

ON THE THIRD DAY, DAD RETURNED TO pick me up on his way home. He arrived late afternoon in the middle of a cloud burst. The Miller family and I were sitting in canvas chairs on the veranda where we'd had lunch, trying to talk over the noise of the rain on their tin roof, the water pouring off in one long waterfall the width of their house. Dusty and Hazel senior were sipping on their pink gins and the three of us – Rose couldn't resist returning home in time to meet this boy her big sister had told her about – were drinking our Colas.

Dad was supposed to have returned in the morning so we would do a daytime drive home, but he'd been delayed. Now, much of our drive would be at night making the going tougher. The teeming rain turned torrential, the sky a swirling slate grey and the prospect for a successful arrival home tonight getting worse by the minute.

I didn't want to leave. I was having a wonderful time with Hazel. It was a bit like love, I thought, but I was much too scared to say the word 'love' out loud.

"I'll write you a lot, Haze, I promise. I hope to see you again these hols but if not, then there'll be a lot to look forward to returning to school."

"Hmm," she said, "who'd have known we'd actually be happy to return to that place?"

With Dad having said a quick 'hello-and-bye' to my hosts, he ran back to the Land Rover. I followed, with Hazel in tow still holding my arm. But I'd become sodden with the amazingly warm rain as had she, so, I mouthed goodbye then broke free and ran towards the Rover which Dad had idling. I glanced back as I ran and saw Hazel, still standing in the downpour, drenched and blinking furiously. As our eyes met and through her blinks, she mouthed the words, "I love you." The words were as unmistakable as though she had screamed them from the roof tops. My heart skipped several beats. I moved to go back to her but she turned on her heel and ran to join her parents and sister who were watching from the shelter of their veranda. From there she gave a last wave.

FATHER HAD BEEN WHISTLING THE OPENING MOVEMENT of *La Traviata*. Whistling his beloved opera music was his habit while driving. There was not a chance one of those new fangled car radios would work in Tanganyika; certainly not in the Southern Province anyway. Then he had a thought:

"You're very quiet," called Father over the noise of the downpour and the Rover's engine. We'd been jogging along the soaking track of a road for an hour or more. "Nothing to say? Nothing wrong, I hope? Enjoyed your trip?"

"No, Father, nothing wrong," I sighed and clung on tight.

"Pretty keen on Hazel?"

I wasn't expecting that from him. We never talked about things like girls.

"Yes," I called back in my raised voice. "How'd you know?"

"When a boy and a girl are keen on each other it shows. Everyone can read the body language."

"Oh."

"You'd better keep this hush-hush from your mother, chum," Father was almost shouting. "She's not keen on you having romantic ideas at your age. Thinks you should focus on studying. Girls are way too much of a distraction."

"Hmm."

"I agree with her for that matter. You really would be wise to focus on school and hopefully university and leave the girls alone until you're old enough."

"Can't hear you, Father."

"I know you won't, of course," he carried on. "You'll just have to learn the hard way like everyone else. You should try to keep everything in balance and give prime importance to school work and, if you can, keep your girl-friend relationship as secondary. Anyway, I'm not going to tell your mum, I like to keep peace in the household."

"Mum's the word, right, Dad?" I yelled.

"Mum's the word," he yelled back.

The Land Rover was bucking and sliding over the saturated track, throwing black cotton mud in every direction. Our vision was constantly obliterated with the windscreen being coated with the stuff as we nosed into troughs and the mud drenched like a bow wave in a heavy sea. Only because of the torrent washing the screen could we keep going. We were the only ones out it seemed, with no other traffic in either direction. The road, no more than a track at the best of times, was now just an elongated swamp running down the middle of a rain forest. Other than for our headlights we were surrounded by total blackness. Father had engaged four wheel drive and it was a relief when it had cut in. But even so we could get bogged down and we both knew it.

"We're averaging about fifteen miles an hour at best," he shouted. "At this rate there's no hope for getting home tonight. It's as well I phoned your mother at the office this morning and alerted her this might happen. There's certainly nowhere to phone between here and Lindi. There was a warning that bad weather was on the way."

As Father said that, there was an enormous thunder clap that made us jump out of our seats.

"Jesus Christ!" he cursed.

"Yikes," I followed up.

This was followed in seconds with brilliant forks of lightning not a mile away. Then, unbelievably, it got worse. It was as though we had driven into the very heart of the storm. Suddenly there were lighting bolts all around us. The rain became so hard the windscreen wipers all but stopped.

"Do you think we're going to make it, Father?"

"Inshallah, chum, Inshallah."

A tree, not fifty yards ahead, was struck by lighting and exploded into brilliant flame, soaring skyward.

"Oh my gosh, please don't let it fall across the road," I exclaimed.

"It's leaning the other way, I think it's falling away from us," called Father, as he slowed to a halt. The tree crashed away from the road.

"Thank God for that," he muttered, then continued. "I don't know exactly but it should be about twenty miles ahead." As he accelerated again he explained, "There's a bush hotel not far away – what's it called? Hmm, McKinnon's Rest."

"Yes, I remember, we passed the sign on our way to Nach."

"I just hope we can make it that far. If we do we'll stop there for the night."

"You've stopped there before haven't you, Dad?"

"Actually no, at least, not overnight. I stopped for a drink once but that was about it. If I stop over for the night it's usually at a place west of Nachingwea, nearer the halfway point between Lindi and Songea. Oliver's Road House. Good chap Oliver. Unusually intelligent. Not sure why he buries himself in the bush but somehow he's amazingly informed. Through some freak of nature he gets a good radio reception most of the time from the B.B.C. Maybe that has something to do with it. Other than that it's as bush as it comes there. But he's a fine fellow, his wife too."

"Do you know the people at McKinnon's Rest?"

"Only from that brief visit when I downed a couple of whiskys. Near as I can recall he was a large man, his wife half his size; Yanks, I think."

"What's his name, Dad?"

"Can't remember for the moment, it'll come."

Our conversation lapsed as Father, concentrating on the driving had all his skills tested negotiating the abominable surface. He resumed his whistling; this time from *The Marriage of Figaro*. I was thrown around in my seat like a rag doll and barely remained in place. My muscles ached from holding on. Somehow, we didn't get stuck. Dad just kept that Rover on the road with our headlights flashing from trough to skyward every second or two, while I thought how glad I was that I didn't have to travel from Songea on roads like this.

Relief at last. For a brief moment our headlights lit the sign at the roadside, *McKinnon's Rest*. It was 9 p.m. and we were exhausted.

"I've got it, his name's Shelby," said Dad, as he steered off the road and bounced into the driveway, "Shelby McKinnon."

McKinnon's Rest consisted of five thatched, single-roomed rondavels in addition to the main larger one. It was set in heavily encroaching, impenetrable jungle, quite literally in the middle of nowhere. The rondavels boasted whitewashed mud walls, with holes for windows, and there was a one drop toilet for all, located about 25 yards from the nearest rondavel, in the Gaboon viper-ridden bush.

We splashed our way to a stop at the main entrance. Our headlights had lit the reception inside so the proprietor came strolling to the door to see who was arriving at this hour and in this weather.

"Hi you guys," he yelled above the roar of the wind and the thunderous rain. "Lookin' for a room, are yuh? You've come to the right place."

Dad and I scrambled, grabbing our bags and rushed, shoulders stooped, heads bowed in the downpour, through the small, single door entry to the welcoming dryness of the hotel's interior, the proprietor stepping deftly aside as we did. We came to a stop, dripping, briskly shaking the water off ourselves like a couple of dogs, with Dad saying we must change out of our shirts before anything. While we did that and donned dry replacements, Shelby McKinnon introduced himself and his wife, Dakota, as they looked on.

Shelby was a bear of a man, with sparkling brown eyes and a ready sense of humour in a gruff sort of way. I couldn't get over the size of his arms, complete with tattoos, must have been four or even six of mine to one of his.

Dakota reminded me of Annie Oakley. She wore a similar skirt, and blouse topped by a leather bolero with tassels and her hair was tied back in a pony tail. All she needed was the cowboy hat and spurs; oh, and the guns maybe. We finished rubbing our hair with dry towels proffered by Dakota.

"God, it's terrible out there," we agreed. "Worse than usual. Shouldn't be so bad at this time of year."

Now, as I buttoned my shirt and felt comfortable again, I could concentrate on my surroundings. We were standing in the hotel's entrance, but also in its reception, bar and dining room all at once. This one rondavel was 'it,' aside from the guest bedrooms.

"What's your poison?" Shelby asked Father.

"Whisky, please, with soda. Make that a double, will you."

"I guess you mean Scotch right, not Bourbon?"

"Er, yes, please," said Father recognizing the American's hesitancy between what to us was whisky and what was Bourbon. "A Johnny Walker will do fine."

"And you, son, what's your name?" asked Shelby, as he pulled the soda water syphon from the paraffin fridge.

"Edwards, sir."

"Your first name, son, and don't call me, sir. I'm nobody's sir."

"Tony, sir."

"Pleased to meet you, Tony. I'm Shelby, from the great State of Wyoming," he said in his American drawl. "That's all you need to know. You can call me Shelby." As he said this another guest got up from his chair and came over to join us. "And this here is my guest Bobby – do you know Bobby?"

Father regarded Bobby quizzically as if he should know him. The man was tall and lean, almost gaunt with a slightly hawked nose and a hat that was falling apart from years of use but which was just about managing to remain tethered to itself. He wore a white shirt under a thin pullover – what on Earth he needed a pullover for I couldn't imagine, and in any event it had been got at by moths and was threatening to disintegrate. Long light-coloured trousers, rather than shorts, completed his ensemble but his heavy boots seemed in the best condition.

"Not C.J.?" Dad asked.

"The very same," said Shelby. "Meet C.J. Ionides, known to the local gentry hereabouts as Bwana Nyoka."

"But Bobby will do," reassured C.J. "That's the name I go by to my friends. I hope I can count you both as new friends?"

"I'm sure you can, sir," I answered for Father, "but what do we have to do to be friends, sir?"

"You have to like snakes, young man," replied Bobby. "Anyone as doesn't like snakes is no friend of mine."

"He means it," said Shelby. "You guys havta like rattlers and such or he'll have no time for yuh."

"There're no rattlers in Africa!" asserted Bobby as he rose to the bait. "Quit trying to get my goat."

I think Shelby, this garrulous, transplanted American, built like a tank, was trying to make light of the notion that if we said we didn't like snakes it could make for a difficult and unfriendly evening; therefore, he hoped we would like snakes, if only for tonight. As it happened, Father was well-read on them and possessed a fair knowledge on herpetology. Before you could look round he and Bobby were off and running, knocking back whiskys and having a conversation like they were long-time friends. Meantime Dakota, Shelby and me were getting to know each other.

"Father said you're Americans?" I asked.

"Thet's for sure, son, we are thet. Or were. We're kinda displaced now livin' out 'ere an' all. Gave up on the States a long time ago. Came 'ere to get away from the crap. Mind you, Wyomin's all right... only place that is, really, but it's surrounded by crap."

"Oh you hush yer mouth, Shelby McKinnon," Dakota jumped in. "I'm from the great State of Georgia, Tony, and I liked it just fine. Don't ya'll be a listenin to anything my husband says, he don't know what's good ner bad."

Shelby laughed out loud.

I just smiled and said, "Oh."

And Dakota continued, "Anyway, ya'll must be hungry? Don't suppose y'ad dinner being as where ya'll hailed from?"

"No, miss. My girlfriend's mum *(Gosh, that felt funny saying 'my girl-friend' like that; that was a first, formalizing it for adults, made for a feeling of excitement in my chest)*, that's to say Mrs. Miller in Nachingwea, did make us a sandwich for the road but Dad had urged her not to go to any trouble as he thought we'd be home by this time. Not only that, but the drive was so rough that now we're starving."

"Well, you guys are a bit late for dinner, but we can rustle up some eggs, can't we, Dak?" Shelby interjected. "'Ow about some of 'em scrambled eggs filled with cheese and veggies and stuff?"

"That would be wonderful, sir. For my father too?"

"Of course, and quit callin' me *sir*. Wanna 'nother Coke?"

"Yes, please, sir."

After popping the top off a Coke, Shelby and Dakota disappeared behind a curtain into their kitchen, while I sidled over to listen-in on the conversation between Bobby and my father.

"So anyway," Mr. Ionides continued, addressing Dad but glancing at me once or twice, "there's this literary fella out from the U.K., you know, some sort of writer or somin; name's Wykes, yes, that's it Alan Wykes, he's bin writing a book 'bout me. He's shacked up at my place in Liwale and been living the experience, he says. Can't imagine why. Have no idea who'd want to read about me. They should have better things to do."

"Well, I don't know so much, Bobby. The work you've been doing for these many years is not only commendable and a great service to the local population but you're advancing the world's knowledge about these creatures; you're contributing wonderfully to science. Maybe it's just me but I think Wykes is on to something. What's he titling the book, do you know?"

"*Snake Man*. [*Snake Man* by Alan Wykes was duly published.] You know the locals call me, 'Bwana Nyoka.' I told him he should title it that way to be authentic. But he says most of his prospective readers don't speak Swahili, so if he titles it in the native tongue he'll lose sales. Best to use the English translation. How 'bout you, kid, you like snakes?"

"I'm a bit scared of them, sir, but I don't wish them any harm. My friends at school say we should kill every snake we see, but I'm not so sure. I don't like killing them when they're trying to get away. I did nearly get killed by one once though."

"Oh, what happened?"

Father looked at me with raised eyebrows; he hadn't heard this story before.

I went on to tell them the story of the black mamba in the loo on my first day as a Senior at Kongwa. "If I'd taken one more step towards him, sir, I wouldn't be here now."

"Ye gods and little fishes," said Father, "the things you get up to in

Kongwa; you've been saving up that story, I see. You'd better not tell your mother or she'll have you on the first plane back to England."

Ionides, ever on the defensive about his precious snakes, conceded I may have a point. "However," he went on, "you have to realize it wasn't setting out to attack you. The snake had established what it thought was a safe territory, you come bargin' in causing a big fufarar, it's going to defend itself, you understand?"

"Oh, yes, sir. I'm sure you're right, sir. It could have lashed out and bitten me but it didn't."

"Precisely my point. Anyway, I'm glad you didn't get bitten and it all ended safely."

Ionides turned to Father, "You know, Wykes has returned to Lindi for the while I'm in Songea. Normally he comes along with me, calls it field work research, but this time he wanted time out to write. Anyway, there's a village up there, near Songea, got a nest of Gaboon vipers causing mayhem, taken a couple of their kids already. So that'll keep me busy anything up to a week to sort that lot out. But why don't you come to Liwale for a visit after I get back. Wykes will be back then too. I can put you up and you can meet some of my friends. (He was alluding to his snakes.)"

As Father explained later, he was thinking fast on his feet. On the one hand he'd taken a liking to Bobby and wouldn't have minded the experience of seeing him on home turf. On the other hand it was known – indeed Bobby had told him – that he lets some of the snakes roam his house at will.

"They're the tamed ones," he told Father. "I wouldn't let just any old Gaboon viper wander around."

Tamed they may be, I thought, *if you really could tame a snake that is, and Bobby insisted that he had, but de-fanged they were not. If you were to accidentally tread on one's tail while walking around the house, would it remember it'd been tamed?'*

"That's very kind of you, Bobby," said Dad, "but let's leave it open for now. I have a lot of work on at the moment; this stop overnight is going to lose me another day at least, so I'm not sure if or when I could get away. I mean, we're looking at a three-day round trip one way or another, so I'll have to see how things go."

"Please yourself, Les, it's up to you, but consider it an open invitation." At that he slugged back the rest of his whisky, wiped his mouth with the back of his hand and yawning said, "Well, I'm all in. Time for some shut eye. Maybe I'll see you in the mornin', maybe not, but hopefully in Liwale some time."

Shelby and Dakota reappeared from the kitchen with two plates laden with three-egg omelettes, oozing cheese and sprouting veggies, several slices of thick white bread with lashings of butter and sliced mango on the side.

"Night," Bobby called out.

Father and I moved to the dining table and tucked in.

"Mind if we join you guys?" Shelby and his wife invited themselves.

"No, not at all."

Dakota brought three coffees to the table and another Coke for me. "There you go, Les," she said, "but don't drink it if you don't want it; there's plenty more Scotch."

"You know that Ionides fella," said Shelby, "he's British raised, you know, but Greek heritage. Really eccentric... have to be I suppose to do what he does. He was a white hunter back in the day, but he's given that up and in-stead studies and catches the most dangerous snakes of Southern Tanganyika. I reckon they'll kill him one of these days – he's been bit that many times."

"Shelby! That's not nice."

"Well, it's true."

"I've read of him," Dad responded as I drew long and deep on my straw. "I've always wanted to meet him, but I really don't have the time to mess about in Liwale. It's a pity really, wouldn't mind seeing his set-up."

"Just as well ya'll like snakes," Dakota jumped in. "He wouldn't have talked to ya'll if you didn't. I mean that, he'd have turned his back on ya'll and gone to his room. Has no time for anyone as doesn't like those critters."

"He should hang around here more often," added Shelby ruefully. "I've told him often enough we have most of Tanganyika's snakes right here in our back yard."

"He likes to stop by," said Dakota, "but he's always in rout some place else. I guess we need to call him some time to come catch some of ours."

"You guys came from Nach right?" asked Shelby. "That's where old Bobby usually drops his catches. Like now he'll be off on that Songea job real early. Whatever he catches he'll drop off at Dalgety on the way back. He does that, you know, has them shipped to the world's zoos, or universities or wherever from there. Trouble is, he's not real careful how he houses those critters, so sometimes they escape in the store. You can imagine the mayhem that causes." And with that Shelby broke out into the loudest guffaw we'd heard all evening.

The conversation between Father and the McKinnons continued enthusiastically for another two hours, way after our hosts' normal bed time, but it was a fun evening. Sometimes I 'got' the jokes the adults were telling but sometimes I didn't. I listened again to one I'd heard Father tell before; he seemed to like relating it. I never did understand why everyone burst out laughing hysterically at the end. I couldn't see where it was funny at all. Anyway, it seems that the road from Songea to Mbeya was divided by the Njombe Escarpment. This was a road so dangerous that it was a serious threat to life and limb every time anybody drove it. The point of the story though was set at the Inn, as bush as McKinnon's Rest but with somewhat larger premises, with the main building having an upstairs.

"The Njombe Hotel," Father would say, "was good fun at the end of that run. The pub was run by a steadfast colonial with a pukka British accent who didn't give a damn about anything. The billiard room was directly below the so-called bridal suite," he said, "used less by brides than other 'folie à deux' *(expressed with a French accent and rapidly fluttering eyelashes).* But the chalk for the billiard cues was attached to a piece of string and the string was attached to the underside of the bridal bed upstairs, through a not insubstantial hole in the ceiling above the billiard table – hilarious!"

This was the moment everyone broke out laughing. I couldn't see where a hole in the ceiling was that funny. Anyway, apparently the hotel was also home to a tame mongoose which would shell the hard-boiled eggs that were for sale in the bar, by throwing them through its legs against the skirting board... they sold a lot of eggs, and the fat mongoose was always well fed. Now that was funny!

"Time to turn in, I think," said Father after yet another nightcap. "Better get the boy to bed, we're going to have some drive tomorrow, assuming we don't get socked in here."

"I'll get a lantern and take yuh to yuh room," said Shelby. "There's a light in the room but we'll turn the generator off soon as we go to bed; but we'll give you a half hour to get comfortable. I think the rain may have eased for the moment so now's the time."

With that we splashed our way from the main building to our bedroom rondavel which, for a reason unclear to me, was not the closest, even though

Bobby was the only other guest. When we emerged from the main building, the sound of the massive bullfrog population racked up its intensity so loud that I thought I would never sleep. There were bullfrogs in Lindi too but nothing that compared with this lot. Then the tree hyraxes started screeching and set my hair standing on end; they sounded like someone was being murdered. The air was difficult to breathe, it was so thick with humidity, and made more so with the musty smell of soaking jungle, so that it was almost suffocating. With all this I stepped gingerly, thinking about the snakes that lurked in the impenetrable bush that bordered the narrow pathway. "We've got most of Southern Tanganyika's snakes in our backyard," Shelby had said. Exaggerating maybe… but even so, just exactly how many did they have? I was especially alert given, as I'd learned from Ionides, the most deadly of all, the slow-moving Gaboon viper, prolific in numbers, was native to this rain forest that reached to our very door. A bit longer than puff adders, these snakes are fatter and heavier with flattened, triangular heads on a narrow neck. They have two-inch fangs, sometimes longer, that are the longest of any venomous snake, anywhere. It didn't help that, as Mr. Ionides told me, the viper's bite gave off more venom and was more toxic than the puff adder even. And it had the same habit of lying in wait along pathways and not getting out of anyone's way!

> Rikki-Tikki-Tavi
> *At the hole where he went in*
> *Red-Eye called to Wrinkle-Skin*
> *Hear what little Red-Eye saith:*
> *"Nag, come up and dance with death!"*
> — Rudyard Kipling

I watched with the stare of an owl's eyes as we trudged. I thought I would not be walking to the choo during the night. If it came to it, I would just hang on until morning, or piss out the front door if I couldn't wait.

Our rondavel possessed one light bulb hanging from a rafter in the ceiling. I peered into the thatch to ensure there were no snakes taking cover there. Never mind raining cats and dogs outside, in this place it could be raining snakes and frogs inside. Powered by the hotel's small generator, the ceiling lamp fluctuated between brilliantly bright through to almost out. There was a matching sound effect as the generator noise built to a crescendo, or died. Shelby muttered about the carburettor needing cleaning as he showed us the paraffin-powered Tilly lamp.

When we finally got back to Lindi the following afternoon Mother asked Father about this Hazel girl. He was put on the spot with her questions and in the end couldn't help but tell her of my apparent girlfriend in Nach. So much for 'Mum's the word.'

Mother looked at me through squinted eyes and produced a wagging finger. But she didn't come on strong, probably content that, for the moment anyway, I was here and Hazel was there. Father did reassure her that he thought Hazel to be, "A really nice girl, could be good for Tony."

ALL GOOD THINGS COME TO AN END and so did the long holiday. Dad stood watching as I packed my electric trains away, then said, "You know, chum, thinking of trains, while I was on safari last week I called into our office in Mikindani. A fellow came in for supplies and we got talking. Turned out he was working for East African Railways and had been charged with closing railway spurs that had been built for the Groundnut Scheme. I mention it, because they'll be closing the Kongwa spur from Msagali."

"Really! Wow! Does that mean they're closing the school?" I asked hopefully.

"No, chum, it doesn't," Dad replied with a smile. "What it means is your school train will stop going to Kongwa after this Christmas. Apparently the *Kongwa Special* will go to Dodoma from next January on and you'll be bussed to school from there."

"So now I'll be travelling by plane, train and bus to get to school? Crikey, Dad, why not a boat as well? Yish. As if it isn't bad enough already, they have to do that to us. So what about the rail lines, do they just stay there rusting away?"

"No, I expect they'll lift them up and cart them away, probably to be re-smelted in some steel mill. I'm not sure really, something like that."

CHAPTER TWENTY-THREE

SCHOOL LIVENS UP

BACK AT SCHOOL, IN JANUARY OF '56, we found ourselves still reading avidly about WWII. We passed books around as the adventures captured our imaginations. Between the exploits of R.A.F. pilots like Douglas Bader, or 617 squadron of Bomber Command, *The Dam Busters,* or sea stories such as *H.M.S. Ulysses* by Alistair Maclean, there was plenty to get into. Then there was the other side of the story, involving escapes from P.O.W. camps such as *The Wooden Horse, the Colditz Story* and *The Bridge over the River Kwai.* All this came at a time when board games like *Monopoly* were newly popular. Inspired by this, I invented a game that I thought far superior.

One of my keenest supporters was Andrew Burns. He'd arrived as a new boy this term. He was short for his age, blond-haired, good looking, and a tough little bugger when he wanted to be. He was friendly to me and I liked him. Burns was not only in Livingstone but in our house, although in the bedroom at the other end.

I became aware of him at bath time on our second night back at school. There was the usual scramble for the tub and fetching buckets of hot water from the boiler. An impromptu tussle had broken out as new boys had their towels whisked off them in a kind of exposé of what the boy had to offer. Burns had been fighting us off with some success and maintained his towel firmly round his waste.

"What's wrong man, Andy, we're all boys here, what are you worried about?" asked Aranky. "You're not going to go all term without being seen naked."

"There's nothing wrong, man, just hurry up and leave me some water."

"Come in with us, man," Jenner invited.

"No, I can wait."

Then Gunston stole up behind Burns and in an instant had ripped his towel off and stepped back laughing. Burns was exposed, and now we understood what his problem was, although he had nothing to be worried about. He had the longest any of us had ever seen on a boy of his age.

"Wow, Burns, looks more like you've got a middle leg," teased Aranky.

"Makes up for being a shorty," affirmed Berry.

"Gimme my towel back," appealed Burns.

"You've got nothing to worry about," I said. "Why are you so shy?"

"I don't know, it's so… you know. I'm just a bit… you know."

"Here's your towel," laughed Gunston. "You're going to need it. I don't think your trousers are long enough to hide that away."

Burns blushed as he wrapped the towel back around himself.

"Come on," he said, "you've seen what you wanted, now hurry up."

WE WERE ONLY A FEW WEEKS INTO the new term when Burns's parents came for a visit and stayed at the Club. It was always a special time when parents came. Sons or daughters would get a few hours off over a day or two to be with them, and in turn they were allowed to invite a friend to join them. Andrew had invited me and, boy, was I pleased.

The Club had been the hub of the social scene when Kongwa was all business. It was a one-storey, post-modern building, set among a landscape of date palms, flamboyant and jacaranda trees, massive bougainvillea, with numerous flower beds boasting the best and most beautiful of Africa's tropical flowers. Cana lilies were prolific; there were small trees of frangipani, colourful displays of hibiscus, agapanthus, begonias, magnolias, gladioli and oleander bushes. Deep blue morning glory climbing over thick manyara hedging finished off the perimeter.

The Club's main room was anchored by a long bar and cooled by whirling ceiling fans. Outside, umbrellas with bumblebee stripes dotted the terraced patio, and chaises longues were mixed among chairs and tables. Here, bathed in sunshine, was the new swimming pool. It was not Olympic in size but was large enough for good swimming, competition and plenty of fun.

Now, with most of the Club's members gone, it was a gathering place for off-duty school teachers and the few workers left at the P.W.D., and the place for visitors to stay the night. The pool's busiest use was our swimming lessons.

This Sunday, Burns and I rushed down after church, rolled up towels and cosies under arms and arrived at the patio, panting in the heat, where we found his parents. They were relaxed by a poolside table, an umbrella keeping off the sun's rays and sipping an exotic-looking drink, appearing most content.

"Hello, Andrew," he was greeted warmly by his parents, "and who is this handsome young friend of yours?"

They were off to a good start with me.

"Oh, Mum and Dad, this is Tony. He's my friend."

"Pleased to meet you, Tony. We've read about you in Andrew's letters."

I smiled my thank-you.

"Well now, you two look pretty thirsty to me," said Andrew's dad. "I imagine a Coca-Cola will go down well?"

"Oh yes, please," Andrew answered for us, "and you know what, Tony? They have refrigerators in the Club, so they'll be cold."

"Mushee," I said.

"Let's go and change," said Andrew full of excitement. "I can't wait to get in the pool and cool off."

"You two run along and have fun," said his mum. "We'll keep the colas here in the shade."

With that we were gone, changed and into the pool and had so much fun, having the pool to ourselves that, by the time we came back for a drink the cola had warmed up.

"We'll ask for more ice," said Mrs. Burns.

We enjoyed lunch on the terrace. Mr. Burns had promised we would love it, "They serve excellent food here," he said. "They have an exceptionally talented chef who was recruited when this place was hopping. It seems he's chosen not to leave. Must like it here."

After our lunch had gone down Andrew said, "You know Mum, Dad, Tony's good at telling stories. I think he could write books for boys when he grows up."

"Really?" replied Andrew's mum. "What stories do you tell?"

"Oh, it's nothing really," I said modestly. "Anyone could do it."

"Come on, Tony, you know you do," responded Andrew. "He tells them at night after lights-out. Sometimes I go to where his room is so I can hear them. Trouble is I get sleepy and have to go back to bed before he finishes."

"Well, I should think so," said Mrs. Burns. "You need your sleep, young man."

"And another thing," went on Andrew, "he's invented this game. It's a board game and we play it all the time. It's really mushee, you should see it."

"What's it about, Tony?" asked Mr. Burns. "Can you describe it?"

"Oh yes, sir, I can. It's all about this P.O.W. camp in Germany and it's full of British prisoners and the objective is to try to escape and get across the border to neutral Switzerland."

"Oh really? What does it look like; I'd like to see it. I don't suppose you brought it with you?"

"No, sir, I didn't, the board is too large to carry around but I can describe it. See, there's this board, I've made it with card, and it's larger than a *Monopoly* board. I've divided the whole board into half-inch squares. Then I've drawn over some of them the layout of a P.O.W. camp like you see in books, but larger; I have a road and a nearby village; there're landscape obstacles, a river to cross and other things before trying to cut through the barbed-wire border fence to Switzerland, or even bluff your way through the frontier post. We use the tokens from a *Monopoly* set to move around in any direction but if the game was made by a company they'd be little men dressed as P.O.W.s or as German officers. Anyway, we use dice and I've made two sets of cards, a bit like Chance and Community Chest except the wording is geared to my game, of course. We throw the dice and move our tokens. Now the thing is, you can move your token in any direction you chose except you cannot march straight through a barbed-wire fence or the border post. When you reached the wire you'd have to stop and go back on your tracks... unless you have wire cutters. Also, you can't go through the border post unless you have a passport. The objective is first to escape the camp and secondly to cross the frontier into neutral territory, so choice of direction to move is very important."

"How do you know when and which deck of cards to chose from?" asked Mrs. Burns.

"Well, Miss, about two-thirds of the small squares are blank but the others have a question mark in them if you're within the camp or an exclamation mark if you're outside. When you land on a square with one of those you have to pick a card from the correct pile and see what it says."

"Tell them some of the cards, Tony," Andrew encouraged.

"Well, for example, within the camp there are good ones that say, 'Proceed directly to the beginning of a tunnel of your choice.' You see, there are three tunnels that lead from the prisoners' barracks to outside the barbed wire fence but you have to get on them at the beginning point and tell the other players that you're going to follow that tunnel out if you can; there are rules about that, of course. Or, you might get a card that says, 'Insulting a German Officer, return to barracks and miss a turn.' Another one might be 'Wire Cutters – good for one time use.' With those you could walk through the fence and therefore escape. They'd also be good for cutting through the frontier fence. If you've escaped the camp, you might turn up a card that says, 'Given a Passport by Underground Partisans, retain and use to walk through border post.' Another says, 'Caught, return to camp and solitary confinement, miss three turns.' There's even one that says, 'Shot... leave the game.'"

"Oh no," said Andrew's mum. "How sad."

"It's got to be like the real thing, Mum," Andrew assured her.

"It sounds interesting," said Mr. Burns, "and cleverly thought up, well done, I must say."

"It's a great game," said Andrew, "'cept for one thing."

"And what's that?" asked his mum.

"Well, to be honest with you, all the others have managed to escape at some time, even if they got caught again, but I've never even got out of the camp. But I tell you what, I will sooner or later."

"It sounds fun," said Andrew's mum, "but anyway," she said glancing at her watch, "are you two going to have another swim? We'll have to be leaving soon or miss the train, so now's your chance."

Andrew turned to me, "You know what they say about the pool, Tony?"

"What?"

"They say eighty-two lengths equals one mile. So swim eighty-two lengths without a stop and you'll have swum a mile non-stop."

"I already swam that far in Lindi Bay once."

"Really, did someone test you? How do you know it was a mile?"

"Well, I swam alone so I can't say for sure. Have you swum that far?"

"Yes, not in this pool, but I have, haven't I, Dad?"

Mr. Burns smiled indulgently and nodded. Just hearing that came across as a challenge.

"Well," I responded, "there's no chance of swimming eighty-two lengths any other time, so I'll try it now, while I'm out with you. You can be my counter, if you like, so no one can say I cheated."

"Okay," said Andrew, "let's watch you go then."

At my fortieth length Andrew called, "My parents have to leave now, they have a long journey, so it's time to say bye."

But the parents had followed to watch me briefly and Andrew's father called out, "Don't stop your challenge, Tony, we'll just say bye from here. Nice meeting you. Don't stop swimming; you've got many more lengths to go before your mile is up."

"Thank you so much for having me," I called out, "and for letting me do all this swimming. It was nice to meet you too. I hope you have a good ride home."

"Thanks and bye."

With that they wandered off, with Andrew escorting his parents to the Club's car that would shuttle them to the station. Andrew returned and resumed the count; I told him I'd done two lengths while he was gone.

As the afternoon wore on several off-duty teachers arrived. They'd heard how two boys came to be at the Club, normally out of bounds except for swimming class, and were used to the routine of the occasional parent turning up and giving their child and friend a day at the pool. But now the parents were gone. Miss Strong was there, along with Miss Hurley and Miss Bayliss relaxing in their colourful cotton frocks and seated around the concrete tabletop close by the pool. They said nothing for a while but at my sixty-seventh length, Miss Strong called out my name. I kept swimming as I turned my attention to her.

"It's soon going to be bath time, Edwards, and Burns's parents left some time ago. You're not supposed to be here once the parents have departed. I think you two should be getting back to your house."

In between breaths and continuing to swim and taking in a few mouthfuls of water, I called back politely, "I've got this challenge on to try to swim eighty *(gulp)* eighty-two lengths of this pool because that equals one mile. I will get out, of course, Miss Strong, if I must but do you think it would be possible for me to complete my challenge first, now I've got this far?"

I kept swimming pending an answer; I wasn't going to give Andrew a reason to count me out.

"Well, I don't know," she turned to talk to her two companions and after a few moments called back, "How many lengths have you done so far?"

"This is my sixty- *(gulp)* eighth," I called back, as I touched the end and pushed off again for my next length.

"All right," said Miss Strong as she received nods of assent from her colleagues, "you have permission to finish your challenge at eighty-two and then you must leave the pool and get back to your phase."

"Yes, Miss Strong. Thank *(gulp)* thank you very much."

Not long after that Andrew called the eighty-second, I jumped out and soon we were hurrying through the newly-arriving crowd of yet more teachers including Mr. and Mrs. Moore.

"I was wondering," said Andrew as we hurried back to our house, "do you think you could tell us a story tonight?"

"Yes, if you like."

"But it must be different this time. You know, your usual stories are kind of a bit far-fetched; they're fun but, well, you know."

"Something more realistic you mean?" I asked. "A story that's adventurous but could be true; could really happen in Kongwa nowadays?"

"Yes, you know, true to life. People would believe you if you told it to them."

"I'll see what I can come up with... I'll think about it."

✦ ✦ ✦

WE WERE OUT-OF-BOUNDS, THE OTHER SIDE OF the donga and far round the west side of Church Hill. We were exploring newly-found empty houses for the first time. Doug and I were joined by Paton, Ivey, Burns, Aranky, Berry and Goggles as we explored in search of trouble, we didn't know what. Buried in the thick outcrop of trees and scrub, we found more dilapidated buildings. Because we were risking serious trouble, we stole up to one particular house with great care; it was set away and out of sight of the others and surrounded by thick, dead forest. Unusual for Kongwa, this house was an L-shape rather than the usual shoebox. Head bowed low, Doug admonished, with finger to lips, to be quiet. This was serious stuff after all, as there could be bad people behind every bush.

He crawled to the house, slowly easing himself up at the wall, then peered in the nearest window. After a while he lowered himself and stole quietly to one side as he began circling the building, I assumed, because he disappeared. First in line behind Doug, I wondered what was keeping him; surely he should have reappeared and given the sign to close in by now?

After an age, Doug came stumbling through the bush, hunched low and found me in position. I expected him to confirm the house was abandoned, no one there. Instead, with a blanched look he said, "I think somebody's been living there. I can't believe it in this place, it's so wrecked but I'm telling you there're signs there were people in that house not long ago. In one room there's a dining table and chairs, they're dirty and rotten, but they're there anyway and there're dirty plates."

"Wow," I responded. "So what do you think we should do, Pepsi? Shall we tell the others?"

"Yes, but not yet. There doesn't seem to be anyone there now. First, I'd like to circle the house one more time and make completely sure there's no one inside. Can you tell the others not to move in 'til I've finished casing the joint?" Doug liked that expression. He'd picked it up from an American gangster film and was his favourite, especially appropriate at a time like this.

"Whatever you say, Peps, but don't be too long. I don't know how long I can keep the others from following."

Doug moved away to case the joint again, while I moved to our friends bunched a little further back, away from the house, and let them in on what I knew.

"Golly," said Paton, "do you think they're real gangsters or criminals or something?"

"What would they be doing in Kongwa if they were?" sighed Berry, with his intellectual air. "They'd have places to go other than Kongwa, I'm sure.

Certainly better than a dump like this. If there were people there, they were probably Africans taking shelter."

Well, that was deflating and took the edge off the excitement. Why does Berry have to be so bloody practical? There was a surprising rustle in the bushes that startled us but it was Doug returning.

"There's no one there, so if you want we can go inside. Are you game?"

A chorus of *yes* and *let's go* followed, so we followed Doug's lead and found ourselves at the front door. Doug turned the handle slowly and pushed. The squeaky door opened easily enough. We entered cautiously, peering around, ears tuned to the slightest threat that would cause us to scatter.

We moved from room to room, pushing aside spider webs, glancing at the geckos riding the walls and came across several sleeping mats on the floor, with blankets set aside. They didn't look recently used, like last night, but they were not as dilapidated as the house. Someone had been here. The dining table Doug told of was in the room next to the kitchen. There were dirty plates with remnants of bone and covered with cockroach droppings. In the kitchen, the log cooking stove was cold, but its ash tray was full.

"Better not touch anything," I said. "It might be best if no one knew we've been here."

"Assuming whoever it was comes back," said Berry. "This looks to me like somebody squatted for a while, seeking shelter maybe, eating a meal then moving on. We've seen Masai from time-to-time, a long way from home; they'd need somewhere to sleep the night."

If Berry was the intellectual, Paton knew African customs and lore. "Masai wouldn't be seen dead in a European building like this," he said, "and they certainly wouldn't be cooking food on a wood stove. They'd be after the nearest cow from which they could draw blood to drink. Then they'd sleep under the stars with their animals, having first built themselves a boma. No, it's definitely not Masai."

"Well, it's hardly likely it would be locals, Paton," Westley responded. "After all they have their own kijijis. This has been shelter for someone passing through, someone not normally living here. It wouldn't be Europeans, I'm pretty sure."

I stepped through a back door off the kitchen, and looked around outside. "Nothing suspicious here," I called. Ivey and I took a closer look at what was an over-grown driveway. It hadn't been used regularly for a long time and was almost hidden. However, I found flattened saplings, as though something heavy had rolled over top. A car maybe? We wandered back inside and told Doug.

"I'll take a look just now, Tony."

Goggles had been sifting through the stove's ashtray. He'd picked out a few half-burned scraps of paper. They had nothing on them except for one piece slightly larger than the others. Goggles peered through his thick lenses at something written.

"Pepsi, look at this," he called over.

We crowded around to see what Goggles had found. The paper was scorched from the heat. Clearly it was part of a larger sheet now in ashes. But the writing on it was legible, if you could read Morse code... and we could.

-. . -..- - | -- . . - .. -. --. | -- .- .-. -.-. .... | | - .... | ..--.. |

"Gosh," said Aranky, who read it the fastest, "it reads, 'Next meeting march 13th.' Do you think this message was transmitted or received by someone here?"

Goggles ran a hand through the ash feeling for more scraps but didn't find any.

"What do you think, Peps? Next meeting March 13th? Would that be this coming March 13th – it's February 20th today. Could they mean this coming March 13th and do they mean they'll get back together here?" I asked, looking around at the others.

"I dunno. I suppose it could," Paton responded. "The food and dishes look like they're a couple of months or so old, not a year or two, so it could mean this year... and this place."

"I think we should keep watch, you know, check on this house from time to time and especially around March 13th." Aranky said.

"You blokes are nuts," said Berry. "This is old hat. You tried this Morse code trick on before, Aranky, when we were Juniors; you should come up with something new, man."

"I didn't do it, I swear I didn't," Aranky assured us in protest. "I didn't know we were going to come here today. None of us did. It wasn't even my idea to come here. I didn't even know this house existed."

"That's true," responded Burns. "None of us knew of this place. Still and all, why would you think something sinister? Are you saying some crook has been transmitting messages in Morse? Seems to me, now you know the houses aren't haunted, you want there to be gangsters around every corner. This is Kongwa School, you know."

"You may be right, Andy," said Doug, "but I think it's suspicious. It doesn't hurt to keep an eye out, and if there's anything happening, we'll find out in March."

"And another thing," said Berry, "if someone was transmitting messages, wouldn't they do so in Cigogo or Swahili; if it was Africans sending them, that is?"

"There are many dialects, Stew," I said, "and many African languages. English is a common language over much of Africa, even the world. Who knows who they might be sending messages to?"

It had been mid-afternoon when we'd set out. Knowing how quickly it got dark, Goggles had brought his torch; it would be scary battling our way into bounds and over to our houses in pitch black. Now, Goggles suggested we get back before we were missed. He switched on his torch in the half light, then flashed it around the room in the descending darkness. Suddenly he exclaimed, "Hey, what's this?"

It was less the wire itself than its shadow from the torch that he'd noticed. The wire was similar to the aerial wire I used for my radio.

"Follow its course," Doug said. "Let's see where it leads."

In one direction the wire led outdoors, high above the roof line and disappeared into the branches of a tree, out of sight in the descending gloom. Indoors, the wire had been dropped to the floor and hidden behind a white-ant eaten skirting board. It reappeared with a few inches of it showing from behind the skirting board in the small bedroom at the far end. It was a room none of us had spent much time examining because there was nothing there except a small table and chair.

"You could stand something on that table," said Ivey furtively, "like a radio maybe and it would be connected to that aerial wire."

"Or a transmitter," added Burns.

"I've been thinking, it would be strange to write the message in Morse," Ivey mused. "You know, you'd tap out the message in Morse but you wouldn't normally write it in Morse, would you?"

There was a thoughtful silence at that, then Burns said, "To be honest with you, you might if you weren't very good at it; you know, a learner or something and you tried writing out your message first before you transmitted it."

"Yes, like *we* did," I added, "when we were learning. First we wrote it out." Then, on further thought I asked, "But how would they transmit without electricity?"

"Easy," said Burns. "They could have some small hand-crank generator with them, you know, like gramophones have, or maybe even a battery like you've got with your radio."

"And anyway, why use Morse, isn't that a bit old hat?" asked Berry.

"Yes," added Goggles, "wouldn't they use radio?"

"It is," I responded to Berry's question, "but they might think their messages could be listened into more easily… it's easier to send a short Morse message, maybe with a few code words, you know, like they did in the war and not give away their location."

"What about its range?" Goggles queried. "Wouldn't there have to be a receiver somewhere not far away?"

We looked around at each other; none of us had a ready answer, except Burns, who told us that some radio messages can carry pretty far; "take the B.B.C., for example."

We all paused to think on that for a moment. Then Burns said he'd look it up in the library and see if he could find out something about small transmitter wave ranges.

"Well, anyway," said Doug, "we'd better get going or we'll not be ready for dinner. We can talk later. Come on."

By March 13th most of our group had lost interest or had other plans. Berry was convinced we were reading too many spy novels and let us know we could count him out. Paton found himself out for the day on a geology exercise with a few others and a teacher. Ivey had been caught out of bounds on a separate occasion and, having received a caning, was also writing lines every spare minute he had for both his Housemaster and his house prefect. Burns, having got interested in a girl, was spending every spare minute he could with her rather than us; however, he had checked up on radio transmitters in the library. He'd told me that as near as he could work out, it shouldn't be difficult to transmit Morse from a small portable in Kongwa to somewhere several hundred miles away. That would mean a signal from a small transmitter could easily reach places as far as Nairobi, in Kenya.

"It's only about four hundred miles from here," he'd told me.

Aranky couldn't join us because Fergie had him putting in extra cricket practice in the nets. So it was left to Doug, Goggles and me to follow up.

After church we collected our lunches, then sidled nonchalantly to the donga where we quickly dropped down its sides and hurried along. Under the Baobab root bridge we swung clear, my heart skipping a beat as I glanced at where Hazel and I had first kissed.

Neither Goggles nor I knew how far along this donga we'd walked last time before climbing up its side, but Doug knew. Trees and bushes were like road signs. He seemed to remember them all and which were good landmarks. I'd brought my Scout's handbook with its Morse code alphabet. Goggles carried his torch. Doug brought his field glasses and we all had sheath knives hanging on our belts. To complete our armament, we'd brought our catties with pouches of carefully chosen rocks.

Doug found the place. Without hesitation he said, "This is where we left the donga last time. From now on we must be dead quiet. I mean, who knows if there's anyone there or whether they've been and gone already but what we don't want is to get into trouble. Even if there are people, they may be there with the owner's approval. I don't want to get socked with being caught out of bounds. So, you two follow me, watch my rear and do exactly what I say, all right?"

"Will do, Pepsi."

With that, we clambered up the side. As we caught our breath, Doug peered into the shade of the enclosing trees, thick with dead leaves, the residue of the rainy season. The wine of a diving mosquito ended abruptly as it landed on my forearm. My slap broke the quiet.

Doug whirled. "Sssshhh, what did I tell you?"

"Sorry, Peps. Mosquito, what must I do?"

"Don't slap it, squash it if you must, but don't make a noise," he urged.

"Sorry."

Doug moved off into the dried magugu grass, skirting bushes with long thorns, and we followed. Soon we were shrouded in what had been lush, overhanging greenery, now dead but thick. Brilliant streams of light penetrated gaps in the withered foliage, creating sunny pools on the forest floor. Trapped mosquitoes alerted us to beautiful, rim-lit spider's webs when we found them entangled, helping us avoid a face full of web or the bite of a dismayed spider.

In the trees, vervets screeched a warning of our approach.

"I'd no idea there were monkeys here," I thought. "They weren't here last time; must keep well away from the school. If there are people at the house who can read the sounds of the forest, we could be in trouble."

It wasn't long before Doug glanced back, finger to lips, with a signal to crouch low. I was five yards behind, and Goggles another five behind me.

"Wait here," he silently mouthed, "until I get back."

Doug melted into the woods leaving us shrugging at each other.

We were restless by the time he reappeared.

In a crouch he returned breathlessly. "You're not going to believe this," he panted, "but there really are Africans there. I only saw one but I heard conversations using a mixture of Kikuyu and Swahili rather than Cigogo like the locals speak, so they're not from here. And there's smoke coming from the chimney."

"What did they say?" we asked earnestly.

"Oh, nothing much. It had to do with gathering wood. I didn't catch it all. But there's another thing; they have a pick-up with them. They found a way through the overgrown drive that ends up at the back; remember we thought that was a driveway when we were last here? Well, anyway that's how they got here."

"What do you want to do, Pepsi?" asked Goggles.

I looked at Doug, frowning. "Yes, what do you think? I vote we get closer. I want to know what's going on."

"So do I," replied Doug, breath coming a little easier, "but we must be careful. There may be several of them and if they're up to no good and they see us, we'll be in trouble."

"I want to piss," said Goggles with sudden urgency.

"Well, hurry up then… and don't piss into the wind," Doug stage-whispered after him, as Goggles moved for privacy behind a tree.

"What's the plan, Peps, what do you want to do?" I asked again.

"First we'll stay together 'til we get close. Then, I'll circle to the left, past the front door and under the living room window. I'd like you to move to the right and reki that small bedroom. I want Goggles to stay at the spot where you and I move off, so that he can watch, and run like hell if anything goes wrong. All right with you?"

"Yes," I said tremulously. It was suddenly so deadly serious. "But how close do we get and what will we look for?"

"We need to find out who they are. If they are just regular wanaume then that's an end to it. If there's anything going on, like if they're thieves or something, well, we'll need to find out. Then depending, well, I s'pose we'd have to tell a teacher."

"But they'll punish us for being out of bounds; I don't want a thrashing for that."

"Nor do I but we'll have to take our lumps if it comes to it. We can't not tell them if there's something bad here."

"Maybe they'd forgive us if there is?" I said.

My heart beat fast. I felt its thumping in my chest. It may be that the Africans were just poor, out-of-work homeless people looking for shelter. But yet, what about that Morse message? That's what was making the difference. And Doug said they had a pick-up. This wasn't our imagination. There was something not right... and it was nerve-wracking to think of it, out here, with no one knowing where we were. Well, Berry and the others did, sort of, but could they find this house again?

Doug brought me back to focus.

"You ready, Tony? Here comes Goggles."

Doug told Goggles the plan. I think Gogs was relieved at being the watch; then we moved off as quietly as we could, following Doug towards the house.

We smelled it first. The wood smoke from the stove was drifting languidly through the trees for there was little wind. The vervets had quit their warnings or we had moved beyond their territory. It was quiet except for the raucous laughter coming from the house. It was reassuring to start with. These were happy people. *Happy people wouldn't be up to no good, surely?* Finally we were within sight of the tree line, the edge of the clearing in which the house stood. *Thank goodness the trees are close in so we have cover,* I thought nervously.

"Now, Goggles," Doug turned to him, "this is where you should stay and keep watch. Keep to the shade. If there's trouble, leave quietly, make your way back to the houses and fetch Mr. Moore or any other teacher. Can you do that?"

"Yes, of course."

"No problem finding your way?"

"No, it's not dark. I'll be all right."

"Good, right then, keep your head down and watch 'til we return. Tony, are you ready? I'm going to peel off to the left; you'll go off that way, to the right. You'll find the window of that small room at the end of the house, the one with the small table and chair and the aerial wire. Only when you've listened carefully, for everything and anything, try for a look through the window. Be *very* careful when you do. They'll be able to see you more easily outdoors in the sunlight than you can see them indoors. Let's go."

With that we split up and moved off. I headed at an angle towards the right of the L-shaped house. Doug was heading towards the living room where, he said, most of the laughter and conversation was coming from. As he was more adept at Swahili, or Kikuyu that I knew little of, it made sense that he should go where the talk was.

Just then an African emerged through the front door. I froze into a haunch hoping Doug had seen him too. The African was young and looked strong. His skin was a deep, rich brown and reflected a high sheen in the sunlight. On his top lip was a moustache and a wiry beard was slung below his chin. He wore a dirty American T-shirt that had once displayed an advertising message for Michelob beer, and a pair of khaki shorts. Feet were shod in sandals. In what was for me an unfamiliar dialect of Swahili he called back to his comrades as he emerged, "I'm going for a pee. We'll talk of the plan when I return."

With that he walked over to the tree line, unbuttoning the fly of his shorts as he walked.

I held motionless in my crouch, peering through a brown, leafy puzzle. Halfway through his pee, the African, who had been gazing around him in every direction, seemed to rest his eyes on the bushes behind which I was hiding. Fortunately, he didn't peer too hard or apparently recognize that I was there in all my frozen Sunday whiteness, for he finished relieving himself and walked back to the house calling out, "Right then, let's get down to business."

I waited after the door had shut to make sure none of the man's comrades decided to do the same. When they didn't, I moved toward the room I was to check on. Fortunately, from this end of the house I'd be out of sight except through the one window if someone just happened to be looking.

I emerged from the woods and stepped deftly to the wall, flattening myself against it. I sidled along its side then went into a low crouch, inch by inch, until I was almost under the low-slung, open window. I heard someone in there. There was shuffling of papers, movement of feet, a short cough, but no conversation. Whoever was there was alone. Nervously, I moved my head from around the window frame to peer inside. If anyone was looking out, they would see me and the alarm would be sounded. I was as tense as a drawn bow string, ready to scarper for the slightest reason.

I peered through the grimed glass. It took moments to focus because it was so dark compared with the brilliance of outdoors. Then, through the gloom, I saw an African, seated at the table. I jerked my head back. But even as I did, I realised he wasn't facing me. His back was to me. Slowly I peered again. The man was relying on the daylight over his shoulder to see what he was doing. When he turned to his side to sift some papers, I saw a transmitter key. I jerked away and flattened myself to the wall again thinking, *That can't be right. What's he doing with that? I think they're up to no good after all. Bloody hell!*

I heard the scrape of a chair and the squeak of a door. Slowly I peered through the window once more. The man had left the room. There was the key and papers in plain view. I tried to read the top ones but the writing wasn't in English and too far away anyway. I needed to tell Doug. There was no point staying here. I couldn't get into the room through a door and it would be too dangerous to climb through the window. But I'd seen what I came to see. So I withdrew to the tree line, then made my way towards the other side of the house.

There was Doug, clear as day. He was lying below the low-silled window, flattened against the crumbly exterior wall. The windows he was lying under were wide open. If anyone came to the window and glanced down, Doug would be in trouble because the burglar bars had been removed. The occupants could climb through and be all over him in seconds. I caught his eye. Doug put out a hand gesturing me over but to circle and stay low. There was only the one angle to approach and not be seen and it meant being visible from the front door. I took my cue. He was beckoning again, he must have reason to think no one was about to exit through the door. Stealthily I emerged into the open, came to the wall, went down on all fours, and crawled around the corner to join him. There was much talk inside, fortunately loud and involved, so we could safely whisper. I told Doug of my discovery.

"I knew it," he said. "Ssshh, listen now."

"Let me take you through this one more time, Kinoyo," said voice number one in Swahili. "We're not going to take aggressive action like capturing or killing any of those European totos... yet. That will be for you to do when the time comes. We're here to establish a cell, recruit people, train them and then we'll move on. You're our first recruit. But, you must do exactly as we say. If not, or if you betray us, you and your wife and your kids will have your throats slit... or worse. Do you follow me, Kinoyo?"

"Yes, of course," replied Kinoyo, his Cigogo dialect evident. "I'm sorry to sound impatient. I just want to get this going, but I'll do whatever the great Kenyatta says."

"Silence!" interrupted voice number one angrily. "You're never to speak that name, do you understand? Never! There must be no knowledge that we're seeking to expand Mau Mau into Tanganyika. You will never speak of him, or his lieutenants, or of Mau Mau. When you recruit your people, you'll not tell them of this either. When the time comes we will tell you what to say."

Voice number two jumped in. "One of our leaders will be coming here for the first meeting by the second moon. By that time you'll need to have recruited up to six potential operatives. We expect no less than three. Do you think you can do this? Are there enough discontent people who might readily join up?"

"I'll find some," replied Kinoyo. "Most of them seem to be fat and happy enough with the Europeans, I have to say, but still there is discontent among a few of the young. I think I'll not have any problem finding four, maybe six."

Doug and I looked grimly at each other, silently mouthing, "Mau Mau!" That was big trouble. Everyone knew of the atrocities going on in Kenya, the most awful, savage cruelty and bestiality, mostly Kikuyu to Kikuyu but of course involving Europeans, especially farmers and their animals. And this meant we'd be in serious trouble if we were caught.

Another voice called, "I have kukuu na chipsi cooked up. Bring your beers and let's eat before we go over any more details."

"There's one thing I have to do first," said voice number one. "I need to let Thika know we're on track. They want to be kept informed and I have a time call to send a message... Let's see now, what is the time? Yes, in the next few minutes."

Yet another voice said, "I've got the transmitter ready; let's do that first."

Doug and I looked at each other and mouthed "Thika?"

"I've heard of that place," I whispered.

"Yes," he whispered back, "not too far from Nairobi. We must get out of here before someone comes out... I want to see what happens with the transmitter."

That's the place where Elspeth Huxley said her parents lived? I thought, as we turned to crawl away and go to the other side of the house. *I hope they're all right.*

Most of the occupants had moved to the kitchen, where the fresh cooked kukuu na chipsi awaited.

We melted into the trees in a crouch. Doug followed me as I led the way to the window. We stayed hidden but could hear the slow chatter of Morse being tapped out; the operator was inexperienced, that was certain. We didn't catch the whole message, it had taken too long to get here, but we did catch the last of the transmission.

"... successful stop next meeting with new recruits and first training session on Sunday April 10th. stop over stop."

The incoming response was faster, the operator more skilled, but it was short. "... message received stop good work stop Uhuru stop."

The stutter of the incoming ended abruptly, and was replaced with silence. Then voice number one said. "Good. Let's get some of that kuku. Now, where'd I put my beer?"

Doug whispered, "Did you catch anything?"

"Mostly the end, although their Swahili seems to include Kikuyu, but I got the drift. I wrote down everything I could; the last word was Uhuru. That's the Mau Mau's war cry of freedom, isn't it?"

When we felt sure the two had left the room, we left our cover and moved in so Doug could take a look through the window and see the transmitter key. Satisfied, we returned to the seclusion of the trees and made our way to Goggles.

"What happened, who are they, are they crooks?" Goggles blurted.

"Sshh, quiet," Doug and I urged in unison.

"Not crooks," I whispered. "Terrorists."

"We both heard them," said Doug in a low voice. "They were talking in a Kenyan dialect of Swahili. Almost certainly they were Kikuyu; *Mau Mau*, I think. We know they were not Wagogo; well, one of them was because he was from here. But the rest were Kikuyu, although one may have been Luo on account of the melodic way he talked. Come, let's get out of here. We can talk more later."

We paused to eat at the root bridge, and discussed what we'd heard. We'd not eaten our lunches, at least Doug and I hadn't; Goggles ate his while keeping watch. As we did, I leaned against the spot where I'd kissed Hazel; it was taking on a nostalgic memory for me. *What a difference, eh? First her and now this.* We downed our lunches fast as we were in a hurry. We wouldn't feel safe 'til we got back home.

"So what are we going to do, Peps?" I asked.

Goggles and I looked intently at Doug.

"We have to report this. There's no choice. This is very serious. I suggest we go to see Mr. Moore right away. Okay with you?"

"Why not your Housemaster?"

"Well, for one thing Hobbs is away in Arusha or somewhere, a rushed visit to do with family, I think, and also there're two of you from Livingstone, so I suppose Mr. Moore is as good as any."

"I agree."

"Makes sense."

We circled the girls' phase keeping well clear; we weren't looking for more trouble than we could already be in. After crossing the paved strip we arrived at the driveway to Mr. Moore's house, and knocked on his front door. Mrs. Moore answered, her smallest in her arms gurgling happily; she brightening with a smile as she recognised our faces.

"Edwards, Venables and who's this?"

"Westley," I said. "He's from Wilberforce, Miss."

"Oh, hello, Westley."

Mrs. Moore was a nice lady and seemed to like us a lot. Perhaps it was because she had two girls of her own and more recently a baby boy, I don't know, but anyway she was always pretty decent. Mrs. Moore didn't use make-up and wore her hair short and curled in the fashion of the day. Her short-sleeved, thin dress was wide at the neck and flared below her waist, stopping short a little below her knees. Her dress was colourful and bright and matched her kindly manner.

"Is Mr. Moore in?" I asked.

"No, I'm afraid not," she responded smiling, "although I'm expecting him any time now. What's this about? Can I help you?"

"It's very serious, Mrs. Moore," interrupted Doug. "I think we should wait for Mr. Moore. We can wait outside until he arrives."

"Why don't you come in?" said Mrs. Moore. "I'm not used to young boys coming to the door with very serious stories. Perhaps I can offer you some lemonade while we wait, or I have Tizer."

We were soon ensconced, Doug in a deep arm chair and Goggles and I on a settee drinking cold lemonade from tall glasses. Very welcome, considering we hadn't drunk for hours.

Judi and Stephanie ran giggling through the house into the garden as Mrs. Moore returned from putting Alan down. She couldn't contain her curiosity and asked, "You know, Mr. Moore and I haven't got any secrets. I'm sure he wouldn't mind me knowing whatever it is you intend to tell him."

We looked at each other exchanging glances then Doug said, "We went the other side of the donga, Miss." This was followed by a guilty-looking pause.

A disappointed frown overtook Mrs. Moore's face.

"That's not good, is it, isn't that out of bounds? ...But then, it's not all that bad either. Actually, I'm a bit surprised you would even tell me. Were you caught by somebody? Did they send you to Mr. Moore to own up?"

I jumped in.

"Actually, that's not the reason why we've come to see Mr. Moore. We've come to tell him what we found the other side of the donga, that's the bit that's serious," I assured her with gravity.

"Well, do tell," she responded, with a curious frown. "Let me be the judge of how serious it is. You never know, I may be able to save you from a hiding."

At that moment, Judi and Stephanie ran back indoors, full of excitement, "Mummy, Mummy, you should see the snake the 'boy' killed outside, you're not going to believe it, it's soooooooooooo long."

"Just leave it alone, darling, promise me, don't touch it, all right? Now I need you to run along for now, while I have a talk with these boys."

Judi gave us a huge smile while Stephanie looked curious. "Who's that one?" she asked, as she raised her little arm and pointed a finger at Doug.

"That's Westley," replied Mrs. Moore. "He's in Wilberforce, now run along, please."

I started again to tell Mrs. Moore what we'd seen and heard. Then Doug

joined in and Goggles followed with his slant, filling in details. It was noticeable how serious Mrs. Moore's face had become. Clearly she was shocked.

"Are you certain of this?" she asked when we'd finished. "That's what
you want to tell Mr. Moore? It could be serious indeed if you're right. You're
not having me on, are you? If you're playing a game you realise you'll be in
serious trouble with the Head as well as Mr. Moore for being out of bounds. I
don't like my boys getting caned, but I worry you may have it coming."

The sound of the Jeep drawing up outside indicated Mr. Moore's return.

As he walked in he showed surprise at two of his charges and one other
sitting in his sitting room sipping on his lemonade.

"Hello, Maurice," Mrs. Moore began. "These three have a rather serious
story to tell and I'm not sure I—"

"—It is true!" I said. "It really is, Mrs. Moore, we wouldn't lie about this.
We know we'd get a thrashing if we did. But we're not, truly."

"Hello, Kathy." Mr. Moore gave his wife a peck on the cheek. "Now
what's this about?" he asked, turning to us.

"They've got quite a story, Maurice," said Mrs. Moore. "I'm going to get
you a drink – you'll probably need it."

We told Mr. Moore what had happened. Venables brought out the charred
piece of paper with the coded message and handed that over.

"I must say this does seem unlikely," said Mr. Moore. "Are you quite
sure this is not a game? It'll be six of the best for you from the Head if it is."

"Please, sir," I said. "We can take you to the kaya. We probably shouldn't
go today because the wanaume are still there, but we could take you tomorrow. They said they were leaving after their meal, sir, and getting together
again, with their new recruits on April 10th, sir. We can show you the signs
they were there, sir."

Mrs. Moore returned to the living room with whisky and soda for her
husband and a plate of biscuits for us.

"Thank you, Kath," said Mr. Moore, as he accepted the drink, then took
another look at the charred piece of paper.

"Here, have a biscuit, boys. I must say I was shocked when you told me;
I thought you must be having me on. But hearing it again and hearing your
answers to Mr. Moore's questions, I'm inclined to give you the benefit of the
doubt. What do you think, Maurice?" she addressed her husband.

"I'm inclined to believe them too, Kath, if a little sceptical. The one thing

I know is the authorities are worried because the Mau Mau has made incursions into Tanganyika on our northern border. We've been encouraged to arm ourselves, as you know."

"Yes, and my dad even bought a gun because of that, sir," I added enthusiastically. "I saw it last hols."

"Of course, we'd never suspect anything in Kongwa," Mr. Moore continued, "but this signature, Uhuru, is worrying. That's the Mau Mau war cry. Hmm. If what you say is true, then we have time. The Kikuyu will probably have left by now. In any case a platoon of police could never be rustled up at short notice. I doubt we have more than half a dozen askaris and a commanding officer in Kongwa. I imagine any intercept would have to be done with police brought in from Dodoma. Leave this with me, boys. I'll talk it over with the Head. You three are not to discuss this with anyone, under any circumstances. I don't want this story being repeated around the school, do you understand me?"

We nodded, grimly.

"This could be exceptionally dangerous. Even the boys you went with the first time must not know. If they ask how things went today, you are to say nothing happened and there was no one there. Do I have your word on this?"

"Yes, sir," we chorused, looking at each other in *told you so* excitement.

Around the dinner table that evening, Angel-face remembered to bring up the subject.

"So how did the crook hunting go today, huh? Did you make any arrests?"

The other three at the table laughed.

"Yeah, Edwards, Gogs, how'd it go?"

"Oh, nothing. There was no one there," we said, as we glanced furtively at one another. The others dropped the questions with self righteous smiles.

Next morning, during French class with Miss Hurley, Mr. Moore entered the classroom, whispered a few words in her ear, and on receiving a nod, turned to face me and Goggles and gave us the 'come hither' sign with curling finger. We stood in silence and followed him out of the classroom into the sunlight, followed by twenty-nine sets of eyes wondering what trouble we were in this time. Outside, we found Doug waiting, already called from woodwork.

"Let's find some shade," said Mr. Moore. "I think the baobab next to the admin block."

We followed and ended up in a circle under the tree.

"The Head and I have agreed I should follow up on your Mau Mau story immediately. If I am persuaded by what you show me, we'll take it from there. I want you to take me to the house you told me of, following exactly the route you describe. Do not miss out any detail. I expect you to follow the same precautions you did before when approaching the house, just in case any have remained behind. If this is true, we do not want to reveal ourselves."

Forty-five minutes later, we were walking around the house from room to room. There was no one there now but there were signs of newly-discarded chicken bones and cold chips on tin plates. The cockroaches were having a field day. One plate had been left in the bedroom where the transmitter had been. Mr. Moore noted the dust on the table was still there but had clearly been disturbed. The sleeping mats were there, although they'd now been placed in an untidy pile to one side. And the aerial wire remained in place. Before we'd entered, we'd found tyre tracks from the wanaume's pick-up. Around the front, clearly visible in the sand, were fresh footprints from large, unshod feet and one set of sandal imprints.

"I have to say, all the signs suggest that people were here. Whether or not they're up to the nefarious activities you claim I don't know because this is all circumstantial. But, your story holds together and on the face of it there's reason to believe you. So, I'm swearing you to continued silence. We'll be in touch with the police, whom I imagine will be watching on April 10th. At that time we'll find out if these men, if they return at all, are indeed Kikuyu and potential terrorists, or whether that part of the story is a product of over-vivid imaginations. Now, let's return to school."

That night I swore Berry to absolute silence. He'd watched as Goggles and I had been summoned out of Miss Hurley's French class, and he'd seen through the window Doug waiting outside, so he knew something was up. "Promise me on a stack of Bibles?" Then I told him what we'd found.

The next day I caught up with Hazel during mid-morning break.

"Hello, silly boy," she greeted me. "Haven't seen you for days."

"No, I know, it's been difficult to get away. But let's not talk about that, I've something important to tell you. I'm not supposed to. Mr. Moore made us promise. But, well, you're very special and I can't not tell you any longer."

"Sounds exciting," Hazel responded. "What do you mean, 'Mr. Moore made you promise not to tell anyone'? That sounds weird."

"It won't when I tell you."

"Well, tell me then, and hurry up – break's not that long."

"Hazel, you have to promise me. I'm really serious; you've got to keep this secret. I'm already telling you when I'm not supposed to, but, well, you're not just any girl, you know, you're special."

"Cross my heart and hope to die," said Hazel. "I won't tell anyone if you're really serious about this. Don't worry, I can keep a secret you know. I know you think girls can't keep secrets, most can't actually, but I can, at least if it involves you."

"Well, here it is then." And with that I told Hazel our story from beginning to as far as it had got. Hazel's jaw dropped open, eyes widened, a hand went to mouth in horror several times and all this was supported with several "*Oh-my-God*s."

"So, anyway," I concluded, amid the sound of the end-of-break bell clanging in the distance, "that's as far as it's got. April 10th is the big day. We'll see if anything more is said between now and then. I just hope we're proved right, because otherwise, the three of us could find ourselves bending over in front of the whole school."

"Oh, they wouldn't do that, would they?" asked Hazel alarmed. "At the very least they know you had the best intentions, even if you were mistaken."

"Yes, but we were out of bounds and the Head takes that seriously."

"Oh, I don't believe it, they couldn't," said Hazel. "If they do, I certainly won't attend, I promise you that, I don't care how many demerit points they give me. Anyway, we have to get back to class. Let's try to get together later."

The next thirty days passed slowly. Keeping the secret, together with Mr. Moore's and the Head's decision to believe us and call in the police, proved an agonisingly long wait. Finally, April 10th came... and went. There was no word. Neither on the 11th nor the 12th. Mr. Moore didn't say anything, the Head didn't say anything; but then, neither did he summon us for a caning. The five of us, including Hazel and Berry, were on tenterhooks.

Then, on the Wednesday morning, April 13th during morning break, as we were playing nyabs in the morning heat, we looked up to watch three 'boys' under the guidance of the Head, and the assistant Head, Mr. Shuttleworth, carry out a temporary dais to the centre of the open ground next to the flagpole.

"Now what's that all about?" queried Ivey, as Berry and I exchanged frowns.

Before we could speculate, the bell for class was rung prematurely and was followed by the Headmaster standing on the dais and calling through a bullhorn.

"Gather round, please, everyone. Yes, you too, young ladies. All girls and boys gather round, please. I have an important announcement and I want you to hear this. Gather round, gather round, come on now. Tighten up there."

With the aid of prefects and teachers, like sheep dogs rustling up the herd, gradually the Senior school was packed around the dais within general hearing distance of Mr. Gillham. He was flanked by Mr. Shuttleworth, Mr. Moore, Mr. Hobbs, the head boy and the head girl. Moments later the conversation died and Mr. Gillham stepped forward to begin his address. Before he could say anything, Miss Strong came quickly to the dais, escorting Kongwa's European police captain. He looked posh in his khaki shirt with short sleeves, khaki shorts and highly-polished, red leather, shin-high boots. He sported a number of medal bars on his chest, a peaked cap on his head, braid through his epaulettes, a swagger stick tucked under his left arm and a holstered gun on his belt. He stepped to the dais and joined Mr. Gillham with a whisper – running late, I suppose – but the Headmaster was clearly expecting him.

"This last Monday," Mr Gillham began as he addressed the school through the bullhorn, "a terrorist cell, in the process of being formed by certain Kikuyu men, was interdicted by the Tanganyika police. The arrests took place in a house to the west of the donga, around the back of Church Hill."

There was a big, "Ooooh!" at that, as most of us turned to look at each other in amazement; then an immediate murmur of conversation erupted. I felt the hairs on my arms and back stand on end – I had no idea there would be this kind of announcement. Berry and I were wide-eyed.

"Silence, please, I have more to say. The arrests were made without incident and all is well. The purpose in telling you of this, aside from the fact that it will shortly become public knowledge, is because we have to thank three boys from among our number who were instrumental in discovering this cell and tipping off the authorities. Will the following boys please step forward and join me here on the dais... Westley, Edwards, Venables."

I was shocked to hear my name called, it was the last thing I expected.

I did wonder why we'd not heard anything but now it was coming out. Followed by a couple of hundred pairs of eyes, I made my way towards the dais, converging with Pepsi and Goggles along the way. We stepped up, and were clustered together to face the school's Senior boys and girls, embraced by the arms of the Head.

"These three boys broke school bounds," he began. "In doing so they incurred what would normally result in a mandatory punishment. However…" he paused as he surveyed the earnest faces of the crowd, standing there, anticipating witnessing a public caning with the kiboko, " …and as it happens, the result of their misbehaviour is so very good, so excellent, so much in the tradition of what I would hope for and expect from my boys in the way of astuteness, tenacity and backbone that I intend to forebear in the circumstances."

Kongwa's collection of Senior school pupils exchanged surprised glances and whispers, and I thought I detected a sigh of relief from the girls. It was definitely not like the Head to do that.

Mr. Gillham then went on to relate the detail of our detective work, something like we had told him. I was quite surprised. We knew Gillham's spoken English to be impeccable but he used it now in a creative way, embellishing if anything on the excitement of the story as we had told it. In some parts I almost didn't recognise it as he rose to the occasion.

"Westley, Edwards and Venables," he concluded, "demonstrated courage in confirming a Mau Mau-like terrorist cell in the making. They were able to persuade their Housemaster, Mr. Moore, of the validity of what at first seemed more like an April fools story. Mr. Moore and I in turn contacted Kongwa's police officer-in-charge here," he turned and acknowledged the policeman by his side, "Captain Brise-Norton, who opted to give the boys the benefit of the doubt. He set a trap for last Sunday when the boys said they expected the cell members to return, supported by a platoon of askaris from Dodoma. The four suspects did return, along with four locals whom they had since recruited, and the police made eight arrests. I'm now going to ask Captain Brise-Norton here to say a few words… Captain?"

"Thank you, Headmaster," began the Captain after taking over the bullhorn. "I would like to echo all that you said. This incident is the first reported of potential insurgent activity this far south in Tanganyika. The authorities have been at great pains to ensure the troubles in Kenya do not spread across this country, so it was disappointing to learn that the cell was in progress.

However, it is our hope that, due to its failure, this may be the end of it. We like to think we've nipped this in the bud. If we have, then the plaudits due to the three boys here know no bounds. With that in mind I have suggested to your Headmaster, and he has concurred, that we recommend to the Governor-General that these boys be nominated for the George Medal for meritorious service, the highest award for civilians, for valour and selflessness in their actions."

A spontaneous outburst of cheering and clapping followed, during which the Captain handed back the bullhorn to the Headmaster. Mr. Gillham held his arms up requesting silence and as the hubbub died he continued.

"I want you to know that Captain Brise-Norton has my unqualified support. These boys were astute and intrepid. I heartily support his commendation as I am sure all of you do. Therefore, I would like you all to join me in expressing your support for your brave colleagues. Let's hear three resounding cheers for these courageous boys of whom we all should be justly proud. Westley, Edwards and Venables."

"Hip hip, hooray! Hip hip, hooray! Hip hip, hooray!"

The entire school cheering made for a noisy few moments, yet their cheers evaporated into the background for me as, from my vantage point on the dais, standing there and squirming in my embarrassment, my eyes came to rest on Hazel, a beaming smile on her lovely face, gently wiping away her tears....

"...Well, chaps, what did you think of that one? Made a change from my usual stories, don't you think?"

Silence. I became aware of the heavy breathing of sleep.

"Oh, come on... someone must be awake. You wanted a real-life, believable story, didn't you? You can't all be asleep! Andy, man?"

But they all seemed to be.

"Andy, you need to wake up, man, and get back to your room."

"I'm awake," said Burns sleepily, as he got up from where he'd been lying beside Aranky on his bed. "Your story was neat," he whispered over his shoulder as he shuffled down the corridor to his bedroom, "but I don't think you should end it with a girl crying."

CHAPTER TWENTY-FOUR

REGAL TIME OUT

W E WERE NOT LONG INTO OUR SECOND term of 1956, when we learned that in October, Princess Margaret would make a Royal tour of Tanganyika. We guessed that would make for at least one day off to honour the visit, but I became more excited when I heard Lindi was on her schedule. There was precedence for chaps to be allowed to visit home for two or three days for a Royal visit, which wasn't often, and this being the case I wanted my moment of glory. So I was overjoyed to read in a letter from Mum that, in view of she and my dad being on the list of dignitaries to meet Princess Margaret, I was to come home and celebrate this auspicious occasion. A day later, Mr. Moore called me to his house after class.

"Ah, Edwards, yes, I did send for you, didn't I? Now what was it I wanted to speak to you about, let me see, uh, er…."

"The Royal visit, Maurice," asserted Mrs. Moore, baby Alan in arms, no sign of the girls. "You received a letter from his parents?"

"Yes, that's it, thank you, my dear. You may or may not know," he said, turning back to me, "that Princess Margaret is making a Royal visit to Tanganyika. This will include a number of smaller towns. It seems that your home town of Lindi is on the schedule. I have received a letter from your parents, asking that you be allowed to journey home, for a quick visit mind, so you can be present for the ceremony."

"Thank you, sir. Yes, my mother wrote me that she'd be in touch with you."

"Yes, well, this is going to occur next week… bit inconvenient really, middle of the week and all, not even half term, but there you are, we'll have to see what we can do. Mrs. Moore will set up the arrangements for your train ticket and plane flight. You will overnight in Dar es Salaam with people you know? The Kherers?"

"Yes, sir, I know them well. I always stay with them to and from school."

"Very well then, they will meet your arrival, and put you on the train again on your return. But anyway, that's enough for now. Mrs. Moore will call you when she has the details and an itinerary. Any questions?"

"Not for now, sir, thank you sir. Should I go now?"

It had been an uneventful drive in the milk gari this time. I'd left Kongwa earlier than before because the train schedule had changed and now left Gulwe at 11 p.m. I was excited as it trundled into Dar es Salaam on the Wednesday afternoon. I leaned out the window on the platform side and soon saw the Kherers, anxiously surveying the carriages as they rolled by. I had become most fond of Franz and Jean; they were always so kind that my overnights in Dar were the highlight of my trip. Amazingly, the train came to a halt when I was immediately in front of them, so we did a big hug through the window and Mr. Kherer nearly pulled me through.

"Wow, you're bigger than ever."

"Hold on there, Franz," Jean said to her husband. "I don't want you putting your back out. Tony's way too big for that now and anyway I expect he's got luggage with him as well as a suitcase in the guard's van. Just you put him back again so he can gather up his things, and we'll meet at the door down the end."

I gathered my carry-on and a small case that had been lent by Mrs. Moore, scooped up my chameleon that was trying, unsuccessfully, to match the colour of the maroon leather upholstery and then rushed down the corridor to the exit.

"No, I've no other luggage. The trip is so short. I've brought my tie, blazer and trousers for the ceremony. I've got clothes in Lindi if I need them."

"Good, that makes it easy," said Jean in her broad Dutch accent. "Let's make the most of what's left of the day. Franz has to return to the office, I'm afraid, but we'll have some fun, Tony. Tell you what, Franz, why don't we drop you off right away, I'll keep the car and Tony and I'll start off at the ice cream shop. You've had lunch?"

"Yes, thank you, Mrs. Kherer, I had it on the train, but I'd like an ice cream. We never get ice cream at school, you know."

"Oh you poor boy, you are deprived," said Mrs. Kherer in mock sympathy, followed by a chuckle. "All right then, we'll do that first, then what, a swim maybe?"

"That would be nice, oh, except I didn't bring trunks with me."

"You can go in your birthday suit. We'll go up past the Club. There's no one on the beach up there, so you won't be seen."

Actually I would be seen, by Mrs. Kherer, and I did feel shy at the idea of being seen in my altogether. But, she was such a nice lady, and the thought of the swim in the warm ocean so tempting that I wasn't going to say no. In any case, she politely averted her eyes while I slipped off my khakis and waded in.

At 6 p.m. we met Franz for dinner at the new, pride-of-Dar es Salaam, the super posh Intercontinental Hotel. After an evening drive, when the Kherers showed me some of the more beautiful parts of Dar at night, we ended up at their home where Juba, their Mpishi, had prepared a tasty, late supper followed by more ice cream and jelly. I felt spoiled, thinking of Hazel and my friends dining on school food and not having any fun. I wished Hazel could be with me.

THE 6 A.M. FLIGHT THAT TOOK ME to Lindi departed on time. It was crowded, where normally there would be a few empty seats, but I supposed there were many flying in for the ceremonies. By mid-morning I was home.

"You've brought your best clothes, I see," said Mother. "That's good; thank goodness you didn't forget them. You may get the chance to be introduced to the Princess tomorrow so we want you looking posh. You need a hair cut too. We'll get that attended to in the next hour or so as there'll be no time in the morning."

I walked to the Goan barber shop. On my return I checked my clothes to make sure my shirt had been laundered and the grey trousers, tie and blazer had been ironed. The shirt looked whiter than usual; the dhobi in Kongwa failed to remove the salmon pink that was the residual colour of Kongwa's whites.

The following morning was a flurry of preparations. We walked the waterfront to stare at the Royal Yacht *Britannia* moored in Lindi Bay. Then we made our way to the boma and its open space, reserved for anything from flea markets to a new car sales park. There was a long and wide dais, with tall poles supporting a white marquee. The awning was striped; the poles reminiscent of the masts of tall ships, and gaily coloured bunting, pennants and streamers lent a festive air. The raised dais was skirted similarly. Away from the dais, in the hot sun, were neatly laid out rows of chairs for the guests. Dad showed me where to sit as he and Mum would be seated elsewhere.

The ceremony started with the marching band of the Royal Scots Grenadiers. After a while they stopped, as VIPs arrived and took their seats on the dais. Sitting among them were Father in suit and tie, with Mother by his side. Mother was smart in a colourful morning dress, hat and gloves. Front and centre were people whose roles I could not guess but who looked important. They too were dressed in white, wore fancy white helmets, a sort of over-sized pith helmet from which sprouted plumes of ostrich feathers. On some of the gentlemen, ceremonial swords hung at their sides. The ladies looked wonderful, dolled to the nines in breezy colourful morning dresses, stockings, high heels and hats with nets. And there we sat, wilting in the late morning sun, wishing the Princess would arrive so we could get on with it.

A caravan of limousines rounded the corner. I wondered if they'd been brought on the Royal Yacht because I didn't think there were cars like that in Lindi. The Princess stepped out, and after a round of handshakes took her seat. Speeches were spoken, more band music played and then the area before the dais was cleared to make way for the African dancers.

The dancing was led by a troupe of watoto whose traditional act to the beat of their fast playing drums was impressive. This was followed by exotic female dancers who arrived after an extended pause. I think the delay was unexpected because I detected signs of restlessness on the dais. The ladies were exuberant as they arrived, ululating at a high pitch and working themselves into a frenzy. Last came the adult males, dancing in a vibrating, thundering, escalation of sight and sound, kicking up sand which, to the regret of some I'm sure, drifted towards the dais. I think there was an absence of forethought there because I noticed the Princess waiving her fan with a little too much enthusiasm for regality.

The moment I was waiting for arrived, the food and drink part. We drifted to the marquees, resplendent in exotic foods and wines laid out on white tablecloths with all the best silver and serving tureens.

"No, you may not," replied Mother, in response to my request for a half glass of wine. "There's plenty of juice and soft drinks over there."

I took a plate of morsels and tried nursing a tall glass of chilled lime juice. I found a spot to pause, the edge of a table that supported a huge vase of flowers, where I could set down my plate and glass for a moment and take in the scene. To my astonishment, Princess Margaret, closely escorted by white-dressed men in plumed helmets walked close by. She noticed me and turned just as I was looking up, perhaps because I was the only child present.

"Hello, young man, what's your name?"

I looked around, startled. *Are you talking to me?* I thought.

"Yes, I'm talking to you," she smiled, as she seemed to be reading my thoughts. "I hope you're having a good time."

"Oh yes, Miss, er, I mean Princess, my name's Edwards, Miss, Tony Edwards," I said, not having been coached on how to address a princess. Clearly no one thought I'd be engaged in conversation this way. "It's just wonderful, and a smashing ceremony; have you been to some like this before?"

She chuckled at that. "Oh yes," replied the Princess, "once or twice. Now tell me, how do you come to be here today, no school?"

Oh, that inevitable question. There I was trying desperately to forget there was even such a thing as school, only to discover that princesses are just like every other adult; they always ask about school.

"Oh yes, Miss, I mean Princess, I am at school, that is, I am normally, but I was allowed to come home from Kongwa to be here for the celebration and because my father's very important."

"Oh, is he indeed, and what does your father do that is so important?"

"He's the past mayor of Lindi, Princess, and chairman of the Chamber of Commerce." I glanced around. "See he's over there – that's my mother with him."

"I shall have to tell the former mayor of Lindi and your mother what a fine young man they have for a son," said Princess Margaret. "Now tell me, Kongwa, you say, is that where you go to school?" At that moment her equerry whispered something in her ear and the Princess went on, "That's where they have all the groundnuts?"

"Yes, Ma'am, that is, they were supposed to have but not as many as planned, that is to say, from what I know."

"Yes, I'm sure you're right, Tony, I believe that is so. And tell me, is this your school blazer you're wearing?"

"Yes, Miss."

"It's most handsome," said the Princess, "and a handsome young man too."

At that moment her equerry whispered into her ear once more.

"Well, nice to have met you, Tony."

She held out her hand and I mine. It was a thrilling handshake, and with that the Princess moved on.

CHAPTER TWENTY-FIVE

BUSH SCOUTS

I'D RETURNED TO SCHOOL SO QUICKLY, IT seemed I'd hardly been away, and yet the trip was an excitement that lingered. Now it was Friday afternoon and we Scouts were getting ready for a weekend camp.

"Tell us again what happened," asked Aranky, pulling his kerchief through the leather woggle as he dressed in uniform. "Was she as beautiful as princesses are supposed to be?"

"I thought she was nice," I replied, as I slipped my shirt on. "I don't think she was like you see princesses in story books, but she certainly was neat and so was everyone else."

"And you talked with her too," interjected Burns, as he wandered through from his room, canteen dangling from his belt, arranging the whistle in his breast pocket.

"That's more than I got to do," said Berry.

Stew had gone home to Mwanza, and returned on the day I'd left for Lindi. "I was just sick the whole time," he said. "It wasn't even fun being home and I never got near the Princess."

"But you know what," I said, "Tony Firth and Titch Rogers were part of a Boy Scout welcoming group that greeted her off her plane when she landed in Mbeya. Did you know that?"

"Yes, I knew they were going," Berry replied. "They live in Mbeya, so they'd have got to see her either way."

Sometime later, the Scouts rendezvoused outside the mess, where Mr. Brownlow was waiting with the school gari. Burns was a troop leader like me, as was Aranky. There were three troops under the leadership of Mr. Brownlow, our Scout Master. Each troop leader was in charge of seven Scouts. Our uniforms were covered with pockets, the sleeves and epaulettes emblazoned with badges signifying status and achievements, our green kerchiefs around our necks, and a whistle, secured by a white braid cord, tucked into our breast pockets. We carried our own drinking water, in a canteen hanging from our belt. Our khaki shorts had upturned cuffs, we wore strong walking shoes and putties to protect from snake bite. Our dashing slouch hats with military-style upturned side kept the sun off our faces. We kept our snappy maroon berets for ceremonies and when at our den.

We left the gari at a baobab landmark, on our bush-bashing route towards Kiboriani. We weren't going to climb the mountain but Mr. Brownlow had decided it was a change of scene from Kongwa Maji, our common destination, because it lay on the fringe of the Masai Steppe with its vast savannah landscape and infinite variety of animals. I recognised the area where we left it because we'd passed this way on the zebra hunt. However, Mr. Brownlow had plans for a different direction, once we were walking.

We scout leaders pored over the map Mr. Brownlow spread on the ground.

"Over the next couple of days we'll be walking in an octagon-like circle so we end up back here Sunday afternoon," he said. "We'll be trekking on set bearings for given periods of time before changing bearing, each time to our left."

We hoisted our bergens, Mr. Brownlow slung his Lee Enfield over his shoulder, and we trekked for an hour until there was just enough light of the day left to set up first camp. He chose ground close to the base of a kopje, not unlike Snake Rock, and we now set to assembling our tents.

"I'll be watching your knots," called Mr. Brownlow. "I hope your prep has been done and the correct knots used for the right applications."

That done, Burns, Aranky and I set out to find firewood for the evening cooking, taking with us a few Scouts who could handle either cutting or hauling large tree limbs, preferably fallen as a result of elephant activity. The younger ones scoured the campsite for tinder and grass. The light was fading fast, as we prepared to cook our boerevors and beans. The good thing was, we'd brought our food and water with us. Living off the land was not planned. Soon, each troop had a fire roaring, our pots dangling from the makeshift frames over them. The beans and sausages would not be long in heating. The first new lesson for the younger ones came at washing up time.

"Keep quiet now, troop leaders, I want to see if our newer Scouts can work this out," said Mr. Brownlow. "Now tell me," he asked, "how are you going to wash your plates and cutlery?"

"We need water, sir," answered one.

"And a bowl, sir," said another.

"Maybe even soap suds," ventured a third, "like our 'boys' use at home."

"Our what?" asked Mr. Brownlow, with an annoyed frown.

"Sorry, sir, our servants, sir, not 'boys.'"

"That's better. But, has anyone got a bowl?" he asked.

"No, sir," they chorused.

"And have we got water to spare for washing up?"

"No, sir," they chorused again.

"Or even any soap suds?"

"No, sir."

"Very well," he continued, "how will we wash our dirty plates and cutlery?"

The question was followed with a circumspect silence. How indeed? All the usual conditions were not present.

"Can we find a river, sir?" came one small and hesitant question.

"Have we crossed a river today, can you see one, or hear one?"

"No, sir."

"Then we cannot clean up in a river, can we?"

"I suppose not, sir."

"All right, I'll show you what we're going to do to make everything clean again," observed Mr. Brownlow. "First gather up a pile of loose sand from around you. Tell me, what are your plates made of?"

"Aluminium," came back the answer.

"Good. And you've not left any large gobs of food on them, right? Now, sprinkle your plates with a good layer of the sand that you just gathered. Scrub them with that sand and the flat of your hand."

As the Scouts did this, he continued, "See how the residue is scoured by the sand? Now, shake off the sand, then take a dry cloth and wipe away the powdery residue. See, you have clean plates. Now, anyone want to tell me how to clean your knives, forks and spoons?"

"Yes, sir," piped up one, who proceeded to describe a similar process for the cutlery as he'd been shown for the plates.

"Why don't you take a fork and try it?"

Of course the Scout couldn't get the fork clean. It wouldn't retain any sand and the food between the prongs remained in place.

"Doesn't seem to work quite that well, does it?"

"No, sir."

"Here's what you do. Find an area where the sand is soft and deep rather than hard-baked. There's usually loose sand lying in pot holes or between the undulations of the terrain. Then, take your cutlery, one at a time, and push them into the sand. See what I'm doing? I'll take this dirty fork and push it into the sand, well past the prongs, making them completely submerged like so, pull it out again and there you go, the entire food residue is gone. I can wipe the thin film of dust with a dry cloth, and then I'm all set for the next meal."

"All right, Scouts," I followed up. "Finish cleaning your plates and cutlery the way you've just been shown."

Later, we selected one of the three campfires and built it up so that our three troops would blend and we'd enjoy a singsong, but not before we'd had a draw on who would be paired with whom to be on guard duty over-night, in two-hour shifts.

I was awakened by the squawking of a million kasukus overhead circling and landing on the several baobabs among which we'd camped. I pushed through our tent flap and stretched, surveying the new day, the sun rising in my eyes, its heat already noticeable as it burned off an overnight mist. I noted Aranky was awake and tending the fire, he'd been at it since 5 a.m., he told me. He'd told Baker and Rogers who'd been on guard duty to get another couple of hours kip while they had the chance. He'd stoked the embers of the old fire and the new one was building with a pot of water perched over top.

"So why were you up so early, Ken? Didn't you have a midnight watch?"

"Yep, but I'm always first on camping trips. I didn't sleep well – did you hear the noises?"

"Yes, there were hyenas all over the place for one thing. Good thing we posted guards."

"They kept the fire going," said Aranky. "Around 5 a.m. there was quite a breeze. Our tent flap worked loose and was fluttering much better."

"Yes, I heard it too," I replied. "Anyway, can I help get things going for breakfast?"

As I worked with Aranky, prepping for breakfast, I felt excited. I looked around and savoured the landscape. I realised I had really come to appreciate Africa. It was an early morning romance for me to discover how pleased I was with everything I saw, with the excitement of the trip, with the camaraderie of my friends. And of course Mr. Brownlow; he was great. And then my thoughts drifted to Anthony Paton. After all, if it wasn't for him, I wouldn't be a troop leader yet. We hadn't had a lot to do with each other, Paton and I, with him being in house four and all, but we were friends. What was amazing was his knowledge of bush craft and his love of animals. That's why he enjoyed being a Scout. I wondered why he hadn't returned to school this term. Just like most others, I supposed. Got home, found out his parents were on the move again, back to the U.K. most likely. That's the way it was. Most boys and girls were here for only a year or two, depending upon the length of their dad's ex-pat contract. Good friends left school saying, "See you next term," didn't return, and you never saw them again. As a result of his not coming back, there'd been a vacancy for a troop leader and I'd won the promotion.

Snapping out of my thoughts, I asked Aranky, "What would it be like to be a Boy Scout anywhere else in the world? They would never have the real thing like we have.

"Yeah, well, Africa is where Lord Baden-Powell created the Boy Scout movement. His whole idea was to do with surviving in the bush like this."

It wasn't long after that, breakfast complete, the three troops broke camp before circling up to receive directions for the day.

"Here's what we're going to do," Mr. Brownlow began. "Today we're going to trek north-east of Kiboriani, see it in the distance there, until we find a location for our second camp. We're taking everything with us, so make sure you've packed your bergens well. Now, here's the interesting part. We're not just going to walk. I want everyone spread out in a wide, thin line, about fifteen feet apart from each other so we can conduct a sweep. We're going to be searching for tracks. You see, we know that there's been trouble from a lion pride in the region all right, and it's become our duty to find those lion tracks so we can set off in pursuit. So I need all of you to scout the ground as we walk, looking for tracks of any sort, so that we can come together and sort out what animal they belong to and see if we can identify the lions we're looking for. And no, I'm not expecting real lions in this area so you don't need to be worried. Now then, you all have your tracks recognition booklets with you?"

"Yes, sir," came the chorus.

"And hopefully you've studied that booklet, like I asked you to at our last den meet?"

"Yes, sir."

"Good, then if we're ready, heft your bergens. Troop leaders, spread your troops into one, long, wide line for the sweep."

It wasn't long 'til we'd spread out to a good 375 feet wide, with Mr. Brownlow in the middle. Then he gave the order, "Right, Scouts, forward march."

We troop leaders had our instructions. As ones who knew at a glance what track was which, when someone did spot a track, only the Scouts from our own troop would stop to regard it. If it was a rare track then we might all cluster and inspect but Mr. Brownlow didn't want twenty-four of us gathering around every dikdik track.

Soon after we'd moved out, the first tracks were spotted. It belonged to a hyena cackle, likely the ones who'd kept some of us awake in the night. Because hyenas were so common it was important to recognise them, so we gathered around for our first inspection.

Back on the trek, it wasn't long before there was a call from the troop in the middle, "Looks like it may be a snake track, sir, it's kind of slithery."

Mr. Brownlow went to inspect. "Good lad, Rogers, well spotted. I think you should all come and see this," he called. "Stand back this way, I don't want you walking over it."

We took turns in a close-up inspection, then stood back. "It doesn't look much like a snake track," began Mr. Brownlow, "but would anyone like to venture if it is and, if so, what sort?"

There was silence, in which the Senior Scouts would give the Junior Scouts first chance to answer, but when there was none I spoke up.

"Yes, sir, I think I may know."

"All right, troop leader, let's hear it. Tell us what the track tells you."

"Well, sir, although on the one hand the track suggests it may be a snake, it's not distinct. Most snakes wind their way across the terrain. As they do, the rear part of their body follows along in line with the front end of their body, traversing the same ground, thus leaving a clear, winding print. In this case the track is not clear. So I think this snake was probably a puff adder because the track is wide. The puff adder is slow-moving and kind of hauls its body along; sometimes it has a slight wriggle, but mostly in a straight line, quite unlike what thinner snakes do."

"Excellent, troop leader, and tell me now, is there other information you can glean from this track?"

"Yes, sir. Nothing has crossed the track. If it was old there should be other tracks over top, such as hoofs. Or you'd think there would be beetle prints or ants that had crossed the track but there's none. It's clean. The other thing is, while there's not much wind now, sir, it was windy in the night. Our tent flap woke me along with the hyenas. If this track was old, or made during the night, it would be erased by the wind. That hasn't happened either."

"Champion, champion. Your conclusion, Edwards?"

"The puff adder's not far ahead, sir. As it's going in the same direction as we're walking, we're likely to catch up with it, sir, so we'd better be careful."

"First rate, troop leader Edwards, I hope you all heard that," Mr. Brownlow turned to catch the eyes of the group. "An excellent analysis and one hundred percent spot on, I've no doubt. So, we have not only learned a lot about puff adder tracks this morning, but we have been alerted to proceed with great caution; we may soon come across the snake. When we do I want it to be because we have seen it first, not because someone has trodden on its tail. We have no way of getting any help or of getting to hospital for another day and a half, so, no bites, please."

"Good job, Edwards," said Burns. "I didn't know you knew that much about snakes."

"It's not a lot really. I am interested in them and my dad has some books about them that I've read. Then of course I met that chap I told you about, the one the Africans call Bwana Nyoka, what was his name…? Iondes, Inedis, Ionides, that's it, CJ Ionides, but, you know, you pick up tips along the way."

"Still and all," said Burns.

It wasn't long before we came across the puff adder. It was changing direction at the time and had veered to our right. The shout went up, "Snaaaake!" And soon we were taking turns examining it as it continued to haul its way along its intended path. No one got too close, and after a while we left it and moved on.

By mid-morning the sun was scorching. We rearranged our kerchiefs into the back of our hats to drape over our necks so we wouldn't get burned. We waded through grasses once more, tall, scorched and dead. We found plenty of droppings, and hoof prints here and there, enough to work out what animals had last been here and even how recently. After a while we found ourselves walking a small plateau, devoid of acacia or other trees until we reached its end through a steep descent into a shallow depression. Here the acacias and baobabs and the grass returned and looked a little less dead. With the magugu grass quite green we would pull a stem and chew on it to get refreshment from the moisture inside.

And then they were spotted; several baboon troops of sixty or more animals, with babies galore. Mr. Brownlow raised a hand and called out, "Troops, halt."

We huddled, while surveying the scene. Mr. Brownlow knew well of baboons' reputation and wanted to give them a wide berth. Having scoured the area with his field glasses, he unfolded his map of the region, a map that might have been drawn by David Livingstone himself, for it was singularly lacking in detail but all there was to be had. He called the troop leaders to pour over it, made notations about where we'd come from, compared these with compass bearings, the map's topographic details such as they were and where we'd been and where we were going, and then called our complement to attention.

"I have no wish to get close to the baboon troops," he said. "We need to change direction now from our present north-easterly course, to a northerly course."

While wiping his over-heated neck, Mr. Brownlow pointed towards the low hills we could see ahead and noted the stand-alone outcrop in the mid-distance, saying that this would be our new bearing.

"We'll resume our sweep towards that kopje. We need to keep changing our bearings anyway in order to return to our point of departure by tomorrow afternoon. We must be sure to reach it in time."

It was amazing there'd been no sign of them when we were on the high ground. But now, in the thick glades of acacias, we found hordes of animals browsing the sweet grass and taking shade. We'd been spotted some time since and so, as we approached the hundreds of browsing wildebeest, zebra and antelope, they moved off at about the same pace as our arrival, keeping a respectful distance between them and us. Mr. Brownlow called us to bunch up from our sweep; I think he must have worried about lions, they being prone to following herds. Soon we'd formed our own small herd, marching resolutely towards where the animals had been seen, although now they'd disappeared into the tree line.

The grass was short, evidence of extended grazing. Animal tracks were so concentrated that we could rarely separate one from the other, so spotting them became futile. And in any case, we now needed to be alert, looking ahead and around rather than watching the ground.

We heard them first; the unmistakable thrashing about among the trees that indicated elephants. The ground shook, tree limbs snapped as they were ripped or came tumbling down; there was the feel of movement everywhere. Mr. Brownlow brought us to a halt, arm up. Without a sound he turned, finger to lips. He lifted his field glasses and scanned the heavily-treed veld ahead. But soon he dropped them again.

"Can't see a thing," he muttered. "Trees too thick. But they're there," he whispered. "Can you hear them?"

Those of us closest agreed we could. By now there was a nervous expectation. We knew elephants were near but couldn't see them. It was likely they had a better fix on us. This called for keeping a cool head. Mr. Brownlow brought his Lee Enfield down from his shoulder, checked one more time that it was loaded, and held the weapon at the ready. He decided we'd best remain still, and silent, until we could determine where the animals were. Using sign language, he bade us crouch low, hide as best we could and keep quiet.

I moved up close to Mr. Brownlow and whispered, "Sir, I think they're ahead and off to our left. The wind is coming from our left so they may have heard us but not got our scent. They'll become alarmed when they do."

"You're probably right, Edwards. Trouble is, it sounds as though they're right in front."

"I agree, sir, but I think that's because of the breeze that's come up. Look," I said in a loud stage whisper. Ahead and off to our left, we could

make out the unmistakable hide of a huge tusker emerging from the undergrowth, walking directly across our path. He didn't stop to watch our human
crowd, being bent on pulling down a tasty morsel he'd found on an acacia
limb.

"He seems unaware of us," I whispered. "Or if he is, he's not alarmed."

Mr. Brownlow nodded, then looked around him intently to make sure
his charges were still crouched, un-moving and quiet. As the tusker moved
more into view he was soon followed by several females and two of the tiniest elephants I'd ever seen. They were frolicking, enjoying themselves with
never a care in the world.

The old tusker paused and the herd came to a halt, although they kept
munching on thickets of grass or low hanging limbs that were prolific with
leaf. Now he looked in our direction; perhaps he had our scent, or a suggestion of it. We froze, all of us, disciplined, quiet and un-moving. The tusker
flapped his ears as we met his gaze, nodded his head up and down, threw
up his trunk but then seemed to calm himself. He didn't trumpet, the sound
I was dreading, because it would herald a charge. If he decided to do that
we'd probably scatter and then who knew how that might end. With minimal
movement Mr. Brownlow brought up his rifle, flipped off the safety and took
a line on the tusker.

"You're not going to shoot him, sir?" I queried in a worried whisper.

"Of course not, if I don't have to. But if he charges, I need to be ready."

I don't know if you'd call it a stand off. We didn't move. The tusker
seemed to suspect we were potential trouble, yet was unwilling to start something that might end badly for both parties. I got the sense he was thinking
things through, pondering leaving well alone in the interests of his females
and babies. Elephants don't think like that as far as we know, so perhaps it
was a result of our quiet and absence of movement that led him not to take
action. It was as though he'd made up his mind to move along, for the tusker
suddenly turned away and ambled forward at a brisk pace, as though to clear
the area, the females hurrying along behind and the babies positively running
as fast as their little legs would carry them, to keep up. We remained still,
until the noise of the elephants receded and we could no longer see them.
Signalling us to remain quiet, Mr. Brownlow beckoned.

"What do you think, Scouts? Was that not an impressive experience?"

"Yes, sir," we chorused quietly.

"This is what it's about, you see. This is the real world. You against nature. By practicing great prudence and thanks to your superb discipline, we witnessed a wonderful experience that few others will ever know. And we did it safely, by remaining quiet, lowering our profile and keeping *very* cool heads. I'm impressed with you all. Now let's resume our pace, keep close together until we reach our landmark; once there we'll make camp."

We resumed our trek, and after a while our group became stretched out. Mr. Brownlow was a hundred yards ahead, surrounded by some of our most enthusiastic younger members holding him in conversation, while we troop leaders did the opposite, bringing up the rear, making sure there were no stragglers we could lose along the way. After a while, Aranky muttered an aside about a smell coming from some of the Scouts in front.

"I know we didn't bathe last night," he said, "but we shouldn't have chaps smelling high this soon?"

"Yuk," joined in Burns. "It's potent, what can it be?"

"Can you tell which blokes smell the most?" I asked.

Aranky pinpointed it. "It's the chaps carrying the meat rations. The rest of the boerevors that we saved for tonight must have gone off in the heat, especially if it wasn't that great to start with."

"We'd better tell Mr. Brownlow," Burns suggested. "It must be inedible by now but also carrying that smell with us will bring all the hyenas in the world."

Even as Burns uttered those words, movement out of the corner of my eye made me turn and watch as several marabou storks landed on the topmost limbs of nearby acacias. Marabous and vultures are the garbage cleaners of the veld and it was a bad sign that they were already on to us.

"Why don't you catch him up and tell him, Andrew. I can't imagine Mr. Brownlow wanting to do anything but dump the stuff. I'll single out our meat carriers and get them and their bergens aside 'til you get back."

Mr. Brownlow brought the group to a halt and hurried back, while at the same time Burns was called away by his troops.

"I can't believe the food has gone off that quickly," he worried as we unpacked the smelly bergens and wrinkled our noses. "All right, discard the meat and the bergens, in fact anything that's tainted. I don't want that smell following us around. Oh dear, this is bad luck. We have no other meat for dinner and not a whole lot of beans either. All right, I think this presents a fine challenge. We'll keep our eyes peeled for game, something small that will provide sufficient meat for one night. We'll bag something suitable if we can, in which case we'll eat well this evening. Otherwise, I'm afraid, it will be three hungry troops who return to school tomorrow evening."

With that, Mr. Brownlow lifted his field glasses to his eyes and scanned the landscape.

"Excuse me, sir," Burns had returned. "Baker and Rogers just showed me tracks they've found which they thought were Thomson's gazelles, and I think they're right. Come and see."

Burns showed us the tracks, quite distinct from the many old ones. "Not only that but there's fresh droppings here too."

"I can't believe it! That's amazing." Mr. Brownlow got excited, uncharacteristically for him, as he inspected the tracks. "They are Thomsons. You're quite right. What a spot of luck. Well found, you two, you'll soon be enjoying promotion at this rate."

Baker and Rogers smiled proudly.

"Now to see if we can catch up with them."

Mr. Brownlow was tall and well built. But, even though he was fit and agile, it didn't stop him, as he gathered up his things and set off after those tracks, from tripping over a protruding baobab root and falling hard to the ground.

"Godverdomme!" uttered Aranky, the first to recognise our situation if Mr. Brownlow was injured. "No, man. We can't have Mr. Brownlow hurt."

But he was. Both arms had gone out to save himself and break his fall. But it left two nasty lacerations from the palms of his hands up to his elbows and one long and deep cut that was bleeding freely. Bending over him, I asked, a bit pointlessly, "Are you hurt, sir? Are you going to be all right?"

Aranky moved in to remove the rifle that had slipped into an awkward angle, and would inhibit Mr. Brownlow getting up.

"I'm not sure," he grunted. "I think I've twisted my ankle, it's very painful. Here, help me get to my feet."

Mr. Brownlow struggled on to one knee. As he put his weight on the offending ankle, he gave a stifled yell, and fell forward, grasping heavily on me as he did so to brake another fall and dripping blood on my uniform.

"Damn it!" he said. "This is the last thing we need… sorry about the use of bad language there… no excuse."

"Where's the large First Aid kit?" I asked no one in particular. "Our personal ones won't do for this. Quick, let's get it from whoever's carrying it."

Burns set off calling out, "Who's carrying the main First Aid kit?"

"Sir, can I get you to sit down," I asked, "so we can give you First Aid? That's what we need to do before anything."

"Quite right, Edwards, just the way you've been taught, good for you. All right, look there's a mound over there that would be easier to sit down on and get up again. If I can just lean on you and Aranky to get me over there?" he grunted again in his pain. "Did you check the safety is on?" he asked as a follow-up to Aranky taking the rifle.

"Yes, sir, it's on."

Burns returned, with Baker bearing the kit.

"All right, Scouts, this is a real world field exercise," said Brownlow, once he was ensconced at the mound. "I'm going to act like I don't know what to do, say nothing while you attend to my injury. I'll speak if you do something wrong, not otherwise."

First Aid was Burns's strong suit. Aranky and I held back and let him carry on, cleaning the wound with the antiseptic, applying ointment and bandaging cuts.

"To be honest with you, I think you may need stitches in the arm with the deep cut, sir," said Burns professorially, "but we'll have to wait and see what the Doctor says."

The bruised and bloody grazes of which Brownlow had several, he left open after cleaning them and applying iodine. Forgetting who he was talking to, Burns said, "This is going to sting quite badly, I'm afraid. Try to grip your fists and concentrate on something else."

"Yes, Doctor," said Brownlow, only half bemused.

Aranky left with a couple of Senior Scouts to look for a branch they could cut that could be fashioned into a crutch. While he was surveying the trees, one of them came up with a discovery.

"Look," he said, "this limb has been torn down by elephant. There's sufficient of a notch left on the one end where the limb was part of a fork in the tree for an under arm crutch. All we have to do is cut the other end to the correct length, then whittle in to shape."

"Great find," Aranky said as they withdrew their sheath knives and set about stripping the branches. Not long after, Aranky brought the crutch to Mr. Brownlow for measuring against his size to get the right length.

"I need material to wrap around the crutch end so it's comfortable in your armpit, sir."

Mr. Brownlow removed his shirt and then his vest, handing the latter over. The assembly wasn't perfect. There wasn't a handle for Mr. Brownlow to hold on to with the crutch under his arm so he had to twist his wrist to grip the main staff. "But," as he said, "it's a fine job given what we have to deal with. You Scouts make me proud."

"Are we going to have to cut short the weekend now, sir, what with you injured and all?" asked Burns.

"No. I think we may as well press on. We've about passed the point of no return anyway."

"Pardon me, sir?"

"Point of no return. That means we've reached a point in our trek where it would be as far to return the way we came as it would be to continue on. Actually it may even be a little shorter, so there's no point. Secondly, I'd like to muddle through if I can. I don't want to lose you Scouts your weekend. Furthermore, this incident presents new challenges, which so far you are responding to as well as any adult would. We must turn this misfortune into a positive experience."

Aranky asked, "Still and all, I suppose you're not going to be able to shoot, sir?"

"Not likely now. I'd have to be propped up and rest the gun barrel in the fork of a tree or something then wait for a suitable animal to walk right by me. Could take days if ever. Not going happen now and we don't have time to try."

"Well, sir, I may as well tell you, sir, I can shoot," said Aranky.

"You can?"

"Yes, sir."

"Game?"

"Well, the fact is I've never shot game, sir. But I have done tons of target practice, sir. My dad's been training me for when I'm old enough. With his gun, I can put a bullet within three or four inches of a target bull's eye at a hundred yards, sir."

"You can?"

"Yes, sir. Well, that is, with his gun, sir. My dad owns a Holland & Holland. I don't know how I'd do with your Lee Enfield, sir, but maybe it's worth a try?"

"It's an old gun," Mr. Brownlow told him. "Military, you know. It's a Number 5 Mark 1. They were called 'Jungle Carbines,' specially developed for bush conditions in Burma and Malaya, very accurate. I've owned it many years and believe me I have the sights well honed. All right, you and Edwards take Baker and the three of you proceed at a faster pace. Follow those gazelle tracks and see if you can get close. You, Burns, seeing as you're our on-the-spot doctor, I'd like to remain with me... er, just in case. Now remember where you are," he addressed us again. "Watch out for snakes, especially puff adders. Monitor the wind. You'll get nowhere near the gazelle if you're up-wind. See what you can do, nothing too big mind, we can't cope with it, and stay close to our planned route; we must catch up before long and certainly well before dark."

Mr. Brownlow grimaced as he shifted positions and put weight on his ankle again.

"Better get on with it," he said in obvious pain. "Take the gun, there's spare ammo in my top left pocket here, and we'll see you later. Any problem at all, shoot two shots in the air in rapid succession so I know and have a direction to march towards. Edwards, you'd better take my field glasses. Oh and, Aranky?"

"Yes, sir."

"Watch out for the kick or you'll throw your shoulder out."

We'd started off fast, Aranky, Baker and me. It wasn't long before we spotted the herds where we hoped to find those gazelle. Keeping acacia trees in the line of sight, and frequent checking to make sure we were downwind, we finally drew close; not close enough for a shot, but well positioned to see the choice we had. I peered through the glasses. There were those Tommies milling around in the foreground, chewing grasses, hundreds of zebra and wildebeest beyond. Even further away were a few giraffes nibbling on the acacias. One of those Thomsons would be ideal. I passed the glasses to Aranky.

"You're right, Edwards, there's quite a few of them. Seems like there's a vlei there, there's more grass than anywhere else. How's the wind?"

"We're still downwind, nothing's changed."

"My guess is we're about five hundred yards away," said Aranky. "I'm going to get closer, very slowly, keeping behind tree cover for as long as possible. If or when I think I've been noticed, I'll go to ground and crawl the rest of the way. If they don't catch my scent and if I'm not seen, I think I can get within range. I'm just going on what my dad taught me so I don't know, but it's our best bet."

"You're right, man. We have nothing else to go on. Baker and me will wait back here and watch. There's nothing we can do but give the game away."

"Not another pun, Edwards?"

"Sorry."

We watched Aranky disappear into the trees, moving stealthily through the grasses, from one acacia to another, closing the ground between himself and the Thomsons. With the field glasses I panned between him and the gazelle as I anxiously waited to see signs of their alert and probable alarm when they would take off and that would be the last we'd see of them. And true enough, one of the Thomsons, on the outer fringe of the herd, clearly did see something for he became suddenly alert, his chewing stopped as he waited for confirmation of movement. But none came. Aranky must have realised and was lying low. After some time, the Thomsons, not detecting danger, resumed foraging.

I was getting tense. I could no longer see Aranky and realised he must be crawling. But could he see what we could see? Was he crawling in the right direction?

"I don't know," said Baker. "What's keeping him?"

"This is something you can't rush," I responded, while I peered through the glasses, as much to reassure myself as Baker. "So long as the herd isn't alarmed, we have to assume that—"

Bang! A single shot recoiled across the plain, reverberating through the trees and set the entire herd into alarm, beginning a stampede in the opposite direction from which we were coming and kicking up a massive cloud of dust. At the same time that happened, the Thomsons I had been watching leapt into the air like a springbok, and then fell to the ground, apparently dead on the spot.

Elated, Baker and I broke cover and rushed forward, running through grasses, leaping across downed tree limbs, round ant hills until we caught up with Aranky, getting up from the ground and rubbing his shoulder.

"Jeez, that gun's got a kick," he greeted us. "That bloody-well hurts."

"Are you all right, not injured or anything?"

"No, I'll be okay," he said, rubbing his shoulder all the while. "Just bloody sore. Godverdomme, man, that recoil's a bastard, eh."

We joined up and made our way to the dead gazelle. Aranky had placed a bullet through its skull.

"What an incredible shot. I can't believe your accuracy. Your dad's going to be proud of you when he hears of this."

When the Scout troops caught up an hour later, with us waiting in the shade of an acacia, Mr. Brownlow, still limping, was not only impressed, he liked the vlei too so it was here we set camp. It was as though the site had been designed for camping. The acacias were well formed and spaced and the grass between them greener. The golden afternoon sun, lower in the sky now, was streaming through the branches, silhouetting the trees with a bleach white rim, highlighting the gossamer wings of dragonflies darting between them and revealing massive spider webs strung between many.

While some were lighting a fire and hewing a rotisserie, we troop leaders gave the rest a lesson in skinning and preparing a gazelle. A long wooden skewer was fashioned from a heavy branch, on which the gazelle was impaled and then, with much hefting from the stronger Scouts, was placed onto the two support forks either side of the fire. A rotisserie handle had been created out of branches and a supply of cord was used to lash the handle to the skewer. With everything of wood, we worried about whether the gazelle would be cooked before the skewer burned, but we needn't have. The sun disappeared, the sky still sheets of crimson, orange and yellow. The insects were starting up, there was a light evening breeze that was wonderfully cooling and the roasting of the meat was nearly complete.

"That aroma is stunning," said Burns. "I'm famished."

By now the work was done as our entire complement stood around and watched the final stages. Mr. Brownlow was propped against an acacia, his slouch hat pulled low to keep the sun out of his eyes, watching the goings on and leaving us to look after the roast.

"Aranky gets first pick, any cut he wants," I suggested. There was a chorus of approval. I went on, "Then we give some to Mr. Brownlow, then Burns, Baker and me and if there's anything left, you blokes can share it between you and the hyenas!"

A groan of boos followed that witty remark.

That evening was the most pleasing, the most satisfying and most enjoyable time I'd ever had at school. For my part I felt like a man.

"No adult could have done better than you did today," Mr. Brownlow told us. "You Scouts are in the best tradition. I'm sure if Baden-Powell was still around and knew you, he'd be the proudest man alive."

We'd joined in enthusiastically as we watched younger Scouts replenishing our bonfire with fuel and others leading the sing-song. Mr. Brownlow had nodded off, satiated from a fine meal and exhausted with hobbling on his sprained ankle. Later, along with everyone else, he'd crawled into his tent to sleep. Only Burns and I remained awake, taking first watch, gazing into the fire and chatting until the inevitable subject arose.

"The only thing I miss about this," I said, "is that Hazel isn't here to enjoy it. This is such a great evening, I feel so good, it's a shame we can't share it."

I took a slug of water from my canteen.

"You can't have girls in Boy Scouts, Tony; that'll never, ever be allowed."

"I know, it's just that…."

"So howzit going with her anyway?" asked Andrew. "How long is it since you two got together? I s'pose it's quite a while really, before I arrived in Kongwa?"

"Two, maybe three terms." I threw some sticks into the blaze. "How about you and Avril Jenner? You were pretty keen on her for a while?" I asked.

"Uh huh, but it didn't last. Hmm. I must admit, Berry and I thought it would never last with you either, she being older and all. What's it like, you know, really?"

"What's what like, Andrew?"

"You know, having a steady and all. Berry told me how keen you weren't when she first proposed… that's funny isn't it, *she* first proposed. To be honest with you, I didn't believe it when he told me. I'd heard about Pepsi with Pam, no doubt about them getting on, and he's still going strong too. You both seem to have keepers or something."

"It's difficult to say, Andrew. It's more a feeling than anything. You know, I enjoy being out with you a helluva lot like I do with Berry. We get on just fine and I wouldn't change that. But it's a different relationship somehow. My heart beats so hard sometimes when I think of her and it doesn't do that for boys, no matter how much I like them."

"And you snogg a lot, of course?" asked Andrew, with a wry smile.

"Yes, that's definitely part of it; the fact that she's a girl, you know."

"Avril didn't want to kiss, that's why I dropped her. Said it was too soon. I mean, what's the point otherwise?"

"I suppose."

"Does she make you randy?"

"Andrew! How could you ask that?"

"Well, you know, have you ever been further than kissing?"

I was shocked at the question.

"Of course not, Andy. I mean, I couldn't, could I? I respect her too much to try anything on."

"Just wondered."

CHAPTER TWENTY-SIX

DOUBLE DATE

SINCE THE AGE OF ELEVEN SENIOR BOYS were allowed to take Sundays to go for long picnic walks. It wasn't quite like the adventures of Scouting in which we went further afield, but the joy in the walks was that, although one or two teachers might come along, depending on where we were going, they also might well not. All we had to do was let our Housemaster know the general direction we intended walking, more or less, and with whom. Sometimes we followed the railway track, but more often we'd make the five-mile trek to Children's Mount. Once there, we'd decide whether to climb its two thousand feet and eat at the top, or stay at its base with our lunches, and goof around in local dongas.

In the early days, the girls had not been allowed to do the same thing; after all, they were girls! However, with the passage of time, the change of Headmasters and perhaps a prescient view of the future, that rule was re-laxed to where they could walk to the mountain too, so long as they went in large groups. Often, boyfriends and girlfriends would team up as we walked. Climbing the mountain might even become a race when girls might challenge boys to the top and sometimes they'd win. What wasn't done was that a mixed pair would split from the group, and go off by themselves. At least, it wasn't done by most of us. It was done, of course, by Doug and Pam, she being free of boarding constraints making it easier. As my relationship with

Hazel strengthened I would mutter about how lucky Pepsi was to get away with his time alone with Pam and how difficult it was for me.

"Well," he said one Saturday, "I've tried to get you to come with Pam and me before, so, I say again, split off from the chaps tomorrow and come with us."

"How could I do it safely, Peps, without getting caught? I mean, think about Hazel, it's so much more difficult for her," I said. "Berry won't like it either. We usually do things like this together. We've already agreed to team up for tomorrow's walk."

"But you go with several blokes, don't you, not just Berry? Burns's one, it seems to me, and Ivey and what about Goggles, Maclean, Aranky and Muddle?"

"Yes, they'll be there, and others like Jenner, I suppose."

"All right then, here's how we can do this…." And with that Doug laid out an idea he thought would work.

"All you have to do," he concluded, "is talk to Berry about it. He's a good sort and he knows about you and Haze. It's not like you'll be leaving him alone by himself. You may even want someone who would cover for you if questions were asked."

"Questions?" I frowned. "Who's going to ask questions?"

"Well, that's just it, you see, you never know which prefect's looking for trouble. I always have a cover, just in case."

"Oh, I see what you mean; all right, I'll talk to Berry."

That evening I got Stewie aside.

"Gosh, you've caught it bad, eh?" was his initial response. "Gotta be with her all the time, huh?"

"Hardly, Esperer. I don't really see all that much of her, not for any lengthy time at any rate. I spend much more time with you and the others."

"Anyway," said Berry, "it doesn't matter; of course I'll cover for you. What's the plan?"

"Pepsi and I'll start out with you lot on the walk to Children's Mount. When we get to a place he knows, we'll peel off; it's a particular baobab, he says, one that seems to have a triangle of acacias around it."

Berry looked quizzical for the moment, "I'm not quite sure which one you mean, but that's all right, I don't need to know. So you'll do that but what about her? The girls only go out as a clan."

"Hazel won't join them. She's going to tell them she's spending the day with Pam at her parents' house. Some of the girls will know what she's up to, but hopefully none of her prefects. As soon as the group have left, Pam and Hazel will set out to join with Pepsi and me. I haven't seen it but there's a shallow Donga which we can duck into and not be seen. When we've teamed up, we'll follow the donga for a while to keep below the horizon. You know both Mr. Moore and Mr. Brownlow bring field glasses with them."

"Field glasses aren't much use in the bush."

"I know, but Doug doesn't want to take chances. When we come out of the donga we'll head in the direction of Two Tits."

"That's quite a way," said Berry. "I'm not sure you could get there and back in the day without driving."

"I said we'll be heading in that direction. We won't reach Two Tits. Don't even want to. Not taking our girls out there to climb a mountain."

"Uh huh," said Berry with a smile and a wink, "I should have known. Okay, like I said I'll cover for you." And then he added conspiratorially, "You'll have to give me all the juicy details of what happens."

ON THE SUNDAY, BOYS AND GIRLS WERE clambering down the brilliant white, mica-strewn rocks of Church Hill after the service. Pam had teamed up with Hazel and the two girls, looking lovely in their best Sunday frocks, were scrambling over the rocks, ignoring Doug and me only yards away. At the base Hazel said "bye" to her dorm compatriots and then with Pam, split off in the direction of her parents' house. We went with our friends to collect our packed lunches and set off. We soon rounded the eastern base of Kongwa Hill and headed south towards Children's Mount.

I was tense at the start because there were more teachers than usual. Shutty and Miss Strong had decided to join the walk, as well as Mr. Moore and Mr. Brownlow, field glasses swinging from their necks. Mr. Brownlow was carrying his Lee Enfield resting casually on his shoulder which he supported by the barrel. The teachers were involved in conversations with other boys or girls, however, and paid no attention to us as we dragged our feet and fell behind.

We found ourselves a little off course. Then Doug spotted the baobab he was looking for over to our right. After a brief whisper, we feigned weariness and said we were going to rest, then sat down, backs against an Acacia trunk. I gave Berry the nod so he knew this was it.

"Well, I'm not waiting for you two," he said out loud, encouraging the others to follow him. "You chaps can catch up later."

Burns hesitated. He'd been talking with Doug and me and was ready to hang back. But Berry gave him the look and said, "Come on, Andy, we don't want to goof around with these two… do we?"

Burns got it. "All right," he said cheerily, "kwa heri sasa. See you later."

Soon the stragglers among the boys had left us behind, now hidden among the grasses and trees.

"We need to get over to the baobab fast," said Doug.

We made our way in a crouch, heads low, to the baobab with the acacia triangle.

"Good, now I know where I am," said Doug. "This way and keep it quiet. We have no way of knowing if there are prefects or masters lagging behind the main crowd so we need to be careful. That's why we can't call out to the girls by the way. All right, no talking. Just follow me."

Before long we'd found the donga and were right on target; the girls were ahead of us. It was exciting to see them sitting there, looking so maradadi in their best Sunday frocks, resting in the shade. They hadn't heard us and were startled when we jumped from the donga's edge to its base, and there they were. We gave each other a quick hug, but Doug wanted to move on right away; he didn't feel safe and wanted to get away from the area as fast as possible. The punishment for the boys, if we were caught, was six of the best and being expelled.

The base of the donga was full of droppings, but there were few fallen trees or obstacles in our path. Not nearly as dramatic a donga as the one close to the school. We must have been walking a good twenty minutes, brushing away flies and slapping at horse flies before Doug stopped, suggesting a short rest.

"God, it's hot," he said, pulling out a hanky and wiping his neck. "We're okay so far. From here the donga curves northwards which is not where we want to go, so we must get out of here. But first, let me check it's safe."

With that Doug scrambled to the top. While he was gone we wiped our necks, and faces, Hazel borrowing my handkerchief. I glanced up to where

Doug had climbed when movement caught my eye. I peered through the brush, unblinking, not wanting to miss even the tiniest thing; I'd seen something. Where was it? *I'm sure something up there moved. There! There it is, I can see it now, just. It's a twig snake!* It looks so much like the twig of a dried out tree you'd never ever see it, unless it moved. And it moved, right into where Doug had clambered up.

"Pepsi!" I called in a stage whisper, conscious of his instruction to keep quiet but at the same time needing to warn him.

"What?" came back the whispered response. "Ssshhh!"

"It's a twig snake!"

"What, where?"

"Right where you climbed up. You mustn't come down the same way, see. Those things could kill you if you're bitten this far away from the hospital."

"Thanks, man."

It wasn't long before Doug clambered down, several yards further up.

"It's clear," he said. "I couldn't see or hear anything. Let's go."

Doug and Pam set off in the lead, holding hands and walking fast. I caught Hazel's hand and did the same, hanging back a little.

The bush was thicker now. As we walked we skirted low-slung acacia branches, strode through grass thickets and pushed through intertwining branches of thorns, scaled minor dongas more frequent than they were deep and constantly circled the ever present msasas. After a while we came across a vlei. The grass was almost green; it was cool to look at and to the touch.

"Let's take a rest," said Pam. "I don't know about you but I'm bushed."

Hazel and I came staggering up looking for shade.

"I vote we have lunch," Hazel said, first wiping her forehead once more with the back of her hand, then shaking out the skirt of her dress to cool her legs from the heat and perspiration. Pam had brought extra rations. I'd noticed her carry bag looked heavier than our lunch loads and when she brought out some of the contents I understood why.

"Wow, Pam, you've done us proud," said Doug. "Up to your usual standards."

"Thank you, kind sir," she said in mock flirtation. "We try to please."

We tucked in to the extra lettuce, tomatoes, olives, cheese and crackers as well as our packed lunches, and soon found ourselves harassed by flies. They too loved this cool area and no more so than when we brought out our food.

The others drank warm water from Coca-Cola bottles, I from my Scout's flask. When we'd finished we sat back to rest.

I'd wondered what was going to happen next. When I was with Hazel alone and we had the chance, we'd kiss and caress and enjoy snuggling. But now we were in someone else's company. My upbringing had it that physical touch with a girl was something strictly private, something that would never be done in public.

Hazel and I were propped against an acacia, swotting flies. Then, before our eyes, Doug, who had been lying down on the greenish grass next to Pam, each of them gazing at the sky, rolled over onto his side with an arm over her chest and began kissing her. She put up no resistance and was clearly returning the favour. At first I was embarrassed and hardly dare look at Hazel. But I couldn't take my eyes off them and the pleasure they were enjoying, so I flicked my eyes sideways to see what Hazel was doing. Hazel was looking straight ahead, obviously taking this in but pretending not to, making no move.

I slowly reached out a hand. Our fingers touched, then we clasped. After a hesitant pause I pulled her hand and she moved towards me, making no resistance. Then I slipped an arm around her back, pulled her in tight, gently lifted her chin and kissed her. I'd been waiting all day for this. This is what I was out here for, to be with Hazel.

After a while Doug and Pam came up for air, as casual as you like and as though nothing exciting had happened. "Okay, you two, want any more to eat?" asked Pam.

Hazel and I broke off our embrace and turned, embarrassed at having been seen kissing.

"I think they're rather busy at the moment," Doug chuckled.

"Not me, thanks, I had plenty," Hazel said as she straightened up with a weak smile.

"Me too."

"Just as well, because there isn't anything," said Pam having checked her bag. "Except for the Smarties that are probably soft by now."

Doug was watching me wryly. He knew I felt awkward for the moment and was enjoying my embarrassment.

"What would you like to do?" asked Pam. "We can stay here all afternoon and, you know, be together, or maybe we can—"

"—Ssshhhh, what's that?" questioned Doug.

We fell quiet, listening.

"It's drums," I said, "That's African drums."

"Yes, it is," said Doug, "and not far away."

"There must be a kijiji around here."

Hazel chipped in, "Maybe they're going to have an n'goma. I went to one once with my folks in Nach; maybe these people are going to have one too. If so it could be fun to watch for a while."

"Will they let us watch their n'goma?" I asked. "Maybe they don't want Europeans interfering with their traditions."

"Maybe not," said Doug, "but the Wagogo are pretty friendly. I don't know why they wouldn't unless there was some personal private ritual involved. Shall we see if we can find them and ask?"

"Hang on," I said. "I just heard something else."

We lapsed into silence, to hear the clanging of cow bells and the bleating of goats. We stared in the direction the sound was coming from and before long, the advanced guard of goats made their way through the trees and grasses to be followed by the first tossing of the head of long horned ng'ombe as the lead animal wandered, nodding, into our domain. He came to a halt at seeing us, the goats bleated and after them a couple of watoto emerged through the tall grasses. Covered in a red ochre of dust, both boys were dressed in a ragged vest and European style shorts that seemed to have more holes than cloth. They each carried a mkuki.

"Jambo, bwana," they greeted us respectfully.

"Jambo, habari?"

"Salaam. Eeeh."

"Let's ask them if they know what the drumming is about," suggested Pam.

"Why don't I be translator," volunteered Hazel. "I'm probably the most fluent of the four of us."

"Nawauuliza watoto, mnakaa kijijini hapa karibu?"

"I asked them if they were from a kijiji near here," Hazel told us.

"Ndyio memsahib," replied the one toto.

"Hicho kijiji ndicko ambacho tunasikia sauti a n'goma."

"Ndyio memsahib."

Hazel turned to us, "I asked him if the kijiji they are from is the same as where the drumming is coming from. The boy said, yes, the drumming is from his village and its quite close by."

"Can you ask him how far away the village is?" asked Doug.

"Well, I can try," replied Hazel, "but these watoto probably don't know how to measure distance or time and they certainly don't carry watches. Let me see what I can get out of them."

She turned back to the watoto. "Kijiji chenu ni mbali na hapa?"

A third toto materialised, mkuki in hand and watched. The first one shrugged in answer to Hazel's question.

"I know," said Hazel, "I'll try something else."

"Umetoka kijijini leo asubuhi pamoja na ng'ombe na mbuzi?"

"Ndyio memsahib."

Hazel turned to us. "You want to do a little mental arithmetic. They left their village this morning with the herds. They might average 1 mile an hour at best as they wander through the bush, maybe even less. What's the time now, 1:30p.m? Okay, say seven hours at a half mile an hour, that would put them at three and a half miles away, if they walked in a straight line. So, probably less than that."

"Ask him to point out the direction of his kijiji, Haze, I'll bet he knows that."

Hazel turned to the boy, "Kijiji yenu ni upande gani? Unaweza kunionyesha?"

The toto half turned and pointed in a direction for which there was a clear landmark. In the far distance, perhaps three miles away, was a low hill. Somewhere between here and that hill, lay the village.

Hazel turned back to the boy. "Kutakuwa na n'goma kijijini?"

"Ndyio, memsahib."

"Unafikiri kwamba wazee wenu watakubali tukienda kuona hiyo n'goma?"

"What did he say, Haze?" I interrupted. "I'm not following."

"Well," said Hazel, "I asked him if there's to be an n'goma at his village and he said yes. When I asked him if he thought the elders would mind if we visited and watched for a bit he said he didn't think so."

"Ask him what's the n'goma's about," said Doug. "It's almost always a celebration to have an n'goma, I wonder what it is."

Hazel asked the boy, "Sababu gani kuwe na n'goma kijijini?"

"Wameua simba, memsahb," replied the toto, "alikua anaingia ndani ya boma usiku kuua n'gombe wetu. Sasa simba ameuawa, memsahb."

Hazel turned and told us the story. "It seems they killed a lion that had been getting into the boma at night, killing cows and goats."

"Sounds like a good enough reason for an n'goma," said Pam. "I vote we go and watch it if they'll let us."

"We can do that, Pam. But don't forget, where one lion has come from there's likely to be others."

"Oh my gosh, I didn't think of that," said Pam. "Oh my gosh."

"Well, let's not get too worried," I said. "There's always the chance of coming across something out here. Heck, we've more than our share of hyenas at night."

"Hmm, well, that's not quite the same thing as a lion," Hazel asserted. "But anyway, we're here now, so let's go on. I think if there were lions close by they'd be attacking the watoto cattle before they'd bother with morsels like us."

With that we thanked the watoto, "Asante sana watoto, asante sana," gave them the box of Smarties, all we had left from our lunch, packed up the remaining rubbish and shoved it in the cleft of an acacia and started out fast, arm in arm in spite of the heat, heading for that hill.

We'd been walking a little over a half hour, when we smelled the wood smoke. The sounds of multiple drums throbbed louder with every step and we became excited about the prospect of the n'goma.

"The sad thing is, I don't think we'll get to watch the actual n'goma," Hazel volunteered a little breathlessly. "It seems to me they hold the celebration at night and we'll have to be back at school before then. What we can probably hear is the drummers practicing, or working themselves into the mood."

It wasn't long before the bush opened abruptly into a clearing. There were several dozen kayas, apparently unprotected, although set back among them was the boma, surrounded by a five-foot-high fence of acacia thorns and scrub. The village was in preparation. Males were daubing others with paint, women were helping each other with their hair, while others were keeping the pots boiling and the ugali stirred. Over to the right a circle of drummers, daubed in celebration paint, clothed only in red ochre'd loin cloths, were drumming at a furious rate, as though in competition with each other to see who could go the longest without missing a beat, or the fastest, or the loudest perhaps. The drum beats reverberated through my body, stirring excitement and sending my skin super sensitive, as my arm hairs stood on end.

It was a while before we were noticed, so absorbed were the villagers. But then an alert was called and in seconds a crowd of tribal members, jabbering ninety to the dozen, approached and surrounded us. Moments later the circle parted and through the gap walked a tall and handsome-looking African, well dressed in white shirt and shorts, amazingly clean tennis shoes, given the red dust, and white socks to his shins.

"Hello, boys and gels," he greeted us kindly with a smile and in almost immaculate English, "what brings you so far from home? I take it you're from Kongwa?"

"Yes, we are," replied Doug. "We've chanced by in this direction and earlier met watoto from your village with your cattle and goats."

"Oh, yes, that would be Mathew, Christian and Joab. Were they well?"

"Oh absolutely, very nice boys, very polite."

"Good, we try, you know, in the mission."

"Anyway," continued Doug, "we came across them, and of course we heard your drums. The watoto told us you were celebrating the killing of a lion that had been raiding your boma. We're keen to watch your n'goma; if we'd be allowed to that is."

"Well, we'll have to talk to the Chief about that. I am not he as I'm sure you realise. But I am his first born. I teach at the Catholic mission, several miles away, but I like to come home on the weekends to visit him and my mother, all my sisters and, of course, my daughter."

"Is that the mission with Father Doherty?" I asked.

"Yes, how do you know of him?"

"I was out with a group hunting game once and we stopped by the mission. They were very kind; gave us a drink of fabulous, fresh-squeezed lemonade.

"Ah yes, the sisters have a special recipe. It's not just any old lemonade."

"And Patrick gave us some ideas where we might find game," I continued.

"He's a good supervisor, Patrick; I think they're very happy with him."

"You said you visit your family which is mostly sisters?" I asked. "No brothers?"

"No, just sisters and one daughter. It means attending an awful lot of weddings these days I can tell you," he laughed good naturedly. "Anyway, what are your names?"

We introduced ourselves.

"That is good. My name is Paul Madinda. Anyway, let me bring you to the Chief and we'll ask him if you may watch for a while. I don't know if you realise but the n'goma will begin properly tonight when I expect you will be back at your school, but it is starting up now, mostly practicing and will continue non-stop for the next two days."

"We'll be happy to watch the preparations for a while," said Hazel. "It's already exciting as it is."

We followed Paul through the break in the line and down a path marked by a row of warriors either side, each with their mkuki at their sides. At the end of the line stood the nymba ya mtemi, the Chief's house – "Also known as a boma," whispered Hazel.

We came to a stop short of the door, where two askaris barred our way, arms outstretched, clutching their mkukis at the hilt and resting the tip of the handle on the ground. Paul had already passed them and turning briefly said, "I'll be out in a while. You wait here, please." And with that he stooped low and disappeared behind the leather curtain into the Chief's home.

"I thought a boma was a cattle corral?" I whispered to Hazel.

"It is," she whispered back, "but it's one of those words, like we have in English where the same word means something different. It depends on context."

"Oh," I whispered back and then, after a pause, I said, "I heard my dad once talking with friends and they were joking about the boma in Lindi. They had me believing that someone with a sense of humour had adopted the boma name for the D.C.'s office on account of its full of civil servants; you know, civil servants, cattle?"

"That's a good one," Hazel chuckled. "Maybe. But I don't think so. More likely they adopted the word because a tribal chief lives in a boma therefore the Africans would relate to their European counterparts calling their local chief's offices a boma."

"Ssshhh," whispered Doug. "I saw the door flap move, I think they're coming."

Paul returned, bursting quickly through the low doorway in a stoop, pushing back the leather flap as he did. Then he straightened and, talking

352 ♦ ANTHONY R. EDWARDS

through the crossed spears, he said, "The Chief is treating you very well, I hope you appreciate it. He is coming out to greet you, personally, himself."

While Paul stood off to the side to await the Chief's arrival, the four of us looked at each other.

"Wow," said Pam, "it's not as though we're anyone special. I think that's really mushee. Hope he doesn't take too long though, the time is passing and we'll have to start our trek back to school soon."

Then an askari held open the flap for the Chief as he emerged. He laboured under his old age and leaned on a fimbo for support. Another placed a stool for the Chief to be seated. The Chief took a deep breath, looked up, waived away the askaris and beckoned us closer. He spoke but his voice was quiet and his words unclear. Paul suggested he act as interpreter. Then the Chief spoke again.

"Ninyi wavulana wawili na wasichana wawili mnafanya nini hapa mbali na shule yenu?"

"The Chief asks: 'What are you young boys and young gels doing out here so far away from your school?'"

"Please tell the Chief we're allowed out on Sundays. We teamed up to go somewhere different and came upon his grandchildren in the bush tending the cattle and goats. They told us there was to be an n'goma at this kijiji and we could hear the drums. So, we thought we would come and visit and hope to be allowed to watch for a while."

"Mnatazamiaje kuwa hai huku porini kama hamna mapanga wala mikuki ya kujilinda?

"The Chief says: 'How can you expect to stay alive in the bush if you haven't got any spears or pangas to defend yourselves?'"

"Please tell the Chief we are not expecting to be long in the bush. We are only on a day trip and brought food with us. We will return to the school in a while."

"Je hamjui kuwa ni hatari huku porini? Simba hawako mbali. Walikwisha wavamia ng'ombe na mbuzi wetu?"

"The Chief asks: 'Do you not know it is dangerous in the bush? There are lions not far away. They have attacked our cattle and goats.'"

"Please tell the Chief we know this now but did not know this when we set out. But we are not frightened. We will go home carefully bearing in mind the chief's warning."

"Umepata chakula cha kutosha. Au una njaa sasa?"

"The Chief asks: 'Have you had enough food. Are you hungry?'"

"Please tell the Chief we've had our lunch, even shared a little bit with the chief's grandchildren."

"Umewapa chakula gani?"

"The Chief asks: 'What food did you give them?'"

"Please tell the Chief that we shared our Smarties, chocolate sweets. Does the Chief know what Smarties are, Paul?"

"I will explain it," replied Paul.

"Unataka kukaa kwa muda gani kuenye ngoma?"

"The Chief asks: 'How long do you want to stay at the n'goma?'"

We huddled to agree on the time and how long it would take to return. We wouldn't be stopping to eat like we did on the way out, so it shouldn't take more than two hours.

"Please tell the Chief, unfortunately most of the day has passed and we have a long walk back. We think maybe one hour is all we can take."

"Unaweza kukaa pale, karibu na mke wangu wa tatu"

"The Chief says: 'You may take a seat over there,'" Paul pointed to what were clearly a number of tribal leaders taking their seats already, watching the drummers and what appeared to be an assembling of dancers, "with his third wife – my cousin."

"Kama uko tayari kuondoka, lazima unamwambia mke wangu. Yeye atasema na askari na utaonyeshwa njia ya kutoka. Sitaki uwe hatarini kwa hivyo nitatuma askari wangu wenye nguvu zaidi kuwasindikiza ninyi mpaka shule ya Kongwa."

The Chief says when you are ready to go, you should tell his third wife. She will tell her askari and you will be shown the way. The Chief says he does not want you to be in danger, or to get lost when darkness falls, therefore he will assign his strongest warrior to come with you, and escort you to the boundary of Kongwa School."

We broke into big smiles at that, thanking Paul and asking him to thank the Chief for his generosity and kindness. Then, after bidding the Chief, "Kwa heri sasa, asante sana, asante sana," we followed Paul who said, "Ah, I see my cousin coming this way. There she is, over there."

Our eyes followed his gaze and settled on an incredibly beautiful and shapely young Gogo girl, who didn't look to me much older than Hazel.

She was walking in our general direction. The girl was draped in a colourful kanga and supported a huge gourd upon her head. As Paul approached she broke into a demure but wonderful smile. She was almost regal and could even be a princess, I thought, she was so elegant, with her flawlessly smooth, matt, light brown complexion. Paul and she spoke a few words, she lowered the gourd from her head and set it down near a kaya doorway. Then she turned and smiled at us and beckoned us to follow.

Yikes, the old chief has such a young girl for his third wife, I thought. *I wonder what she thinks of that?*

"I have to get back to the mission," Paul said. "Which, as you know, Tony, is in a different direction from the way you'll be going... and a bit further. So I'll be changing into something very light and then running all the way."

"Oh my gosh, running all the way?" asked Hazel. "How far?"

"Oh not very far really, about ten miles. I'll be back soon after dark. Kwaheri sasa." And with that he was gone.

As Paul disappeared, the drums, which had quieted for a while, burst into sound again, surging through our bodies making me feel week at the knees. Paul's cousin gestured us to be seated on a line of stools and then took her place alongside us, rubbing shoulders with me. I was in awe of this girl's radiance and wanted to strike a conversation or ask her name but wasn't sure if I should.

But then I did. "This is very nice of the Chief to let us watch your ceremony," I said. "My name is Tony, what's yours?"

She turned, gave me a beaming smile and said, "Miriam, please, my name-e is Miriam Madinda.

Then the dancing girls came on, interrupting the moment. They were not like any dancing girls I'd seen in a Warner Brothers musical. Travelling in line like a slithering python, these beautiful young African girls, bare-breasted, wearing only tiny skirts of beads as well as jewellery and ornaments about their heads, ears and legs, came ululating out from behind the kayas in a spectacular co-ordination of dance and sound. They were thrilling to watch and became the more so as they picked up the quickening beat from the drummers, until they were moving in little short of a frenzy.

I sat watching wide-eyed, stupefied. The school's end-of-term dance was nothing like this! Pam and Hazel glanced at Doug and I as the girls came shimmying up close and our eyes widened with the bouncing of their breasts.

"Enjoying ourselves, are we?" they asked knowingly, as Douglas smirked and I smiled, slightly embarrassed.

It seemed like only a minute rather than an hour, when both Pam and Hazel announced in unison that our time was up. "We must leave now or there's no hope of getting back to school in time for our baths. Then we'll be missed by Matron, then questions will be asked and before you know we'll have been discovered. We must leave now."

"Okay," said Doug, "let's go."

"We must tell Miriam," I reminded, "the protocol is most important. We mustn't give offence."

I turned to my side and whispered into Miriam's ear. She looked up and over her shoulder, clapped her hands and an especially tall warrior, with a longer handled spear than most, eased his way through the crowd to her side. She gave him instructions in Cigogo, way too fast for me to understand but I took it that she was repeating the Chief's instructions.

"Okay, you may please go now," she said slowly in stilted English. "My askari is the biggest and strongest one. He will take you to your school."

We thanked her profusely, "Asante sana Miriam," as she gave us her lovely smile one last time. The askari beckoned and we set off at a fast pace.

"Pretty girl, Tony," said Hazel with a knowing look, as we left the ringside.

"Er, um, which one did you mean?" I stammered.

We made good time considering how hot it was, even at this late hour. It was getting on for 5 o'clock and, as we made our way, realised we'd travelled further than we remembered. The sun was setting, its blinding rays directly in our eyes. Darkness would soon be upon us and make it harder. But our askari knew exactly where he was. It was strange to think he would be the person who'd face the fight if danger threatened.

After an age at a fast pace through the tinder dry brush, up and down the sides of dongas, skirting outcrops of thorny bush, resting briefly against the trunk of baobab trees, and watching the setting sun's orange streaks give way to darkness, our askari came to an abrupt halt, announcing that we were at the boundary of Kongwa.

"Kwa heri watoto," he said perfunctorily, as he turned on his heel and disappeared into the descending gloom.

"Asante," we called after him, "asante sana."

Because it was so late we barely recognised where we were and might not have done but for the silhouette of Kongwa Hill in the near distance, against the not quite blackened sky. I thought about how, but for the askari, we'd not have found our way home, certainly not in time. We made our way along the beaten path that ran close by the phase 5 boys houses of Nightingale, then Curie, because there was no way of circumventing them.

"Keep in the shadows," I urged. "We don't want to be caught now."

At one point there was muffled conversation between Hazel and Pam, ending in titters and suppressed laughter as they tried to be quiet while enjoying a joke.

"What's so funny?" I whispered. "We must be quiet."

"Oh, we were just speculating on what it would be like to burst into the boys' houses round about now," whispered Hazel. "You know, bath time and all."

"I'll tell you something," Douglas smiled. "The boys wouldn't mind."

With that we chuckled, then refocused our concentration as we came close to being visible to a pair wrapped in bath towels standing outdoors near their hot water boiler. Hazel and Pam couldn't keep their eyes off them as we snuck by. I suppose they hoped the bath towels would fall off.

Doug and I had to pass Livingstone and Wilberforce, of course, because both girls lived further away, Hazel in phase 3, and Pam in her parents' home that wasn't far from phase 2. Although the girls urged Doug and I back to our houses while the going was good, we wouldn't hear of leaving them by themselves.

"No, we insist on seeing you back safely," Doug and I asserted. "There's not a chance we're leaving you on your own."

Doug and Pam eventually peeled off in the direction of her parents' house. Hazel and I, with farther to go, continued cautiously, nipping in a crouch across the tarmac strip, dashing from bush to tree, as far as either of us dared to the very edge of the girls' phase. There we came across her house some thirty feet away. Her friends were moving around inside and out, the light spilling through the open door onto the darkened ground. I pulled Hazel close and gave her a bear hug.

"What a great day it's been," I said. "I hope you've enjoyed it as much as I have."

"It's been fab, Tony, really. What a great idea. Thanks for such a super time."

And with that I enjoyed one long, last, lingering kiss, before Hazel broke away. Keeping to the shadows, she disappeared from view until suddenly re-appearing at the brightly lit door of her house, as casually as though she'd been there all evening.

> *Funga safari, funga safari.*
> *Funga safari, funga safari.*
> *Hamari ya nani? Hamari ya nani?*
> *Hamari ya Bwana Kapteni, Hamari ya keyaa.*
> —From the regimental march of the King's African Rifles

CHAPTER TWENTY-SEVEN

LOVERS' TRYST

TORRENTIAL RAINS WASHED THE FIRST TERM OF 1957. Arriving by bus at 2 a.m., we'd not got a chance to see the changed countryside, but boy, what a sight when we woke that first morning. Green was everywhere. Not like the coast, of course, not the lush, verdant green of Dar; but green by Kongwa standards. Msasa and acacia were prolific in their miniature leaf; the magugu grass was taller and thicker than ever. Rivulets and mini dongas were formed, leaving the ground like a dried-out delta until it rained again. Insects and reptiles seemed limitless, especially snakes driven out of their underground retreats.

A couple of weeks into term, Doug and I had strolled to the playing fields to watch the school's rugby team practicing for a match between Kongwa and the Indian School in Dodoma. As with cricket, the Indians all-too-often won, no matter how hard our team trained.

"Have you heard from Berry?" Doug asked as we stood and watched from the boundary. "He left at the end of last term, didn't he? I know you two got on."

"We were good friends, but no, I haven't heard from him. He was going to Britain, you know, and then returning to Uganda, I think – no, it was Kenya, Kisumu, but he's going to school in Nairobi."

"Good luck with that," said Doug. "From what I hear of Nairobi schools, I think it'd be a whole lot better to be in Kongwa."

I lapsed into silence, pensive, as I thought about Stewie. I'd been dismayed when he'd announced his last term. My friends were forever leaving Kongwa, as their parents moved on. He'd promised to write, just like with Ivey who'd left at the same time, but I hadn't heard from him either. Berry said he'd write to me first because he hadn't known his new address yet.

Then I noticed the darkening horizon and it snapped me out of my thoughts. "Look over there, Peps," I said, pointing west. "Looks like another storm coming."

"And how," Doug replied. "Boy, is that sky black."

The sun was burning overhead as ever, even though we were moving towards late afternoon. For now, the sky in front of the oncoming storm maintained its deep cerulean blue as we sweated buckets in the unusual humidity; it was a certainty we were not going to see it much longer.

"What do you want to do?" I asked.

"Let's watch the practice a bit. The chaps are doing well. If they're as good as this when they play Dodoma they could win."

"That would make a change."

Doug grimaced. "Not much help from your house, Tony; only chap from Livingstone on the team is Alan Alder."

"Yeah, I know. It's dominated by Curie as usual."

"And Wilberforce!" added Doug indignantly.

"And Wilberforce," I conceded.

"Gosh," I said, "that storm's coming fast. It's going to be a heavy one."

We watched as the earlier thin line of deep black spread across the sky, racing closer and forming a dark and brooding anvil at its thunderhead, while sheet lightening lit the roiling clouds into a threatening, deep-slate grey.

"Did you see that!?" I exclaimed as it was followed by a massive charge of forked lightning hitting the ground in a dozen places, followed moments later by the not-too distant crash and rumble of thunder.

"I wonder if the ref will stop the practice?" asked Doug of no one in particular.

Then the sun was gone as the ominous black clouds bore down and blacked it out. The smell was intoxicating with the wind carrying the rain's fragrance ahead of it; so welcome; so inviting.

And then it was upon us. Those few, first, tepid drops, those scouts, those huge pathfinders would hit in the eye, or splash off a knee or hit in the back of the neck. Then a couple more; then wider as you could count the drops making craters in the dry, red soil, like the landscape on Mars. Then the torrent arrived, one moment it was something to watch, just five feet away, the next second you were possessed within its warm, watery and pelting embrace, instantly saturated, hearing overtaken by a tempestuous roar amid breaking thunder.

"Maybe we should find cover," I yelled into Doug's ear. "Rugger practice is bound to stop now, we can't just stand here."

"What did you say – can't hear you," I lip read.

"Let's find shelter," I tried again.

"Let's see what they do," he yelled back, nodding towards the players on the field, "and join up with them when they come off."

I got his drift as we turned to watch, expecting the players to pack it in. But, with grim determination, Kongwa's rugby team kept on practicing through the deluge. We could barely see the ref, the short and stocky Mr. Simms, as he tried to end the game blowing his choked-up whistle through the teeming rain and the blinding water in his eyes. Neither must most of the players; it was certain we could barely see them. Yet they kept furiously at it as they joined in muddy scrums or attempted to beat the odds and score a touchdown.

We started cheering, "Come on, Elwood!" as Elwood Thomson, the team's fly half, who'd just taken a pass from vice-captain Aurelio Balletto, bore down on the ref at full speed, ball tucked under arm, cleated boots splashing explosive mud and, like a runaway train powerless to divert from its course, ploughed into Mr. Simms, flattening him into the ooze, even as we'd seen him blowing silent from his whistle in a futile attempt to close the game.

"Oh my gosh, I hope Mr. Simms is all right." I said.

The fly half spun on his axis, nearly fell flat on his face but somehow recovered and in his momentum vanished into the fog as he raced for the elusive goal line.

"That was a helluva hit," I added. "Wow, will he…?"

"He's getting up," Doug commented drily.

Scrambling unsteadily to his feet, the ref must have been seeing stars as he wobbled about this way and that, eventually retreating to the sideline, guided perhaps by our shapes as his beacon.

"I can't see most of them!" he shouted as he arrived. "And they certainly can't hear me, so I think I'll just leave them to it. Clearly they're having a ball out there… if I may put it that way."

We laughed along with him. "Very well put, sir," we yelled back.

✦ ✦ ✦

MY ROMANCE WITH HAZEL WAS AS STRONG as our new world was wet. We loved to see each other and I enjoyed her company as often as I could. But we didn't have enough time together. With the success Doug had meeting Pam on nocturnal excursions to secret rendezvous, I decided to take my chances at the same thing. We'd got away with several Sunday trips so that gave me confidence. Now, being older, I could delegate a Junior boy to be my cover, just like I had been for older Seniors in earlier years. Annelize's brother, Egbert, was in Livingstone Juniors. I knew him well and could trust him, particularly because of his sister's friendship with Hazel. He'd done the same thing for prefects; still did once in a while.

Hazel and I made a plan. At a place in the donga we judged well away from the girls' phase we agreed on a spot which had a handy young baobab as a landmark, and were excited in anticipation. I alerted Egbert to stay awake.

When all were asleep, I hunched low and darted over to the Junior phase, snuck in the back door of Egbert's house and roused him. The rendezvous was a long walk, especially at night with danger from animals along the route, together with the risk of being discovered. It was with teachers in mind that we took a circuitous route to avoid them. However, we couldn't avoid one particular house.

The moonlight was brilliant. Perhaps it was the angle of the Earth not being too far from the equator. Perhaps it was the clarity of the air from the extended rainy season? But that moon was so large and beautiful you could make out its terrain without a telescope. Beautiful though the night was, it could spell trouble. Our shapes would stand in stark relief against any lit background, meaning we would have to take extra care to keep to the shadows.

We made our way, sometimes crossing open ground heads down and in a crouch, literally darting from bush to tree to anthill to choo depending upon the cover available. At one point we were walking a road hugging the inside curve on the edge of a culvert. From around the corner a car approached at speed, headlights on full beam, stabbing the darkness so suddenly it was inconceivable we didn't hear it coming and been warned seconds earlier. We dived down the culvert's side tumbling head over heels, scraping and sliding, bruising ourselves on the muddied rock but cushioned by the thick grasses of the season.

"Boy, that was close," I said, as I staggered to my feet, coughing and spluttering from the wet sand I'd got in my mouth. "How about you, Egbert, you okay?"

"Yeah, man, I'm fine," he said brushing mud off his clothes, but as he glanced at me he caught sight of blood on my right knee.

"Looks like you gashed your knee, man."

I looked down. I hadn't realised it but I did now as pain set in and I felt the cut throbbing. I pulled out my hanky and wiped the mud away.

"It's tough. I'm not letting this stop me, I'll clean it up when we get back later, we must keep going. Here let me check you over."

I examined Egbert; he'd come off better than me with only a few slight grazes. I looked again at my gash in the moonlight but I didn't see it as serious. We climbed the culvert and resumed our walk, me at a limp. Now we came close to the teacher's house. For some distance in either direction, the ground was impenetrable with thickets of thorns. We couldn't go through that lot and to go around would have taken us well out of our way. There was nothing for it but to sneak through hostile territory.

We darted from the 'boys' choo, to ant hill, to bush, until at one point, the side wall of the teacher's house became the next point of refuge. Even as we were scurrying across open ground, the door of the adjacent kaya opened and a servant emerged. We froze in a deep shadow where in daylight we would have been in plain view. The servant stopped and looked around. He'd heard something and appeared to look directly at us. We could even see the whites of his eyes like penlight beams not ten yards away. How could he not see us? Such is the trick of light with a brilliant moon and the deepest of shadows that apparently he didn't. He looked around to left and right, and then peered again in our direction. It was like he could see something but couldn't make out the shape. Maybe the combined shape of our two bodies close together distorted our appearance so we no longer looked like people. In any event after taking one tentative step forward, he thought better of it, backed up a little to start with and then turned and made back into his kaya.

I waited an age. Then I whispered to Egbert in the dullest tone, "Don't even blink, 'til I say so."

I wanted to ensure the servant wasn't watching from his doorway. Eventually I whispered, "I don't want to hear you breathing even – follow me, keep low, hug the wall, we're going along the outside of the house, under the windows and around the corner at the end there."

We were so low we were almost crawling as we slid by, backs compressed to wall, under the bedroom window. As we continued under the bathroom window we heard movement from inside and then yellow brightness suddenly flooded the area, threatening us with exposure. We both froze in mid movement. We heard the sounds of someone inside, just inches away from us, huddled as we were alongside the outer wall in a denuded flower bed. Ablutions completed, the light switched off and the occupant retreated. After waiting a little longer, I beckoned as we eased our way along the rest of the house. At the end we turned around the windowless side, made a tiptoed dash to the side of the servant's choo for the next house, which I judged empty, and from there slunk back into the cover of small bushes and shrubs.

After crossing the tarmac strip and passing in the shadows of the Junior's classrooms, with the baobab now in sight, I gave Egbert instructions where to stay, and reminded him to watch for adults and alert me if necessary. At the slightest hint of trouble, the warning cry was to be the hyena call. If we needed to run we'd make our way to safety together. So, with that, I stole back into the grass through which I made my way down the donga's side and up the other to the out-of-bounds edge. As I approached, I made a hyena call which, if she was there, Hazel would return along with flashes from her torch.

My heart was beating faster. I hadn't been alone with Hazel for two weeks. I was anticipating that gorgeous face, that lovely smile and those so sweet kisses. There were three short flashes from her torch; she'd arrived ahead of me.

There she was, "Hello, Haze, howzit going?" as casual as you like.

Hazel's scanning mechanism was working overtime. Before she had time to say much she'd noticed the blood streaming down my knee, something I'd forgotten about, and greeted me instead with her routine, "Hello, silly boy, what have you done to yourself this time?"

After a long, warming hug she stood back and said, "Come, let's find a place to sit and let me look at that knee."

Once ensconced, she shone her torch onto the cut which was deep and had rich red blood dribbling out still.

"This is serious, Tony, we can't just leave this."

"You expect me to go to Matron at this time of night?"

"No, silly, you won't have to. I have a First Aid kit with me."

"You what?"

"First Aid kit, you know, tube of antiseptic, bandage that sort of thing."

"But who would think to bring such a thing tonight?"

"I did. I'm a Girl Guide, remember. We carry the small, personal kit like this all the time when we go out on Guide trips – don't Scouts? You know, 'Be Prepared' and all that?"

"Oh."

"You, of all people, should know about these things, just the same as when you're scouting. You know how dangerous it is if you get a serious cut… and that's what you've got here. Anyway, sit still while I get my stuff out."

"Centi kumi will know I never looked after this myself. What will I tell her?"

"Who?"

"Centi kumi, that's our new Matron's nickname. She's out from England; Christine Dove's her real name. She replaced Mrs. Moore on account of her new baby boy, Alan. Anyway, her idea of punishment for things we've done wrong is to fine us ten cents from our weekly pocket money; so we call her Centi kumi."

Hazel smiled, "Well, anyway, I'm going to put an Elastoplast on it," she said, having cleaned the wound with the antiseptic cream and a piece of gauze, removing half of Kongwa's sand from the deep cut as she did so. "It'll be fine for tonight. Tomorrow you'd best remove the plaster in the morning and make sure you hide your legs, keep other boys in front of you so Centi kumi doesn't notice the cut before you leave for breakfast. Tomorrow afternoon, you can go to her for a clean dressing. She'll likely believe you that you cut your knee near the classrooms and washed it yourself."

Hazel was so gentle the way she tended my knee. "It's almost worth hurting myself," I said, "just for you to look after me."

"Silly boy," retorted Hazel. "There that should do you."

"I think you'd make a fine nurse. Maybe that's what you should do for your career."

"No, thank you very much. Tending a wound like this is about my limit. I don't like dealing with blood. Because it was you it was sort of okay, but otherwise…."

"I want to kiss you, Hazel. It's been so long. I can't wait any longer."

"I want you, too. Come, let's snuggle up."

We talked of home. Hazel didn't appreciate being at boarding school any more than I, although we conceded it wasn't so bad these days. It gave us the opportunity to see each other after all. We shared stories of home and the things we did in the hols. Hazel was still living in Nachingwea and we talked of the wonderful days we'd had that time of my visit. But this evening was different and I sensed a quietness on her part. I didn't know quite what to make of it but she seemed subdued, pensive even. Then she looked up and startled me with a new question.

"Did you ever hear about Anthony Paton?"

"No." I frowned wondering why she would ask. "I didn't know you knew him. He didn't return to school last term but chaps come and go all the time. Actually I'm a Scout troop leader because he didn't come back."

"He's dead, you know?"

"What!?"

"Yes, it was pretty well hushed up. I didn't tell you before because I was asked by my parents not to tell anyone, after I found out. But it will all come out sooner or later. I think about it all the time. I have to tell someone."

"What happened, what did he die of?"

"I'll tell you if you promise, cross your heart and hope to die, you'll never tell anyone."

"You can trust me, Haze, you know that."

Hazel gave me that 'you'd better' look.

"Well, the Paton family went to Kenya during the long hols last year. I think they have cousins up there who own a large ranch. It was somewhere near Kisumu if I recall, you know, not too far from one of those rivers that feeds the Nile. Anyway, it was Anthony's sister's birthday and they were on

this farm and not doing anything special so he and his sister 'Kitten' – that's
what her dad calls her although her real name is Susan – well, they went off
into the bush. You know what Anthony is… or was… he just loved being out
in the sticks and was terribly interested in animals; I think he'd have become
a vet when he grew up; anyway they went off exploring together."

"I didn't know he had a sister," I interrupted. "Does she come to
Kongwa?"

"Yes she does, or did. She's a couple of years younger than you so you
probably didn't notice her. She's a lovely girl.

"No. I only notice lovely girls a couple of years older than me."

"Silly." Hazel gave a weak smile.

"He's a good looking boy too," I added, not having yet adopted the past
tense. "And a nice chap actually. I get on well with him."

"Yes, did you notice his eyelashes? Any girl would be as envious as anything of his eyelashes; he was such a handsome boy."

"Was?" I asked.

"Yes… was. I just told you, he died."

"Oh. Yes, you did. I don't think it sunk in."

"Well anyway, this terrible, terrible thing happened. You know they lived
in Nachingwea?"

"No."

"Well they did… do… the family. Anyway, we know them well. But
here's the thing. The Patons had friends who were also friends of ours. They
were visiting us and I heard my mum and dad talking with them one evening.
I'd gone to bed, they thought, and didn't know I was listening from around
the corner outside my bedroom, so I heard all about it."

"So what did happen?" I asked urgently.

"Well, Anthony and Kitten were messing about around the water's edge
of this river. I think it was… no, I can't remember the name of the river…
maybe it was a bit further north, up nearer to Lake Rudolph."

"Hazel, I don't care about the name of the river, just tell me what
happened."

"Anthony was taken by a croc."

"What!?"

"Yes," said Hazel in a suddenly subdued voice, tears welling now that she had said it out loud. She glanced down to look away, fidgeting with her hands as she sobbed for a few moments.

I put my arm around her and gave her a hug.

"Anyhow," she sniffed, suddenly looking up, throwing her hair back and saying, "This won't do; mustn't be silly; it's all over now anyway...."

She paused, then with a swallow continued, "He, that is they, Kitten and him, were messing about at the water's edge. She'd taken her shoes off but not waded in far. Anthony was up to his shins in the water. There were dead tree logs floating by and one in particular. Except it wasn't a log. Suddenly, with no warning, just as Kitten, that is Susan, had looked up at Anthony to call him to come and see something she'd found in the mud, this log turned into the gaping jaws of this massive Nile crocodile. At the moment she saw it, it was lunging at her brother and caught him by one of his legs. Apparently Susan screamed so loud and so shrill and so full of horror that her voice carried quite some distance and her dad and some African 'boys' heard her and came running. But they were way too far away and arrived too late. She watched in horror as the croc dragged her brother under and then did the death roll. You know what that is, I suppose?"

"No."

"She watched that croc roll over and over, its jaws around Anthony's leg and her brother being dragged under water and then surfacing again as the croc rolled, then under, then out again, over and over, she said, it never seemed to stop. The croc was drowning Anthony... that's what they do, you know, they drown their prey. Susan was screaming, screaming, screaming, non-stop screaming in absolute hysterics as her dad and the boys came running. By the time they got to her there was no sign of the croc or Anthony. She couldn't talk except to scream at them, 'Croc! Croc!' They could see her brother was not around. Of course they called out for him but they soon realised what must have happened."

And then Hazel burst into fitful sobs again at the memory of the story, and that she had known and liked Anthony so much, and for the horror that had been Susan's and her parents. I squeezed her tighter as I pulled her hard close to me. I found a handkerchief in my pocket to wipe her tears.

We sat in silence for a long time after that, caring not for the rustles in the grass, the noisy insect opera, or the hyenas' hrummphing. At first I thought one of our lookouts was alerting us to danger and pricked up my ears but then realised the sounds were too far away. It was a real hyena. After a while, Hazel turned her face to mine and we kissed deeply. When we were satiated we leaned back and gazed at the brilliant moon. As she studied it, Hazel asked, "Do you believe in God?"

"I think so," I replied. "At least I'm supposed to. I'm due to become confirmed in St. Andrew's next week and not just by Reverend Beesley either. In fact both Pepsi and I are, some others too."

"Oh, yes, you told me. Well, I hope you pay more attention in that service than you normally do, gazing out the church windows looking for the bus."

"I've only been able to since we started using the church again. I think it was silly using the girl's gym, don't you? I mean, why'd it take so long to come up with the idea of having two services on Sundays so they could accommodate everyone?"

"I don't know."

"Anyway, you're right about the windows. It's all because they stopped the train, you know. Stew and I loved hearing the train. You could hear it reverberating around the hills and then, when it finally got here, it whistled like crazy to let people know to come and pick up the freight and the mail. We thought of it as our connection with the outside, hoping it was bringing letters from home. Now, with the bus, I never hear it or see it, well, except you can see the bus's dust trail from the church when it arrives on Sunday mornings."

"Oh, so that's it."

"Mm hmm. But what I didn't tell you is, we're going to be confirmed by the Archbishop of Tanganyika, Father Trevor Huddleston. How about that?"

"No, you didn't! Why, what makes you chaps so important?"

"Well, I don't think it's anything to do with importance. The Archbishop is coming by on a visit and I suppose they do things like that when the big daddy is in town."

"And Pepsi will be confirmed at the same time?"

"Yes," I said, "although I don't think he'll ever make it to heaven."

We both laughed at that. Doug was such a character and was always in trouble with one teacher or another.

After a long pause, Hazel said, "I don't."

"You don't what?" I asked.

"I don't believe in God. No loving God would have let that horror happen to Anthony."

There was another long silence.

"Actually I think it was worse for Susan," she sighed as she picked up again on her thoughts. "Anthony was soon dead and probably never knew what was happening. But Susan witnessed it all in close up. She'll never be the same again."

"Is she back at school?"

"No, and I doubt she ever will be. She was shocked beyond belief. She adored her big brother, you know, absolutely adored him. They were best of friends. I don't know what will happen to her."

After another long silence Hazel asked solemnly, "What will become of us, Tony? Where will you go with your life? Where will I go with mine?"

I opened my mouth to respond with something thoughtful when suddenly Hazel reached out to me, and pulled me in close saying, "Forget it. No more talk."

I was caught slightly off balance, not to say off guard and as I put a hand out to steady myself it came to rest on her left breast. I quickly withdrew it, horrified that I was going to be in trouble.

"I'm sorry, Haze, I'm so sorry; I didn't mean to do that, I...."

"Silly boy," she said, "I liked it... there's nothing wrong... don't worry." Then she dropped her chin a bit and looked at me in that especially seductive way of hers and said, "I really liked it."

I got the message and gently returned my hand to the blouse over her left breast. Slowly I followed its contour, gave a little squeeze and when I still didn't get my face slapped, moved from her left to her right. She stared at me with that inviting, limpid look that her eyes gave out in the moonlight.

"Don't stop, Tony," she breathed deeply. "Don't stop."

My fingers rested gently on a blouse button. She breathed deeper. I kissed her long and fiddled with the button. No hand pushed me away. The button came undone. I moved up and undid another, then another. I moved my hand to cup a breast covered though it was with her bra and felt such a thrill, such excitement, such stirring where I ought not to be stirring. I completed the undoing of her blouse buttons and Hazel leaned forward to help me remove it.

I reached behind to undo her bra strap but didn't know how the fastener worked. I fumbled for a moment, my excitement rising and then became frustrated that I couldn't unclasp it. I wanted that bra off urgently – I couldn't wait. Hazel was shivering – how could that be in this sultry air? But she made no move to help. I had the thought that even though she was older than me and knew so much more that she'd never been this far with a boy before.

In my urgency I slid her shoulder straps down instead so the bra dropped off her breasts leaving both exposed, her body trembling in excitement as I now sensed, her skin moist and beautiful beyond measure bathed as she was in this silken moonlight. Hazel arched her neck invitingly. At first I just stared in astonishment.

"They're so lovely," I said. "My gosh, you're so beautiful, so perfect. How can you be so lovely?" Then I cupped a breast in my quivering hand and then the other. I stroked them so tenderly, squeezing ever so gently, traced their contours; this was sheer ecstasy, such joy, such happiness. How could they be so firm as well as so soft? Then I stooped to kiss them and Hazel giggled.

For a long time we held together in each other's arms as I caressed her. I was so entranced, in such awe of her comeliness.

"You must be the most beautiful girl in the world," I said. "I haven't seen any girls' breasts before, not even a picture, well, except for statues maybe; but I can't believe there were ever any two more lovely or so perfect."

Hazel smiled with a radiance about her that I hadn't seen before; she said nothing, but I knew she too was terribly happy. Then she asked, "Is that really true, you've never even seen a picture of a naked girl?"

"Of course not. Where would I ever see one? Even in the movies we're not allowed to see a man and a woman kiss, never mind see anyone naked."

"Well, I once heard tell a story of a girl and a boy in a bath together," Hazel smiled a knowing look.

"Oh, please! If you mean Annelize, we were so young then, it wasn't the same and besides which she hadn't... you know."

"Hadn't what?" Hazel teased.

"You know."

"No, I don't know."

"Well, you know; developed."

Hazel smiled. "Hadn't developed, huh? You saw the African girls at the n'goma," she reminded me. "They'd developed all right."

I looked at her in surprise. "I'd forgotten about that. I suppose you're right... and yet... that's different somehow."

I continued stroking her breasts pensively as we half sat, half leaned against the donga wall in silence, and then I continued.

"You know, it really is different with African girls. In their culture they're not ashamed of their beauty. To be topless and to feed their babies in public is completely normal for them. And because of that, seeing them naked up top seems normal enough to me, even though I'm not one of them. But if I were to see a number of European girls dancing the same dances as they do, even out here in the wilds of Africa, it would be a totally different thing. I wonder why we have to be like that. Crikey Moses, what is there to be ashamed about in the beauty of girls?" I asked in a sudden rising of irritation. "It's so stupid!"

As we held together there were more rustles in the grass as an iguana dashed by or a snake wound its way in pursuit of dinner. Our heavy breathing, the sound of our wet lips, the murmurs of pleasure and Hazel's occasional giggles, sounded quite beautiful against the noisy background of the night. I so much wanted it to never end.

Above us on a high branch an owl had landed to rest. It hooted as if in pleasure, as it bowed its head and gazed at us, blinking its huge, yellow eyes at our exhibitionism.

A heavy drop of warm water hit me, then another, then a couple on Hazel too.

"Uh oh," I said, "I think there's rain on the way."

We looked up. There was nothing to see. Where was the moon, where were the stars? A few more fat droplets, then more and then suddenly, as though a stopper had been opened, the heavens opened and our world was full of water as we were drenched in the deluge. We jumped to our feet as the sky was lit like daylight with a fibrous spread of lightning filling the sky, followed seconds later by a massive thunder clap like I'd never heard. There was nowhere to take shelter, what were we to do?

"Mmmm-uh! Mmmm-uh!" The hyena call, this time from close by, called out louder than any hyena would come up with and really only sounded like a human trying to mimic one.

We looked at each other startled. It had come from Hazel's friend who was waiting some thirty feet away.

"That must be Larly," yelled Hazel over the noise of the rain. "I told her to let me know if I was getting too late. She's probably worried because of this rain. We'd better get back before we're discovered, Tony, it really is late," she said glancing at her watch. "I must go."

Hazel was busy lifting her bra back into place as we talked, and then I helped her as with difficulty she pulled on her sopping wet blouse and did up the buttons.

"Who's Larly," I called over the noise. "I don't know her?"

"Barbara Larlham's her name," Hazel called back. "No, you probably don't know her; she's two years behind you. She's a good kid; I know I can rely on her. That reminds me, Annelize asked me to ask you to say hello to her baby brother; your fag is Egbert?"

"Yes, same as before. He's a bit of a skellum, they tell me, but I don't have any problem with him."

"I must go now, I'm sorry, Tony!" We were shouting to be heard.

"I know, I know, gosh, Haze, I don't want to go!" I yelled back.

"We must, we must. But we'll get together again soon, all right? See you in the break tomorrow."

Rain was pouring off Hazel's head, eyelashes fluttering, her saturated blouse and skirt clung to her body. I stretched out for her and gave her a last and wet lingering kiss before she turned towards the donga.

"Hey, where are you going?"

"I have to cross the donga."

"But you can't," I yelled. "You need Larly with you and, in any case, look, it's flooding. It must be a foot deep already. Look, the water's a torrent down there."

"Oh my God," yelled Hazel. "What are we going to do? We have to cross."

"You can't, the water's rising by the second," I shouted. "It could be dangerous; you'll have to get back the long way round. There's a road that crosses the donga about a half mile away up that way," I said pointing, "opposite direction to your phase. You'll need to cross there then double back. I'll come with you to see you safe."

"No, you won't, Tony Edwards. You look after yourself and get back to your phase – Larly and me'll manage."

"I'm coming with you and that's that. Now let's go. I just want to see you safe most of the way then I'll return. Come on, let's go."

"What about Egbert?" Hazel yelled.

"Jeez, I'd forgotten him. I'll find him and tell him to make his way back to his house and I'll follow. Wait for me here."

But by the time I'd found Egbert having taken the wrong path at one point because I dare not call out, told him what to do and returned to where I'd left Hazel, she was gone. I started to charge after her in the general direction that I knew she and Larly must have followed, but several minutes had gone and I realised they were too far ahead. Fighting against the soaking bush, the incredibly heavy rain, and the mud that the normally bone-dry red soil had become, all in the blackness of a thickly blanketed sky, had become scary. I knew she and Larley had torches because Hazel had rebuked me for not bringing mine. "Egbert has his," I'd told her, "and the moon was so bright when we left." So, feeling anguished about leaving the girls to fight this storm alone, I turned on my heel and made my disconsolate fight against the elements. I crossed the donga's rushing torrent by 'tightrope,' in a sitting walk across the baobab root in the pitch black and made my way back to my house.

CHAPTER TWENTY-EIGHT

MOVING ON

I T WAS HALF TERM, EARLY APRIL 1957, when I received the letter from Mother. She wrote, '...so in the circumstances, Tony, we think it best if you return to England to complete your education. You have two more years of high school and we think it better that you finish at home. The education is better there and a good school name will look better on your CV. When you pass your 'O' levels, we'd like to see you go on to the 6th form and take your 'A' levels, for university entrance. You'll come home to Lindi, have most of your holiday here and then we'll return to Sudbury Hill in time for you to start at Harrow High.'

I told Hazel, at our first opportunity to get together.

"Why?" she asked. "If your dad's not leaving East Africa, why do you have to go to the U.K.?"

"My parents say they don't think the schooling here is all that great. My marks aren't very good and they think this school may be the reason."

"Did you tell them that last year, a boy in this school won higher marks for maths in the Overseas School Certificate than any student in the entire British Commonwealth?"

"I didn't know that. Who?"

"Don't you know? Balletto, you know Aurelio?"

"I don't know him well, no, although I've seen him around. He's senior to me. I know he's on the rugger team. He's in Curie, isn't he?"

"I think that says something about the quality of teaching."

"Hmm."

We paused to ponder; then Hazel said, "So you're leaving same as me, huh, except you're going to school in England and I'll be starting a job. My dad's got a job opportunity in Kampala."

"In Uganda?"

"Yes, of course; if he gets it then I suppose I'll go with him and Mum and get a job there. It's bigger than Nachingwea so my prospects will be better."

"I don't want to go," I suddenly blurted. "I don't want to leave you, Haze. England is so far away."

"Wherever you are, or I am, is going to be far away. Kampala isn't exactly next door, you know."

"It's a whole lot closer than London. I'm older now. I could get my parents to let me visit you in the hols."

"From what you told me about your mum I'm not so sure."

That gave me pause. "I know," I said. "You're old enough. Why don't you come to London to get a job, then you could live near to Sudbury Hill and me?"

"I don't know, Tony. We'll have to see. If it was easy, if I had the money, I wouldn't hesitate. But I haven't got any money, I'm seventeen, I'll have my 'O' levels, hopefully, by the end of this term but I doubt my parents would let me go by myself what with knowing no one in London, other than you that is. But I'll sound them out, you can be sure of that."

"I hope so, Haze, really I do."

After a long pause, "It's funny, you know," I said, "we were destined never to remain in Kongwa 'til the end of our schooldays... well, that is, I wasn't."

"What makes you say that?"

"I was talking to Fergie about the success of our play and one thing led to another. He told me he'd no longer be putting on plays in the open and building scenery outdoors. He says he'll be using a building that will be a proper theatre. There's going to be a new school."

"What new school?" asked Hazel.

"Well, that's it, you see, that's what I asked, what new school?"

"And?"

"Well, he said Kongwa is closing down during the short hols at the end of 1958. He says they're building a proper school in Iringa, not like this one, and that it will open in January 1959. They're calling it St. Michael's and St. George's. St. Michael's will be for the Juniors, I suppose. In fact this school is sometimes known as St. George's, he told me, that's why the school magazine is called *The Georgian*. He said Kongwa may be renamed St. George's even before it moves to Iringa. Anyway, everything will be moved there, that is everything they want to keep, I suppose, and the students only have to arrive when the time comes."

"Oh my gosh. I'm not sure I'd like that," said Hazel.

"I'm bloody sure I wouldn't," I followed. "There's going to be four hundred really disappointed kids now, well, the boys anyway, I don't know about you girls."

"Four hundred?"

"Yes, that's how many of us there are now, with the late arrival of a new boy in February."

"I hadn't heard that."

"It took long enough to get used to this place," I continued, "but, now I'm older and have you, it's so much better these days. I seem to get on more with the other chaps and even the teachers are nicer. I actually quite like it here."

"That new school will never be the same." said Hazel, "If it's being built as a school that means bye-bye fun times."

"I know it; can you imagine losing all the freedom? We've had new boys from Kenya who went to Prince of Wales school near Nairobi during the emergency. From what they said it sounded awful. I mean, those schools were like being locked up in a P.O.W. camp."

"A prison camp?"

"Yes, you know, kept in by barbed wire and all. The schools up there were surrounded by ten-foot-high, electrified, barbed fences, with lookout towers, searchlights, sand bags, armed guards and armed teachers. Used to be that there were privileges for leaving the school compound and going on forays into Nairobi – then it stopped; wasn't allowed at all. It was just like a prisoner of war camp. I hear it's eased up a bit now, but still and all"

"They had machine guns as well, I suppose?" Hazel smiled the question, not really believing it.

"Yes, I told you, like I said, the armed guards in the towers had machine guns. Just imagine. Behind those wire fences and lookout towers, everything would be concrete and brick or stone and clustered together. There's no getting out. Some of the schools, like Prince of Wales, are boys only or girls only so there would be no chance for you and me in those. And even the mixed schools have the girls so well separated from boys that we'd probably only ever get together in class...."

"Like it's supposed to be here," said Hazel with a smile.

"Yes, but that's the point... supposed to. In Nairobi there's no supposed to about it, it just is so.

"Wow."

"It used to be very different you know, before the Emergency, before the days of electric fences and Mau Mau. They had quite a lot of freedom, like we have. I remember being told one really funny story about going to and from school by train in Kenya. This boy, he was only here for one term, then left again. Anyway, his older brother had been at Prince of Wales in the old days, back before the war. He had a friend named John Cook, who had some amazing stories about the fun they used to have – like ambushing a train filled with girls an' all."

"Ambushing a train full of girls? You must tell me that one," Hazel enthused.

"Well, near as I can remember it, the story went something like this: You've heard of the Prince of Wales, I suppose?"

"Yes, of course. And yes, I do know that Nairobi Girl's High is not far away from it."

"Oh, so you've heard about the 'Heifer Boma'?"

Hazel clipped me round the head. "Don't you call us girls cows, Tony Edwards. Honestly, you boys are so rude!"

I chuckled as I put my hands up, trying to fend off the slaps. "Anyway, the main line of rail used to run alongside the school's boundary. But it had a steep gradient at this point and trains often spun their wheels and had a lot of difficulty getting up the incline. Anyway, as this chap Cook told it, it had been normal for both schools to break up at the same time. Most of the kids lived in or around Nairobi but there were also up-country pupils like we have and boys and girls from different schools would join the mail train that took them home for the hols. But in December one year, the railway authorities reported to the schools' principals that unruly behaviour had occurred on the pre-Christmas journey home and they'd had passenger complaints. So the principals decided that the girls would be sent home on a separate train, two days earlier than the boys at the end of future terms. The boys were devastated by the news, of course, especially as some had girlfriends at the high school. But anyway, about a dozen of them hatched a plan that would allow a swift but amorous rendezvous.

"For about ten days prior to the day on which the train carrying the girls was due to pass by, the boys involved endured dry bread with lunch and dinner, smuggling their butter rations out of the dining room and storing them in their leader's locker. When the big day arrived, the train carrying the girls was due to pass the school at 4:15 p.m. at a time when formal classes in the boys' school were finished and sports about to begin. At 4 o'clock, the boys rushed across the boundary fence and smeared their hard-won butter ration on about ninety feet of both rails. Hearing the approaching locomotive, they dived into cover in the bushes alongside the rail and waited.

"The train was making heavy weather of the steep gradient and no sooner did it reach the buttered section than the main drive wheels of the engine started to spin frantically as the driver applied increased steam pressure and the train came to a steaming, wheel-spinning halt. But the Sikh driver was prepared for such an event. Quite often in the past, early morning rime on the rails in the highlands had caused this skidding and the answer was to spread sand along the affected line to provide grip for the spinning wheels. The driver descended from the engine cab with a bucket of sand and started spreading it on the rails.

"Meanwhile, from every open window in the coach carrying the girls, young heads peered out, curious as to the reason for this unscheduled stop, although they knew they were opposite the boys school, of course. No sooner had the driver – now joined by the guard – gone to the far side of the locomotive to apply sand to the track than the boys broke cover and boarded the girls' coach, to the screaming delight of the girls.

"The couples had so little time. Lots of hugs and snuggles. Exchanges of small tokens of love and then the sound of increased steam activity as the driver began to get the train under way. One final kiss to each of their beloved and the daring dozen leapt from the moving carriage – then standing beside the embankment to wave a fond, but sad, farewell to their sweethearts.

Apparently this little trick happened on several occasions before the authorities finally rumbled it, and the cane was brought out and used on errant suitors."

Hazel chuckled and giggled at the story – we both did, then we fell quiet again as we pondered how things had changed in Kenya.

"Just think," I said, after a while, "poor old Berry's going to school in Nairobi now. He must be in the thick of all that Mau Mau stuff. I wonder how it's going for him?"

"When did he leave... end of last term?"

"Yes, at Christmas. He lives in Kisumu now, that's why he goes to school in Nairobi."

"Have you heard from him, got a letter or anything?"

"No. He said he'd write, but he hasn't yet."

"Why do they have barbed-wire fences?" Hazel asked as if catching up on what I'd mentioned earlier. "Do they have too many boys running away?" she quizzed displaying a mischievous smile while getting in the dig.

"You'd never have known that if I hadn't confessed to you," I said reproachfully. "But anyway, no, that's not the problem. It's the Mau Mau thing. The schools have the fences and guards to keep the Mau Mau out, not the students in."

"Oh my gosh," said Hazel, as if believing what I'd told her for the first time. "Really?"

"Uh huh, that's what I heard from the chaps who'd been there. And I know that the grown-ups in the government are worried that Mau Mau could spread even further into Tanganyika too; that's why my dad bought a gun. They've already crossed the border into northern parts you know?"

"Yes, I remember you telling me. Yikes, can you imagine?" asked Hazel, frowning. "Being in a Nairobi school and being attacked maybe, and you could see and hear all the gunfire and yelling and what-not going on the other side of the fences, with bullets flying around and all, and there you are inside and you can't escape. I don't think I'd like that and I'm sure my parents wouldn't."

"Can you imagine being in this school where we're spread over a couple-a hundred or more acres and have no protection if there was a Mau Mau attack?" I said, as I recalled the story of the Mau Mau cell adventure that I'd told my friends one night.

Hazel stared wide-eyed. "Holy mackerel that would be sooo scary."

"The only reason I'm here is because we're in Tanganyika," I said. "When we were first coming to East Africa, Mum said no to me going to school in Nairobi, because of the Mau Mau. You see, at first they thought that's where I'd have to go. They thought there wasn't a secondary school for Europeans in Tanganyika. Parents used to send their kids to Nairobi or Salisbury in Rhodesia or back to England. If my dad had been sent to Kenya I'd have been left in England like I was when he and Mum were in West Africa. If that had happened, I'd have been sent to Canterbury. Little did Mum think there could be Mau Mau in Tanganyika too."

"Canterbury, huh? I've heard of that," said Hazel. "That's a public school for boys, isn't it?"

"Yes, and disciplined, and rigid, and scary as bloody hell."

"But," said Hazel, "you're going back to an English school anyway."

"Yes, a grammar school but it's a day school, so that's something. That'll make a big difference. I'll travel to and from school on the tube or by bus. At least I won't be locked up behind walls, hidden from the outside world."

"Hmm, see what you mean, but…."

The bell rang for classes. We straightened up ready to get back.

"Want to get together tonight? I can get Egbert."

"I want to," replied Hazel. "I really, really want to… but I can't."

My heart, which had been beating faster at the thought, suddenly sank. "Why not?" I frowned.

"I have to swot, Tony, you know that. In a few weeks it will be exams. I have to pass my 'O' levels no matter what. I'm working hard at it every night before lights-out. You do understand, don't you?"

"That's before lights-out – what about *after* lights-out, that's what I'm talking about?" I asked plaintively.

"After lights-out I swot too, a lot of us do. Once Matron has gone, we get out our torches and do more reading under the sheets 'til we fall asleep."

"I see, Hazel," I sighed, knowing we did the same thing. "All right, I suppose I do understand."

The break area was almost clear of students.

"We'd better get to class. Let's talk later if we get a chance."

"Okay, kwa heri sasa."

The truth was I also had a lot on, especially after class hours with the drama club. We were putting on Shakespeare's *The Merchant of Venice*, and I'd been slacking learning my lines. Mr. Ferguson was showing impatience because he knew I could do it, and do it better than anyone else he said, and yet constantly in rehearsals I was letting myself and them down. I resolved that if Hazel was going to spend all her time studying for exams, than I would throw myself into my part in the play. I was, after all, playing the lead role of my namesake, Antonio.

"I'm sorry, sir," I began, as soon as I arrived at the class, intending to take the wind out of Mr. Ferguson's sails. "I've not studied my lines any better than I did last time. But I'm telling you this honestly, sir, straight out before we get going, because I've resolved that this is changing. I'm getting fully into the role from now on and by the time we next meet I'll have them down pat, you'll see, sir."

"All right," Mr. Ferguson replied, as he regarded me sceptically. "We will see indeed. You can keep your script handy for today's rehearsal but by next week I expect you to know every last word, flawlessly. If you don't, I'm cancelling the play and that will be the end of it. Now, let's proceed as best we can."

I also had end-of-term exams coming up. I found I was vying with myself as to which I was going to work hardest at – maths which was my worst subject, French, Latin, English language, English literature, history, geography, physics, science, biology, technical drawing or the play. It suddenly became a whirlwind of effort, which I could only focus on because Hazel was not able to meet. It was tough enough as it was, whenever the thought of her overtook my mind.

Now that Berry had left, Hazel helped me with maths as often as she could when I just didn't get it, but of course she wouldn't be there when exam time came. Hazel was lucky. Maths came naturally to her, where for me it was a struggle. Doug was never far away. When I wasn't swotting I was out with him breaking some rule or other. And Burns was around, casual, relaxed and a good friend.

THE WEEKS PASSED. THE RAINY SEASON ENDED and the dry heat returned, if a little less intense now, while Kongwa's natural reddish-grey colour reappeared.

The Merchant of Venice had been a great success. Mr. Ferguson had been so pleased the way it came together that he cajoled Miss Strong into letting the girls attend the performance too. I received congratulatory slaps on the back, even from boys who used not to like me much. The funniest thing was with Burns next day in class. He'd played a first class Portia, having replaced Stew as our female lead role in a Shakespeare play. When we reviewed his performance, the girls picked up on it.

Avril Jenner teased him, given that she was once one of his short-lived girlfriends, when she said, "You know, Andy, you were so good at that part, so much like a girl, I think I'm going to have to come to you for lessons on how to be a better girl."

The class erupted.

"I want lessons too," Anita Beyer joined in.

"It's her eyelashes," said Julie Baker. "Sorry, I mean his eyelashes; they're so gorgeous; may I borrow your eyelash brush, Andy?"

"Very funny," smiled Burns, blushing in embarrassment at the teasing and the warm congratulations at the same time.

Pepsi, not to be left out, added, "Hey, Burns, can I date you?"

Roars of laughter.

Mr. Ferguson interluded, "Westley… correct English is, *may* I date you, not, *can* I date you. The issue is not whether you can, we know you can, the question is whether or not the young lady is prepared to participate. You are seeking permission, not to know that you are physically able, therefore the question is, *may I date you?*"

"Yes, sir."

"Get in the queue, you're after me," cut in Jenner.

More laughter from the entire class with Mr. Ferguson chuckling too, letting us have our fun, perhaps because we were close to the end of term now and after all, we'd made him proud to be a drama teacher.

I LAY IN BED LISTENING TO THE others asleep. My mind wandered through the years in Kongwa. There was one more week of term, then, for the last time, I'd be going home for the summer, so-called because it was summer in Europe but really it was winter, such as that was, in East Africa. Thank goodness the heat had dropped. It'll be cooler still in July and August, when we're not here.

I felt overwhelmed with mixed thoughts about leaving Tanganyika. On the one hand, I recalled telling my parents during one of my holidays that I wished I was back in England. They had come up with a number of arguments to do with the exciting life of East Africa and how it lent so much more freedom than would be the case back home.

"How many boys have ridden on a plane?" Mother had asked me. "Never mind flown to school in one."

My glib retort had been, "I think it would be more exciting riding the Underground than one of those smelly, bumpy planes."

Mother didn't have an answer to that. My emotions in those days were not readily assuaged. Now I wasn't so sure. The freedom I'd experienced in Africa was, if not unique, certainly something few children in the West would experience. This school, however, was unique. I'd hated it to start with, but then, I hated boarding school anyway. But it had grown on me, as had Africa. With the passing terms and as I got older, life was less stressful and much more fun... especially with a girlfriend and all.

Africa was where it had all started, where humans had evolved in the beginning, or so anthropologists like Mary Leaky were telling the world. And here, in Kongwa, we lived in a tiny village, surrounded by as much wilderness as there'd ever been in thousands of years, where animals and reptiles roamed free. The Africans in their natural habitat were so at home, self-reliant and such nice people. I'd not known English people as ready to laugh as these Wagogo; mostly the English moaned.

It was dawning on me how lucky I was to have lived in Africa. No matter what became of me, or my life, there was no taking away my school days here, the good along with the bad. I'd spent several months in England a couple of years ago because my grandpa was ill. I'd gone to school, for one term, at Harrow High. The discipline and restrictions in the school were so strong, as were the social expectations publicly that it took little imagination to foresee what it would be like living there; worse yet in a boarding school. And then I thought of Allan House, my pre-Kongwa days, and how unhappy

I'd been. But the worst thought now was in leaving Hazel. What were we going to do if she couldn't come to England?

I propped myself up against the wall and gazed through the mesh and bars at the outdoors that stretched forever. I watched the hyenas sniffing around and never did understand what they found of such interest. I thought about how the females are the leaders and dominate hyena cackles. It seemed strange. Typically in the animal kingdom the male was in charge but not so with hyenas. I'd learned that hyenas' sworn enemies are lions. No one seemed to know why, they just are. A lion will kill a hyena just for fun; they don't want to eat it. Lions don't do that with other animals. That begged thinking about.

The lionesses are the most active, the main hunters in the lion pride too, but in spite of their practical domination, they still defer to the lion. The hyena male on the other hand was nothing except as a source for making cubs. He was lucky if the clan left him enough food to eat. I wasn't sure I'd want to be male if I was a hyena. But hyenas were only one of the myriad species of animals, insects and reptiles that I'd come to know... and love.

I thought about our Sunday trips out and Boy Scout weekends. The fright with the lionesses chasing us, the hunting we'd done, the snakes and iguanas, the mamba in the choo, the openness of the savannah, the water buffalo, zebras and the giraffes, the elephants and the Wagogo kijijis and their ng'omas and not a little shame at swiping some of their mahindi. The wild of Africa was thrilling, the call of Africa, unmistakable.

We European boys had been as much an integral part of the wildness when we'd pursued our unprotected adventures in the bush. Africa's smells, its sounds, its wind and its rains were to be found nowhere else. England was nothing like it. And the Africans? I'd not really had as much to do with them as I'd have liked, yet I had got to know them somewhat. I knew I liked them, found them to be friendly to a fault and with the keenest sense of humour you'd find anywhere. Wherever the Wagogo congregated there was laughter.

The generator noise cut out, bringing me out of my reverie. The electricity plant continued to shut down from around two in the morning, just as it always had during the last – what was it? – five and a half years now. The insects had not got used to this, so when it was turned off, they'd switch off too for a few seconds. Then they'd switch on again, all at the same time. How can millions of insects stop their chirruping and buzzing and whistling at the identical moment and then start up again at the same moment? I didn't have an answer. As far as I knew, no one did.

It was Tuesday and classes were over. We would depart on Thursday, first by lorry to Dodoma, then on the *Kongwa Special*, along with over three hundred of the rest of the school's kids and many of the teachers. A day earlier, the buses that carried north and west-bound students, like Doug and Susan, would depart. From Dodoma they would catch either the north-bound mail to places like Mwanza and Kigoma or alternatively a bus to Arusha or Moshi. Then the buses would return for the girls the following day. I'd exchanged addresses with Doug; we would write to each other. He said he thought he too would soon be returning to England, somewhere in the London area, but it wasn't definite.

Tonight was the big night; the night of the end-of-term dance. I was excited because everyone knew Hazel and I were going steady and that I would be dancing with her all evening, no question. We'd been taught that it is permitted for a man to cut-in in the middle of a dance, forcing the male dancing with the woman to step aside while the new male took over the fe-male partner for the duration of that dance, a matter of etiquette with which those of us with girlfriends did not approve. But then, of course, if it was known you were going steady it was unlikely any boy would take his safety into his hands by being so presumptuous; so I anticipated few problems in that respect. What I was burning to do was hold Hazel tight and close and to have her to myself all evening.

Now I was helping set the dance floor up on the Club's tennis courts. Robert Compaan, this year's Head Boy, was organising and called me over, "Edwards, I need you to go to the end of the net on the other side of the court and unhitch it from its tie at the post."

"Yes, Robert."

"Westley, are you helping or not?"

Doug was heavily into conversation with Pam who, as usual, could get time off.

"Oh er yes, Robert, what should I do?"

"See those boxes over there?"

"Yes."

"They contain the lights I want to string up around the tennis courts. The white ones I want to light the perimeter of both courts. The coloured ones are to be criss-crossed at angles over the top of the courts. I'd like you to start unravelling them and getting them laid out."

"All right, Robert, I'll get going."

"Here, I'll help you," joined in Pam, and the two of them moved off towards the boxes.

Elsewhere other prefect organisers had marshalled boys to carry chairs from the classrooms to our location. Soon there would be enough chairs set to one side of the perimeter to seat the girls. On the opposite side the boys would be positioned without chairs, standing room only. Perhaps it was thought that leaving the boys standing was the encouragement needed for them to select a girl from across the courts and ask for a dance. It was well-known that many of the younger ones were shy, and would need prodding; something I well remembered. Of course, the situation wasn't helped for them knowing that, having summoned the courage to invite a girl to dance, two things could go wrong. The first was that another chap had selected the same girl and got to her before you, resulting in a U-turn in the middle of the floor and having to face your colleagues as you arrived back, looking stupid and feeling sheepish. You could avoid the U-turn by coming to a halt, re-assessing the available talent and determining if there was anyone left that you wouldn't be ashamed to be seen dancing with. But that was embarrassing too, standing there in the middle of the dance floor, eyes wandering left to right as you surveyed the remnants of schoolgirl pulchritude.

The other unattractive outcome was that you arrived at the feet of your heart's desire and made bold with your invitation, only to be declined. The girls were supposed to have been taught that it was incorrect etiquette, not to say un ladylike, to turn down a boy's invitation to dance, but if so, it was a lesson that hadn't always sunk in. Indeed, it had been noted on occasion that a girl, having declined a boy, might be seen, moments later, dancing merrily with another girl. Girls could do that.

So the end-of-term dance was not something everyone looked forward to. But these days I certainly did. In fact Hazel and I had managed a brief get together just yesterday in which I told her I'd been co-opted to help Compaan and could not get away to meet in the donga. She'd said she would come to the courts if she could, maybe she'd help out too if Pam Chambers was there.

Hazel was not able to get away as it turned out, leaving me feeling desolate. We were running out of term. Within a day or two we'd be gone our separate ways, not knowing when we'd be together again. I was desperate to talk to her, to hold her tight, to find some way that we could keep this going.

But evening dinner came, and went, and now it was time to wander down our short tarred road to the tennis courts, now the colourfully-lit dance floor. I left the mess with Burns and Jenner, and Pepsi joined us from the Wilberforce end.

"Let's get down there," said Doug, ready to go. "I'm sure Pam's waiting for me. How about you Tony, Hazel will be there, of course?"

"It's all right for you two," said Jenner. "You two have girlfriends, no concerns at who you'll dance with, but Andy and me, we have to take our chances."

"Handsome blokes like you," said Doug, "no problem. You'll quickly scoop up the best available."

"Thanks, Pepsi," said Burns, ever sensitive to being a shorty, "that's very reassuring, 'til we get there." And then reminding himself that he was usually positive, he added, "Anyhow, you're right, it'll be fun."

"Hey, wait for me." Aranky came running up.

It looked exciting. The white lights of the perimeter contrasted with the coloured lights overhead. Boys were dressed in their blazers. I think the girls brought special dresses with them at the beginning of term especially for the end-of-term dance because I was sure I'd not seen most of the outfits before. The girls were beautiful in spite of there not being a single powder compact or tube of lipstick between them. And their hairdos, considering there were no hairdressers, were amazing. Clearly there was much co-operation, helping each other out. Maybe that was why Hazel hadn't turned up in the morning – she was helping her friends too.

This was the first term that the school had acquired a HiFi stereo system. The machine ran off electricity, it played LPs and it had large extension speakers with one placed at one end of the floor and the second speaker at the other. Music for the first dance was playing but the boys were slow to get started. Pepsi was having trouble picking out Pam in the crowd. I hesitated. I'd spotted Hazel, I wanted to dance but, golly, I didn't want to be first on the floor with the whole school watching. What must I do? *I can't wait much longer.*

Thank goodness, Senior prefect Keith Jones led the floor with his partner. The two were quickly followed by Robert Compaan and his girlfriend, a pair of prefects, then another, then Mr. and Mrs. Moore. I moved, strolling boldly across the floor, eyes fixed on Hazel, although out of the corner of my eye I knew Pepsi was on his way too, as he'd spotted Pam. As I approached, Hazel returned my gaze, demurely she dropped her chin, looking seductive and lovely in that gorgeous, flouncy dress that I'd not seen before, and a beautiful hair do.

On reaching her I stopped, with hands at my sides I bowed with a nod of the head, the way we were supposed to, then enquired politely while extending a hand, "May I have the pleasure of the next dance, my lady?"

Hazel held out a languid arm, a hand for me to take, and then as if sniffing the air, "I'd be delighted, kind sir," she responded. And with that I led her to the floor where we waltzed to the songs of Ella Fitzgerald or the music of Johann Strauss. We didn't leave the floor for forty minutes. A long play record lasted about that long playing both sides, so we took a breather only when it had come to an end and Mr. Brownlow was changing to a new disc.

By the end of the second forty minutes, the air was electric. The volume had been cranked and when *The Gay Gordons*, that had drawn practically the entire school to the floor, came to a final crescendo, we took a rest.

"Come," said Hazel, "let's go for a while. I want you to myself."

With the lines between boys and girls now blurred it was easy to slip away without being noticed. Immediately beyond the perimeter of white lights, the darkness was absolute.

"Oh, that was wonderful," breathed Hazel, puffing and still out of breath. "You're not a bad dancer, you know?"

"That's because I have the inspiration with you," I coo'd my reply. "Without you I am as nothing," I said with an affected Latin accent.

"Silly boy," said Hazel and then dropped her chin, but too late for I saw sadness in her eyes.

"What's the matter? Why are you sad? Come on, there's grass just behind the gladioli bed. Let's sit down there."

"I got a letter from home today," sniffed Hazel as we sat close. "My dad said *no*," she came out with it bluntly. "I wrote to my parents to ask them about London, you know?"

"No, I didn't know you'd written. Actually I thought you might ask them once you arrived home."

"Well," said Hazel, "I thought about that too, of course, but then I thought I'd give them some thinking time. I expected more of a *we'll see* kind of response, because, you know, Mum really liked you, but it was a flat *no*."

"Do you know why? Does your dad have a particular reason, like money, or is he guarding his precious daughter?"

"Probably a bit of both, although he blames the money situation mostly. He says they have a big move coming that's going to cost them a lot; I told you about Kampala, didn't I? He wrote that he couldn't afford to maintain two households, especially not a second one in London. It's a whole lot more expensive there. He said he knows I'd get a job and contribute but that I could never afford London by myself. He wrote that when I can afford to do the paying by myself, then it would be my choice. Until then I should remain at home."

Hazel looked at me with huge sad eyes, tears running more freely down her cheeks. "What are we going to do, Tony? I can't bear the parting!"

"Good night, good night, parting is such sweet sorrow," I said with the affectation of a stage play.

"How could you be so unconcerned, Tony?" Hazel frowned. "Is that all you feel?"

"I'm sorry Haze, really I am – too much Shakespeare with Fergie, I expect. I didn't mean to be flippant, you must know that?"

"Yes," she sniffed.

"Well then. We'll have to think. For the moment we'll have to keep closely in touch, write letters, wait for time to pass and then we'll find a way. Isn't that what they say, love finds a way."

"I suppose so," sniffed Hazel. "I know in the war young couples were parted for years at a time, hardly ever got letters from each other and yet somehow held on until the soldier boy came home… if he came home."

"Well, there's no war on now, I don't think, now that the Suez crisis is over, more or less… Come here," I said, as I snuggled her up tight, then kissed her long and sweet. She returned it with increasing passion until we were all over each other.

Out of the blue, even I wasn't expecting it, I said, "I love you so much, Haze."

Hazel just looked into my eyes at that, with so much caring, but, all choked up, she waved her hand in front of her mouth and said weepily, "I love you too."

In the distance we could hear the music playing as enthusiastically as ever.

After a long silence I changed the subject and said, "Brownlow did a great job with the music this year, don't you think?" I so wanted to make Hazel happy. We couldn't part being sad.

"Yes, he did," she said suddenly perking up. "This won't do. I can't believe I'm being this silly. It's not the way to be. And in any case we'll see each other on the train."

"Yes, although I don't s'pose we'll get a chance to be alone," I replied. "But yes. And then again on the plane. You'll be flying off to Nach the next morning and I'll be en route to Lindi so we can sit together."

"Yes, we will. You won't have to fight for the seat with Annelize, now that she and her family have moved to Dar. Do you know that her dad is now Head Chef at the New Africa?"

"No, I didn't. Good for him," I said.

"Annelize says she likes Dar much better, she's happier there."

"Let's get back to the dance – maybe we'll feel better if we do," I suggested.

"What time does the train leave, do you know?" Hazel asked as we got up, brushing off the newly slashed grass and strolled towards the lights and the music.

"We're supposed to leave Dodoma at 2:00 p.m. like last term. We'll be getting on the lorries at around 10:30 or 11 o'clock and arrive in Dodoma around 1:00."

"Lorries? Who travels on lorries?" Hazel feigned superiority.

"Oh, excuse me," I retorted in exaggerated tone, "I'm soooo sorry I forgot you poor girls have to travel in namby pamby buses. You can't rough it standing in the back of an open lorry like boys have to."

"Well, we're special," said Hazel with a pout. "And in any case, there's nothing namby pamby about it. The buses' bench seats are made of wood as hard as rock and there aren't any cushions. We have a real bum ache by the time we've bounced our way to Dodoma. Not only that but it hasn't got any windows either so all the dust flies in all over you unless you roll down the canvas blinds - and then it's stifling and you can't see anything."

"Yes, well, we have to try to remain standing the whole way and be blown by swirling dust for what is it, fifty miles?"

"Fifty-seven, according to Massowia."

"Massowia! Who's Massowia?"

"One of my friends. You don't know her, but she knows all that sort of stuff."

"Well anyway, once we arrive," I continued, "and brushed off the dust, that'll leave an hour, maybe a bit less, to load. Then it'll be the usual over-night train ride. They don't want us arriving in Dar at 2 a.m. like we do coming here. The parents would have something to say about that! We should arrive around eight in the morning, after breakfast."

As we walked back around the bushes towards the dance floor, my mind drifted to memories of that train journey and what a happy occasion it always was....

From the time the huge Garrett locomotive slipped its brakes, those mas-sive drive wheels skidded for traction, and the extended shriek of its whistle echoed through the streets and alleys of Dodoma, the atmosphere was elec-tric. Everyone was happy and there was never a quarrel. Teachers might frown benignly at some mild transgression which, at another time, would warrant chastisement. We'd be up from our bunks before dawn in anticipa-tion of arrival and anxious for breakfast before we pulled into Dar es Salaam at eight o'clock.

By half past seven the rail line was once more hemmed by the vivid ever-green of the coastal rain forest, our first view of a deep, lush green in almost six months. A hundred and fifty or more children would be leaning out the windows on each side of the train, staring ahead in anticipation of being the first to see Dar es Salaam Station in the distance. With hair streaming and eyes screwed up at the rushing wind, the feeling of elation was palpable. The very engine seemed to be racing as though it too was excited. The near con-stant whistle, *hoot-hoooot, hoot-hoooot*, must have been warning Africans who used the railway as a footpath, and cars and lorries at the unguarded crossings that we were coming fast, but to us it was a happy engine driver entering into the spirit of bringing us safely home for the holidays… and not a minute to spare.

Now there was a general movement to the right side of the train. The platform was always on the right, so half as many children again would leave the left side and the corridor to squeeze in beside their friends in the compartment, seeking a piece of that precious open window space so that now there would be three hundred and more young faces smiling and waving out the one side.

Hoot-hoooot, went the whistle before level crossings with cars and lorries stopped, awaiting patiently the train's passing as we flew by, doing nearly forty miles an hour on the down grade. Drivers waved; smiling faces from behind the windscreens, some climbing from seats to lean on their open door and watch the amazing sight of hundreds of children waving and cheering.

Then, at long last, we rounded the last corner, *hoot-hoooot*. The train would slow to a crawl, in the distance the terminus in sight. As we drew close, chuffing triumphantly towards its shady embrace, you couldn't see the platform for adults; two hundred or more sets of parents standing there, anxious and excited to greet us home. The train inched alongside the platform, with three hundred sets of eyes searching for parents. Mothers craned their necks, hoping to spot their offspring; the dads stood back, looking stoic, it not being good form to show too much emotion. Whoops and screams of recognition overtook the fading gasps of steam. At last the train drew to a squeaky halt.

I was never met by my parents but with the passage of time Franz and Jean Kherer had become warm substitutes. I loved those two and got almost as much pleasure when we would finally sight each other….

Then my reverie was interrupted.

"Hello, anyone at home? I'll give you a penny for them," Hazel said, running a hand in front of my eyes. "Boy, you were far away."

"Oh," I said, "I was just thinking about the train journey and how exciting it is."

"I know, isn't it great? I love the ride too – especially on the way home."

We rejoined the lights and sound of this most successful ever end-of-term dance. The music was loud, the air sultry, everyone drenched in sweat, the beads of perspiration reflecting like spotty kaleidoscopes under the coloured lights. The girls' hair was becoming unravelled, boys had loosened their ties and shed their blazers, the insects were trying to overcome our noise for a change, mosquitoes were being slapped on necks, teachers were frowning at couples who were snuggling too smoochy on the dance floor and, if you had any pocket money left, you could still buy a warm Coke from the stand set up by the duka's proprietor.

Back on the dance floor, we held each other close as Frank Sinatra crooned his melodic voice into our hearts and memories. Hazel laid her head on my shoulder and as she did an overwhelming feeling of love and at the same time sadness washed over me. I lifted Hazel's chin to kiss her slow and sweet, taking a chance we'd be spotted, and then I simply hugged her tight. After a while she pushed me back gently as she felt my shiver of sadness, then gazed into my eyes and watched the tears running down my cheeks. With that lovely smile of hers she shook her head gently.

"Silly boy," she said.

EPILOGUE

THERE IS A SCHOOL IN KONGWA ONCE more, this time for the Africans. Called Mnyakongo, it caters to eight hundred local boys and girls. Four hundred receive a primary education each morning and the other four hundred each afternoon. It is very poor and has only been connected with electricity since 2010, the P.W.D. electricity plant that we knew having long since been shut down. Until recently it didn't have any desks and chairs either. The children sat on the same concrete slabs of the buildings we studied in. Those buildings have long since fallen apart but new ones have been built on those same foundations.

A cohort of ex-Kongwa school kids in Britain, Australia and the USA (Mnyakongo School Project) have been devoting time, money and fund-raising efforts since 2008 to help Mnyakongo obtain services and better cater to their children. Tanzania has a national grid these days and the Mnyakongo School Project negotiated a contract to bring electricity to the school boundary. This is now complete. During two visits in 2010, groups connected with the project returned to the school with volunteers and some students from San Diego State University with boxes of donated books for a new library; to complete the orders for desks and chairs; to paint buildings; to get the school wired for electricity and connected to the grid; to improve plumbing services and to present to the school its first computers.

If any reader would like to know more about this project and the current activities of the Kongwa contingent, please check out the website: http://kongwaconnected.org and/or the project founder, Barbara Laing, at laing.b@sky.com.

The author is donating 50% of the profits from sales of this book, to the Mnyakongo School Project.

KONGWA PHOTO ALBUM

Kongwa facing south from Number 2 Unit. The low, dark hill at left is Kongwa
Hill. The low hill foreground to the right almost lost against the larger hill
behind is Church Hill. The large hill behind at right is Leopard Hill. The
pointed tip in the distance is the tallest in the region at about 2000 feet and
known to us as Children's Mount. It is part of the Kiboriani range five miles
to the south of Kongwa. The Groundnut Scheme's encampment, eventually to
become the school, was set the length of the base of Kongwa Hill and stretched
to the base of Church Hill   *Photo by Hugh Prentice*

Most of the Kongwa School teachers 1955

Some of my teachers at Kongwa in 1955

Tony at age 13,
dressed for dinner

Douglas and Susan Westley

Livingstone House Seniors, 1955

From back left: 1. Sigurd Ivey; George Vorias; Gordon Von Staden; Alan
Alder; Mike Gunston; Anthony Edwards; Mike Delpeche; Jack Allan; Graham
Muddle; Ian Priestley

2. Joe Grandcourt; Norman Vutirakis; Rolando Keller; Coen Compaan; Louis
Mukabaa; Edwin Vutirakis; Pete Bekker; Alan Jones; Neil Thomson

3. Graham Russell; Stewart Berry; Ian Cook; Mike Jenner; John Punter; Donald
McLachlan; Peter Taylor; Henry Rushby; Zbyszek Mieszek

4. Robert Compaan; Keith Jones; Mr Brownlow; Mrs. Katherine Moore;
Maurice Moore; Michael Holiday; Pete Gemmell; Brian Marriott

Ian Cook   Stewart Berry   Sigurd Ivey   Hazel Miller

Kongwa Hill with Kiboriani Range in background and Mount Sang'anga (Children's Mount). *Photo taken in 2010, courtesy of Ian Cook*

Our favourite climbing baobab

The mountains Goggles and Tony faced.
Photo courtesy Ian Cook

Sheba's Breasts.
Photo courtesy Ian Cook

Kongwa Club pool, with possibly Miss
Strong, Miss Taylor and Miss Currie

The duka

Dar es Salaam rail station

Kongwa's rail station.
Photo by Barb Laing

Train safari to school

The Mess

A Seniors' classroom block - with
cinema screen

Seniors' phase – author's house,
rear entrance

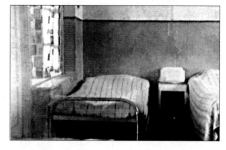

Author's bed

Author's house – front
entrance at far end

The author atop Snake Rock

Mickey Thomas, Roger
Nicholson, Rena Neish,
Maxine Meerloo and
Biddy Goodricke

Constantinides on the school
milk gharri

Lucy Ptnashnik, Marie Ebner,
Hannah Bayer and Lesley Evans

Donald McLachlan, Stewart
Berry and Tony Edwards

Judi Moore with puff adder
and Stephanie (Steve)

Bobby Van Weiden, Robin Hoy,
Marzio Zanardi, Vico Mansutti, Jimmy
Richmond

Nadia Aranky

Ian Cook and Tony Edwards crossing
the donga on the baobab root

Cub troop
Back: Six names-unknown
assistants
Middle: Peter Curly, Clive Knight,
Robert Seabrook
Front: Kenneth Aranky, Alex
Morrison, Billy Neish, Sigurd Ivey,
Cubs Akela Miss Hambleton

E.A.R. Garrett Locomotive
with water tender

The Beach Hotel,
Lindi

Hazel at right, with friends, at
Nachingwea Airfield

Carrying Sheddy's kasukus and
cage to the plane

Tony, Rolando, Egbert and Annelize
at Lindi airfield about to board the
E.A.A. Dakota to Dar es Salaam

Walking to E.A.A. flight at Lindi
Airfield. Annelize second from right,
her mum, me, Tony with dog Binty,
my mum in background. Girl at front
right thought to be Pat Kerswell, with
her mum at far left

The New Africa Hotel, Dar es Salaam

Office and godown for the
Twentsche Overseas Trading
Company in Lindi, 1953

T.O.M.'s block of flats in Lindi. Ours was at top

Left: The living room with Figaro

Mum and Dad entertaining the
McNeils and unknown on the
balcony

Dad crashed in his car to the base of this escarpment

Dad standing on the balcony of the ward in Nairobi Hospital

Lindi street scene

The wrecked dhow on Lindi Beach

The Hon.
Leslie Edwards,
Mayor of Lindi

Lindi Beach

A Tanganyikan road

McKinnon's Rest

On Safari. The main highway to Songea.
Author seated on Land Rover

Celebration for Princess Margaret – she
is seen shaking hands with a VIP

Two of the three sailors from *HMS
Liverpool* with me and Mother

See more Kongwa School photos at http://kongwaconnected.org which
is the website for former Kongwa students who are helping Mnyakongo
School which occupies the same site.

GLOSSARY

ablution	performing ablutions is the act of washing oneself
aloaceous	scrub growth from the aloe family
armoured spider	spider with hard, fluted shell on its back
asante sana	*Swahili* - thank you very much
askari	*Swahili* - guard
baobab	the baobab is called the tree of life. It is capable of providing shelter, food and water for the animal and human inhabitants of the African savannah regions.
Bell and Howell	16mm film projector
bergens	SAS military or military-style rucksack
biltong	cured, dried meat that originated in South Africa. It is similar to beef jerky in that both are spiced, dried meats. Biltong does not have a sweet taste.
bioscope	*South African English* - cinema
boerevors	*Afrikaans* - farmer's sausage
boma	*Swahili* - stockade, fortress. The word was adopted by the British in East Africa as a name for the town hall or government offices.
bwana	*Swahili* - mister, master. Used as a form of respectful address in parts of Africa.

casuarina tree	a striking, graceful tree that grows in lower tropical elevations, particularly around the coast
centi kumi	*Swahili* - ten cents
chakula	*Swahili* - food
chammy	chameleon
choo/dub	*Swahili* - outhouse toilet
chumba cha kulala	*Swahili* - bedrooms
coin with a hole in the middle	East Africa's ten-cent coin had a hole in the middle for stringing together in the absence of pockets in clothing
cosies	swimming costumes, trunks
coupe	twin bed compartment, on a train
dahabieh	a traditional Egyptian sailing boat
dawa	*Swahili* - medicine
deep square leg	cricket term for a particular fielder's location
dekko	look, as in take a look
dhobi	*Swahili* - laundry
dhow	generic name of a number of traditional sailing vessels with one or more masts with lateen sails used in the Red Sea and Indian Ocean
dikdik	small antelope
dishdashas	a long white robe usually worn by men in the Middle East
dom	*Afrikaans* - dummy, foolish one
donga	*Swahili* - river bed, dried up
Dover stove	brand name for a wood-fired cooking stove
duka	corner store
Dunhill	brand name, cigarette lighter
dustbins	garbage can

fag	a boy required to fetch and carry for an older boy, usually a prefect (has nothing to do with sexual orientation). Fag is also a cigarette.
felloes	metal rims around wooden wheels to reduce wear
fimbo	*Swahili* - walking stick
fly nut and butterfly nut	wing nuts
francolins	birds, members of the pheasant family
gaboon viper	an especially dangerous/poisonous snake
gari-ya-moshi	*Swahili* - steam train
godverdomme	*Afrikaans* - goddamnit
habari	*Swahili* - abbreviation of habari gani – how are you doing?
howzat	how was that? – a term shouted by the fielding team in cricket when they think they have caused a batter in the opposing team to be out. The referee decides if the batter should be out.
humpy	*Australian* - tiny cabin in the outback. A humpy is a small, temporary shelter made from bark and tree branches, traditionally used by Australian aborigines.
hyrax	a small, thickset, herbivorous mammal. Hyraxes are well-furred, rotund creatures with short tails that measure 30 to 70 cm long and weigh 2 to 5 kg.
hyena cackle	cackle is the collective name for hyenas
in rout	phonetic American pronunciation of en route
jambo	*Swahili* - greeting, how are you, abbreviation of hamjambo
jigger	the chigoe flea is a parasitic arthropod found in most tropical and sub-tropical climates
jong	*Afrikaans* - young one
juju	(originally West African) witchcraft

kanga	a colourful garment worn by women throughout Eastern Africa
kanzu	a kanzu is a white or cream colored robe worn by men in East African countries. In English, the robe is called a tunic.
kasukus	*Swahili* - parakeet
kaya	*Swahili* - household
kelele	noise, uproar, shouting, din
kibandas	hut, shed, cabin
kiboko	*Swahili* - whip, made from hippopotamus hide, also known as a sjambok
kijiji	*Swahili* - village
kikois	*Swahili* - Masai garment
kilemba	*Swahili* - head garment, turban
kwa heri sasa	*Swahili* - goodbye now
Liverpudlian	anyone who hails from Liverpool in the UK
magugu	a tall grass found in Tanganyika
mahindi	*Swahili* - maize, corn
manyara	(hedge) prostrate herb with big tuber
maradadi	origins unknown - beautiful
mdogo	*Swahili* - small (as in child)
memsahib	*Hindi* - lady, Mrs., madam
mopani	tree grows in hot, dry, low-lying areas. The tree only occurs in Africa.
mkuki	*Swahili* - spear, javelin
mpishi	*Swahili* - cook
msasa	medium-sized African tree having compound leaves and racemes of small, fragrant green flowers. The tree is broad and has a distinctive amber and wine red colour when the young leaves sprout during August and September

mundu	*Swahili* - a sickle, bill-hook chopper, a hand-fashioned slashing tool to cut long grass. A type of scythe
mushee	good, neat, cool
mzee	*Swahili* - elder, older, respected person
mzuri sana	*Swahili* - good, very good
Nach	Nachingwea – town in Southern province of Tanganyika (Tanzania)
ndege	*Swahili* - birds, airplanes
ndyio	*Swahili* - yes
nguvu	*Swahili* - strength, force, power
ngoma	*Swahili* - drumming celebration
ng'ombe	*Swahili* - long horned cattle
nyabs	marbles
nyoka	*Swahili* - snake
OFC	Overseas Food Corporation
panga	machete
posho	*Swahili* - an East African dish of maize flour cooked with water to make a porridge – also called ugali
punda or punda milia	*Swahili* - zebra
PWD	Public Works Department
redoubt	a militarily defended encampment. May consist of an enclosed defensive emplacement.
rondavel	circular, thatched, cabin
salaam	*Swahili* - peace
scarper	get out of here, leave, depart (in a hurry)
scoff	food
scrumping	stealing apples from an orchard
shamba	*Swahili* - plantation/garden/yard

shamba boy	the servant who looked after the garden/yard
shenzi	*Swahili* - barbaric, uncouth, uncivilized, savage, barbarous
shinty	variation of field hockey
Shutty	abbreviation for the teacher Percy Shuttleworth
silly mid off	cricket term for a particular fielder's location
skellum	*Afrikaans* - rascal, rogue, scamp
slops	slip-on sandals
stink bugs	commonly referred to as shield bugs, chust bugs, and stink bugs. There are about 7000 species divided under 14 to 15 families.
stoep	*Dutch* - veranda
Southern Africa	general term - embraces several counties in the southern portion of the continent
tackies	gym shoes, runners
Tizer	brand name - Tizer is a mix of citrus and red fruit with a refreshing sharp twist
Tommies	Thomson's gazelle
tuck	food, sweets and candies. A tuck shop is a small, food-selling retailer.
ugali	an East African dish of maize flour cooked with water to a porridge – also called posho
units	land divisions, as in units of 100 acres
vervets	monkeys
vijana	young boys
vlei	*Afrikaans* - flatter area, valley, depression
voetsek	*Afrikaans* - away with you...
waar is die slang?	*Afrikaans* - where is the snake?
waar is hy?	*Afrikaans* - where is he?

wallah	*Arabic* - a person who is associated with a particular work or who performs a specific duty or service – usually used in combination
wanaume	*Swahili* - men
watoto	*Swahili* - children (one child = toto)
wembembe	*Swahili* - killer bees
woggle	a device to fasten a Boy Scout's neckerchief

ABOUT THE AUTHOR

ANTHONY R. EDWARDS

Tony was born in London, England, in 1942. He spent many formative years in Africa and was drawn to return in 1962 after completing his college education.

Tony's professional life included photography, television, advertising and anthropological research. It turned out Tony was born a bit of a nomad, following, as he did, his career to Britain, Rhodesia, Zambia, South Africa, the United States and Canada. Fortunately for him or perhaps because it was meant to be, Tony's wife, Imelda, whom he met in South Africa, enjoyed the same wandering spirit.

In 2004, Tony and Imelda settled on Salt Spring Island in British Columbia, Canada.